the SON *&* *his* HOPE

NEW YORK TIMES BESTSELLING AUTHOR

PEPPER WINTERS

The Son
&
His Hope

by

Pepper Winters

The Son & His Hope
Copyright © 2019 Pepper Winters
Published by Pepper Winters

Published: Pepper Winters 2019 **pepperwinters@gmail.com**
Cover Design: Ari @ Cover it! Designs
Editing by: Editing-4-Indies (Jenny Sims)

www.pepperwinters.com

OTHER BOOKS AVAILABLE FROM PEPPER WINTERS

Ribbon Duet
The Boy & His Ribbon
The Girl & Her Ren

Dollar Series
Pennies
Dollars
Hundreds
Thousands
Millions

Truth & Lies Duet
Crown of Lies
Throne of Truth

Pure Corruption Duet
Ruin & Rule
Sin & Suffer

Indebted Series
Debt Inheritance
First Debt
Second Debt
Third Debt
Fourth Debt
Final Debt
Indebted Epilogue

Monsters in the Dark Trilogy
Tears of Tess
Quintessentially Q
Twisted Together
Je Suis a Toi

Standalones
Destroyed
Unseen Messages
Can't Touch This
The Son & His Hope

*****

Part One

*****

Prologue

DELLA

* * * * * *

TODAY I MUST watch my husband die all over again.

I tried to refuse. I pointed out how cruel it would be to relive the worst part of my life—the life that never managed to heal. I don't have the strength to watch my love story, curse my life story, cry at my broken romance.

In a way, I wish I'd never penned our tale—that I'd kept it treasured and secret. Then again, the words I chose were just for us—it was Ren who decided to share. Ren who immortalised our love in page and movie screen.

I had him all to myself for thirty-three years, yet for the past four, I've had to share his memory with countless strangers.

Our tragedy is tattered pieces of history that I'm never free from. And I don't want to be free from it because there will come a time—soon but not too soon—when we will meet again. That belief—that faith—is what keeps me going on the darkest of days.

One of those days being today.

I wish I could fast-forward, claim illness, be firm enough to say no.

But it's expected.

The invitation was sent. The date set in stone.

And so, I'll go.

I'll swallow my tears, bind my lonely heart, and be brave, all because he is brave. So eternally, amazingly brave.

Jacob.

Our son.

He is no longer a boy, but he isn't quite a man.

He has so many things to learn, yet somehow, he's wise beyond his age.

He is extraordinary and brilliant, and now...he has his own tale to tell.

Jacob is just beginning his story, and I still have a part to play—at least until he no longer needs me. When that time comes, his existence will eclipse mine. His successes and mistakes will take centre page—a new generation of heartbreak.

Ren and I…we are no longer needed.

But I've said too much; taken up too much of your time.

This book isn't about me—it's about him.

And don't worry, I have no warnings to give you. No caution-filled paragraphs or ominous foreshadowing.

You don't need anything to fall in love with my son.

Our son.

Because he's special.

Just like his father.

And just like his father, the love he has to give comes with torture and torment, and I pity the poor girl who falls for him.

Chapter One

JACOB

* * * * * *

Fourteen Years Old

I WAS FOURTEEN when the movie came out.

Fourteen when I was forced to watch my dad die all over again.

And fourteen when I met Hope, only to curse her name for the rest of my life.

Thanks to being a teenager, I believed I knew better than everyone. After all, my father ran away from horrors and looked after himself and a baby when he was only ten. If he could survive with nothing and no one that young, then I was sure as hell old enough to protect my mother.

I'd done my best to prevent us from being here. I'd seen her fear about attending. Even Grandpa John and Aunt Cassie had stood by my side and told her it wasn't weak to refuse. That just because her first three objections weren't accepted didn't mean she couldn't ignore them.

Ever since she was contacted about movie rights, I'd tried to keep the actors, screenwriters, and directors away from my family. I'd even gone as far as placing animal snares around Cherry River, snagging a producer's ankle before he could barge into our home, armed with a spiel to guilt-trip my mom into allowing my father's death to be glamorised by Hollywood.

In the beginning, Mom said hell no, Cassie threatened to sue them, and Grandpa John got his shotgun. It didn't matter that Dad had all but prophesied this would happen and written the final scene of the movie himself.

But then the social media pressure began. The constant emails, letters, tweets—all of it begging to have *The Boy & His Ribbon* transformed onto the big screen.

The offer kept growing in digits, and the producers became

more insistent until finally, Mom agreed. But only if the money went to the kids who'd been hurt by her parents, the evil Mclarys.

That alone earned her more news time than a local political scandal—catapulting our family into the spotlight and guaranteeing that the tragic love story of my parents was one of the most anticipated releases this year.

Filming began the moment Mom signed their nasty paperwork. That day, I'd used my slingshot to fire pebbles at a few of the suited execs as they left, smug and patting themselves on the back. I might have also stabbed a BMW's tyres with the Swiss Army knife Dad gave me on my tenth birthday.

Afterward, things were quiet for a while. Mom pretended the movie wasn't in the works, and I did my best not to plan revenge on the men who'd badgered her until her 'no' became 'yes.'

We'd all agreed to stay well clear of everything to do with it, but that was before the phone calls started. The 'oh, we were just wondering what sort of backpack Ren carried you in, Della?' 'By the way, how old was Ren again when you first found the Wilsons?'

To start with, Mom was polite and answered them. But then the phone calls turned to visits, then literal kidnapping as they stole her away to offer set advice on a farm only a few miles down the road.

They'd deliberately filmed the movie so damn close that history reached out and sucked Mom into the past. That wasn't the only time they asked for her help, and her visits on set always left her shaky and strung out. Her eyes haunted with memories; her thoughts distracted and sad.

I *hated* those movie people.

I cursed what they did to her—making her relive the beginning, the middle, and the end. And I hated them for my sake too. I loved my parents. I missed my dad like crazy, but to see actors play out scenes where my parents were my age made me feel weird—like I shouldn't be seeing such things.

Plus, I despised the actor who played my dad. I hated the way he smiled at my mom. I hated how he talked to her like someone would talk to a timid animal. I loathed how his eyes lingered on her when she made excuses and extracted herself from their painful conversation.

"Jacob. You're going to crack your teeth." Mom's fingertips tapped my jaw where I clenched as hard as I curled my fists.

Her touch dragged me from the past year of hell and into our current nightmare. "Can't we just leave?"

"You know we can't." She sighed heavily. "A couple of hours and this will all be over. They've finished filming. They'll leave us alone now."

"Yeah, right." I rolled my eyes. Didn't she get that the premiere was tonight, which meant the movie was only just releasing? We were in for a whole new world of awful once the public claimed it as their own.

"Stop looking like you want to murder everyone."

"Can't hide the truth," I muttered, eyeing up the actors in front of us as they oiled their way up the red carpet. We stood in the shadows, waiting for our turn to walk the paparazzi gauntlet. I wished there was a back entrance. Better yet, I wished I was at home away from this madness.

Mom looped her arm around mine, tugging me forward.

I pulled against her for a heartbeat, fear and anger a rich recipe in my chest.

Touch.

The worst curse in my life.

My new black blazer was too tight—probably from breathing so hard. My glossy shoes too stiff—most likely because they weren't my scuffed-up paddock boots.

"Come on," Mom whispered, pulling me into a walk. "Let's get it over with."

My feet unglued from the ground, and I moved with her.

Walking toward the flashing cameras, I was no longer a kid hating everyone. I was a son protecting my mother from leeches.

I stood taller, glowered harder. I was my mother's date and bodyguard.

For four years now, I'd taken the place of my father—keeping my promise to him. My oath that I'd given while we'd sat squished together on the tractor on a long summer night a year or so before he died.

He'd told me, man to man, that he needed me to look after Mom. That he expected me to be there for her when he couldn't. I'd kept my tears at bay and shook his hand solemnly. I'd sworn that I'd never let him or Mom down and would do whatever it took to make her smile when she was sad and keep her safe when she was in danger.

And Dad had trusted me because he knew I wasn't a moronic kid who didn't have the skills to uphold that promise. He'd taught me to be self-sufficient. He'd made me exactly like him.

"Smile, Jacob." Mom pinched me as the first cameraman angled his intrusive lens in our direction. I smiled, but my thoughts were still in the past. Still lingering on that summer when Dad dropped the pretences of treating me like a kid and trained me like a man.

Around Mom, he chose what he said—to stop her scolding him for telling me things I shouldn't know at such a young age.

But when it was just us?

It didn't matter I'd been a quarter of his size and worshipped the ground he walked on. I was worthy and wise in his eyes, and he told me things in black and white.

No protecting me. No faking or lying.

He'd told me about puberty and sex on my seventh birthday; his cheeks pink with a story of how he'd wished someone had been able to tell him. He'd sat me down and discussed death when the kids at school horrified me with tales of him dying and coming back to eat me as a zombie.

He'd let me fall, allowed me to make mistakes, and permitted me to figure things out before stepping in if I needed his help or staying out of it if I didn't.

He'd prepared me for the day when he wouldn't be there.

He'd done a good job, but it didn't mean the pain was any less. That his loss didn't hurt every damn day. It didn't prevent my eyes from tracking to the blown-up photo in the living room of him, Mom, and me when I was five, all dressed tidy-like against the barn. We were smiling, even knowing what we were about to face.

He was the best person I knew, and this damn film was a mockery to his memory.

He should never have published Mom's book. He should never have hired a ghost writer to type his dictated chapters. He should never have gotten sick and died.

"Della!" a cameraman yelled. "Mrs Wild, this way. Are you looking forward to seeing the meadow scene?"

Another called, "Will you cry when Graham Murphy playing Ren and Carlyn Clark playing yourself find each other again?"

An awful one shouted, "Do you wish you could die so you could stop being so sad?"

I jerked.

What a jackass.

I was standing right there!

I'd already lost half my family. I wouldn't be strong enough if I lost the other half too.

My throat closed around pain and fury. My muscles spasmed in Mom's hold.

She looked at me under mascara and eye shadow. "Ignore them, Wild One. They don't understand." I matched her in height, and her blue eyes glowed with unshed tears. "I'm not sad because I have you, okay? I'm not going anywhere."

I gritted my teeth until they crunched.

Being her red carpet date was proving to be harder than I thought.

I loved movies.

I adored when we'd have burgers and fries and see the latest blockbuster.

But this was different.

I didn't *want* to see this movie.

Because the actor they'd cast to play Dad…he'd never beat the real thing. Whatever parts of the book Hollywood had chosen wouldn't reveal a tenth of what Mom and Dad had gone through.

But most of all?

I was sick at the thought of the ending.

The ending that the screenwriters had insisted on including.

A scene where my mom died.

Where she went to find my dad.

Where I became an orphan all for disgusting ticket sales.

Chapter Two

JACOB

* * * * * *

"THIS WAY, MRS Wild, Jacob." A guy in a navy uniform motioned for us to follow him down the wide gold carpeted stairs toward the middle, where the row of velvet chairs had the most leg room.

The cave-like blackness of the cinema ought to promise good things, but tonight, it was like stepping into a tomb. A tomb filled with ghosts and forest funerals.

My fingers ached from curling into fists. My skin crawled with the urge to rip off my fancy new clothes and bolt.

"Thanks." Mom nodded politely, squeezing my arm and letting me go. "After you, Jacob."

I took the first step, my gaze locking onto the crowd already gathered below. The producer I couldn't stand, the director I wanted to kill, and the cast of this monstrosity.

My feet froze. My heart ordered me to run in the opposite direction.

Mom tapped my shoulder, urging me forward. "Go on."

I wanted to refuse. I needed open fields and night sky.

But what I wanted always came second best. Always had. Always would.

My promise.

My oath.

Protect her.

This movie wasn't about me.

Life, in general, wasn't about me. It was about upholding my vow to a father who'd been my everything, then left me with *way* too much responsibility. Did he understand how hard it would be? Did he get that putting me in charge of my mother's happiness was sometimes too much to bear?

Some days, I wanted to run and never come back.

Some nights, I *did* run, but by morning, I returned to my room before Mom noticed my absence.

It didn't help that I looked exactly like him.

People often did a double take these days. I had dirty blond hair instead of dark, but my face was his, my voice was his, and my loner tendencies were his. Even my eyes were his.

When Mom looked at me, I knew I caused her both comfort and grief. Sometimes, if I took out the trash without being asked or cranked up the diesel tractor to row the meadow, she'd suck in a breath as if she'd seen her husband and not her son.

She often told me my habits were his habits. The way I moved. The phrases I chose. And just like I caused her comfort and grief, she caused me the same. Even though it comforted me to know how similar I was to a parent I'd never see again, it also grieved me to know I wasn't truly my own person.

I wasn't *me*.

I was a lacking replica who constantly reminded people of what they'd lost.

I was living in his shadow, doing what I could to be him, but constantly aware I was only letting them down because I *wasn't* him. I would never *be* him. I would never be as *good*.

"Jacob," Mom hissed under her breath, nudging me again. "Get down there."

She broke the thick wave of self-pity.

And I was grateful.

I didn't know where such selfishness came from. I'd never let myself acknowledge the truth before. Never allowed the sensation of suffocating pressure knowing I would never be enough.

Four years was a long time to uphold a promise.

A lifetime was forever to live in memories.

Flicking her a look over my shoulder, I hid my desire to run. "Sorry."

"You okay?" Mom's face softened, her eyes searching mine, doing her best to extract my secrets when I'd become a master at hiding them.

I grimaced. "Course."

For a second, her fear about seeing this movie was overcast by her worry for me. Something I couldn't allow. She had enough hurt without me causing more.

"Stop." I smiled broader. "I'm good, Mom. Quit worrying."

Her lips pressed together, but she nodded reluctantly. "I don't believe you but this isn't a place to argue." Tilting her chin at the awaiting crowd, she said softly, "Two hours of agony and then it's done."

"Two and a half hours, actually." I grinned wryly as if it were a laughing matter. "Long movie."

Before more pain shattered Mom's heart, I turned around and followed the attendant down the stairs. With each step, my back straightened, gathering the strength to face the imposters who'd broken yet another piece of our life.

As we drew closer, I made a promise to myself for a change. For the rest of the evening, I would do my best to behave.

I was done arguing.

"Hello again, Jacob. Della." Graham Murphy's signature half-smile slid over me to lock onto Mom. He had the audacity to gather her in a quick hug.

I glanced away, uncomfortable. Whenever people who weren't family touched my mother, my skin crawled.

I felt guilty.

Guilty for letting others touch her. Guilty that I didn't stop them from sharing what once had been my father's.

Dad said he was always watching, listening, and protecting—even if we couldn't see him. Well, what the hell would he think if he could see us laughing and hanging out with other people without him?

It'd be a slap in his face, and I hated that Mom didn't think about that as she patted Graham's back and withdrew as quickly as possible.

Then again, maybe she did. She certainly cringed when others touched her. "Hello, Graham. Nice to see you."

"You, too." His half-smile widened a little. "I hope the limousine was on time collecting you."

"It was. Yes." Mom nodded. "Very considerate to pick us up. We could've just driven—"

"On opening night to your own movie?" Graham's eyebrows shot into his brown hair. "No way."

He acted as if a limo could solve world hunger. Didn't he get that Mom and I didn't care about that sort of thing—glitz, money, possessions. It meant nothing in the scheme of things. Just stuff that didn't make you happier.

Awkwardness fell.

Mom smiled, forcing past the discomfort. "Well, thanks again."

Graham reached out and touched her forearm, his eyes warm

and worried. "Don't do that. I know what tonight means to you guys and—"

"You know, do you?" I snapped before I could stop myself.

Mom stepped away from Graham's touch as I sized him up. That touch was more than just politeness. It bordered on inappropriate. It reeked of a wannabe friend.

"Jacob," Mom said sternly. Glancing at Graham, she rolled her shoulders a little. "Sorry, it's not easy for him being here."

"Not easy for you either." I glowered.

"That's not the point, Wild One." Her eyes met mine. "The point is none of what we're feeling is anyone else's fault. Don't take it out on—"

"So you're saying it's Dad's fault?"

What am I doing?

What happened to my vow to behave?

Her entire face shattered only for her gaze to fill with ice. Her temper I could handle—I was well acquainted with it. At least it stopped the sorrow. "We'll talk about this later."

"Can't wait."

She stared as if she didn't know me.

And in a way, she didn't. *I* didn't know me. I'd promised to behave, yet for some reason, I grew angrier every minute.

I didn't want to be here. I didn't want to see this. I didn't want to *hurt* anymore.

I broke eye contact, looking at the floor. "Sorry."

Before Mom could forgive me—which she would, she always did—Graham shifted on the spot and rubbed the back of his neck. "Eh, sorry if I caused any issues."

"You didn't. It's fine." Mom shook her head, reaching out to squeeze my wrist to let me know she accepted my apology. "Just…you know how it is."

"Yeah." Graham's voice softened. "Actually, I do." His smile was less perfect for the cameras and more honest with history. "When my wife died, it took two years for me to feel halfway normal."

He just played the dead-spouse sympathy card.

Wow. Jackass.

"I'm sorry, Graham," Mom murmured. "It's the hardest thing."

"It truly is." Graham's gaze lingered on hers. "Time helps, but it never truly heals. I'm here for you if you ever want to talk and…things."

The offer made me hate him ten-fold because it wasn't a secret Graham felt something for my mother. He wanted liberties she'd never give him.

I'd noticed it a couple of months into shooting. I'd told Mom my suspicions, but she was either blind or stupid. It wasn't until a reporter asked if something was going on with her and Graham that she believed me.

When Graham was asked the same question, instead of a sharp disbelieving laugh like Mom gave, he looked directly into the camera and said that playing Ren Wild had been the hardest of his career. Especially because spending time with Della on set meant the script became a little too real, and he developed off-screen feelings for her.

It had caused even more buzz around the movie.

People swooned at the thought of Mom finding a second chance at love with the guy who played her dead husband. Meanwhile, Graham Murphy was lucky he survived to the end of filming.

I might be young, but I knew how to wield a knife. I knew how to take a life—thanks to Dad's hunting lessons. I wasn't squeamish, and I wasn't exactly tolerant.

While the internet had polls on whether Mom and Graham were an item, I had my own poll on which way I would murder him.

The only thing that stopped me was Aunt Cassie.

She said there could be a hundred men in love with my mother, but it wouldn't make a damn bit of difference. No one could ever hope to compare to the ghost that haunted us.

I liked Aunt Cassie.

She didn't hide things from me and treated me like an adult rather than a silly kid. She listened to me when Mom wouldn't and didn't pussyfoot around when talking about the past. If Dad was a part of whatever memory she shared, she'd tell me—the good, the bad, and the idiotic. Mom, on the other hand, would gauge me, assess me, make me feel as if I was this broken thing who needed protecting when really *I* was protecting *her*.

Clearing his throat, Graham pointed beside him to the red velvet chairs with our names pinned to the top. "Your seats are next to mine."

Good job at pointing out the obvious.

"I'm glad." Graham gave Mom a sympathetic look. "It means I'm close if you want to discuss the movie while it's playing."

My knife grew heavier to be used.

Local magazines might call him a heart-throb, but I called him a cheap imposter. He was the same height as Dad with similar bronze-brown hair, but the similarities ended there.

He'd had to wear contacts to change his green eyes to the correct dark shade, and his contract meant he bulked up for the first part of the movie—doing his best to convince an audience he was a natural born farmer—only to lose weight as the plot progressed.

I'd stopped going on set when that happened.

Actually, I'd stopped going when the coughing started.

The tiny hint of what was to come.

The awful curse that would come true.

The first time he coughed, delivering a line to his co-star Carlyn Clark, my chest felt as if someone had punctured it with a pitchfork.

The second time, laughing with the actor playing Grandpa John, I stumbled beneath pounding memories of what it was like to live with a dead man walking. A dead man who struggled to breathe and coughed to stay alive.

The third time, as Graham buckled under a coughing fit in the stable, something had happened that I wasn't proud of.

Grief that I still hadn't processed, stress that I still hadn't let go of, and memories that I'd done my best to forget all flooded my brain and broke me.

Tears came.

Rage followed.

And I'd bolted from the stable—running from fake stalls, fake hay, and even faker people—vanishing from the past and those who replicated it.

I couldn't stop hearing my dad coughing.

A ringing in my ears.

A barking in my mind.

For years, I'd cringed every time Dad coughed. My reaction to his coughing steadily switched from a simple flinch to outright panic.

Thanks to Graham, I remembered it far too well.

I'd hidden from Mom for hours, only coming out of the forest because I'd made a promise, and that promise was more important than me.

So what if I had an issue with coughing?

Mom was alone.

And it was up to me to make sure she didn't feel lonely.

When she saw me, she fussed and questioned, but I brushed off her concern. I argued that I was fine. I did what Dad expected and assured her everything was okay.

But she didn't believe me. Instead, she told me we all had triggers. Some more than others. A trigger from trauma ingrained in our psyche with the power to override everything else.

Love was a trigger of mine—though I didn't understand that until much later.

And coughing was another.

It didn't matter if it was a stranger in a restaurant or a family member. If someone coughed, my heart galloped and palms sweated and all I could think about was death.

Mom swallowed hard, wincing a little at the red velvet chairs waiting for us to occupy. "I think I'll have my eyes closed through most of it. Doubt I'll want to talk, I'm afraid."

Graham groaned under his breath. "Yes, of course. There I go again, saying things that make me sound heartless."

Mom didn't reply, leaving Graham floundering for a new topic.

Unfortunately, that new topic was me.

He made eye contact, his green imposter gaze looking me up and down. "You're very suave tonight, Jacob."

Mom relaxed, glad to no longer be centre of attention while I stiffened under the spotlight. Crossing my arms, I glanced quickly at my wardrobe. Black blazer and shirt, black jeans, stiff new cowboy boots and silver string tie.

Mom had offered to buy me a tux.

I'd refused.

When I didn't accept the compliment the way society said I should, Mom glanced at me in reproach and ran a hand nervously over her hip, smoothing the glittery copper of her dress.

Her gaze begged me to put aside my inherited loathing of crowds and conformity and be normal—until we were back on the farm and away from people at least.

Forcing myself not to roll my eyes, I said, "Thanks."

"Welcome." Graham grinned, relieved.

That damn awkwardness descended again. I actually wanted the movie to start so we could get this over with and leave.

"Oh. My. *God*. What a *night!*" Blonde haired Carlyn Clark bowled into Graham, breaking apart our tense trio. "This is *insane*. Isn't it, Graham? I mean, I knew the media would be in a frenzy seeing as this is based on a true story and all, but *wow!*"

Graham accepted his co-star's air kisses, half glad to have someone easier to talk to and half annoyed at the interruption.

"Oh, hi, Della." Carlyn floated toward Mom and pressed against her in a weird Hollywood-type hug where no body part touched. "How are you? Aren't those paparazzi questions prying? It's madness, I tell you." Without missing a breath, Carlyn blew me a kiss. "And Jakey! How *fabulous* that you came too. Get to see your parent's love story. How romantic." Her face melted as if it was the best thing in the world for me to watch my parents get together, have me, then be ripped apart forever.

I gritted my teeth to keep from saying something I shouldn't.

Carlyn beamed as she sipped her champagne like some crazed hummingbird. "God, Graham, those reporters for *You, Me, and Them* are *relentless*. They want to know if I'm the secret mother of your daughter." She giggled. "As if I'm old enough to have a ten-year-old."

Some magazine had crowned her prettiest actress last year, but her lipstick was too pink, her hair too bleached, and her legs too short. She might've played my mom in this god-awful movie, but she'd never compare to the real thing.

Graham stiffened. "They know who Hope's mother is. And they definitely know it isn't you."

In terms of personalities—despite my dislike of Graham—he was tolerable, Carlyn on the other hand? She might play kind and supportive in the movie, but in real life…she was a self-obsessed nightmare.

"I know, but they're *desperate* for us to be in a real-world relationship after being in this movie together." She wafted at herself as if she was the hottest thing in the theatre. "I mean, the amount of fan mail I receive saying we should get married and pretend a new version of Ren and Della lived happily ever after is in*sane*. They're all begging for us to fall madly in love and make a new ending, and the movie isn't even *out* yet. It's crazy!"

Mom winced.

My temper lashed out in protection. My ingrained promise to stop what was hurting her exploded. "Shut up. Just *shut* up."

Carlyn froze. "Did you…did you just *growl* at me?"

"Just shut up."

Mom gripped my bunched forearm. "Wild One—"

"Jacob, she didn't mean—" Graham held up his hand.

"How *dare* you!" Carlyn bared her teeth. "You can't talk to me like—"

"Daddy, what's going on?" A brown-haired girl in a princess silver dress interrupted the fight, forcing curses to be swallowed and tempers to be smothered.

Carlyn whirled away with a huff, and Graham instantly changed from actor to father.

The polish he wore vanished. The fakery he held like armour disappeared. He wasn't some Hollywood superstar; he was just a Dad.

And I was jealous that the kid who'd just interrupted us still had one.

One who loved her a lot, judging by the way he dropped to a knee and cupped her face as if she held everything he ever needed. "Where did you go, Little Lace? I was getting worried."

The girl threw me a look, her fingers twirling anxiously in her poufy silver outfit. "I went to see if they had ice cream. Keeko took me." She pointed over her shoulder at a Japanese woman who smiled gently.

Obviously some sort of nanny.

The woman shrugged. "Sorry, Mr. Murphy. I didn't mean to worry you."

"You didn't. It's fine." Graham stood, dismissing the nanny and gathering the tiny girl against his side. "And did you find this elusive ice cream?"

She wrinkled her nose. "Nu-huh. They only have fancy names like crème something and toffee whatever. I just wanted vanilla." Her eyes landed on me, locking us both into place.

My muscles tightened, sensing danger, yet I couldn't look away.

She was tiny, yet her gaze was powerful enough to evoke chills up and down my spine.

For the longest moment, no one spoke.

The girl kept staring at me, her forehead furrowing with intensity as if she could set fire to me just by glaring.

What the hell?

Mom came to my rescue. "You know what? Jacob likes vanilla, too." She flicked me a look then glanced back at the girl, probably wondering why I was suddenly the most fascinating thing to this kid. "In fact, when he was about your age, he had a vanilla pony birthday cake that he smeared all over his face." Her voice stayed steady while bringing up that terrible, *terrible* evening, but her eyes glistened.

Why the *hell* had she mentioned that?

What was she trying to do? Make this evening that much harder?

My cheeks heated as pain drenched me. My shoulder blades hurt as memories prickled. I *hated* remembering. I wished I could delete the night of my tenth birthday forever.

How we'd gone camping as a family.

How we'd had cake and Dad told me not to take the small stuff for granted.

How we'd gone to bed and I'd woken at midnight to something that, to this day, still haunted my nightmares.

Sobs.

My parents sobbing as they said goodbye.

Mom didn't know.

I'd never said anything.

But I'd heard them.

And it was a secret that scarred me, scared me, and silenced my deepest sorrow.

I never wanted to feel the agony that my parents went through that night.

Ever.

"Oh, yeah?" The girl never took her green gaze off me. Green like her father. Brown hair like her father, too. However, where his nose was straight, hers was button and her cheeks were rounder. "I love vanilla. It's the best thing in the *world.*"

What was I supposed to say to that?

I liked the stuff, but it wasn't that amazing.

And she still hadn't stopped staring at me, staring as if I belonged behind bars as an exhibit.

I narrowed my eyes, doing my best to tell her to back the hell off without adults scolding me.

"Jacob…" Mom commanded. "Be nice."

I sighed, accepting defeat in the form of having to entertain a child all evening when really, I couldn't afford to. I had a job to do. A job to protect my mother from whatever crap the director had stitched together. "I guess vanilla is okay."

The girl stuck out her hand, swishing toward me in her over-the-top dress as if I'd proved myself worthy of being her friend just because we shared similar taste buds. "I'm Hope Jacinta Murphy."

I stumbled backward, studying her miniature grip as if it held spiders.

I didn't like spiders. Just like I didn't like strangers. Especially tiny girls with staring problems. "Good for you."

"Jacob." Mom hissed, poking my side.

I rolled my eyes, reaching out to shake the hand of some crazy child of Hollywood. She'd been raised in a city, lived in a fairy-tale, and believed money was infinite. She didn't look like she'd been muddy or sunburned or exhausted in her entire life.

She wouldn't last a day in the real world.

Squeezing her midget fingers, I let her go as fast as I'd touched her. "Nice to meet you, Hope Jacinta Murphy."

Even though it's not nice at all.

Her cheeks pinked as she looked me up and down, once again staring in that freaky way. "What's your full name? Daddy always told me to tell someone your full name so they never forget you."

"Believe me, I won't forget you."

"So what is it?"

"What's what?"

"Your name?"

"Jacob."

"No, your *full* name?" She planted a hand on her hip with attitude. "My first name is Hope. My middle name is Jacinta for my mommy." Her lip pouted. "She died when I was seven. I wanted to change my first name to Jacinta, but Daddy said there was only one Jacinta, and I have to stick with Hope." Her cheeks whitened before she pushed aside the sadness that I was well acquainted with and nodded firmly. "And my last name is Murphy because we all need last names as there are so many Hopes in the world but not that many Hope Murphys and only one Hope Jacinta Murphy."

Her shoulders rolled. "Uh-huh…" Her confident outburst folded into pink embarrassment. "So…anyway." She shook her head, turning away from me as if she no longer wanted to know my full name.

Which was fine by me.

But Mom answered for me, pitying the poor kid as she scuffed her shoe into the gold carpet. "His name is Jacob Ren Wild." Her voice hitched a little on my dad's address. "But you can call him Wild One if you want. It's kind of a nickname." Bending closer to Hope, she asked gently, "Do you have a nickname to go with your pretty full name?"

Hope glanced at me with intense green eyes before answering politely. "Lace. Daddy calls me Lace."

"And what a pretty Lace you are." Mom grinned, something flashed blue in her blonde hair.

A blue ribbon I'd seen her wear every day of my existence.

"I call her Lace for the tatty shawl that her mother used to wear around the house. Hope kind of claimed it after..." Graham cleared his throat, sharing a look that I didn't like with Mom. A look that said, 'I understand your pain. I have the same kind.'

My hands balled.

It wasn't fair that Graham knew my dad called her Ribbon. It wasn't fair he knew so much about us when we knew nothing about him. He believed he stood a chance with my mother just because he'd played my father.

Once again, awkwardness descended, saved by the little weirdo Hope Jacinta Murphy. "Jacob Ren Wild, why aren't you wearing a tuxedo like everybody else?"

I flinched at my middle name. "What?"

"All the boys are in shiny suits with bows. You have that string thingy and boots. Wait..." She tilted her head as shoulder-length brown hair cascaded with gravity. "You look like those cowboys on TV." Her eyes widened in worry. "Oh no, do you have horses, or do you just eat them?"

"Wait, *what*?" It was my turn to stare at her. Stare at a crazy child who now gawked at me as if I was a monster. I glanced at Mom, wanting to see if she'd heard that ridiculous question.

Mom just snickered. "She means the cake. The vanilla pony cake I told her about."

"Ah." I stuck my hands into my pockets, wanting to talk about anything else but that night. "Right."

"So, do ya?" Hope demanded. Her gaze laser intense and unyielding.

My skin crawled again as if she had some magical way of touching me just by looking. "Yeah, I have a horse."

"Oh, wow. You do?!" Hope bounced in her stupid dress. "I've always wanted a pony, but Daddy says I can't."

Graham shrugged. "I work so often on location that Hope is home-schooled so she can come with me. We don't have time for a dog, let alone a horse."

"You should have brought her to Cherry River while you were filming." Mom's smile was genuine as she drank in Hope. "My sister, Cassie, and I run an equestrian facility. We have a few suitable ponies for a beginner to learn on."

Before Graham could reply, Hope froze in that uncanny way

of hers. "Really?" Her mouth parted. "Like really, really? Could I pat them? No, I mean could I *gallop* them? I *really* want to gallop. And jump!"

Mom laughed. "Once you've mastered the walk, trot, and canter. Galloping isn't something you do on your first try, but with your determination, I'd say you could learn to jump very quickly. I started riding a lot when I was your age. It didn't take long to master." Her eyes grew wistful, her thoughts once again belonging to the past and Dad.

I was used to her drifting off.

It was a regular occurrence.

"I didn't know that." Graham reached for his daughter's hand. "Do you offer lessons too? I have a couple weeks off before my next commitment. Perhaps, I could bring her one day and let her try?"

Mom nodded. "We actually started a boarding facility a year ago. During school holidays, we have a maximum of four children come to stay in the stable bunkroom. They learn how to look after the horses, do daily chores, and get to ride in the morning and afternoon. It's good character building as well as a way to feed that pony addiction."

"Sounds great." Graham grinned. "I know it's not school holidays, but would you mind if I brought her—"

"It's the start of summer," I interrupted. "Mom and I are busy with other chores. We have hay to bale and a farm to—"

"You're the one running that these days, Jacob. Not me." Mom cut in. "I'm sure Cassie would love to teach Hope. Perhaps put her on your old pony, Binky."

My heart raced with possession.

Not for the white plod of a pony I'd long outgrown but for our farm.

I didn't want trespassers on it.

I *definitely* didn't want trespassers who knew our entire life story. Who had acted it out and believed they knew us.

They would *never* know us.

I crossed my arms, wanting to argue but knowing better. "Fine. But don't expect me to teach her."

"I didn't say that, did I?" Mom scowled, her tolerance waning.

As if I'd commanded the night to get worse, the huge screen erupted with colour and noise, showing the audience how lucky we were that the cinema was equipped with 'all-around sound.'

I gulped.

The urge to run returned a thousand-fold.

"Guess we better take our seats," Graham murmured, pushing his daughter into the one reserved next to my chair.

Great.

Just great.

Not only had this actor played my dead dad but now I had to chaperone his strange kid.

Hope patted the red velvet next to her. "Come on, Jacob. You look sad. Do you want a hug? A hug makes everything better." Stretching out her arms, her face stayed serious and not in the least bit mocking. She genuinely believed a hug could fix me.

Not just strange.

Delusional.

If coughing was an emotional trigger for me, so was affection of any kind. Even Mom struggled to hug me.

There was no way Hope would manage it.

"I'm good. Thanks." Sitting stiffly, I blocked her from my mind as the opening song blared, the title splashed across the screen, and my worst nightmare began.

Chapter Three

JACOB
* * * * * *

Fifteen Years Old

"YOU'RE GOING TO school, Jacob, and that's final."

"But it's a waste of my time! I hate being stuck in a classroom. I'll never need trigonometry or stupid science. My brain doesn't compute that way." Stalking around the living room, I glowered at my mother. "I don't belong there."

Up until a year ago, I thought I belonged at Cherry River Farm. I believed my life was owned by the same fields and forests where we'd scattered Dad's ashes.

But that was before the movie.

Before my dad died all over again and my 'on-screen' mother committed suicide by pill to join him. Hollywood had forced me to watch an alternate universe.

One where I was an orphan and not wanted.

One where I was on my own because loyalty meant nothing anymore.

Ever since that night, I'd had nightmares of Mom dying. I'd wake drenched in a cold sweat and bolt from my bedroom to the forest. I'd stay there until daybreak, fighting the urge to keep running.

To leave before she could.

To break my promise to look after her because I sucked at it anyway.

I'd be free.

Free from *everything*.

I could just be me.

Not sadness.

Not pity.

Not their son.

I wouldn't have to be someone I wasn't because I would never live up to him.

But I wasn't the only one struggling.

Mom barely slept. She'd stopped going online to avoid the messages, emails, and tweets. My ability to hide a lot of my own issues faltered, which meant our matching tempers clashed far more than normal.

I hated that I upset her. But I also hated that I couldn't figure out the crap inside my brain and go back to how I'd been.

For years, I'd been a master at putting aside my grief so Mom wouldn't have to worry about me. I'd taken pride in shouldering as much responsibility around the farm as I could—routinely asking for more chores.

But these days?

The rage from the premiere still festered—even after a year—chewing holes inside me until I became volatile and surly.

It was just a stupid movie. But it had played out my darkest fears.

Luckily, a year was an eternity in the scheme of a movie's shelf life. The phone no longer rang, and our town was forgotten as a tourist destination.

Life moved on.

But it didn't mean emotions faded.

Dad had always been a third wheel in our world, but lately, it was as if his ghost was touchable. A physical presence patrolling the corridors at night.

When Graham had coughed around tears on the big screen; when the camera zoomed close and he gasped, *"Come find me on the meadow where the sun always shines, the river always flows, and the forest always welcomes. Come find me, Little Ribbon, and there we'll live for eternity,"* I'd almost punched everyone in the theatre.

Almost stabbed the director.

Almost strangled Graham Murphy.

Dad would never have said that directly to Mom.

He knew better than to be so cheesy.

Instead, he'd written her a letter.

A letter hidden in the back of the book he'd secretly published.

So many things Hollywood got wrong.

So many things they'd changed.

And it made me so *angry*.

Angry that they'd hurt Mom, Aunt Cassie, and Grandpa John. Angry that they'd hurt everyone I cared about, and I wasn't able to stop it.

"You're fifteen, Jacob." Mom stomped from the living room to the kitchen. "You're not dropping out of school. No matter how many times you bring it up."

"I'm not dropping out. I'm moving on with my life."

"And I repeat. You're fifteen. You have your entire life ahead of you. A couple more years won't hurt."

Yeah, they will. I'm hurting all the damn time!

Swallowing hard, I muttered, "I know what I want. And school isn't it."

Mom rested her palms on the wooden countertop as if weary fighting with me. I was tired fighting with her too.

This was not a new argument.

Every Monday, I pleaded my case. And every Monday, I lost, but it didn't stop me from trying. I had to try because I couldn't keep this up for much longer.

I knew I was young. I knew I should chill the hell out. And I knew I was being the opposite of a good son. But I also knew something inside me was growing. A need. An urge. A demand for…for—

Ugh, I don't know.

"No one knows what they want at your age." Her eyes fell to her fingers and the wedding ring she never took off, doing her best to hide her lie.

"You did. You knew." Thanks to the movie, I knew just how young Mom was when she fell for Dad. I knew a bit too much about their relationship these days.

Her gaze flashed back to mine. "Yes, and I made myself very unhappy."

"Well, I'm unhappy now!"

"Welcome to the club!"

We both glared, breathing hard.

I backed down, scrambling to fix what I'd done. "Look, I'm sorry, okay? I just…I'm not saying I'll stop learning. I just don't want to go to school. I'll study something else."

Mom inhaled deeply, doing her best to shed her temper like me. "Study what exactly?"

"I dunno." I resumed my pacing, kicking my school backpack resting against the couch on my way past. "I could do an agricultural degree."

"You couldn't enrol until you're older."

"I could be an apprentice to some farmer."

"You already know more than what most could teach you."

"Exactly!" I pointed through the glass doors to the rolling meadows beyond. "I have all the education I need for out there. I know how to fix a broken tractor. I know when the grass is ready. I know—"

"Yes, but none of that is practical in a city or an office or—"

"I'm never going to live in a city or work in an office."

Mom scowled, her fingernails digging into the countertop. "You don't know that. One day, you might."

"I won't."

"I just don't want you boxing yourself into a corner, Jacob." She sighed. "The future you want now might not be the future you want in ten years' time."

"So what? It's not like school is gonna shut down in ten years."

Her lips flickered with a smile, despite herself. "No, but if you don't have the grades, you won't be able to get into universities or colleges."

I strode around the coffee table, and faced her over the counter.

I tasted her defeat. I just had to push a little harder. "I'm not into words like you are, Mom. I'm not interested in being a doctor or a lawyer." My eyes drifted to the greenery outside again, feeling the familiar kick in my heart. A year ago, I was content believing I would be a farmer all my life. Dirt ran in my DNA. I'd been born into this and *wanted* it.

I did.

Truly.

But thanks to that god-awful movie, my contentment now mixed with a terrible sensation of being trapped.

Our tempers cooled as Mom reached out and patted my hand.

I hid my flinch from her touch.

"I'll make you a deal." Her blue eyes met my dark ones. "Keep going to school—"

"Really? Are you not listening? I can't—"

"Ah-ah, quiet. Let me speak." She turned her 'Mom' voice on, silencing me. "Keep going until you're sixteen. If you still feel this strongly on your sixteenth birthday, you have my blessing to leave."

"That's a year away."

"That's the deal."

I scowled. A year was an eternity. She was asking for too much.

"Sixteen, Wild One. Those are my terms. Like it or lump it."

I slouched onto the counter. "I don't like it."

She chuckled, coming round to squeeze my shoulder.

I tensed, unable to hide it this time.

She noticed. Dropping her hand, she respected the unspoken boundaries I'd erected since that fateful funeral. "Yes, but you'll lump it. For me."

I stood taller, shifting to face her. Her arms widened a little, her gaze eager for contact after our fight.

For a hug.

I shivered at the thought.

It wasn't that I didn't love her. I did. I loved her too much. And I wasn't naïve to think if she died like in the movie, I'd feel the same pain I felt when Dad died.

But just because I knew that didn't mean I wanted to make my pain greater by giving in to physical contact.

She smiled sadly, arms dropping to her sides.

It made regret burn. I'd hurt her all over again.

Why did I keep doing that?

Why was I such a terrible son?

Shoving aside my own selfish needs, I steeled myself and reached out to hug her. Her body was slight and stiff. She flinched in surprise, then squeezed me as hard as she could.

Even though instincts screamed to pull away, I didn't. I was taller than her now and with growth came an even greater responsibility to protect her.

"Sorry," I mumbled into her hair.

She hugged me fierce, rubbing my back. "Don't ever be sorry for asking for what you want." Pulling away, she kissed my cheek. "I know life seems hard and messy and frustrating. I know a year stretches into infinity, but when you're older, you'll realise how short the days are, how fast the months go, and realise a year is nothing."

I knew she thought of Dad again.

Her thoughts were never free.

"You have your entire life ahead of you, Wild One. All I ask is…try not to rush it. Be grateful for each day, even the dark ones."

Chapter Four

HOPE

✴ ✴ ✴ ✴ ✴ ✴

Eleven Years Old

"SUBJECTS YOU ARE not allowed to bring up…" Dad looked at me, splitting his attention between me and the road. "Don't talk about Mom. Don't mention the movie. Don't bring up his dad. Don't—"

"What's the use in speaking if I'm not allowed to?" I pouted, crossing my arms. I'd been up for hours—way past my normal wake-up time—thanks to pure excitement for what today held.

Horses.

Lots and *lots* of horses.

Riding horses.

Gonna be so much fun!

I didn't care I had to wait over a year for this to come true. Today was the day, and it was going to be amazing!

"Hope, don't give me attitude." Dad frowned, slapping on the indicator of our expensive black 4WD that he'd bought Mom because she wanted to travel in style. That was until she was stuck in a coffin. "Just please, talk about horses and anything else you want, but not about death or dying. Okay?"

I pinched my forearm, reminding myself that those thoughts were not acceptable.

Dad and that strange woman who said she was a doctor and smelled of apricots had warned me to stop thinking about corpses.

But that was the thing. I couldn't control what my brain decided to focus on. And it was stumped. Stumped on a question even Dad couldn't answer.

Why?

Why had Mom gone?

Why were we born?

What was the point? The goal? The *purpose?*

When I'd asked those questions, I'd gotten odd looks, whispered remarks, and worried shushes. Apparently, I was too young to ask. Too young to know, anyway.

I didn't tell Dad when I thought about coffins and cemeteries now because I was sick of him telling me that it wasn't a subject for little girls.

Growing up on set and being around more adults than children meant I was confused about where I fit in.

I found kids my age stupid. And adults found me stupid.

I didn't really have anyone to talk to. And being told to keep my thoughts on more suitable subjects…well, it was hard.

I bit my tongue a lot.

But I didn't want to disappoint him any more than I already had. And besides…today was for me. I wanted him to know how thankful I was.

"Okay, Daddy." I smiled as he turned down a long gravel driveway. "Lips sealed."

He flicked me a glance as if he didn't believe me but then nodded. "Good girl."

But what if there was a sick horse?

What if there was some animal dying out in the paddock?

Could I ask what happened to the soul then?

Could I enquire if there was a horse heaven or if they went to the same place as humans?

And if they did, where *was* that?

I wisely kept those thoughts to myself as a large farmhouse came into view with pretty gardens and a wraparound porch. The kind of house Dad had filmed in, but we never lived in. The kind that made me jealous for normal families while we lived in hotels and fancy trailers.

A sign with an engraved galloping horse next to a big barn pointed the way to Cherry Equestrian, guiding us farther onto the farm and around a bend, then down a small hill to yet another huge barn. Outside, horses were tethered to a long pole, some with saddles on, some without. A round yard glinted with a wooden fence, and a square arena held brightly coloured jumps on white sand. All of it was surrounded by the loveliest green meadows that made my mouth literally water.

Immediately, my fascination with the afterlife vanished, replaced with the urgent need to leap from the moving car and squeeze one of those cute ponies.

"Ohhhhh." I wriggled in my seat, pressing the window button for it to go down and bring in the delightful smells of whatever deliciousness was out there.

Sweet.

Musty.

Free.

"Ahhh!" I inhaled deep, unclipping my seatbelt and sticking my head out. "This is *amazing*. Can we move here, Daddy? For like, ever. Not just for today?"

Dad snickered, grabbing hold of my jeans waistband to keep me from climbing out the window. "Wait until after you've been for a ride and you're covered in mud and manure and all your muscles hurt."

"I'll want to stay even more then." I beamed as a woman with brown hair glittering with red strands came out of the large barn and waved.

I waved back like a lunatic. "Come on. Hurry up. I needs to be on a pony."

"Needs is not a word, Hope." He chuckled, though, some of his familiar tension fading. "Why am I forking out tuition fees if you can't even speak correctly?"

"I can't speak correctly because you don't let me speak at all."

His eyebrows shot up. "Well played, Little Lace."

I blew him a kiss.

Dad parked and released me.

I shot from the glitzy glamour of our car and skidded through dust and dirt, loving it so much more than the red carpets and polished tiles of our world. My hair flew wild and my arms spread wide as everything was suddenly so much more *alive*.

I careened to a stop in front of the woman, breathing fast, smiling huge.

She laughed as a cloud of driveway muck wafted around my boots, and I shivered in joy at ruining my wardrobe's perfection. "Well, I'm guessing you're Hope." She smiled while looking me up and down, hooking a bridle over her shoulder with the reins dangling down by her thigh. "Della said you'd be coming. So, you're the kid of the actor who played our Ren, huh?"

I bit my lip. I wasn't allowed to talk about the dead.

"Silent type?" The woman cocked her head, the bridle slipping a little. "If you're not who I think you are…who are you?"

It didn't matter who I was. All that mattered were horses.

My eyes locked on the bridle.

I knew the lingo.

I'd asked Keeko to Google and teach me every piece of tack, part of the horse, and common riding term.

I might be an utter beginner, but no way did I want to come across as a moron.

Especially to Jacob Ren Wild.

Last year, he'd looked at me like I was a silly bug bouncing around and annoying him rather than recognising how brave I was with adult conversation. I hadn't talked about any topics I wasn't supposed to. I'd behaved and kept my death questions to myself even though Dad acted in a movie where the main guy died.

Before the premiere, I'd seen Jacob occasionally on set. I'd peered through my trailer window while Keeko drilled me with math and English and spied him skulking about while Dad delivered lines filled with coughing.

I wasn't allowed to officially meet him, but I'd follow him on the rare times I had a lesson break. Stalking him, I'd dash between props and director chairs, trying to see if he knew more about this dying business than I did.

Jacob hadn't come by much, but on the odd times he did, he fascinated me. He was just a boy, yet the crew treated him with utmost respect and suffocating pity. He barely said a word and glowered at most of the actors, but no one ever reprimanded him.

He was everything I wasn't allowed to be.

Mud covered his jeans, stains painted his T-shirt, his dark blond hair was shaggy, hands dirty, and face tanned from the sun. I'd been envious of his freedom. Jealous that he was permitted outside while I was stuck in the air-conditioned shadows of my flashy trailer.

Even with the strange look in his eyes—the one that warned he'd be friendly but wouldn't let you get too close—didn't stop me from fantasizing what it would be like to be that messy. What it would feel like to be dusty and barefoot and grass-stained.

Now I knew—standing there with a layer of dirt on my brand-new boots—and it was *so* much better than I imagined. Jacob should know how lucky he was to live here.

I'll tell him.

"Where is he?" I blinked, glancing behind the woman as if she were hiding him.

"Where's who?" Her forehead wrinkled.

"Jacob Ren Wild."

A small flicker of pain ran over her face, only to vanish. She tugged on the bridle over her shoulder. "Do you two know each other?"

"I know he ate a vanilla horse once. And I know he's sad."

The woman froze. "You do, huh?"

"Yep." I nodded importantly. "Death always makes people sad. It made me sad too, but now I'm just annoyed that no one can tell me where dead people go because I'd like to talk to my mom, you know?"

"Ehh…"

"Sorry. *So* sorry." Dad slammed to a stop beside me, clamping a hand on my shoulder, locking me in place with a physical leash. His eyes blazed from above. "Hope, what did we *just* talk about?"

I dropped my gaze. *Ugh, it slipped out.* "Sorry."

Dad squeezed me hard, shrugging in helplessness at the woman. "I'm sorry again. I don't know what to say. Her mom passed away and—"

"She died," I clarified helpfully. "Like Jacob's dad."

"Hope!" Dad shook me, rattling my teeth. "Not another word, you hear me? Otherwise, this horse day will be over before it's begun."

True panic filled me. I swallowed back what I wasn't allowed to say. "I promise. I'm sorry. I-I didn't mean it."

"It's fine." The woman shook her head. "Nothing much shocks me these days. Kids and their strange conversations."

Dad laughed under his breath. "Yep. She's keyed up about riding today. When she's excited, she's a little too talkative about subjects that shouldn't be mentioned." His fingers squeezed again, talking to me even though he spoke to the woman.

"Death is a part of life. It's natural to want to know more about it." The woman bent a little, holding out her hand. "I'm Cassie Collins. But most folks round here know me as a Wilson. Call me Cassie, though, okay?" She grinned. "How about, once we've been properly introduced, we have a more personal conversation later? That work for you?"

Dad pushed me forward, letting my shoulder go. I took the hint to be on my best behaviour.

Taking Cassie's hand like I'd been taught, I curled my fingers around hers and shook solemnly. "I'm Hope Jacinta Murphy. Jacinta is my middle name because—"

"Okay, Hope. That will do." Dad chuckled. "Not everyone needs the saga on your full name."

I nodded, standing taller. Horses. Horses were the best thing in the world, and I was here to ride one. Nothing else mattered. "I'm ready to ride now, please."

The woman frowned, her eyes never leaving mine. "You are?"

"Yep. I want to gallop."

"Patience isn't her strong suit, I'm afraid," Dad cut in.

Cassie kept her gaze on me. "Ah, well, galloping takes practice. How about we focus on the basics first, okay?"

I chewed my cheek, doing my best to be polite, grateful, and normal. I didn't want basics. I wanted everything. All of it. *Immediately.* I wanted knowledge and answers and experience. But I merely nodded and smiled sweetly. "Okay."

"Great." Straightening up, Cassie asked, "Just so I can assess your level, have you been around horses before?"

"Nu-huh." I shook my head. "But whenever a horse comes on TV, I get butterflies in my belly." I glanced longingly at the closest pony—a black and white thing with a big butt and long tail.

I melted on the spot.

The woman laughed as my feet drifted forward, my eyes wide with longing. The reins and leather of the bridle creaked by her side. "Wow, you're in trouble, Mr. Murphy."

Dad cleared his throat. "Excuse me?"

"She's in love, and she hasn't even touched one yet. You're in for an expensive hobby."

"If it makes her happier, then I'm okay with that."

I flicked a look over my shoulder. Dad's tone sounded weird, and when I caught his eyes, they were full of worry. Worry I'd put there because of my stupid questions about dead people.

My heart sank. I'd hurt him. I'd hurt him when he'd given me what I wanted most in the world. Running back to him, my face slammed into his chest as I threw my arms around him. "I love you, Daddy."

No more, okay? I promise I'll never talk about dying again. Not to you or adults, anyway.

I didn't want him to worry about me like he had to worry about Mom for so long. I'd heard the rumours that she'd been mentally unstable toward the end. And I guessed they were right because no one mentally stable would've done what she did. But I wasn't like her. I wouldn't do something so silly.

Dad's arms latched around me as he bowed and kissed the top of my head. "I love you too, Little Lace. You can talk to me about anything, all right? I'm sorry for making you feel like you can't."

Pulling away, I smiled bright and brave. "Can I go ride a horse now?"

He grinned, once again that concerned sadness I'd caused gleaming in his eyes. "Sure, go and have fun. I'll stay out of the way, but I'm close by if you need me."

"Okay."

"Aunt Cassie? Where the hell did you put—" Jacob stormed from the barn a few metres away.

I froze.

He was taller than a year ago. His hair just as untamed and eyes just as guarded. But instead of red carpet clothes, he wore leather chaps over Wranglers, a grey plaid shirt with its sleeves rolled up to his elbows, and a tanned cowboy hat.

He suited this outfit so much more. He was cleaner than a lot of the times he'd been on set, but his chin had a smear of earth and his hands were filthy.

Same old surly boy even if a year separated our first official meeting.

His gaze landed on me, and just like in the cinema, something tingled down my spine. Something warm and wary. Something that said he was different and not necessarily in a good way.

Once, when Dad was filming in some town, a stray dog slinked on set. All bones and matted fur; the adults wrinkled their noses at it and shooed it away.

I'd slipped from Keeko's ever watchful care and chased after it. The poor thing growled at me. It'd tried to bite me when I reached out to pet it. It snarled when I offered some of my sandwich.

But I wasn't afraid.

Its violence was because it was scared. Somehow, I knew that without being told, and I didn't run away. I merely sat down, placed my chicken sandwich between us, and waited.

I waited a while.

More patient than I'd ever been.

But slowly, the dog swallowed its terror and crawled toward the food. It devoured it in two wolf-like gulps. Afterward, it sniffed me from afar, then claw by claw, it inched closer.

The first time it let me touch his dirty head, my heart was heavy and light and hurting and happy all at once. I hated what he'd been through, but I was glad he was with me now. It hurt thinking about his hardship but I was grateful to be able to fix it.

For three months, I smuggled food out for him. He still growled occasionally if I moved too suddenly, but in the end, he would lick my face all over and fall asleep with his head on my lap.

When Dad found me, curled up with a feral stray on the night of the wrap party, I'd exploded into tears as he'd yanked me away. I wanted to keep the dog. We'd bonded. We'd built trust. We were friends. But he called the shelter, and they took him away.

He promised they'd find him a good home. But I heard that some shelters killed unwanted animals. So the dog I saved became yet another victim of death that I couldn't understand.

That was how I felt about Jacob.

I pitied him yet was grateful for him.

I was wary of him but brave enough to face him.

He might bite but only because he was afraid.

Rolling his eyes, he broke the trance between us, muttering under his breath, "Nope." Turning on his heel, he lifted a chap-wrapped leg to head back into the barn.

"Oh, no you don't, Jacob Wild. Come here. Meet your new student." Cassie clicked her fingers as if he was some skittish horse and needed encouragement. "Come on. Don't be rude."

Perhaps, I should've brought some carrots and apples, not to treat the ponies but to bribe Jacob to be my friend.

His shoulders slumped before turning again and exhaling in a heavy puff. With hands balled, he stalked toward us.

Even though I thought of him as a beaten stray, my skin still prickled with rejection.

What had I done to annoy him so much?

I'd barely said anything to him. So many days separated our first meeting. The only thing I'd done was told him my name so he wouldn't forget me. What was so bad about that?

Yes, his dad had died like my mom, and that sucked. But he was older. He knew more about the hows and whys than I did. He would have answers that I'd been denied.

He should have it figured out.

I'd stared at him that night, wondering if he held the secrets I needed. Hoping I could make him like me enough to share those secrets.

But he'd just glared until my scalp prickled.

When he'd moved to sit beside me, I'd wanted to whisper in his ear that Keeko read an article online about ghosts. I'd wanted to ask if he'd seen his dad's ghost. I wanted to tell him I knew what it was like to be a kid and worry about the parent left behind.

But then I caught the sad glisten in his eyes masked by cold anger—a look I knew well from Dad's grief—and my pity ordered me to offer a hug.

The same physical touch I'd offered the stray that'd growled and snarled and threatened to bite, but in the end, loved me as much as I loved him.

But unlike the dog, Jacob looked repulsed.

He glowered as if I'd done something unforgivable.

A hug was something *everyone* wanted. It cured most things. Or at least, that was what Dad said. But to Jacob, I might as well have thrown those fancy-named ice creams in his face.

Dust plumed around his boots as he came to a stop beside Cassie. His jaw worked before he forced politely, "Hello again, Hope Jacinta Murphy."

I beamed, despite my fear that I'd offended him. "You remembered."

"Told you I would, didn't I?" His forehead furrowed before he looked at my dad, and his face blackened even more. "Graham."

Dad nodded, his back straightening like it did when he met well-connected directors.

Huh, that's strange.

He gave respect to a grumpy kid instead of requesting he show better manners.

I knew he'd played Jacob's dead dad. I knew he liked his still alive mother. And I knew playing that part had changed him and not in a happy way.

It'd reminded him of true love.

That he'd lost it.

And so had the woman called Ribbon.

But still…to see him submit to a teenager was *huge.*

"Jake. Good day for a ride." Dad cleared his throat. "Nice weather."

"It's Jacob. And yeah, it is." Grabbing the bridle from Cassie's shoulder, he fisted the whole thing in one hand. "Been looking all over for this."

"I was going to tack up Binky before Hope arrived."

"I'll do it. The sooner we get the lesson done, the better."

"Whatever you want." Cassie smirked, her gaze jumping from Jacob to me. "Take Hope with you."

"Next time." He stalked off without looking at me.

I refused to be so easily intimidated. I'd faced down a rabid starving mutt. I could face a snappish boy. Leaving Dad without a backward glance, I skipped to his side.

His body tensed, his stride lengthening as if he could out run me.

I just skipped faster. "Can I help?"

"No."

"Why not?"

"Because bridling isn't something a beginner does."

"But how can I learn if I don't do it?"

"You'll learn later. Once you've mastered the basics." He strode faster, his chin tipped up and eyes narrowed against the sun.

I kept pace, my heart twirling in happiness as we moved closer to the horses. "What are the basics?"

"Other stuff."

"What other stuff?"

"Stuff you'll learn. Now git. Go back to your dad. Your horse isn't ready yet."

"I want to watch."

He sighed heavily. "Why? I'm just gonna put his bridle on."

"I need to watch so next time *I* can do it."

"If there even is a next time. And besides, it's not that easy." He scowled down at me. He was rather tall; all legs and length. "You have to make sure not to clack their teeth with the bit, to thread their ears through the headstall, and to cinch the buckles to the right length."

"Okay. Got it."

"It's not a matter of 'getting it.' It's a matter of experience."

I smiled. "Experience you'll teach me."

"Ugh." He looked at the sky. "Fine."

"Great!" I clapped my hands as we approached the black and white big-butt thing, but then my smile fell as we skirted around it to a tiny white pony that had its nose almost touching the dirt, fast asleep.

It was nothing like the black noble Pegasus I'd envisioned, flying over fields and through forests, the world a blur.

"What's that?" I planted hands on my hips.

"What do you mean, what's that?" Jacob laid his palm on the tiny pony's rump, scratching him gently as he moved to its head.

The horse blinked sleepily, lifting his long neck as if it was the biggest chore in the world.

And then, it yawned.

Yawned as if it would rather be in the paddock munching grass than about to create magic with me.

A horse yawning was *ugly*. All teeth and tongue and eyes rolling back.

Eww.

"I'm not riding that."

Jacob snickered. "And I say you are."

"But I want a fast one."

He wrapped his arm around the pony's head, positioning him while slipping the bit into its mouth and securing the bridle so smoothly and quickly, I was left a little in awe.

He was right. Watching hadn't taught me a thing. He was way too fast. He had an otherworldly way with these critters, and I had yet to touch one.

Raising an eyebrow, Jacob turned to face me, allowing his body to fall against the pony until it held his weight. The pony didn't flinch or protest at being used as a leaning pole; if anything, it nickered quietly and huffed in contentment as if they did this a lot.

"A fast one, huh?" He ran a hand over his shaggy, dirty blond hair. "Fast ones are dangerous."

"I don't mind danger."

He looked me up and down, from the brand-new cowboy boots with their turquoise faux snakeskin to the freshly pressed jeans and matching turquoise shirt with pearl buttons.

I'd picked this outfit from an online catalogue stating that true horse girls mucked out barns and rode champion rodeos in impeccable outfits.

I shivered as his gaze burned into me, dark and distrusting with a hint of—okay, a lot of—dislike. "You would handle one lope of canter before squealing to get off."

Crossing my arms, I cocked my chin. "Try me."

"My aunt would kill me." He chuckled under his breath. "And as much as I'd love to prove a point and chuck you on Forrest just for fun, I won't. You'll start with Binky." He elbowed the white pony keeping him upright. "This is Binky. He's trustworthy, sane, listens, and looks after beginners."

"So everything you're not," I muttered, eyeing the horse and thinking what a stupid name. It was a kid's name. I didn't come here to be treated like a kid. Especially not by him.

He might have the adults fooled, but I saw who he truly was.

He was more damaged than the stray. More lost than any

abandoned dog. More likely to lash out than any mistreated beast. "I thought you might be happier than last year at the movies. You're not."

Jacob stiffened. His jaw locked; eyes narrowed.

When he didn't say anything, I added, "Time is supposed to stop the pain of losing someone." I looked at the ground. "I guess it has for me, but some days are bad." I dared look up. "Are you having a bad day, or are you always like this?"

His eyes darkened to dangerous black. "Are you always this nosy?"

"Most of the time." I nodded. "I have so many questions to ask you. When we left the movies that night, Dad told me we could come for a ride the next week, but then he got another job which started straight away. My questions had to wait. But I've been dying to come ever since your mom told me—"

"Enough. You're not here to talk. And I'm not here to listen." He grabbed a brush from the ground and swiped it hard and fast over the pony's mane.

His back moved with jerky yanks. He muttered something I couldn't hear.

Despite his prickly attitude, I wanted to hug him. To deliver what I'd offered at the cinema. To give in to the undeniable urge to just reach out and *touch* him.

I might be killed for it, but what if it helped him?

It made no sense. Apart from Dad, I didn't really like touching people.

Not after what happened with Mom.

But him…yeah, he needed to be hugged.

"…so that's the plan. You ready?"

I shook my head. "Umm, what? Were you talking to me?"

"God, weren't you listening?" He sighed in annoyance, spinning around and throwing the brush on the hay-littered ground. "Great. I give you the rundown of what's about to happen, and you just stare off into space like a—"

"Sorry, okay. I'll listen to everything you say from now on." My temper—that I'd earned from my mother, according to my father—spiked. "Just repeat and let's get this show on the road."

"You're not in the movie business here, *Hope*." He bit out my name. "Don't get pushy with me."

I narrowed my eyes, not liking his tone—the sharpness or intolerance.

I wanted to argue. To tell him even though he thought I was

some Hollywood brat, I was more than that. He should give me a chance instead of making up his mind about me. I wasn't ten anymore. I knew more things than I did a year ago.

But then my temper smoked, and my shoulders slouched.

Just like I didn't blame the stray for growling at me, I couldn't blame Jacob Ren Wild. He was right. I'd been too pushy. I'd ruined this all over again.

Suddenly, riding didn't seem all that fun after all.

Looking at Binky's hooves, I asked softly, "What exactly did I do wrong?"

Silence fell as Jacob pushed off the pony and stood upright. "Excuse me?"

I dared look at him. "All I did was be nice to you at the movie premier, and you decided to hate me instantly. You might see a silly kid who you don't have time for, but I'm not. I'm studying high-school level stuff, according to Keeko. I ask questions no self-respecting adult should ask, according to Dad. And…well, I kinda don't have any friends. I just wanted you to like me so…"

"So what?"

"So I would have someone to talk to."

"I'm not interested in conversation."

"I'm getting that." I huffed, kicking dirt, silently pleased when more dust settled over my pristine boots. "Anywho…Binky. He's safe. I'm a beginner. I'm stupid and not to be trusted. I get it." Stepping away from him, I looked at the arena to the side. "Are we going in there? Should we get started so you can do other stuff rather than hang with me?"

I made the mistake of looking at him.

He stood rooted to the ground, eyes wide, head cocked as if he couldn't figure me out.

My tummy tumbled as he licked his lips. "Huh." Disbelief was heavy in his tone. Shoving both hands into his back pockets, he drifted toward me, his chaps whispering together. "She has a backbone. Who knew?"

"What?"

He ignored me. "What questions?"

"Huh?"

"You said you ask questions that no self-respecting adult would ask." He rocked back on his heels as if my answer was no big deal but couldn't hide his interest. "What questions?"

"Oh, no. This is a trick." I glanced over my shoulder to where Dad and that Cassie woman were still talking. "Dad told me those subjects are off-limits. For once, I'm going to behave."

Dad caught my eye, waving across the yard.

I waved back just as Jacob muttered, "What subjects?"

"Nothing."

"It's something." He scowled. "Tell me."

"Can't."

"Why not?"

"'Cause it's not suitable conversation."

"I don't care. I *like* unsuitable conversation." His shadow fell over me, locking me in place.

He wasn't that much older than me, but the authority in his voice and the desire to obey were a little too hard to ignore.

He crowded me. "Tell me."

"No."

"Yes."

I pouted. "I won't be allowed to ride if I do."

"Tell you what." He leaned closer, threatening and conspiring all at once. "I promise to give you a lesson if you tell me. Despite what the adults say."

"Promise?" I blinked, goosebumps once again erupting at his closeness.

"Hope to die."

I cocked my head at the phrase. Funny how something related to keeping a promise had my name in it tied with death.

Maybe that was why I was so fascinated by the subject.

Taking a step back, I hesitated. Wasn't this what I wanted? To talk to a fellow kid who'd lost half his family and seek answers? Narrowing my gaze, I nodded. "Okay."

"Good, spit it out." He removed his hands from his pockets and crossed his arms, a half-smile on his face. "Go on. What stuff aren't you allowed to talk about?"

"Stuff like death and things."

He froze. "What about death?"

"Forget it. I'm—"

"Interested in dying?"

I nodded, focusing on Binky who'd gone back to sleep.

"What about dying?" he asked quietly, shooting the adults a look. For the first time, he accepted me as part of his inner circle instead of keeping me pushed out of it.

I liked that.

I liked that too much.

It made me want to give him what he asked for even though

it would mean breaking my promise to Dad.

I glanced over my shoulder again. Dad had finished his conversation with Cassie and headed to the car, no doubt to get his phone to take photos of me and catalogue this whole riding afternoon.

I had precisely two minutes alone with Jacob before I'd have my watcher back in place.

The dark questions shouldn't be in my head, but I couldn't kick them out. When I'd tried, they only became more persistent.

If I talked about them with Jacob, maybe they'd stop hounding me so much.

Stepping into Jacob, I sniffed the rich leathery smell of him. Sweet grass and hot sunshine mixed in my nose, making me that much more jealous of where he lived versus my home on the road. "Mom committed suicide a week after my seventh birthday. She took pills like your mom did in the movie."

"Wait, what?" His face went monstrous. "My mom is *alive*. She would never be weak enough to kill herself."

I cringed. He just called my mom weak.

He moved to speak again, but I whispered in a rush, "I found her in bed when I got home with my old nanny from tennis practice."

Jacob sucked in a breath, his eyes still black but not as murderous. "You found her on your own?"

"Yes." I nodded, biting my lip against the memories of her cold waxy hand, and her glazed hazy eyes. "I thought she was napping, so I curled into bed with her. Nanny went to make dinner, leaving me with her for an hour. It wasn't until Dad came home and found me snuggled with a corpse that I understood why Mom was so cold—despite the blankets I pulled over us."

Jacob gulped. He opened his mouth as if to request more morbid details, but Dad appeared. His hand clamped on my shoulder, squeezing in love, layering me with guilt for doing something he'd asked me not to.

I shouldn't have done that.

I shouldn't have said one stupid word.

Stepping away from Jacob, I swallowed back the strange prickles of sadness and confusion I always felt whenever I thought about that day and beamed guiltily at the best parent in the world. "Hey."

"Hey." Dad smiled back. "Ready to ride?"

"Yep!" I bounced on the spot, overacting a little but oh well.

Best he thought I was an overexcited girl than someone obsessed with stuff no sane person should be. Best he believe I hadn't just betrayed him.

"Great." He turned his gaze to Jacob. "All good to go?"

Jacob cleared his throat, his gaze lingering on me. "Sure. Uh-huh." Moving away, he gave me another odd look before heading to Binky's tether, undoing the rope, and rousing the dopey pony into a plod.

Dad held me back as Jacob guided the white horse around us toward the arena.

As Jacob went by me, his face mixed with disbelief, grudging respect, and a familiar tinge of worry.

Worry for who I truly was.

I'd revealed my strangeness.

And just like the adults, he'd judged me.

I guessed I wouldn't be getting answers from him, after all.

My heart sank to my toes, and I just wanted to forget this day, this moment, this mistake.

With my hand in Dad's, I followed the boy I no longer wanted to talk to and the pony I no longer wanted to ride into the arena.

Chapter Five

JACOB

✶ ✶ ✶ ✶ ✶ ✶

"NO, STOP THAT. God, how many times do I need to tell you—"

"You suck at teaching," Hope grumbled as Binky ignored her commands to turn right and headed toward the triangle of barrels instead.

"Left leg and right rein. Otherwise, you're gonna" —I slapped my forehead as the screech of metal met Binky's chest— "crash."

Hope bent in the saddle, lying over the pony's neck as her hands stroked, searching for injury. "Oh, no. Poor thing! He ran into the barrel."

"He didn't. *You* did." Storming over to her, I grabbed Binky's bridle and marched him—with his tiny passenger—back to the centre of the arena. "Listen to me and collisions won't happen."

I wouldn't tell her that Binky had done that deliberately. It was a trick of his to get out of lugging beginners around. Giving him a secret pat, we eyeballed each other, on the same wavelength about how annoying newbies were.

When I'd learned on Binky, I'd lasted one afternoon doing walking aids and tolerating the basics before I'd unclipped the lead rope that Mom had me hooked to, then kicked that fat little pony with my short stupid legs.

Binky had been younger then and up for an adventure just as much as I was.

I still remembered Dad's shout as I galloped past him. He'd been building the fence and rail for the new arena, but instead of chasing after me like Mom did, he merely laughed, snagged my mom around the middle as she bolted behind me in panic, and let me make my own mistakes.

I'd like to say I stayed on for the entire gallop.

I didn't.

Halfway through the meadow, Binky decided he was having way too much fun to share with me and bucked me off.

I'd landed in a thicket of wildflowers, winded and bruised but on such a high I felt drugged. When Dad appeared above me with his dark eyes glittering and hand outstretched, I'd prepared for a telling-off. Only, he'd hauled me up, checked me over, and ruffled my hair with a whispered, "Living up to your name, aren't you, Wild One?"

I couldn't remember what I'd said, but I'd been drunk off adrenaline and hated when Mom had caught up, huffing and puffing, running her hands down my arms and legs for broken bones.

Dad had coughed and cleared his throat, giving me a wink as he said sternly, "Don't be so reckless again, Jacob. You hear me?"

I heard him, and I knew his command was purely for Mom's benefit because after she assured herself I was in one piece, Dad and I walked back to the barn together while Mom went to wrangle Binky who had his head in the wildflowers.

He'd rested a hand on my shoulder, squeezing man to man. "I'm proud of you, Jacob. You're not afraid to try new things but don't forget that fear is sometimes the difference between life and death. Don't ignore that voice when it's important."

"Let go of him." Hope swatted my head with her small fingers, tugging on the reins and slamming me back into the present. "Please."

I blinked as she flapped her legs in some imitation of asking the horse to move forward.

"By all means, try again." I snickered at how bad she was. "Perhaps the twentieth try will be the one."

"You're so mean." She stuck her tongue out, flapping her legs again.

"Not mean. Just pointing out the truth."

"You could try *helping* me instead of telling me off all the time."

"I am helping." I crossed my arms as Binky decided the same as me—that her aids were shocking, and he was going to ignore them all—and promptly pawed the sand, looking for a nice place to roll.

Darting forward, I grabbed his bride again. "Oh, no you don't." Pulling him into a walk, I looked at her. "Close call and you don't even know it. See? I *am* helping."

"What? What was he about to do?" Her face whitened under her helmet. "Rear?"

I rolled my eyes. "No, he wasn't going to rear. He was going to take you for a roll." For dramatic effect, I added, "You could've been crushed."

"Oh." Hope's eyes drifted to where her dad leaned on the railings, watching us and occasionally snapping photos. "Thank you…for not letting him crush me."

She didn't need to know if he had gone down, she would've just tipped out of the saddle. Leading her forward, I expected more attitude, but when she stayed quiet, I glanced back.

Her shoulders drooped lower the longer I led her around the arena. She looked dejected. Pissed off. Over it.

Guilt prodded me.

Clearing my throat, I searched for something to say. Normally, she was the one jabbering away. My gaze landed on the wooden bridge and barrels. "Eh, see all this junk in here?"

She bit her lip, looking at the flags and fake bull in the corner with barely any effort. "Yeah?"

"That's for Working Equitation. Perhaps, when you can steer a bit better, you can have a go at an obstacle."

I fully expected that promise to cheer her up. Working Equitation was awesome.

But it didn't.

"Umm, ca-can I get off?" Her chin tucked, and she pulled on the reins instead of using her seat like I'd told her.

"What? Why?"

"Stop." She pulled harder, then remembered her manners. "Please."

I stopped walking, and Binky let out a soft sigh. Little asshole knew he'd won.

Without waiting for me to help her down, she swung her leg over the saddle and leapt before taking her other foot out of the stirrup.

She tumbled toward the ground.

Instinct made me leap forward and half catch her, half act as a landing pad as her weight tripped me sideways.

"Oof!" I crunched into the dirt with her on top of me.

"Oops!" Her knee caught me in places it shouldn't, and her elbow jabbed my throat. "Sorry, I—"

"God's sake. Stop squirming." I clamped my hands on her shoulders, holding her in place while I made sure she wasn't tangled with any tack and Binky was a safe distance away to shove her to her feet.

Helping her upward, I stood as she swatted at sand and dust on her no-longer-new jeans.

Arching my spine, working out the kink she'd left me with, my gaze trailed to something lacy and black left on the ground.

Scooping it up, I narrowed my eyes at the tatty piece of torn something or other.

Fast fingers snatched it from me, then stuffed it into her back pocket.

"What was that?" I dropped my hand slowly.

"Nothing."

"It was something."

"Forget it." She stomped toward her dad, undoing her helmet and letting it swing from dejected fingers.

What the hell had gone wrong?

She'd been all over this thirty minutes ago…and now…she acted as if I'd forced her onto the damn horse.

I whistled for Binky who trailed after me without having to hold him. Together, we followed Hope while I did my best not to eavesdrop.

"Lace? What's up?" Her dad put his phone into his pocket and went to open the gate to exit the arena. He grabbed her in a hug, pressing her face to his chest. "Something happen?"

Hope sighed heavily. "I suck."

Ah! So that *was what was going on.*

"You don't suck." He chuckled, which was probably the worst thing he could do. I knew because it all made sense now.

Hope had been one of *those.*

The type of rider who watched so many programs and movies and dreamed about riding, they thought they'd hop on and it would be natural. That the horse would do what they wanted when they asked, and it would be a seamless bond between human and animal.

Silly girl.

"I do. I'm terrible. I don't want to do this after all." Hope tore herself out of her dad's embrace. "It was stupid to come."

"You waited a year to try horse riding. Don't give up after a few minutes." Her dad glanced at me lingering with Binky.

Hope shook her head vehemently. "Don't care. I suck and want to leave."

Her dad clucked his tongue. "Ah, now, everyone sucks when

they first start."

I groaned under my breath as he said yet another wrong thing.

I didn't want Hope hanging around Cherry River, but I didn't want to crush her dreams either.

I'd been semi-responsible for her disappointment.

I'd let her fumble around like a moron without giving her proper guidance.

This was my fault.

I wanted to keep my mouth shut and celebrate that she was about to leave, but the longer I watched her, the more guilty I became. So guilty, my stomach churned and the heavy presence that I always felt when I screwed up whispered down my back.

Dad hadn't told me off often when he was alive, but his ghost was judging me now. Arms crossed, head shaking, reprimand bright in his dark gaze.

"Yeah, yeah." I sighed at the sky. "I know."

"Did you say something?" Graham looked up, worry etching his eyes as Hope brushed by him, her boots kicking dirt with frustration.

"Yeah, I did actually." Grabbing Binky's reins, I pulled them over his head and passed the worn leather to Graham. "Hold him for a sec."

Without waiting for his reply, I jogged past him and caught up with Hope. "Giving up, huh?"

She glowered with angry green eyes. "Just realised horses aren't for me."

"I call bullshit."

"Don't swear." Her hoity-toity nose rose. "Dad will hear you."

"Don't care. And I can swear. This is my home. My rules."

"And now you get your home back, don't you?" She sneered, no longer the sweet kid trying to be my friend. "We're leaving."

"Not yet, you're not."

"What?"

"Wait here."

"Nuh-uh." She crossed her arms, planting herself to the ground. "I want to leave. Right now."

"Two minutes." I held up two fingers, then took off toward the back meadow.

My legs stretched as fast as they could, chewing up the ground I'd raced over so many times before.

Aunt Cassie saw me charging past the barn, her hand raised then dropped, realising where I was going. "Jacob, no." She shook her head. "Don't."

Mid-sprint, I merely shrugged and kept on running.

I bolted down the driveway, vaulted over a wooden gate, charged across the front small pasture and over another fence until finally, I slowed and snatched the rope halter off the ground where I'd tossed it last.

Forrest, my trusty roan who had mood swings like the devil and wings in his hooves, snorted at my sudden arrival. Prancing away from me, he didn't like the blast of my nervous energy.

"Don't be a dick." I grabbed a handful of grass and lured him toward me. "Come on. Ten minutes. Then you can come back and stuff your face. Deal?"

He eyed me with a snide, almost exasperated look.

I chuckled, giving him a scratch as he let me loop the halter over his velvet nose and fasten it. "We're a bit too alike, you and me. And that's not a good thing."

He let out a massive breath, his lips fluttering and green goo from mulched grass spraying my chaps. "Great. Thanks."

Tossing the lead rope over his neck, I tied it back on itself to fashion basic reins, then fisted a handful of his mane. "Ready?"

Forrest side-stepped, already getting antsy.

"I take that as a yes." Lurching myself upright, I folded over his bare back, then pushed upright.

The moment I found my centre, he took off.

Wind instantly howled in my ears as we went from zero to warp speed. Grass blurred, and the fence came closer and closer.

My thighs squeezed, my hands clutched rein and mane, and I kicked on the final stride, encouraging him to scale the obstruction, sailing us up and over as smooth as a cresting wave.

"Good boy."

My praise meant everything, and his entire body shivered. He put his head down, activating more muscles to run faster.

Me and Forrest…we were an enigma. He'd come to Aunt Cassie to be broken in after other trainers had tried and failed. No one could get him to move forward. He'd just prop on two legs or scurry backward until he fell over or the rider hopped off.

Cassie had tried to fix him. Even Mom had had a go. But no one could get through to the mess of him.

He was never meant to be mine.

It'd happened by pure stupidity on my part.

I'd had a bad day at school. Dad had only been gone two months. I was sick of crying, sick of missing him, sick of worrying about Mom.

At three a.m., I'd found myself running from my demons, desperate to find somewhere to shut up the voices and grief inside my head, only to run into Forrest's paddock.

He'd been called Speckles then.

He'd galloped away from me, and because of the rabid mood I was in, I'd chased him. Wanting him to be afraid of something, just like I was.

I was afraid of everything.

Dying.

Loving.

Family.

I chased him for hours until I finally had nothing left and collapsed jelly-legged in the grass. Dawn crested, and as the moon lost to the sun something amazing happened.

Forrest came toward me, nudged my panting, sweaty body, and didn't leave my side until I was ready to sit up in my pyjamas and stroke his nose.

I patted him for ages before I hauled myself upright on aching bones, knowing I had to head home before Mom noticed I was missing. She'd have a breakdown if anything happened to me...especially after losing Dad.

Only, the horse followed me. He didn't let me out of his sight.

By the time I got to the gate, he wuffled and nickered, and the loneliness in his eyes matched the loneliness in my heart.

And I couldn't leave him.

I climbed the fence and waited for him to come close enough, then threw myself onto his back.

I fully expected him to buck me off.

Instead, his nose turned to snuffle my foot, his body twitched for command, and his ears stayed forward and attentive.

I'd squeezed my legs.

Bridleless, saddleless, fearless.

With no experience other than on a silly pony and no tack to control, I gave my life to the creature as we broke into a gallop.

No walking or trotting for us.

We ran.

Ran from things we didn't fully understand. And unlike me, who was exhausted from chasing him all night, he had energy to burn.

So we did.

We flew around that paddock until the grass churned into mud with hoof prints.

I forgot about everything.

The demons in my head fell quiet.

But then Aunt Cassie and Mom found us, and I'd been grounded for a month. In the end, I'd offered up my entire lifesavings of pocket money to buy him because I overheard Aunt Cassie on the phone saying Speckles wasn't suitable and would end up hurting someone.

They'd mentioned dog food.

I'd told them I'd run away and never come back if they did.

The old owner accepted my piggy bank of change just to be rid of him.

And I'd found my only friend who helped remind me that school and the current crap I was living was only temporary. That soon, I would be a farmer full time, and we'd spend all day together.

"Git. Go on." I growled. "Faster."

He hauled his bulk to an insane speed, just as crazy as me.

I merely held on, allowing him to race.

I let him race because when I gave my very existence to him, I found the freedom I was missing. I wasn't thinking about Dad or Mom or school or gossiping townsfolk.

All I thought about was grass and horse.

Forrest's hooves thundered to the final fence blocking off the turnaround bay by the stables.

Aunt Cassie ran toward us in the distance, sprinting like she always did to try to prevent me from doing what I'd been doing for years. "Jacob. *No!*" She reached the gate, hauling it open. "Come this way. For the love of God!" She waved her arms, but Forrest was locked on a different location.

The fence at the highest point on the crest of the hill.

"Do it." I flattened myself on his back, forced my legs long and low, held my breath, and died, lived, laughed, cried as he flew over the final fence, sharing his power with me as he clattered onto the pebbles, kicking up stones as I sat up and finally took control, bringing him to a trot, then a walk just in front of Hope.

Her jaw landed in the dirt. Her eyes bugged.

Leaping off, I grabbed her inert hand, wrapped it around the halter of my heavily breathing crazy horse, then vanished into the stable.

It only took a second to grab a Western saddle with a high horn and deep seat and the lunge line. Squinting in the sun, I was back outside and tossing the saddle onto Forrest before Hope had uttered a word.

Cinching the saddle into place, Forrest danced on the spot, not used to being so roughly tacked up—and without a brush— poor him. But he tolerated my snappy behaviour as I snatched the halter from Hope, clipped the lunge line onto it, then grabbed her around the waist and hoisted her up.

"Wait, stop—" Her hands planted on my shoulders, fingernails digging deep as I shoved her into the saddle. My arms shook under her weight, struggling with how tall Forrest was.

"Leg over," I grunted, breathing hard as I waited until she did as I asked.

"No, I don't—"

"Just do it." I boosted her the final way.

She cringed, hunkering into the saddle as Forrest pranced, making her clutch onto the pommel with white knuckles.

"Let me down." Her face turned colourless. *"Please."*

"Jacob, what the *hell* do you think you are doing?" Graham tried to grab Hope, but Forrest shied away, his metal shoes clattering on pebbles.

Hope squealed, jamming her knees into the horse, the stirrups far too long for her.

Graham glowered at me. "Get her off that thing. *Immediately.*"

"No." Clucking my tongue, I urged Forrest into a trot, whisking Hope away from her father and out of reach of Aunt Cassie as she jogged toward me, about to prevent me from doing something I most likely shouldn't do.

Hope whimpered, clinging to the saddle horn as she bounced.

"Jacob. *Stop!*" Aunt Cassie shouted, angrier than she'd ever been. "This is insane. Get her off that creature!"

Ignoring everyone, including Hope as she sniffled on top of my horse, I guided Forrest as fast as I could into the arena, made my way to the centre, then uncoiled the lunge line and looked at Hope.

Her eyes met mine, terrified and wide. "Jacob—"

"Just trust me."

Adults gave chase.

Curses were screamed.

I had only a few seconds to get things organised before they ruined this.

Hope wasn't wearing a helmet.

She had no experience.

She was on a horse everyone said would be better in a can than being ridden.

But this was what she needed.

"Ready?"

She shook her head furiously. "No! Let me down."

"Can't. Not yet."

"Wha-what are you going to do?"

"Give you what you want."

"I want down!" Her cheeks flushed red with rage.

"No, you don't." I stepped away, putting distance between me and Forrest's legs. "You want this."

"No. *Stop.*" She squealed as I clucked my tongue, and Forrest immediately kicked into a lope. A nice easy canter, forward and smooth. *"Ahhhh!"*

I didn't let her screams stop me. I didn't let the pressure of disappointing my dead father make me second-guess. He was all about pushing limits and being brave.

This was Hope's moment.

"Jacob!" Aunt Cassie yelled from the arena entrance, knowing better than to run into the circle of a lunging horse. "Stop this before you hurt her!"

"She won't get hurt!" I yelled back before shutting her out and focusing on Hope and only Hope. "If you listen to what I tell you, you'll be fine."

Hope merely shook her head in panic.

"Sit deep. Push your heels down. Hold on to the horn. Ride the wave. Don't fight it. You don't have to worry about steering. I've got him. You don't have to worry about speed. I'm in control. All you have to do is ask yourself if this is what you were looking for."

A full circle at a canter and she hadn't fallen off or burst into tears.

She was pale as milk and stiff as a door, and Forrest snorted at the strangeness of carrying her and not me. His ears flicked back and forth, getting pissy but obeying me to keep cantering.

"Listen to me, Hope. You're fine. He won't do anything. You asked for this, remember? You wanted to be galloping by this afternoon. Well, it's this afternoon, and you're cantering. Three circles, Hope, and you're still on."

A ghost of a smile twitched her lips.

Another circle.

Still hanging on. Still white.

"Let your lower spine go loose. Rock your hips. Let the saddle swallow you up."

She dared look at me instead of keeping her eyes glued to Forrest's wither. For a millisecond, she obeyed, unlocking her spine and riding with the horse instead of fighting it.

But then she lost it, seizing up again, bouncing on his back. "Stop. *Stop!*"

"I won't stop. Not until you learn."

"I don't *want* to learn!"

"Stop this nonsense this instant!" Graham tried to get to me, but each time he charged forward, Forrest was there, cantering around me, blocking me in the circle.

"Jacob. Don't do this. Teach her the normal way. You're terrifying her!" Aunt Cassie commanded, her face red with rage.

"The normal way sucks," I called back. "She has to accept that riding is hard, it's scary, and it's not at all like the movies." I narrowed a look at Hope. "She has to know this isn't choreographed like the sets she lives on. It's not point and shoot. If she wants to ride, she has to *ride*. It's not fake or made up. She rides, or she dies." I shrugged. "Injury versus staying on-board."

"Jacob…" Hope moaned. *"Please."*

I'd lost count of how many circles Forrest had cantered. He could go all day. The only way this was stopping was if Hope listened to me or if she fully accepted that she'd been lying to herself about needing this.

"Listen to the horse, Hope." I clucked my tongue, making Forrest go faster.

She squealed, holding on harder, bouncing like a potato.

"I'll stop him if you can sit to the canter for two beats. Just two. Got it?"

She clamped her lips together, yanking herself deeper into the saddle but not using any leg strength.

"Clutch with your thighs. You don't need your hands. It's all in your seat."

"I'm not you!" Red patches glowed brighter on her cheeks. "I can't do this!"

"You can. Rock. Relax that spine. Ride, for God's sake, don't just bounce there."

Forrest pig-rooted as Hope's legs dangled by his side.

She screamed.

Cassie yelled something.

Graham bellowed.

And I kept Forrest cantering. Placing the long lunge line on the ground, I tucked the end under a rock. The minute it wouldn't drag behind Forrest, I sprinted toward girl and beast.

"What are you—"

Hope never finished that sentence as I vaulted up behind her.

I'd leapt on Forrest many times while he was mid pace. Some I'd landed, some I hadn't, all of them a gamble of faith.

This time, I had something to hold on to, and I wrapped my arms around Hope as I settled behind the saddle on Forrest's rump.

He snorted but kept running.

"Ride with your hips, Hope." Clamping my hands on her waist, I pushed her down, stopping her bouncing, forcing her to rock with the beat.

Instantly, her spine unlocked, her body swayed, and her tension unravelled like a seasoned rider.

"Oh…"

"Yes, oh. Feels good, huh?"

I kept holding her, letting her feel the undeniable freedom and connection of riding with the horse and not against it.

She was tiny and fragile in my hands but strong and steel-willed too. She was a kid who'd napped with her dead mother. A kid who was brave enough to ask a total stranger about death. A kid who didn't have anyone else to talk to in her fake world of movies and actors.

If she didn't annoy me so much, I might've felt sorry for her.

But then her tension came back, reminding me she sought me for a friend but she didn't listen.

"I want to stop now."

I smirked. "You didn't say please."

"Please."

Chuckling, I nudged Forrest a bit faster. "Not yet."

My thumbs dug into the small of her back, forcing her to unlock her hips again.

With a sharp breath, she relaxed and trusted, and the difference in her riding was night and day.

The moment her body naturally lengthened and sought the pace again, I whistled under my breath, bringing Forrest to a complete stop.

She breathed hard in front of me. Her back touching my chest with each inhale. Her brown hair crackled from flying every which way and sweat glistened on her young face.

But she was alive.

And the look in her eyes was no longer defeat but utter awe.

I leapt off, wiping heat from my forehead and looking up at her with the sun blinding me. "Now, tell me you didn't feel that."

Her gaze was glossy, wistful, addicted. "I felt it."

"Good."

She swayed in the saddle. She looked as if I'd just gotten her drunk on illegal substances.

And in a way, I had.

Horses were pure addiction.

"Wow."

I grinned, enjoying how the tightness and nervousness in her mellowed into shaky joy.

Graham skidded to a stop, shoved me to the side, and yanked his daughter from my horse. Wagging a finger in my face, he snarled, "If you *ever* put my Lace in danger again, I'll skin you alive."

Aunt Cassie penned in my other side, disappointment and anger all over her. "What were you *thinking*, Jacob?"

I smiled wider, my eyes not leaving Hope's as she gawked at me from her father's arms.

She might be a child of Hollywood, but for the first time in her life, she was more than what she'd been born into.

She'd had a taste of freedom. And good luck to anyone who tried to tell her she couldn't have more.

Tipping my hand to the rim of my cowboy hat, I saluted my young student. "You didn't die. Congratulations."

Her eyes flared. Graham's jaw clenched. And I stepped the hell away from furious adults.

"That was a stupid, *stupid* thing to do." Aunt Cassie growled under her breath.

As I backed toward the arena exit, I kept my gaze on Hope's wild one. "Stupid, maybe. But at least she knows now. She knows what she wants."

I turned around, whistled for my horse, and didn't say goodbye as Forrest trotted after me. Aunt Cassie yelled an obscenity, and Graham dragged Hope across the gravel, stuffed her into his flashy 4WD, and shot from Cherry River without a backward glance.

Good riddance.

Chapter Six

JACOB
✶ ✶ ✶ ✶ ✶ ✶

Sixteen Years Old

MY FINGERS FUMBLED with the last piece of sticky tape as I finished wrapping the small gift.

It wasn't pretty or neat, but it would do. At least it hid the swirly silvery scarf I'd bought Mom and a new pair of sunglasses with diamante horses on the sides. They were cheap, but I hoped she liked them.

After all, they were a thank you.

A gift of gratitude for putting up with me…and for letting me drop out of school. She'd had a fight with the education board but she'd made me a promise and kept it—signing paperwork to officially free me.

Finally.

"Wild One, where are you?" Mom's voice trailed down the corridor to my room.

"Coming!" Launching off my bed where scissors, silver wrapping paper, and a black ribbon lay, I met her on the threshold just as I was closing my door.

Her eyes narrowed, trying to look past me to the navy painted walls and blue bedspread. She'd let me decorate the room myself after Dad passed away and we both wanted a new start. She'd painted their bedroom a slate grey, which she said was calming but I called depressive, and I went all blue as that was my favourite colour.

Or it was six years ago. Now, I leaned more toward greens, but I had no plan of repainting anytime soon because I wasn't a student anymore. I wasn't a kid. I was a full-time farmer as of Monday, and full-time farmers needed their own home.

Not that I'd told her I was moving out yet.

That would come later. I'd already pushed her further than I should.

"What are you doing all secretive in there?" She pursed her lips and crossed her arms. "Is there a girl in there with you?"

I rolled my eyes, snorting under my breath. "A girl? Seriously? There's a lot of things to worry about where I'm concerned, but girls? Not one of them."

Mom flinched. "You know…you can, um, date, right? I know I was strict when you were younger, but, well, you're officially an adult."

I chuckled, lacing my voice with sarcasm. "Gee, thanks for the permission."

She sighed with a smile, knowing my sarcasm was for all the things I did *without* her permission, but she loved me anyway. The long weekend camping trips alone. The reckless riding I indulged in more and more with Forrest wearing no saddle, bridle, or gear whatsoever.

I'd developed a taste for adrenaline, and she didn't like me searching for it by soaring over fences and dangerous obstacles.

Her nose wrinkled a little as if nervous to broach the next subject. "You know…if you had a boy in there, I wouldn't mind."

My eyes flew wide. "A boy?"

You know?" She coughed delicately. "If you're more interested in them than—"

"Whoa, Mom." I held up my hand, keeping my room obstructed. "I'm not gay."

"Ugh, I know that." She looked at the ceiling as if asking Dad for strength. "And really, you're still too young for that sort of thing. I just…I just want you to know…I'm open to you having a girlfriend, boyfriend. Hell, even a friend at this point. You should really make more of an effort. You're going to be working a lot on your own from now on. It's important you have people your age to hang out with when you want to see a movie or party or whatever."

I kissed her temple fast, a flurry of affection that didn't hurt me too much and gave Mom the contact she needed. "I'm fine, Mom. Honest."

She sighed again. "Are you ready to go?"

"Yep. Just need to change real quick."

"Okay. I'll leave you to it even though I'm still suspicious. Gonna tell me what you're up to?"

"Nope." I grinned, backing into my room and closing the door slowly. "You'll have to wait and see."

"Five minutes," she warned as my door clicked closed.

I darted back to my badly wrapped gift, finished tying the bow, threw on a pair of jeans that didn't have grass stains on, sprayed some deodorant under my black T-shirt, then glanced warily at my door again.

For moments like this, I wished I had a lock.

My heart gave a little kick as I headed to my wardrobe, stepped inside the shallow cupboard, and dropped to my knees. There, I used the tip of my Swiss Army blade to ease up the floorboard I'd loosened and stashed things I knew would hurt Mom.

Things like the letter Dad left me under my pillow the night he died, as if he knew he wouldn't see morning. The stack of photos I'd taken on the old cell phone I'd had as a kid and begged Grandpa John to take me to the store to print off. Photos of me and Dad in the field, by the pond, cooking a barbecue, him hugging Mom in the kitchen, him laughing with Aunt Cassie on the deck, him kissing Mom as starlight kissed them both.

A treasure stash that would only cause her more grief.

And there, beneath the junk of old barn and gate keys, random pieces of hay, and a harmonica Dad tried to teach me to play and failed, was a plastic bag with four small packages.

Packages that had kept me up at night with curiosity, begging me to open them but knowing I never could.

Because they weren't addressed to me.

Tipping them out, I shuffled them around until the scribbled numbers on top faced upward.

All four, wrapped in blue satin paper, glinted in the evening sunshine streaming through my windows. All were about the same size but with different numbers setting them apart.

Today's number would be the first I had to give.

When I first found the bag, stashed in my wardrobe inside one of my old paddock boots a month or so after Dad had gone, I'd been desperate to grow older just so I could watch Mom open them. For a long time, it'd added to my desire to leave school. But then my own desires meant I couldn't face going to class any longer and today was the day I was both no longer a student and could finally give Mom her first gift from the grave.

Putting the box with 'number one' inked in black pen onto my knee, I smoothed out the letter that came with the small bag.

Hi Wild One,

I didn't know how to do this without hurting you. Should I have told you before? Should I not have done it? I still don't know the answers to those questions. And I'm sorry if this is hard and unfair. But I know you're brave and strong and such an awesome son that you will understand and be kind enough to do this for me.

Enclosed are four packages for your mother. But she's not to have them now. It's up to you to hide them until things come to pass, okay?

You're to give them to her as gently as you can. No explanations. She'll figure out the hows and whys for herself—she always has. Also, don't make a big deal out of it, but if she hasn't cut a piece of her blue ribbon lately, perhaps replace what I'm sure is looking pretty tattered when you give each of these.

The only rule is this:

Don't, under any circumstance, *give any of these to your mother if she has found someone who loves her as much as I do. If she's with someone else, I'm happy she's happy. If she's not, I'm happy I still have her heart. But regardless if she's married or dating or only just met someone who makes her smile again,* do not, *I repeat,* do not, *give her these.*

Bury them in the forest and forget about them. I hurt her enough when I left too soon. I refuse to hurt her more while she's still living.

Okay, Jacob?

I know that's a hard thing to ask of you, but I'm trusting you to do what I say. And I'm also trusting you to accept someone new into the family if that is where her happiness lies. Promise me you won't make it hard for her. Yes, you and your mother will always be mine.

Even gone, I'm not giving her up.

But I can share her for a little while if that makes her life more bearable.

With that uncomfortable rule out of the way, here are the instructions:

Box number one is for when you graduate high school.

Box number two is for when you meet the girl you're going to marry.

Box number three is for your wedding day.

Box number four is when you have your first child and make my beautiful Della Ribbon a grandmother.

You got all that?

I know you do.

There is no one else I trust more than you to do this for me.

I love you, Jacob.

With all my heart.

Forever.

I'm so proud of the man you're becoming and so grateful for how well you look after your mother.

Love, Dad.

* * * * *

"Congratulations to Jacob. For leaving behind the rank of student and becoming a fully-fledged farmer. Heaven help you, son." Grandpa John chuckled as he toasted me with his beer. His white hair and beard made him look like some plaid wearing Santa Claus. "Heaven help you for the pre-dawn wake-ups, the midnight close-ups, the constant hunger from working so hard, and the never-ending war between you, Mother Nature, and her seasons."

Aunt Cassie laughed as Uncle Chip stole a wafer from their daughter, Nina's, chocolate sundae. "You're taking on a lot, Jacob." Aunt Cassie's eyes twinkled. "You sure you're ready for this?"

I nodded, taking a sip of my third Coke of the night. "More than ready."

"Ready for the mowing and raking and baling and seeding and—"

"I'm ready." I grinned.

"Ready for the cut palms and boot blisters and—"

"Nothing you say will change my mind, Aunt Cassie."

She raised her glass and clinked it to mine. "I know. Just teasing. You were born ready. Ren made sure of that."

The small inhale around the table was the only sign of pain talking about a ghost.

I looked into the fizzy depths of my drink, reminded all over again that Dad's gift and mine still hid wrapped in my hoodie on the floor. It was like he was there with me, watching and waiting, just as anxious as I was to see how his gift would be received.

Throughout the meal, I'd tried to find the perfect time to give them, but there never seemed to be one.

Stupid to think I could give something so personal in a diner full of chattering people.

Mom had arranged this family get-together to celebrate my leaving school. It'd been an easy evening with greasy, yummy food, lots of laughs—mainly at my expense—and a sugar rush from the massive banana toffee pie I'd had.

We had a booth at the back of the restaurant where the jukebox played random tunes, keeping us private but still part of the atmosphere. But no matter how comfortable I was hanging out with my family, I never fully relaxed in this place. In this town. Not because I didn't like the people who lived here, but because *they* didn't like *me*.

Or some, anyway.

I was the odd one out even though I was born here and had as much claim to this land as anyone. I was a Wild. And being a Wild came with history.

All my life, no matter how often Mom and I would eat at this diner or Grandpa John took me to the farm and feed store, I always knew I was 'different.'

Most of the older folk knew my parents, which meant all of them had opinions.

There were two categories.

Camp number one were overly friendly, kind, and treated me with syrupy sweetness for losing my dad.

Camp number two avoided me, gossiped about me, and glowered as I walked past. They believed I was the spawn of incest and could barely look at me without disgust.

Mention the last name Wild in this town and *everyone* had an opinion on whether Mom and Dad were siblings.

The adults might glare and whisper, but the kids?

They were the mean ones. The ones who took great delight in saying I was special and not 'right.' That I wasn't meant to be alive. That I wasn't *normal* like them.

Well, good.

I didn't *want* to be normal.

It was yet another reason I hated school. Not that I ever told Mom that. It also didn't help that I'd overheard my teacher saying that Grandpa John was wrong to split up Cherry River and give Mom and Dad land. That my parents had arrived from nowhere and nothing and didn't deserve to have what others couldn't afford given to them for free.

It was never free.

It came with the biggest price tag in the world.

"You okay, Jacob?" Mom touched my forearm, snapping me back and making me wince at the physical contact. She immediately removed her fingers with an understanding smile. I'd forgotten how kind she was with my need not to be hugged or kissed. I knew she would like more affection between us, but she didn't push.

My heart swelled with love and shame for everything I'd put her through.

I hadn't been easy.

I'd probably never be easy.

But she put up with me unconditionally.

Leaning forward, I kissed her temple for the second time today.

Her cheeks warmed with happiness. "What was that for?"

"For being the best mom in the world."

She smiled wide. "It's easy when I have the best son in the world."

"I'm not even close—"

"Hey, we've got to push off. Nina has her gymnastic tournament in the morning." Aunt Cassie stood, brushing burger crumbs off her black dress. "It's getting late."

Chip stood too, helping Nina upright and looping his arm around his daughter's waist as if it was so easy and natural. I found it unnerving to be so close to another. I found it...distressing.

"Okay, no worries. Thanks so much for coming tonight." Mom caught Aunt Cassie's hand and kissed her forearm. A random place to kiss someone but Aunt Cassie just smiled, bent over, and kissed Mom on the head.

So much affection.

So much love.

So much to lose.

I shifted uncomfortably in the booth.

I felt eyes on me.

Grandpa John watched me; his forehead furrowed and gaze worried.

What was his deal?

Keeping his stare, I sat taller, daring him to say tonight had been anything but great.

For a second, he challenged me. He stared as deep as he could, ripping at my secrets, tearing at my fears, but then Aunt Cassie ruffled his hair, dragging his attention to her. "I'll drive you home, Dad. Jacob and Della can get their own way back." Aunt Cassie threw Mom a knowing look.

I narrowed my eyes, sensing this departure to leave Mom and me alone was choreographed for some reason.

Ah well, suited me.

I could finally give her the gifts.

Grandpa John cleared his throat as he lugged his old bulk from the booth. "Alrighty." Inching slowly into gear, he placed his huge, hot hand over mine on the table top.

I stiffened instantly.

My skin revoked the sensation of another's heat. My heart scrambled to hide from love. But I stayed sitting and plastered a smile on my face. "Night, Grandpa."

He squeezed my hand for a tad—a lot—too long. "It doesn't hurt, Jakey."

I knew he meant touching.

And he had it totally wrong.

Yeah, it does. It's excruciating.

I nodded, keeping my truth buried.

He was the only one allowed to call me Jakey. But tonight, he was pushing his luck. All I wanted to do was wriggle my hand out from his and blow on it to remove the lingering knowledge that he was getting older. He wasn't immortal. He'd be leaving soon, and there was nothing I could do to stop it.

There would be no hand touches. No hair ruffles. No gruff kisses. Not when he was dead.

Why couldn't Mom and Aunt Cassie see that?

Somewhere behind me, another diner coughed, slicing through the strains of conversation, injecting me with ice-cold panic. I sucked in a breath, hunching over as the stranger's cough morphed into my dad's cough, echoing over and over in my ears.

Grandpa John squeezed my hand again, trapping me between two evils.

I struggled to keep my unravelling mess a secret. I smiled weakly. "Thanks for coming. I'll keep Cherry River running. You'll see."

He smiled sadly. "I have no doubt about your ability to run the farm, my boy. I only doubt your ability to allow others to help if you need it."

Before I could reply, another cough ripped through the restaurant, and Aunt Cassie ushered the last remaining Wilson and Collins through the exit.

For a long minute after they'd gone, Mom and I just sat in silence, waiting for whoever was coughing to shut the hell up.

It took a while, but finally, the god-awful noise stopped, and the jukebox filled my ears again. A squeak of the orange booth cut through the music as Mom reached for her handbag under the table.

Giving me a quick smile, she pulled out an envelope and a small box wrapped in green paper. Caressing the green box with eyes suspiciously damp, she pushed both toward me, not caring that salt dusting the table or a dollop of tomato sauce might smear. "For you."

"This is why Aunt Cassie removed everyone, isn't it? So you could give me this?"

Mom half-smiled. "Can't hide anything from you, can I?"

I shrugged, reaching down for my hoodie and pulling the two packages free. "I have my own things to hide." I placed them in front of her.

Her eyes widened. "What are those for?"

I swallowed, unable to look away from the box Dad had bought her before he died. "Um, well, one is from me. To say thank you for letting me quit school. And the other…" I shrugged again. "The other is a surprise."

Good surprise or bad surprise?

She wasn't with anyone, so I hadn't broken any rules by giving it to her. I *had* made her life difficult when Graham Murphy sniffed around, so I hadn't upheld that part of Dad's letter, but I believed Aunt Cassie.

Mom would never find someone else.

It would be like me finding another dad.

He just wasn't possible to replace.

"Which do I open first?" She reached for the silver wrapping and black ribbon.

"That one. It's from me."

"And the other? Who's that from?" Her gaze snapped to mine, studying the blue box with a gleam of fear.

I clamped my lips closed, gave a tight smile, and motioned for her to unwrap mine.

She did nervously, unsticking the tape and pulling out the scarf and sunglasses. "Oh, Jacob. I love them." She went to kiss my cheek, leaning toward me with love in her eyes.

But I ruined it by sitting back. I didn't mean to do it. It just happened.

Instinct.

Self-preservation.

Terror.

She smiled as if I hadn't just hurt her feelings for the billionth time and tapped the envelope in front of me. "I've opened one. Now, it's your turn."

I sat forward again, inching closer to her on the booth so the pain I'd cut her with might somehow be eased. "It better not be homework."

She laughed. "You passed your exams. Not with the best grades, mind you, but your days of homework are over. Unless you want to go back to school, of course."

I chuckled at her enthusiasm. "Don't hope for miracles, Mom. I'm out of the institution. Good luck getting me back in."

She sighed dramatically. "One day you might change your mind."

"Yeah, and one day you might let me enter a team steeplechase."

Our joking faded as she scowled. "You promised me. That equestrian sport is too dangerous. Do you want to break your back?"

I rolled my eyes. "I wouldn't break, Mom. I'd fly."

Not wanting to rehash a familiar argument, I opened the envelope, pulled out the documents, and skimmed the lines of lawyer jargon.

My gaze flew to meet hers. "What is this? You can't be serious?"

"I am serious. It's all legal."

"But...how?"

"I was just custodian of it. The farm belonged to Ren. Not just in title but in blood, sweat, and tears. Now, it belongs to you."

"You're giving me your hundred acres?"

Mom looked at her hands on the table, twisting the scarf I'd given her. "Your father ensured we have no financial worries. The cash will eventually be yours too, but for now, the pieces of Cherry River that John gave us are officially in your name."

"I-I can't believe this."

"Believe it." She reached across and squeezed my hand.

This time, I schooled myself not to retreat but to shift my palm upward and link my fingers with hers. "I don't know what to say."

"Say thank you and accept it."

"Thank you and accept it."

She laughed, pulling away and swatting me on the shoulder. "I love you, Jacob. I don't know what I'd do without you." She sniffled, pride bright in her gaze. "I knew one day you'd take after him and be called to work the land, but I didn't expect it to happen so soon. Cherry River was always meant to be yours—regardless of age."

My heart hung heavy as she reached for the blue box. The box that had the power to hurt her, heal her, break her.

For a second, I didn't want her to open it.

I didn't want old scars to bleed fresh blood.

But I was too late as she tore the paper, gave me a curious tilt of her head, and plucked the lid off the box. She tipped a folded piece of paper into her palm, along with an enamelled blue ribbon scarf pin.

I groaned, wedging my head in my hands.

What could be worse?

I bought her a scarf, and on the same day, my dead father bought her a scarf pin.

A gift he'd bought years and years ago.

I didn't believe in fate, but chills scattered down my spine. I tensed as Mom rolled the pin in her fingers quizzically, then winced as pain shattered over her features.

Her hands shook as realisation slammed into her. She dropped the pin in her haste to read the letter.

Shit, I should've waited.

I should've given it to her at home away from prying eyes, where her grief would be hidden.

As tears sprang like rivers exploding their dams down her cheeks and the lowest groan of despair left her lips, I prepared to kill her even further by pulling a blue ribbon from my pocket. The ribbon I'd cut from the cardboard wheel my father had left behind.

Only, as I stretched my arm toward her, dropped the ribbon on the torn wrapping of my father's gift, and beat myself up with my incapableness at hugging her, we were interrupted at the *worst* possible time.

A shy voice I hadn't forgotten and didn't necessarily want to hear again.

A voice that belonged to a girl who loved puncturing old wounds with my full name.

"Hello, Jacob Ren Wild. Fancy seeing you here."

Chapter Seven

HOPE

* * * * * *

Twelve Years Old

I WISHED I had the power to rewind time.

Before this horrifying moment, I'd wished I could fly, breathe underwater, or become invisible.

But right there, standing at the table where Jacob and Della Wild sat frozen in sadness, I wished I could stomp on the 'stop' button, crank the 'rewind' lever, and prevent myself from ever coming over here.

Dad hadn't wanted to.

He said their conversation looked private, and I should wait until tomorrow when he dropped me off at Cherry Equestrian for my weeklong stay with them.

But I'd been too impatient.

I'd wanted to see Jacob again.

I'd wanted to recall all those delicious, terrifying, addicting, awakening moments when he'd forced me to ride his horse.

He needed to know how much he changed me.

How much he'd taught me in that one ride.

But now, I wanted the ground to gobble me up and never exist as Jacob's dark gaze turned a brilliant black, hard and glittering like some nasty gemstone. "Hope Jacinta Murphy."

I gulped, backing into Dad as he placed a comforting hand on my shoulder. I didn't deserve comforting. I'd just done the *worst* possible thing.

Della Wild looked at me with eyes the colour of oceans. Her cheeks so wet it seemed as if those oceans were pouring out of her and would flood the diner. When she noticed Dad behind me, she rubbed her face, her voice hitching in apology. "Oh, Graham. Hi."

Jacob silently plucked the silver scarf from the table and passed it to her.

Della gave him a grimace, took it, and used it to wipe her liquid-slicked cheeks. On the table something blue glinted along with paper and a green box.

"God, Della. I'm so sorry we intruded," Dad said. "We'll go." Pulling me backward, he muttered an excuse as if he could fix what I'd broken. "We're in town a night early. Staying at the Aces Hotel under my grandparents' name Duffal. If you, uh, need to get hold of us, that is." Tugging me harder, I tripped a little, still mortified and horrified and staring at Jacob.

Staring at the unmasked panic on his face, the unbridled rage, the untempered despair. Somehow, I understood he felt as guilty as I did. That it wasn't just me who wanted a rewind button or magical trap door.

But what did he feel so guilty about?

"No, no. It's fine. Don't be silly," Jacob's Mom said with another hitch. "We were just celebrating Jacob's graduation." She smiled bright and brittle, forcing happiness that wasn't real. "How nice to see you again, Hope."

It didn't look like they were celebrating.

It looked like they were at a funeral.

Had someone died?

And if so…how?

My terrible mind that fixated on death tried to drown me with unmentionable questions.

I shrank against Dad. "I'm sorry for coming over. I just saw Jacob and wanted to tell him…" I had nothing else. My voice trailed into silence.

"Tell him what?" Della swiped at another tear and crumpled up a note in her hand.

"Um…" I glanced at Jacob who no longer looked at me but the table full of used condiments and melting ice-cream sundaes. "I-I…don't remember."

I did remember.

I remembered every word.

I'd wanted to say them for an entire year, but how could I cough up such things when I was an intruder on something I didn't understand?

Instead, I made an even bigger mistake by pointing at the green box. I wanted the attention off me. I didn't think what I was doing by directing it onto something else. "What's that?"

"Hope." Dad's fingers dug into my shoulder. "That's none of your business."

"But it's a present." I turned to face him, begging him to help me repair this. "Presents make people happy, right? Maybe someone should open it."

Jacob muttered something not nice under his breath as Della sighed heavily. "You're right. It is a present, Hope." Her gaze landed on her son. "And Jacob *should* open it. After all, I just opened one from the same giver."

Jacob froze. His eyes locked on the box. "You mean…it's from him?"

His mom nodded, biting her lip to stem more tears.

"Right, well, we're leaving now," Dad announced loudly, reminding the Wilds that this wasn't a private moment for them. That they had an audience. But either Jacob no longer cared or he couldn't stop himself because he snatched the box, tore the paper, and opened it before I could catch my breath.

He tipped a large silver disc into his hand, fisting it tight. His head bowed as he inspected it.

Despite myself, I leaned forward, desperate to know what it was.

"A compass," he breathed. Turning it over, his face scrunched with pain. His thumb ran over an inscription. *"If school isn't your path, then find your true one. Wander far. Wander wide. This compass will make sure you never get lost."*

Della pressed her face into the silver scarf again. Her body shook as a slicing sound of heartbreak made my hair stand on end.

Dad let me go. Shooting toward her, he slipped into the booth, and wrapped his arm around her shuddering form. "It's okay, Della. It's okay."

The last thing I saw before I was knocked on my butt and got an eyeful of the diner's dirty ceiling was Jacob launching from the table and bulldozing me to the ground.

He'd vanished out the door before I could climb to my feet.

Chapter Eight

HOPE

* * * * * *

"NO WAY. NO fucking way."

"Language, Jacob Wild. Your mouth is as dirty as your father's." The Cassie woman who owned the equestrian centre argued just as loud as Jacob.

"Well, you're always telling me how similar we are. Guess you have to take the good with the bad, huh?"

"Don't change the subject. Hope is staying and—"

"Not gonna happen."

"It is too gonna happen." Her tone sharpened. "Her father made the booking almost three months ago. I'm sorry I didn't tell you, but she's here for the week, and you're going to be civil—"

My new leather riding boots scuffed driveway gravel as I tiptoed closer, shutting up the voices inside the barn.

Darn it.

I was normally so good at eavesdropping. The number of secrets I'd gathered from slinking around the set and listening to actors, sound crew, and scriptwriters was fascinating. Hearing such juicy things—sexy things, naughty things, funny things—all helped with my own story-telling when Keeko made me do English homework, but today...I sucked at it.

Today, I wasn't listening for secrets; I was listening to see how much trouble I was in, and if it was even worthwhile staying. Every time I thought about last night, my back prickled and tears heated and utter mortification made me nauseous.

Dad had driven us to Cherry River despite my pleas to reconsider. He'd told me either way—if I stayed or left—I deserved to say sorry face to face. He'd parked the car with strict instructions to stay put until he'd spoken to Della—just in case I mentioned the words dead, dying, or terminal.

I'd gotten better over the past year—mainly thanks to living in a country where English wasn't the first language—and I no longer blurted out my morbid fascination with the afterlife to strangers. But I understood why he didn't trust me.

Look at the mess I caused last night.

Of course, staying in the car became impossible when I spotted Cassie and Jacob vanish into the barn. And so, I broke yet another promise.

If there was a Heaven and Hell, I'd well and truly bought myself a one-way ticket to damnation.

But they were arguing.

I needed to know if it was about me.

Boots thumped on cobbles just before Jacob appeared from the shadowy building and caught me red-handed.

Again.

"You," he seethed. "Don't you think you've caused enough damage for one visit?"

I shrank into myself, staring at the ground. "I just came to say sorry. I don't have to stay—"

"Damn right you don't have to stay." He crossed his arms. "Do you find it fun to be the most annoying person I've ever met?"

I shrank again, wishing I could literally vanish into my boots. "I said I'm sor—"

"Hope." Cassie appeared from the barn, running a hand wearily through her hair. Glaring at Jacob, she came directly toward me and scooped me into a hug.

Drinking in the much needed contact, I lagged against her. Tears welled in my eyes as she pulled away and cupped my cheeks.

"You're welcome here anytime, Hope. You know that, right? Last night was unfortunate timing, that's all. Any other night, Jacob and his mom would've loved for you to join them for dinner." Her hands trailed from my cheeks as she stood. "Last night, though…it was hard for both of them. I hope you don't take it personally."

"She stuck her nose where it didn't belong. Again." Jacob eyed me with disdain. "Don't you get taught manners in Hollywood?"

"Jacob." Cassie pinched his side—hard by the way Jacob flinched. "Hope is here for horse camp, not for you to pick on. You will be nice. You will be helpful. You will bend over backward to make her feel welcome as she is our guest. Got it?" She pinched him again.

He parried out of her reach. Rubbing his side, he sent her a withering glare. He didn't reply, but the clench of his jaw hinted he had a lot to say—just not something she wanted to hear.

Pointing a finger in his face with warning, Cassie nodded once, then strode toward where Della and my dad were talking, leaving me alone with rage itself.

For the longest moment, heavy silence choked me.

Then Jacob cleared his throat and said in a robotic voice like any well-trained customer service worker, "Welcome back to Cherry River. I *hope* you have a pleasant stay." With a thin smile that made his dark eyes darker and cheekbones sharper, he bowed, saluted, and turned on his heel and stormed away.

Chapter Nine

JACOB

* * * * * *

THREE DAYS.

Three long, awful days where kids learning how to ride infested Cherry River.

Aunt Cassie's horse camp had become very popular, and before I officially took on the role as head farmer, I'd been roped in each school holidays to help teach, guide, cook, and chaperone.

These days, I wasn't expected to be at their beck and call. I had a new boss now—the land that had my name on the title. The farm that was as demanding as any busy company.

I'd always woken with the sun, and now, instead of being trapped in a classroom, I bolted from the house and was on Forrest checking fence lines or on the tractor doing all the jobs that needed to be done before the sky was fully awake.

I was in my element.

Which meant, I was done with teaching.

Over the years, some of the kids hadn't been too bad. All of them had the life skills of a stuffed marmot, but some were at least polite enough to ride the horses they were given, accept the time they were allocated, and stay in their bunk beds out of sight at night.

That was before Hope came to stay.

Ever since she left a year ago, I'd dreaded the day she'd come back. I'd tensed each time Aunt Cassie read the roster for new arrivals, just in case her name appeared. But with each school holiday where there was no Hope Jacinta Murphy, I'd stupidly relaxed thinking I'd scared her away for good.

That Forrest had done the trick, and she'd sworn off horses for life.

But no.

She had to turn up at the worst possible time and see the

worst possible thing and be the worst possible nuisance.

It also didn't help that my temper had cooled two days ago and that god-awful guilt was back. Guilt for snapping at her when none of that night's agony was her fault. Guilt for not being able to let go of the fresh pain every time I touched my compass, transferring that pain into hatred for the brown-haired, skinny girl who looked at me as if I'd broken her baby heart.

Dad hadn't just entrusted me with gifts to give Mom on milestones of my life, he'd given her some, too. When had she found them? Where? How many did she have to give me? How many more times would I have to go through the loss, the rage, the pain?

I'd hoped running the farm would help settle me. I'd fought for freedom from education because I'd pinned all my hopes on finding happiness in the empty fields.

But I hadn't.

More and more, my eyes trailed to the forest boundary, my ears pricking with breeze-whispered words to *run*. To find whatever I needed to replace the emptiness inside.

Dad hadn't just given me a compass.

He'd layered me with yet more of his own attributes and afflictions. He'd given me permission to search for something I didn't understand, all while shackling me to Cherry River because, despite his command to wander, I could never leave Mom.

No way.

My promise to him was still my biggest and most important responsibility.

And right now…right now, I felt trapped.

Trapped by doing the right thing, the wrong thing, the adult thing, the necessary thing.

I needed to apologise to Hope, yet every time I got close, my throat closed up, my hands balled, and I kept on walking as if I hadn't seen her.

She might be a silly kid, but something about the way she stared at me said she knew more than she should. That my secrets weren't so secret when she was around.

Sighing in the dark, I did my best to let starlight and silence comfort me. I'd had a long day sorting out the hay barn, ready to burn off old season bales to create space for new.

The lasagne I'd swiped from the oven and a bottle of cider from the fridge—that I wasn't supposed to drink—swung in my hands as I traversed the back meadows. The gentle hill made my tired muscles burn, but a smile twitched when Forrest nickered for me.

"Yeah, yeah. I'm coming." Breaking into a jog, I covered the final distance and vaulted over his fence. "Hello to you too."

The gelding tossed his head, trotting over to nuzzle my chest as I dropped into his field and headed toward the large willow down by the creek.

He followed me, sniffing the container full of tomato and pasta and mouthing the top of my cider bottle. He'd had enough swigs of juice and cola that he'd grown accustomed to sharing a bottle with me.

Chuckling under my breath, I pushed his warm bulk away as I dropped to my ass and leaned against the tree. I wasn't afraid of Forrest stepping on me. For such a stroppy, so-called dangerous horse, he looked after me as if I was in need of looking after.

At least out here, there were no people. No kids squealing in joy at riding or crying with homesickness for parents.

No mom, aunt, or family.

Just me, the sky, and Forrest.

The only sound as I opened my packed dinner and used the plastic fork stuck to the lid of the Tupperware was Forrest as he sighed contentedly and returned to munching grass. I ate with him, devouring the delicious lasagne and swigging back the cider— sharing a few mouthfuls with the roan.

By the time I'd finished, my mind wasn't so crazed and my heart no longer so worried.

My thoughts drifted to this afternoon when I'd driven past on the quad as Aunt Cassie taught her four new students. Hope had been assigned a bay mare called Biscuit who we'd rescued last October. She wasn't big but was smart and gentle. A requisite for a beginner's pony.

I'd expected to see her just as uncoordinated and terrible as the last time she'd been in our arena, but Cassie had separated her from the others, requesting her to canter and do figure eights while the rest barely stayed on at the walk.

I'd wanted to stop and gawk. To understand how she'd gone from a kid who couldn't steer Binky to loping Biscuit around with her back relaxed, hands soft, and seat glued to the saddle like any seasoned rider.

On a circuit of the arena, she caught my gaze. Her helmet shadowed most of her face, but my back prickled as she transferred her reins into one hand and waved shyly as if afraid I'd yell at her like I did when she first arrived.

The guilt she caused magnified, and I stomped on the accelerator, kicking up driveway dust as I got the hell away from her.

Forrest ambled back toward me, grass sticking out the sides of his mouth as he nudged my knee with his nose.

"Wanna scratch, huh?" I stood with a groan, my young body already very aware of the long hours of labour I was putting it through.

Forrest wuffled, swinging his rump into my face for scratches. I dug my nails into his huge ass, scratching hard and fast—just the way he liked it. His head stretched upward as his upper lip pulled back from his teeth in an ugly expression of pure bliss.

When he'd first backed into me this way, requesting scratches on the big muscles, Mom freaked, thinking he was going to double barrel me. But I'd just watched his eye and knew he came in peace, not murder.

With dirt from his coat caked under my fingernails, I slapped his butt and pushed him away. "Enough. I have to finish my chores."

He pouted, glancing at the moon as if to say it was inching close to midnight and the time for working was done. But I'd promised Mom I'd top up the feed bins for the horses and the splattering of sheep Grandpa John had bought last year, and I still hadn't done it.

Feeding the four-legged kind I didn't mind.

It was feeding the two-legged that drove me nuts.

"See ya." Giving his velvet nose a quick kiss, I gathered up my empty container and bottle, and made my way back to the stables.

Mom had long since stopped badgering me about being home at a reasonable hour, which meant the farm was empty with everyone asleep. It was my favourite time of day where I could be myself with my complications and concerns and not feel like I had to hide.

On some summer nights, Dad and I had snuck from the house and slept beneath the galaxies in the front meadow. Mom would wake alone in the dark, find us both missing, and drag out blankets to lie with us as the sun rose.

I'd never admit it, but thanks to those unforgettable moments, Dad felt closer at this time of night—as if the veil between wherever he was watching was thinner and maybe, just maybe, he'd give me advice I sorely needed or free me from my vow to do whatever I could to keep Mom happy.

Not that I'd ever stop doing what I could for her—promise or no promise. She was the only person I permitted myself to love deep enough to hurt. Even Aunt Cassie and Grandpa John I held at arm's length. I adored them, but I couldn't let them take another piece of me when they died.

Heading to the truck parked by the stable, I dropped off the remnants of my dinner and pulled down the tailgate where six heavy bags of feed waited to be hauled into the barn.

Bending my knees, I hoisted one onto my shoulder and headed toward the shadowy building.

Even once I'd done this final job, I wasn't ready to go home yet.

I needed open skies for just a little longer.

A hike into the forest where Mom and I had scattered Dad's ashes was my next destination. Who knew? Perhaps I'd sleep out there beneath the tree where I'd carved our initials. Maybe hanging with ghosts would remind me to appreciate the living and take away my guilt at failing.

Dumping the bag onto the cobbles, I grabbed my Swiss Army knife from my back pocket and sliced into the plastic. Picking it up again, I tipped the contents into the large bins, coughing a little at the sweet scent of molasses and grain.

As the last of the feed cascaded, a shadow darted to the left. Something small ran in the darkness, banging into a table full of farm junk, knocking a rusty hoof-pick to the ground.

"Goddammit." Crumpling up the empty bag, I tossed it onto the rubbish pile. The creature was most likely one of the feral cats Aunt Cassie kept to hunt mice.

I got that mice were a problem, but I didn't like cats. Everything had a place in the food chain, and I wasn't opposed to eating meat, but cats were cruel. They played with their food instead of killing it outright. They took pleasure in another's misery.

You take pleasure in causing Hope misery—

I shut that thought up as fast as it arrived.

I didn't like it.

But I couldn't seem to stop it either.

Stalking forward, I followed where the shadow had run to. "If you're busy killing, stop it."

A scurry of footsteps ran into a stall where hay was stacked and waiting to be used as equine bedding.

I chased, fully expecting to catch a tabby with a mouse tail dripping like spaghetti from its lips.

Only, I froze as a girl in pink track pants and a grey hoodie slammed to a halt in front of the bales, trapped. Her eyes were wide as she spun to stare at me, her fingers linking and unlinking as if holding her own hand in support.

"What the hell are you doing in here?" I checked my dinged-up watch. "It's past midnight. You should be in bed."

"I-I—"

"Go back to the bunks, Hope." I crossed my arms.

Her forehead furrowed with false bravery. "You should be in bed too, you know."

I snickered. "Nice try. I don't have a bedtime. That rule never worked on me."

She sighed, her long brown hair untethered and tangled around her shoulders. "Oh."

Stale silence fell as we stared at each other. Once again, those awful prickles danced down my spine whenever her eyes landed on me. The guilt I'd been nursing since I'd yelled at her crushed my chest. I cleared my throat, doing my best to be rid of it. "You'll be asked to leave if you're found out of bed."

She scuffed her pink slipper with a silver unicorn horn into the dusty floor. "That would be okay...I guess."

My eyes narrowed. "You're saying you *want* to go home?"

"I'm saying I don't like sleeping in a room with others."

I sucked in a breath, hating that we shared a similarity. "You don't have a choice."

I expected her to nod and turn tail back to the bunk room. Instead, her eyes flashed green. "I slept in the stable last night. No one noticed or cared." She pointed at a striped blanket that used to be clean and folded on a bunk bed but was now covered in hay and scrunched up by the stable door.

"Wait. You slept out here...on your own?"

Her chin came up. "Why do you care?"

I swallowed hard. "I don't."

She flinched. "Why are you always so mean?"

"Mean?" I pointed a finger at my chest. "Me? I'm not mean."

"Yes, you are. All the time. I said I was sorry for being nosy at the diner. I know I annoy you. I know you don't want me here. And I know you think I'm some stupid kid. But I'm only four years younger than you, and Keeko always says that girls mature faster than boys, so I'm probably like your age or older." She squared her shoulders. "So you can't tell me what to do."

I'd forgotten how odd she was. How chatty she could be when we were alone. Last time we'd spoken without adult supervision, she'd told me about her dead mother, and she didn't even know me.

Now, she'd just admitted she'd slept alone with feral cats and terrified mice for company.

God, if that didn't make the guilt press even harder.

My heart thumped with confrontation, but I kept my steps calm and slow as I moved toward her. Words like 'sorry' and 'I didn't mean to yell' battled with standing my ground against her strange stares. "I'm allowed to tell you what to do. I'm in charge here, and I say go back to bed."

"You're not in charge. Cassie is."

"Yeah, and she's not here, is she? So I'm boss."

"You're a bully."

"What?" I bit the word, hating that she'd gotten under my skin and nailed my behaviour. If Mom knew how mean I'd been to her, she'd be furious. Then again, Aunt Cassie had told her about me blowing up at Hope on the first day, but Mom had just nodded as if she understood my temper and gave me a free pass to be cruel.

Perhaps she shouldn't have.

Maybe I needed greater discipline.

If it took away the stress of never knowing if I did the right thing and paved a path to follow, then I'd welcome it. I'd welcome any guidance on how to be a better son, better oath-keeper, better person.

My eyes locked with Hope's again and my fight dissolved. My spine slouched as I looked at the blanket she'd used and the hay bales she'd no doubt slept on, and for once, I couldn't use my temper as a shield.

Her unicorn slippers were the easiest things to look at as I said the hardest thing imaginable. "Look…I'm, eh, I'm sorry, okay?"

She sucked in a breath. "What?" Her tiny squeak could've been mistaken for one of the resident mice.

I rubbed the back of my neck, then raked my fingers through my hair. "I shouldn't have been so…loud." That didn't really make sense. I tried again. "I mean, I shouldn't have yelled at you. I'm sorry for—"

"I'm sorry too." She rushed out in a massive exhale that echoed with relief. "I didn't mean to be a pest. I swear."

I held up my hand, a sort of smile playing on my lips. "It's fine. Let's forget about it, 'kay?"

She nodded fast, her hair swishing over her shoulders. "Yes, please."

"Anyone ever tell you, you say please a lot."

She frowned, her small cheeks pink. "Dad says I don't say it enough."

"Parents."

She smiled back, both of us aware we didn't have parents. Just parent.

Silence fell again but at least it wasn't so strained.

Tucking hair behind her ear, Hope's gaze found my face again, studying me in that intense, scary way that made me feel stripped bare and lacking.

My hackles rose. "You should go."

"Go?" She stiffened. "As in...leave?"

"No, not leave. Bed. It's late. Aunt Cassie is taking you guys on a long trek tomorrow. I won't be blamed for your tiredness if you fall off."

"I wouldn't blame you." Her voice was quiet. "If I fall off, it won't be your fault." Her body snapped to attention, her hands wringing again as if words battled to be spoken all at once. "Oh! I never got to tell you and I've been waiting so *long* to tell you! That's why I came over to you in the diner. I wanted to say thank you for making me ride your pony. Thank you for showing me what I wanted."

She sucked in a breath, coming closer as if desperate to make me listen. "I was so scared. So, *so* scared. You almost killed me, but you were the only person who pushed me. The adults think I'm this breakable thing 'cause of what happened to Mom and how I found her—"

She waved her hand, breaking off as if she was used to not being allowed to talk about such things and launching into new, acceptable topics. "I didn't know how to ask for what I wanted. I didn't know *what* I wanted. I still don't know. And that's okay. But I knew enough that when Dad accepted a job filming in Saudi Arabia, I was brave enough to beg for horse riding lessons. He tried to say no. He said you were reckless, and riding was dangerous, but I didn't stop, Jacob. You'd be so proud of me. I was um...loud. I didn't give up, and I just wanted to say thank you. It's the only thing that's mine. The only thing where I'm not something to someone else, you know? It took so much convincing…after what you did last time. But I got to ride a few camels, a donkey, and a pretty dapple called Prince of Persia."

"Sounds like you miss it." My jaw clenched. "The glamorous life in some desert."

"It's actually very green over there," she said primly. "I do miss some things. I miss my lessons on Prince. His bloodlines descend from a famous racehorse called—"

"Don't care. It's not like we can provide horses of such calibre."

Her face fell as if I'd stolen her favourite teddy. "I'm trying to thank you, and you're getting mad at me again." She stared in that deep, unsettling way of hers. "Just…let me thank you."

I cleared my throat, suddenly feeling as if we were breaking some sort of rule. "Fine. Glad I could help."

She shrugged. "Anyway…I wanted to tell you more, but I've forgotten. You make me nervous and…"

When she didn't finish, I hid my racing heart. "*And…?*"

She smiled quickly. "And…I don't have any friends. I know you don't like me, and you don't want me here, and you can't wait for me to leave but…" She shrank back as if I'd bite her. "You're my friend. Even if you don't want to be."

She was right to back away because the word friend terrified me. It came bound with other words like closeness, trust, affection. Words that led to deeper ones like connection, love, *pain.*

Any soft feelings I'd nursed slammed back into hard ones. "I'm not your friend, Hope."

She sighed as if she'd expected my answer but hoped for something else. "I know." It didn't stop her big, innocent eyes staring at me, filling me with yet more guilt.

If she kept looking at me like that, I'd have to leave. If she was lonely without her dad or nanny, then she should make friends with the other students.

Not with me.

Hadn't she learned that lesson already?

I wasn't looking for friends.

Ever.

I wanted to get away from her, but she dived into yet another conversation that required little input from me. "Cassie said I can jump tomorrow, now she knows my experience level. Isn't that great?" She hopped up onto the bales behind her, her silly unicorn slippers banging against the golden stalks. "I can't wait. Does Biscuit jump, Jacob? I've jumped before, but it's always scary on a new pony." She plucked a dried piece of grass and broke it in half. "I'm hoping I won't let Cassie down. Show her and Dad that the lessons he bought me were worth it."

I crossed my arms, moving to slouch against the stable wall. Despite the dangerous previous topic, I was happy to discuss horses. She made it easy, chirping away like a garden sparrow. "So your lessons over there took you from barely able to steer to jumping?"

She beamed. "Yes! I was hoping I could tell you all about it."

I should be glad my unorthodox teaching method had shown her a passion for horses, but somehow, it pissed me off. When she didn't elaborate further, I waved my hand impatiently. "Well?"

"Thanks to you, I *love* riding. The horse is my friend. I can tell it anything—even stuff I shouldn't talk about, and they can't tell on me. Not that you told on me. You didn't tell anyone what I said." Her head tilted to the side, her face so young and animated. "You're good at keeping secrets, aren't you, Jacob Ren Wild?" The greenness of her eyes seemed to darken, looking older than her twelve years.

"Don't use my full name," I muttered.

"Why not?"

"I don't like it."

"But it's your name."

"It's my dad's name."

"And your dad is dead." She nodded as if it made perfect sense. "Okay. From now on, you're just Jacob."

"Gee, thanks."

She paused at the raw warning in my tone. But then she grew brave again, sticking her flat chest out with courage. "Why does everyone do that?"

"Do what?"

"Avoid talking about the dead?"

I tensed. "I don't avoid talking—"

"Yes, you do. Everyone does. My mom died, too."

God, she'd done it again; hooked me with hints of inappropriate things. She'd napped beside her dead mother. That was yet another similarity we shared—not that I'd slept beside a corpse—but we'd both seen and touched one.

I'd hugged Dad's cold body as he was loaded into the

ambulance, never to return.

I'd had nightmares over the strange wrongness for years afterward. No one at school had been around a dead family member. No one knew the black emptiness it left you with or how it forced you to grow up.

But…Hope did.

"I want to talk about it," she whispered hotly. "I want to know why she killed herself, where did she go, is she watching me, is she sorry, does she wish she hadn't done it, does she miss me, does she miss Dad, will I see her again, does she hear me when I say goodnight, can she see me cantering, is she proud?" Tears glittered but her chin came up higher, crushing my chest with a power only she could wield. "You're my friend. If I can't talk about this sort of stuff with you, then I can't talk about it with anyone, and I'm so *sick* of not being able to talk about it." She tugged her hair as if her head pounded with morbid questions. "Don't you want to know? Don't you ever stop to ask why?"

I ignored the part where she called me her friend again. My breath came short and choppy. "I know why."

"You do?"

"Dad died because he was sick. Unlike your mom, he didn't want to go anywhere."

I gasped, wishing I could stuff such awful things back into the darkness where they belonged.

But I couldn't, and Hope crumpled on the bale, her feet stopped kicking and her head bowed. "You're right. Your dad is in Heaven. But my mom…she's in Hell."

My knees wobbled, desperate to run but tripping forward instead and collapsing me beside her on the hay. "I'm sorry. I didn't mean…" I held up my hands in surrender. "I didn't mean to say that."

She sniffled, wiping her nose on the back of her hand. "It's okay. I've read stuff. I know that suicide is different from dying. It's a sin." She shivered as if a ghost tiptoed down her spine.

I climbed off the bale again and snatched the blanket from the floor. Shaking it free from as much golden grass as I could, I draped it over her shoulders before sitting back down.

She gave me a watery smile. "Thanks."

I nodded, fighting a war to leave for my peace of mind and staying for hers. I'd been cruel to this girl—cold-hearted, short tempered, and unforgiving—so the least I could do was give her something no one else was prepared to give.

Even if it would kill me to talk about such things.

"You know…" My voice was quiet, hushed, hesitant around the small stable. "I don't believe in Heaven or Hell, so don't worry about your mom, okay?"

Her eyes snapped up, her body turning into mine as if thirsty for anything I could tell her. "You don't?"

I shook my head. "I believe the dead have a choice."

"What choice?"

"The choice to stay and watch the living, or the choice to leave and go to the next place."

"What place?"

"Dunno." I looked at my dirty boots. "Some everlasting meadow where they're always happy? Another life as an animal or tree or human? Who the hell knows. There's no point in thinking so much about death because no one truly knows until they're dead. And then you've just wasted your entire life thinking about something you'll find out sooner rather than later."

Hope went as silent and as still as I'd ever seen her. Her eyes widened as if I'd finally given her something she'd been searching for. "I never thought about it that way before."

"Well, now you have."

She stayed quiet, nodding to whatever thoughts ran riot in her head. Finally, she reached into the baggy pockets of her track pants and pulled out the black piece of fabric that had fallen from her jeans the day I'd given her a ride on Forrest.

I kept my face unreadable as she passed it to me.

I didn't want to take it, but she grabbed my cool, rough fingers with her warm, silky ones and pressed it into my palm. The lace was soft, not scratchy. Frayed and worn as if the owner had rubbed and stroked it to a fine thread.

"That was Mom's." Hope bowed her head, fascinated by the black lace in my hand. She let me go, leaving a trail of pinpricks behind. "It used to be a shawl, but it fell apart over the years." She sniffed, looking up with glassy green eyes. "Do you think she feels me when I hold it and talk to her? Do you think she's in some other place and not Hell?"

So many things were wrong with this situation.

I shouldn't be alone with a girl in a stable at midnight. I shouldn't be talking about death and dying with a child. And I definitely shouldn't feel anything more than annoyance and mild disdain.

But behind her youth and fragility lurked someone far braver than me. She'd not only lost a parent—she'd been abandoned *willingly* by that parent. Yes, Dad had left me and Mom, but it wasn't like he didn't fight, didn't try, didn't clutch every miracle to hang around as long as he could. And now, even gone, he still found ways to remind us he loved us, missed us, and was proud.

The compass sat heavy and accusing in my jeans pocket, nestled beside my Swiss Army knife. Self-preservation demanded I get up and leave, but compassion and something I'd long been afraid of made me stay.

I felt sorry for her.

I was in awe of her.

In awe of the way she kept fighting with joy and happiness. She wasn't afraid to love, even though she knew what it was like to have love change to pain. She hugged freely, welcomed touch from others, and sat close to me with no sign of terror.

Once again, I felt like an utter asshole because her gaze no longer pried open my secrets, doing their best to steal what I hid; instead, she pleaded with me to give her comfort.

Comfort she'd been denied.

Why hadn't the adults seen her vulnerability? Why did they tell her to shut up about this sort of stuff when all she wanted was a frank conversation and some answers to try to make sense of why her mother decided that killing herself was better than a lifetime with her daughter?

I sighed heavily, wrapping my fingers around Hope's sad scrap of lace.

She sensed my weakness, shuffling closer as if needing contact and also to protect the lace locked in my grip.

My skin heated with warning at her proximity, and I fought my instincts to move away. After tonight, I would keep my distance, but there, in the darkness with only hay and mice to hear me, I whispered, "Yes, I believe she can hear you."

She sucked in a breath full of thanks and a slight tinge of disbelief that I'd answered. Her gaze tightened with seriousness as she leaned closer. "Do you talk to your dad?"

"Sometimes." I shivered as a chill walked down my spine. "However, it's more the other way around."

Her eyes bugged. "You mean…he's here…on the farm?"

"Kinda." Words were heavy and unwilling as if sharing this secret would somehow make it untrue. But she spun some sort of curse that I couldn't deny whenever she looked so deep and imploring into me.

Clearing my throat, I tried again—for her. "I feel him. I know when I've disappointed him or when he approves."

She wrinkled her nose. "Isn't that just your con-conscious? Keeko told me if I do something that makes me feel queasy, then I probably did something Dad wouldn't approve of."

I couldn't stop myself from correcting her. "It's conscience. And yeah, I'm sure some would say that. But I know otherwise." Shoving the lace back into her hand, I stood quickly. "It doesn't matter anyway. They're both gone. Even if they can hear and see us, they're not real."

"They were real once." Hope curled around her lace, stroking it with her thumb.

"But not anymore," I muttered.

I'd reached my limit. I'd gone past my tolerance. I needed to be alone. And fast.

"My advice? Move on. They have." Striding toward the stable door, I pointed a finger at her. "Now git. Go back to bed. Otherwise, I'll tell Aunt Cassie you're breaking camp rules."

I didn't wait to see if she'd obey, and my last image of Hope—before I bolted into the starry sky—was her draped in a blanket, hay stuck in her hair, and a pathetic piece of lace clutched tight in tiny hands.

Chapter Ten

JACOB

✶ ✶ ✶ ✶ ✶ ✶

"WELL, THE LAST of them are gone." Grandpa John strode inside, bringing life and vibrancy wrapped up in plaid and denim. "Cute kids."

I looked up from where I carved slices of roast chicken. Ever since talking with Hope in the barn four nights ago, I'd had an undeniable need to be kinder.

Not to Hope—I couldn't stand to look at her in the sunlight after what we'd shared in the dark—but to Mom. To my family.

Hope taught me that just because I struggled with affection didn't mean I wasn't hurting others by denying it.

I'd tried to be better.

But it didn't mean I'd made any progress.

"You're an angel for babysitting the stragglers, Dad." Aunt Cassie smiled from the dining room table. Mom and I had come over to Grandpa John's to hang with everyone. It had sort of become a tradition to celebrate with a roast when the school holidays ended and the horse camp closed.

Aunt Cassie curled up her nose. "That awful man was going to send those poor foals to the slaughterhouse if I didn't go that very minute."

Mom flinched. "I'll never understand how people can be so heartless."

I kept my eyes on my knife as I continued slicing juicy meat.

"All good, darlin' girl. Hopefully, the foster mare likes having two fillies. You might have to bottle-feed, though, to top them up." Grandpa John kissed Aunt Cassie on the top of her head, squeezed Uncle Chip's shoulder as he gave him a beer, caressed Mom's cheek as he passed, and ruffled Nina's hair where she sat on the couch watching some awful reality program.

Everyone got touched.

I stiffened, knowing I was next.

"I know. I've already got the formula. They shouldn't be too far from weaning." Cassie scribbled the new additions into her log book of all the horses she'd rescued—the age, condition, and background. Just like her horse camp had become popular, she and Mom had become well-known bleeding hearts when it came to mistreated cases. Lucky we were well off because most of Mom's disposable cash went to feeding and maintaining the abused.

I sometimes wondered if she protected the sick and injured because she couldn't protect Dad.

Grandpa John made his way into the kitchen, his huge bulk and imposing presence making my muscles stiffen even more. Grandpa John was the most affectionate out of the Wilson's. He was gruff and had teeth that could draw blood, but he also wore his heart on his sleeve and saved every spider and fly rather than squashed them.

Planting a heavy paw on my shoulder, he inhaled deep. "Um, something smells good, Jakey."

I smiled, doing my best to stop my body from shaking as he squeezed me. "Thanks."

He sniffed at the roasted potatoes steaming beside the buttery green beans. "Can't wait."

I didn't like to cook, but Mom had taught me well. She said I needed to know how to feed myself because hunting and cooking were the two things that would keep me alive and healthy if and when I left home.

Talking of leaving home…

I'd been thinking about that and knew what I would do. I just needed to find the guts to tell Mom. Besides, the past few days I'd had my daily allotment of stress thanks to Hope being on my farm.

Not that I'd spoken to her again.

Whenever she'd returned from rides with Aunt Cassie, I'd feel her eyes on me like twin ice picks, chipping away at my reserves, reminding me I wasn't as impenetrable as I hoped.

Three times, she'd almost caught me coming out of the barn, and three times, I'd thrown a wave in her direction and jogged off on some very urgent chore that kept me away from her impossible stares.

But that was over now. At least for a while.

She'd left a couple of hours ago—picked up by her dad, kissed like a loved daughter, and hugged like a favourite belonging.

I didn't say goodbye.

She'd come looking for me, but I'd spotted her before she'd spotted me and I'd left my position at the creek where I was damming an area so the lower paddock didn't flood come the predicted rain next week, and then hid in the trees where I was more at home than in a house with four walls.

She'd traipsed through long grass ready to be baled, her face falling from eager to sad. Something in my belly clenched, my mouth parted to speak, my body shifted to go to her.

But then, she'd coughed.

A delicate cough most likely from pollen but enough to send my heart crashing through my ribcage.

She coughed again, reminding me how explicitly fragile and weak humans were. How breakable. How killable. How temporary.

While memories and unresolved panic ricocheted through me, she'd turned around and returned to where the other kids stood with their backpacks and dirty clothes ready for parent collection.

I'd stayed in the trees for a long time after, doing my best to calm down. To stop the memories. To ignore the fact that coughing meant someone's lungs were irritated. And lungs were so damn useless. And if breath couldn't be caught, then death was imminent.

I wanted to chase after her and demand she see a doctor to ensure her coughing was just a symptom of mild hay fever and nothing like my dad had.

To make sure she wasn't dying.

But in the end, I got a hold of myself and convinced myself I didn't care.

Even if she died and I never saw her again, I'd kept my distance enough not to hurt.

Grandpa John nudged me sideways, his hairy hand reaching for the soap and sink. Turning liquid into bubbles, he gave me a grin, then rinsed the mess away before diving into his pocket for a trusty handkerchief.

Pulling it out, he dried his hands, rolling his eyes as I darted out of his way so he wouldn't touch me again—making it seem like I had to scoop the bread rolls from the oven that very second.

His heavy boots passed me by, depositing him on the seat next to Mom where he took her hand in his and kissed her knuckles.

Mom visibly relaxed, resting her head on his shoulder and soaking in the comfort normal creatures found from being loved.

Meanwhile, I focused on dividing out dinner for the family, my bare feet touching something soft on the lino as I reached for the cutlery drawer.

Looking down, I frowned.

Something black and lacy stared back.

What the—?

Ducking, I snatched it from the floor and froze as if Hope had just magically walked into the kitchen. It was the same worn piece of lace she'd forced me to hold four nights ago.

"Grandpa?" I asked, my voice gruff with confusion. "Did you drop this?"

Grandpa John raised his white head, frowning at the lace in my hand. Slowly, his old eyes lit with recognition. "Ah yes, found it on the driveway. Figured it belonged to one of the kids." Looking at Aunt Cassie, he added, "Perhaps you can get it back to the student who lost it?"

Cassie held out her hand for me to relinquish it. "Odd, I never saw anyone with something like that. I guess I can call around and see if anyone's missing it."

"Wait." Mom's head popped off Grandpa John's shoulder. Biting her lip, she pushed away from the table and came toward me, palm outstretched.

For some reason, I found it hard to let go.

With gritted teeth, I dropped it into Mom's hold. My eyes remained possessively on it as she cupped it tight.

She gave me an odd look, her head tilting as if noticing something new about me for the first time. I glared as if she'd trespassed on something she shouldn't have, even though she'd done nothing wrong.

"I think I know who it belongs to." She opened her hand again, offering it back to me.

I didn't take it, backing away a step.

"You know too, don't you, Wild One?"

I narrowed my gaze. I didn't know what her game was, but I didn't like her tone. I crossed my arms. "Should I?"

"If you have a good memory, you should. Then again, I'm thinking you've seen this before, judging by the way you jolted."

I broke eye contact, busying myself with the chicken again. "Don't know what you're talking about."

"I think you do."

Padding toward the fridge, I yanked out the butter. "Dinner's ready. Who cares about a piece of lace?"

"It's Hope's," Mom said. "Graham calls her Little Lace because of her Mom's shawl. Remember? He told us the night of the premiere."

I couldn't control my shudder. "I've done my best to block that night from my mind."

I hadn't been to the movies since watching my dad die, my mom commit 'suicide,' and that god-awful rendition of their love story.

Going to the theatre was tainted now.

The thought filled me with nervous disgust for how eager people threw money at Hollywood to recreate the pain of others.

All stories—either fact or fiction—happened to real people. And not all stories were good. In fact, most stories *weren't* good. Almost all of them had a family theme, striking you over and over with the lesson that you could be rich or poor, but if you had family, you had everything.

Yeah well, family didn't last.

People died.

Animals died.

Everything died.

Only land lasted forever.

Mom's fingers closed over the piece of lace. "I have Graham's number. You should call Hope. I'm sure she'll be missing it."

Brushing past her, I carried the platter of potatoes to the table, doing my best to hide my anger. "Why do you have Graham's number?"

She followed me. "Because he's a friend."

"He wants more than just friendship."

"Jacob." Aunt Cassie shook her head in warning. "Don't go there. Don't go to places you don't understand."

"Oh, I understand. I get that people move on and—"

"You listen to me, Jacob Wild." Mom stormed in front of me, planting hands on her hips. "Cassie is right. You don't understand. You think you do, but you don't. You think you're protecting my honour and Ren's memory by stopping me from talking to others, but you're not. Men and women can be friends. Especially those who have lost someone they can never replace." Her face whitened as old grief, recent grief, constant grief overwhelmed her. "Until you're brave enough to let someone into your own heart, you have no right to judge. *None*, do you hear me?"

Shoving the piece of lace into my hand, she muttered, "My

phone is in the hall. Graham's number is on it. I expect you to call Hope this instant and tell her you have her lace and we'll post it to wherever her dad is filming next. Got it?"

Our eyes locked. My temper flared. My promise throbbed.

I bowed my head in obedience. "Okay."

"Good." She smiled softly.

And I knew what I had to say back.

The same phrase she and Dad used after an argument or heated conversation. A phrase that was so common but meant so much.

"Fine."

She flinched as the one word translated into *I love you*. I'd stolen something that used to be theirs and made it ours. Her eyes warmed, her anger waned, and the sense that she wanted to hug me made me clear my throat and skirt past her into the hall.

There, I swiped my face with a hand smelling of garlic and rosemary and picked up Mom's phone.

There weren't many contacts on the device. And one, in particular, punched me in the heart when I came across the entry that had been transferred from her old phone to this one but would never be answered again.

Ren.

Scrolling away quickly, I clicked on the entry 'Graham' and steeled myself for a conversation I didn't want.

Voices of my family tucking into the meal I'd cooked made their way to where I sulked against the wall. I waited while the ringing of Graham's phone repeated loud in my ear.

Finally, just before the answer machine kicked in, Graham answered as if he'd been running and my call was highly inconvenient. "Murphy speaking."

I glowered at the ceiling, begging for the strength not to snap at him. "It's Jacob. You know? Jacob Wild?"

He paused before saying warily, "Jacob…hi. What can I do for you? Your mom okay?" His voice turned a little panicky. "Did something happen?"

I punched the wall quietly behind me, Hope's lace itching my palm as I fisted it tight. "She's fine. It's not you I'm calling for, actually."

"Oh? Who did you want to talk to?"

As if he didn't know? There were only two of them. "Hope, obviously."

His tone slipped an octave in suspicion. "Why?"

"Because."

"Because…"

I smirked, throwing Mom's words in his ear. "Because girls and boys can be friends."

Silence was loud in my ear. Finally, he cleared his throat. "Look, Jacob, you're a nice kid, but you're—"

"Just put her on the phone. Or better yet, just tell me your address. She left her lace here. I'm guessing she's missing it."

Graham's entire attitude changed. "Oh, thank *God*. We've been rushing around since we got to the airport. Our flight leaves in twenty minutes, and she was adamant she wasn't getting on the plane without that thing."

I stilled. "You're leaving?"

"Yeah, filming a TV series in Scotland. Contract starts next week."

I didn't know what to say, so I didn't reply.

"Anyway, you're a lifesaver. At least I can stop harassing the airport security trying to find it." He chuckled. "I'll text you the address of the house I'm renting. If you can post it as soon as possible, I'll forever be in your debt."

"Whatever."

"Okay then…well, you have a good night. Thanks again."

The sounds of boarding calls and large crowds echoed down the line, followed by empty silence as Graham hung up.

It wasn't until after dinner, I'd walked Mom home, and sneaked from my bedroom to see Forrest rather than crawl into bed that I allowed myself to admit I'd shoved Hope's lace into my pocket instead of giving it to Mom for safekeeping to send.

Chapter Eleven

HOPE

* * * * * *

TO HOPE,

Your lace fell out of your pocket again. Seems to be a habit with you. For something that means a lot to you, you don't take the best care of it. Because of that, I've done you a favour to ensure you don't lose it again.
　　Enjoy Scotland.
　　Jacob.

I looked up, doing my best not to hug the handwritten note from the most unlikely of pen pals.

Dad kept staring at me, his arms crossed, forehead furrowed, and a look of wary dislike in his gaze. "Did you and Jacob talk much when you were at Cherry Equestrian?"

Tearing my eyes from his, I hid my desperation to see what Jacob had sent and did my best to act normal. "Not really." I shrugged, inching toward the staircase of the cute thatched cottage that Dad had rented for the next year. The renovated eighteenth-century three-bedroom cottage was cosy and adorable and quite a shock.

I'd known his agent had put him forward to audition for the lead in a new period drama but didn't know he'd gotten it. The TV show was open ended, which meant we could be here one season, then two, and three, and…

My shoulders sank.

The chances of riding at Cassie's horse camp again were slim. Sure, there would be other horses in Scotland…but there would be no Jacob Ren Wild.

No…*friend.*

"Well, it was nice of him to find your lace. Surprising that he knew what it was." Dad kept his arms crossed and his stern face on. For some reason, he treated me as if I'd done something wrong.

I looked at the large fireplace with its huge candles and fairy lights decorating the white-washed mantle. "You saw the compass his dad got him. I wanted to show him what reminds me of Mom."

Dad paused, whatever annoyance he had with me vanished. "Of course, Little Lace. I'm sorry." Pinching his nose, he came toward me and kissed my head. "It was nice of him to send it so fast."

I nodded quickly. The long haul flight had been an eternity without my favourite possession. I felt naked and afraid as if any second we would drop out of the sky because I didn't have Mom's protection.

Keeko shot from the kitchen, Dad's ringing phone in her hand. "You left it on the counter, sir."

Dad moved toward her. "Cheers." Tapping the screen, he put the phone to his ear. "Murphy speaking. Ah yes, I'm coming now." Stepping out the warped front door, he waved and latched it behind him.

The moment he was gone, Keeko smiled. "Want me to make you some lunch? Then we can go over your homework and plan next week's lessons."

I gave into the urge to hug Jacob's letter, crushing the plastic postal bag to my chest. I shook with eagerness to see what was inside. "In a bit? I want to check out my room again. Not living in a trailer is awesome!"

"Okay, but just because we're in a new country doesn't mean you get away from doing schoolwork."

"I know." Spinning in place, I flew up the rustic weathered steps, ducked under a low beam, and dashed into the candy yellow and white bedroom with its four-poster bed and gauzy cream curtains.

My battered and well-used suitcase had already been unpacked. My clothes hung in the pretty wardrobe, my books waiting to be read on the side table.

Ignoring all of it, I threw myself onto the puffy mattress, sank into the softest comforter, and tipped out the rest of Jacob's package.

Bubble wrap didn't stand a chance against my eager fingers as I tore at the sticky tape and gasped as a silver chain slithered onto the bed, followed by the heavy thud of a finely scrolled locket.

It was the biggest locket I'd ever seen.

Round and polished and *perfect*.

The fine engravings of filigree and flowers glinted in the sunlight as I tossed away the empty packaging and snatched the locket as if someone would take it away from me at any moment.

With my tongue between my teeth in concentration, I cracked it open and gasped.

Folded neatly and tucked safely in its new silver shell was Mom's lace.

My cheeks heated. My heart raced. My hands shook as I scurried off the bed toward the dressing table and its aged mirror. It took a few goes to fasten the chain around my neck, but once I did, the weight of the jewellery filled me with something I'd never felt before.

Contentment.

Relief.

Acceptance that Mom had gone, and I didn't need to fret myself over answers. There was also gratefulness, awe, and the undeniable need to hug Jacob as hard as I could for such a thing.

What he'd given me in the stables that night had somehow calmed the anxiousness in my brain. To finally be *spoken* to rather than babied made the urge to be close to him squeeze unbearably around my heart. It hadn't been easy for him talking about it, I knew that. But he'd done it anyway.

He'd done it for *me*.

And now, he'd bought me something I would treasure forever.

My fingers stroked the locket reverently.

It was the perfect size to fit in my palm.

It was the best gift I'd ever received.

See, Jacob is my friend. Even if he doesn't realise it.

There was no way he'd send something like this if he didn't like me just a little bit. Only a true friend would've been so thoughtful, so kind, so pure to send me something so precious.

I have to thank him.

Rushing back to my workbooks on the side table, I ripped out a blank page, pinched a ballpoint from my pencil case, and curled up on the hardwood floor to write the most important letter of my life.

A letter that, at the time, I had no idea would set me on the path of utter heartbreak and utmost desolation.

Chapter Twelve

JACOB

* * * * * *

Seventeen Years Old

DEAR JACOB,

Today, Dad took me to a local pub where he let me try Guinness and we played a game of darts where I accidentally speared the pool table instead of the bull's-eye.

I got told off by the pub keeper, but Dad bought a round of drinks for everyone, and they cheered.

It was fun.

I've been riding three times a week lately. A stocky little highland pony called Haggis. He can't jump, but he can hack for miles and is bombproof on the narrow country roads.

You'd love it here, Jacob.

Everything is so green and rugged. There are rock walls made by king's men and ancient castles destroyed by Vikings.

I used to hate history, but now Keeko and I can explore for days, researching Anglo-Saxon wars and royal battles. Sometimes, I can even taste the gunfire when I'm standing on the turret of some ancient fortress where the Scots were tortured and hung by the redcoats.

Dad has signed up for a second season, so I guess the TV show is going well. Have you seen it over there? He's had to grow this shaggy beard and comes home smelling of wood smoke from filming in smoky manors.

Oh, I almost forgot!

I had a small part two episodes ago. I was the tavern's daughter and poured ale for a troop of riders. I would've much rather ridden myself, but it was cool.

Anyway, enough about me.

What did you do for your birthday?

Did you get anything nice?

Are you still farming?
What do you do on your days off?
Do you have a girlfriend?
Been to see any movies lately?
How's Forrest?
Is Binky still around?
I haven't heard from you in a while, and I don't want to bug you, but I'd love to have a letter back!

P.S. It would be a lot easier to talk if you were on Facebook or email. You sure you won't open an account?

Love, Hope.

I sighed as I re-folded the letter and stuffed it into the envelope decorated with Scottish stamps. Hope had been gone a year, and in that time, I'd received thirteen letters.

I'd replied to just three of them.

And only under threat of agony from my mother.

The first had gushed with thanks for what I'd sent her.

The second had begged for a reply.

Now, she just treated me as a diary entry, sharing her world with me when I didn't ask to be a part of it.

"Hope again?" Mom asked as I shoved the envelope into the box I'd packed from my room.

I nodded curtly.

The topic of Hope never ended well. Ever since Mom found out I'd sent her a silver locket that I'd bought from Mr. Pickerings Personals—the only antique store in town—she'd watched me closely whenever Hope's name was mentioned.

To start with, I'd indulged her.

I let her think we were friends and that I had the strength to care about another person who wasn't blood. But as the months went on and the letters kept coming, Mom's questions became more personal.

Twice now, she'd asked if I had feelings other than friendship toward Hope. She'd reminded me Hope was four years younger than me, then advised I should be friendly but not *too* friendly.

It'd been hard, but I kept my temper and didn't yell. I didn't bother telling her that where romantic entanglement was concerned, I wouldn't be getting involved with anyone—let alone a little girl who knew far too much about my family.

Mom gave me a half-smile that pissed me off. A smile that said she didn't believe me and put up with my denials because she thought she knew better.

She didn't know better.

My life was perfect just the way it was. I'd been a full-time farmer for a year. I didn't have to interact with anyone if I preferred not to. I could work as many hours as I wanted. I could hide for however long I needed.

The solitude was good for my sanity, giving me the ability to be a better son when spending time with those I cared about.

I ensured each time I saw Mom, I gave her a hug—no matter that my heart raced with fear of losing her. I made sure to clean the house once a week, so she didn't have to. I put my grubby work gear in the washing machine and made her dinner as often as I could before I passed out on the couch from the early starts.

Mom was busy with her own projects, breaking in the rescues that Aunt Cassie had inherited, tending to her flowers, and caring for all of us. For the most part, our lives brushed against each other in a way that said we were close but not dependent.

So far, I'd kept my promise to Dad.

Mom seemed to be coping, if not happy, and I was able to keep my fears of losing those I loved from prying eyes.

However, despite the fact that Hope was thousands of miles away, she never left me alone for long. Her letters were like clockwork; whenever I relaxed after a few weeks of no correspondence, one would be waiting for me, placed on my pillow by a mother determined to force me into meaningful relationships.

The letter would taunt me with gossip I didn't want to know and stories I had no time to read. Then again, I didn't really mind the waffling news of Hope's new life in Scotland. I was glad she was riding, exploring, learning, growing up. But once she'd filled me in on her world, there were always a hundred questions about me.

Endless questions about what I was doing, how I was going, what my goals and dreams were.

She believed we were *friends*.

And it was all because of that goddamn locket.

What the *hell* had I been thinking?

What possessed me to do such a thing?

Even worse, what made me buy something from the only antique store in town and believe it would stay a secret with the nosy busybodies of this place?

I'd bought it purely out of common-sense. She wanted the lace with her at all times, but a pocket wasn't a safe place for something so light and flimsy.

A locket made perfect sense.

After all, Mom kept a photo of Dad around her neck. It was a place for precious things that needed safekeeping.

It didn't mean anything more than a solution to Hope's problem—not that other's (especially Mom) saw it that way.

"You should write back." Mom kept her eyes averted, folding laundry with the TV on low behind her. "There's been a few now that you haven't replied to."

I merely stuffed the letter farther into the box of random stuff I didn't really need. Things like old running gear from school and the blazer I'd worn to the movie premiere and would never wear again.

When I didn't reply, Mom stopped folding and came toward me. More boxes waited patiently by the front door, ready to move with me now that I was leaving the nest.

She slowed to a stop before me. "Are you sure you're ready? There's no rush, Wild One. None at all." Her eyes glossed with tears before she smiled bright and swallowed them back.

I picked up the box, carrying it to the exit. "It's not like I'm leaving, leaving."

"You are. This house will be so lonely without you."

I couldn't look at her. The eternal guilt of letting Dad down when I made Mom sad suffocated me. "I'm just across the meadow, Mom." I glanced through the open door toward the small cabin nestled, almost camouflaged, against the treeline. "You can still see me. Besides, you knew this was coming. You helped me build it."

In the past year, everyone had chipped in. Even Uncle Liam—who pulled long hours as a cop in the next town over—had come to help hammer nails and cut wood.

The cabin wasn't much.

A two bed, one bath single story dwelling that kept its rustic heritage with simple white walls and a high beam ceiling. The kitchen was modern, along with the bathroom, and my bedroom was four walls of glass, jutting out like a box, the entire room cradled by woodland.

I didn't want to live in a tent fulltime, but more and more, I'd been drawn to sleeping unhindered beneath the treetop canopy.

Now, I could be free every night.

"I should never have helped you get planning permission. Then at least you'd still be living here with me." Mom pouted.

This was one of those times when a hug would be good. A hug would defuse the tension and give her the contact she needed with assurances that just because I wasn't sleeping under her roof anymore didn't mean I wasn't still her son.

But today was a bad day for me.

A bad day for both of us.

Today was the anniversary of Dad's death, and the pain cut me like a thousand blades. Mom and I had already been into the forest to pay our respects to our dead loved one. We'd shared a simple breakfast beneath the initial-carved tree, our thoughts with Dad rather than on conversation with each other.

I was unbelievably cruel to choose this day over any other to move out, but…I couldn't do it anymore. I couldn't sleep in the same house where love and heartbreak painted the walls. I couldn't eat in the same kitchen where laughter and togetherness and family lingered like broken ghosts every day.

This place was too hard.

Too full of affection that I couldn't tolerate a moment longer.

"I love you, Mom," I said softly. "I just…I need my own place, you know?"

She looked at the floor, nodding quickly. "I know."

"You're welcome over there anytime."

"I know. You too. Here, I mean. Your bedroom will always be yours."

I went toward her slowly. "It's not my bedroom anymore. Decorate it however you want. Make it a writing room. A library. Anything you want."

She smiled through fresh tears. "A library could be nice."

I grinned, my heart hurting despite knowing moving out of home was the right thing to do. This was the only chance I had to try to figure out the mess inside me. I would never leave Cherry River because I would never leave Mom. But I needed something of my own. Something where I could let down my walls and just…

Breathe?

Exist?

Fade?

Either way, my path was already laid out before me, and I was content to tread it—as long as I had my own space to hide when the mask I wore to protect those I cared about slipped.

My arm came up, my fingers grasping Mom's long blonde hair and the blue ribbon tangled in the strands. I didn't know if she'd cut a new piece lately or if this was the piece I'd cut for her on request of my dad, but either way…not a day passed when she didn't have the ribbon somewhere.

Last year, puberty meant my height shot upward, putting me a least a foot over her. She said it was the only thing I hadn't taken after Dad. I was taller even than him. And at that moment, I was grateful for the height difference as it meant I could bend close, kiss her forehead, and arch out of her reach before she could return the affection.

Her lower lip wobbled as I backed away with a small wave. "I'll be right across the meadow if you need me."

She nodded.

"I'll have my phone on me at all times if it's an emergency."

She nodded again.

"I'm not truly gone, Mom. I'll never leave you, 'kay?"

Her final nod was obscured as I turned around, scooped up the closest box, and walked out the door.

Chapter Thirteen

JACOB
* * * * * *

Seventeen Years Old

"WILD ONE?"

I looked up from where I had my hands in compost, transplanting seedlings into my first official veggie garden. I'd lived alone in my cabin for three months, and after a long day working the land, toiling with sun and seasons, I'd hoped I'd find some resemblance of peace in my own space.

The opposite happened.

I couldn't relax. The silence was too oppressive. The emptiness too familiar. I didn't like watching TV, so I settled on doing anything I could to keep my mind busy.

I studied YouTube tutorials from how to install an extra skylight in my kitchen to planting a garden full of potatoes, tomatoes, broccoli, and every other vegetable I could think of.

I wouldn't admit it, but I was slowly running out of things to do.

Grabbing the rag that I kept in my pocket for tractor grease, occasional cuts, and farm muck, I stood as Mom stepped off the wraparound deck and smiled at my progress.

"Wow, are you feeding yourself or an army?"

"You, me, Grandpa, Aunt Cassie…" I smirked. "I did kinda go overboard when I bought the seeds. And some won't survive with the colder weather, but hey."

She chuckled. Her skin was tanned like mine from being outdoors all spring, and my dirty blond hair almost matched her lighter strands as she came toward me, holding out a bunch of letters. "I've been meaning to give you these."

I raised an eyebrow, taking the stack. I didn't need to ask who they were from. The Scottish stamps gave it away.

I counted four.

Sighing, I shoved shaggy hair from my eyes, wondering how I could stop Hope from this futile outreach of friendship. The fact that I wasn't on social media should be clue enough that I didn't want to stay in touch with anyone.

Mom cleared her throat. "Write to her, Jacob. She's probably lonely over there on her own. The least you can do is be a proverbial shoulder to cry on."

I looked up. "I don't owe her anything."

"No, but ever since she saw you, she's been rather enamoured. Be kind. She's young and fanciful and will grow out of her little crush, eventually."

"Crush?" I froze. "It's not a crush. It's, um. I don't know what it is but—"

"Believe me, Wild One. I know when a girl is in awe of a boy, and Hope is in awe of you. I'm not asking you to lead her on. In fact, I'm telling you she's too young and at no point are you to contemplate anything more than friendship, but it wouldn't hurt to write her back. At least until she meets her first boyfriend and then you'll be replaced."

I rolled my eyes. "She's just so…young."

"We're all young once." Mom smiled sadly. "But it doesn't last long, and age really doesn't matter when the heart knows what it wants."

"Even more reason for me to ignore her."

Mom shook her head. "Read them. Respond. Just be nice."

With a wave, she left me in the setting sun as I smeared a streak of mud on the pristine white envelope and moved to sit on the fallen tree by the kitchen.

Once again, I cursed that damn locket. If I could rewind time and just send the lace, I would.

I'd caused this mess.

I'd given her the illusion that I was open to more than a casual acquaintance, and I honestly didn't know how to stop her.

The rip of paper sounded loud in the orange twilight as I tore into the envelope and lifted out the first letter.

Dear Jacob,

Still haven't heard from you, but that's okay. I've been busy, busy with my lessons. Keeko says I'm gonna kick ass in my first lot of exams this year, so that's good.

Scotland is still fun despite the mist and drizzle that seems to cover the entire country for weeks on end. I'm used to riding in the rain now. And I own more jackets and scarfs than I ever have, but that's just life in the highlands, I guess.

Um, what else is new?
Not much really.
I guess I just wanted to hear from you.
Are you busy with farming?
Do you still feel your dad there?
Do you think my mom is here with me in Scotland?

I know you're super busy but write back when you can!

Love, Hope.

Placing the letter beneath a rock so it wouldn't flutter away in the gentle breeze, I opened the next one. Determined to read them as fast as I could so I could get them over with.

Dear Jacob,

I have news!
I've officially been given a part in Dad's TV show. I'm playing the daughter of the countess Dad has fallen madly in love with, but she's married (the count beats her, so Dad will rescue her, probably kill him, and they'll live happily ever after). Don't repeat that, though, as I don't want to leak info about the show.

The best thing is I don't have to wear the hooped dresses and crazy gowns that all the other girls have to. My character is a tomboy who wears boy's stuff. Cool, huh?

It's only a few episodes, and I don't have many lines, but I'm enjoying it. To be honest, though, I don't think I want to be in front of the camera like Dad is. I think, once I've finished school, I'm gonna become a scriptwriter and create the dialogue that the actors say, cause some of it is cringe-worthy!

If you were online, I could send a few pics from set. I could even send a video of me jumping a new horse called Polka!

Anyway, how's Cherry River?
Did Cassie have lots of kids for her horse camp?
Did you teach anyone?
Are you riding much or too busy?

Would love to hear from you.

Love, Hope.

My patience waned as I reached for the third one. At least she'd distracted me from staying busy and filling in the holes of solitude. Her prattling letters were almost as if she sat beside me.

Dear Jacob,

I had to type this on my laptop and print it off because I broke my writing arm. I have to have a cast on for six weeks. Boo. I fell off Polka and slammed right into a jump. Dad is furious. He's banned me from riding forever. I know he's just scared of me hurting myself again, but he can't take away the only thing that makes sense.
I need it, you know?
No one else but you would understand that.
Anyway, I don't have anything else to say.

Please…write back?

Love, Hope.

I smoothed the letter onto the other read ones, frowning a little at the thought of her hurt. Horse riding was dangerous and she'd just proven bones broke easily. Hopefully, she'd be more careful in the future.

The last letter slipped from its envelope, and I unfolded it.

Dear Jacob,

Your mom wrote to me and said you're not living at home anymore and mentioned your new address to send my letters to.
Wow, you've moved out already? That's cool. But isn't it a little scary? I'm almost fourteen, and as much as I don't really like moving around so often, I wouldn't be able to live on my own yet.
She also said you've been running Cherry River super well and she's very proud of you. That's nice. I wish I could come see your place. I'd love to ride with you and Forrest sometime.
I know you probably think I'm being clingy or annoying by writing so much to you, but every day, when I touch the locket you gave me with Mom's lace inside, I think of you. I think of you and want to tell you all about my

day. I want to hear about yours and what you've been doing and to be your friend.

But I know you're very busy, so I won't ask for a reply this time.

I'll just finish with another thank you and hope you have a wonderful day.

Bye for now, but I hope not forever.

Love, Hope.

*****

Part Two

*****

Intermission

DELLA

✶ ✶ ✶ ✶ ✶ ✶

THAT SON OF *mine is not easy.*

At school, he made no effort to befriend anyone; at home, he keeps love on a leash; and with Hope, he never let down his walls. Each time he pushes people further away, I fall deeper into the fear that Ren and I failed our son.

That Jacob is screwed up when it comes to love because of us.

That he's allergic to touch and togetherness because we showed him what happens when death severs such things.

Jacob barely had a childhood, thanks to sickness and sadness, and his teenage years weren't normal, either.

But Hope…wow, what a brave little thing.

She is the only one who's dared attempt friendship. She's the only one who sees what I see and is strong enough to help.

Between you and me, Ren would've loved her.

But you know that, don't you? I don't even need to tell you why *he would've loved her.*

It's obvious.

If we'd been blessed with a daughter, we would've chosen Hope.

And who knows?

One day, she might become part of our family.

Because a mother always knows, and I know Hope has a crush on my son.

I wonder if it will grow into more as age slips them from children to adults. I wonder if time will be kind to them in the same way it was cruel to us. I wonder if she might be the one to fix everything Ren and I have broken.

Those questions are what led me to meddle.

I know I shouldn't have, but Hope needed a helping hand. A nudge in the right direction.

So I wrote to her.

I told her Jacob's new address.

I gushed how proud I am of my son.

All while holding back what I truly wanted to say.
Thank you.
Thank you for trying.
Thank you for not taking no for an answer.

Chapter Fourteen

HOPE

* * * * * *

Seventeen Years Old

"BRIAN, STOP. I'M not ready."

"Aww, come on, lass. We've been dating for six months. How much longer do ya need?"

His Scottish twang echoed loud in my ears as I wriggled out from under him and scurried from the backseat of his bronze Vauxhall. "I don't know. But tonight isn't happening." My hands shook as I smoothed the hem of my dress back into position and adjusted my bra where his hands had been.

"But we had a bonny meal. It's our anniversary. If we did it now, it would make tonight so special." He wiped his mouth with the back of his hand, smearing my pink lip-gloss that I'd left from kissing him.

The chilly night air bit at my exposed arms. The grey dress I wore—that I'd hoped made me look worldly and refined—mocked me for thinking I was brave enough to lose my virginity.

It wasn't the thought of being naked and feeling someone inside me for the first time that terrified me. It was the fact that no boys held any value compared to Jacob Ren Wild.

They all seemed so juvenile, so one-dimensional, so frustratingly *simple*.

Jacob was complex and snappish and hard work. And no matter how many times I'd tried peering into the secrets he kept locked around his heart, he'd never let me get close.

Not that it mattered.

I hadn't heard from him in years.

For all I knew, he could be married by now. After all, farmers tended to marry young and have kids early. At least, a lot of the Scottish farmers did.

Brian unfolded his bulk from the backseat, joining me on the pebbles where, during the day, tourists parked to stare at the wild view of highland ruggedness and cliff sides. But by night, it was the well-known 'getting high and having sex' hang-out spot for rebellious teens. "You're just a tease, Hope Murphy. A goddamn tease."

I almost rolled my eyes.

Couldn't he see how cliché all of this was? Girl and boy date. Girl doesn't really like boy, but she's lonely enough to go along with it. Boy thinks he's going to get lucky, but girl decides she's worth more and would rather wait forever than give up everything for nothing.

Ugh, even his argument was cliché.

Hence the reason why I wanted to be a scriptwriter. Humans could only tell so many tales. The well-known tropes of the 'meet-cute, boy-next-door, friends-to-lovers, enemies-to-lovers, and forbidden romance' were all overdone. But within those tropes, variations could make a common love story unique—but only if the dialogue and delivery were special.

And Brian was definitely not special.

"I'm going to walk home." I brushed past Brian to grab my small handbag and plum trench coat from the front seat. The trench I'd bought with the income I'd earned from my small acting parts. I had a habit of buying clothes that were a bit too old and styles too regal for a teenage girl who still had no clue who she was.

Only that she was lonely.

So, so freaking lonely.

"You cannae walk home. We're miles away from the village."

"I *can* walk home. And I'm going to." My nose came up in case he argued again.

I wasn't afraid of the dark or the temperamental weather of Scotland. I'd ridden in far worse. At least horses were there for me—making me stronger in both body and spirit, carving me from a silly child to someone I would hopefully learn to like.

"Well, dannae come crying to me when you get lost," Brian muttered, moving around his car to get into the driver's seat. "We're through, by the way. I'm dumping you."

I couldn't contain my laughter. My snicker was full of months of dating someone I wasn't interested in and finally being set free. "That's the best news I've heard all year."

"You're a witch." He slammed his door and twisted the key

with a jerk. The Vauxhall growled pathetically then squealed like a rat as he spun from the car park.

I coughed a little on the dust left behind. Shrugging into the trench and slinging my handbag over my shoulder, I shoved my hands deep into the warm pockets.

With my mind full of fatherless farm boys, I began the long trek home, all the while concocting believable excuses to hide the fact I'd been up at the lookout after curfew with an unused condom in my bag and a heart still well and truly smitten with a boy I would never have.

* * * * *

Sunday.

Normally, I'd go riding with Sally on the moor, even in the rain, but today, I wasn't in the mood.

Last night, after sneaking home with blisters on my toes from stupid suede boots, I'd made the mistake of pulling out Jacob's old letters.

Not that there were many of them.

I'd lost track of how many I'd sent him, but I could count the number of his replies on one hand.

Only four.

All simple and closed off with an unwritten message to leave him alone.

Hope,

Glad you got the locket okay. Stop thanking me. Seriously. It was just a practical thing—doesn't mean anything.
Happy riding in Scotland.

Jacob.

A few lines of neatly written text in return for three pages of me gushing with thanks for his gift and news about my new life in Scotland.

I cringed as I placed the letter back in its box. I'd been a silly, idealistic little girl. I'd believed Jacob found me as fascinating as I found him, but it wasn't until I started dating Brian and grew up that I'd understood I'd just been an annoying child.

And nothing was fascinating about a child who wouldn't stop asking about death.

God, it was almost too embarrassing to remember how

desperate I was to be around Jacob. How, every day at horse camp, I was more interested in spying where he was than actually riding.

Pathetic, Hope.

Adding salt to my already flayed memories, I opened another letter.

Hope,

Thanks for the news, but honestly, you don't have to keep writing. It's fine. I get that you love the locket and that Scotland is totally different from here.

As for me, I'm good. Horses are good. Life moves forward.

Have a great day.

Jacob.

As I ran my finger over the handwritten letters, heat once again flooded my cheeks. A few years ago, when I'd received this letter, I'd been besotted with everything Jacob Wild. His notes might've been short, but I was a master at reading into them. Painting a picture of him working the land, enjoying a novel where he was sunburned and dirty, watching a movie of him taking a nap between Forrest's legs in lush green grass.

Now, I read the letters how they were meant to be read.

Curt and impatient.

And for the first time, anger twined around my heart. Yes, I might've been young and overly eager, but he didn't have to be so cold. I only tried to be nice. If he'd just given me a few extra minutes of his day, who knew if I'd feel as lonely as I did now.

I'd tried making friends. Dad even let me go to normal school instead of being home-schooled by Keeko so I could mingle with kids my own age. However, they were all so...*juvenile.* So focused on parties and who-liked-who and scrambling to study for exams.

No one had time for me.

And my loneliness grew ever more acute.

Hope,

Sorry to hear about your arm.

Get better quick!

Jacob.

I groaned, pressing my face into my hands. When I'd received that note, I'd read between the lines and believed he wanted me to heal fast, not for me, but for *him.*

Now, I saw two simple sentences sent only to appease a clingy, silly girl.

The last letter was the worst.

Hope,

Yes, I moved out of home. It was time.
Glad you're enjoying acting a little.
That's great.
Awesome to hear you're moving on and growing up.
All the best.

Jacob.

Not one sign he wanted me to reply. Not one of my questions about his life answered. His letters were as unyielding and uninformative as he was in person, and I'd cried after receiving that one.

Because, finally, the blinders I'd been wearing were torn off. Maybe it was the fact he didn't live with his mom anymore. Maybe it'd been because time had already pushed him further out of my reach. Or maybe it was because I was sick of reaching out for a friend only to be hurt by his indifference.

Either way, I hadn't written to him again.

In fact, I did my best not to think about him. The locket with Mom's lace lived permanently around my neck, but I forced myself only to think of her when I noticed it in the mirror after my shower or when I tucked it into my school uniform in the morning.

But thanks to strolling down bitter memory lane last night, I wasn't in the mood to do anything but sulk.

What was so repulsive about me? Why were the boys interested in hooking up but not connecting? Why did girls like me to begin with, then hate me a week later?

At least Scotland's weather matched my despondency, giving me an afternoon of drizzle that was perfect for a bowl of buttery popcorn and a perusal of the DVD cabinet to veg on the couch.

Skimming the shelves of rom-coms, dramas, and sci-fis, my attention latched onto the blue spine with the glittery script of *The Boy & His Ribbon*.

I hadn't seen the movie since the premiere. I hadn't had an urge to. Normally, I didn't like watching the movies Dad had acted in, but…this one was about Jacob—in a roundabout way.

I couldn't stop myself as I grabbed the disk, inserted it into the home theatre system, and settled down to watch what love could be like.

A love I wanted for myself.

A love that any girl—young or old—coveted, begged for, and dreamed of.

No matter the pain in the end.

* * * * *

"Whatcha watching?" Dad strode into the living room as I swiped at my tears, totally suckered into Dad's acting and the agony of saying goodbye.

"Nothing." My hand shot forward for the remote, but it was too late.

He paused, his arms behind him as he shrugged off his jacket. "*The Boy & His Ribbon?*"

I shrank into the comfy couch. "Just fancied a lazy Sunday."

Dad finished taking off his jacket before slinging it over the recliner and sitting down to remove his boots. The beard he'd grown for work was unkempt and highland wild, but he was happy in this role. Completely in his element in the howling winds and roaring fireplaces of the past.

"Heard from Jacob or Della lately?"

I shook my head, hiding my flinch.

Stretching backward, he yawned and rubbed his face. "I'll be glad once this early morning battle scene is done."

Sitting cross-legged, I paused the movie where Jacob and his mom were in the forest with an urn of ashes, stopped comparing it to the rainy afternoon when my mom's casket was lowered into a grave, and focused on my only living family. "Yeah, you've been pulling some crazy hours lately."

Dad gave me a tired smile. "All right. Out with it. What's up, Little Lace?"

"What? There's nothing."

"I know you." He sighed gently. "Something is on your mind."

"I'm good."

"Is it about you sneaking home at ten past midnight last night?"

I froze. "Oh."

"Is it about that boy Brian Regan who is never to step foot in my house again?"

I sat taller, getting defensive. "I didn't do anything wrong if that's what you're implying."

He held up his hands. "Not implying. Just saying if you're out that late again with a boy, you'll be on the first flight back home and locked in a boarding school."

Normally, I'd spit and hiss and argue, but his threat about boarding school wasn't new—he'd overused it when I refused to eat broccoli or didn't make my bed—but today, I simply didn't care if he limited my freedom.

It was all the same anyway.

"Uh-oh. Must be serious if you're not rising to that bait." Dad sat forward, linking his fingers between his woollen breeches from set. "Speak."

I bit my lip, my gaze wandering to the frozen screen where the actor playing Jacob was locked in position, looking at the sky with tears on his cheeks.

Should I ask or not?

Was it my business, or should I leave it alone?

When I couldn't figure out my decision, Dad tilted his head in frustration. "Not like you to be tongue-tied."

I sighed. "You don't like me talking about it."

He stilled. "Doesn't matter. If you need to discuss whatever is bugging you, then spit it out. I know I was hard on you when you were little, but you're a young woman now. Anything you want to know...I'll do my best to tell you." He gulped dramatically, the comedian-actor taking over from the serious. "Unless it's about sex, then it's a totally different story. That topic doesn't exist. As far as I'm concerned, you live in a world where you don't know what boys are."

"Ha ha." I gave him a quick smile. He'd already sucked up his nerves and given me the sex talk when I was younger. He'd done it himself, rather than enlist Keeko. He was a good father. A *great* father.

I was so lucky.

Plucking lint from my jeans, I muttered, "Okay then, um...well, you know how when we lost Mom, it changed us. We...I don't know exactly. We just changed."

He nodded, leaning back in the chair. "I know exactly what you mean."

"Well…do you think losing his dad changed Jacob?"

Dad mulled over my question. He genuinely gave me time instead of brushing it aside like he did when I was a child. "Undoubtedly."

"Do you think it's broken him as a person?"

He sighed. "Who can say what each person can tolerate? You and me, we decided that we wanted to keep going, regardless if your mother left us. We had each other to lean on."

"Jacob has his mom. Why isn't that enough?"

Dad rubbed his nose. "Who's to say it's not?"

I gave him an exasperated look. "I know it's been a while since I've seen him, but he was hurting back when I stayed with them. He hurt a lot, Dad. I don't think you grow out of that."

He stroked the thick weave of his trousers, taking his time to reply. "Each person suffers in their own way. His loss was different than ours. His dad was sick. Just playing that role drained me to the point of depression. Knowing you're going to die, all while fighting it until that very last moment…it couldn't have been easy living in that environment as a kid."

"Mom was sick too. Mentally." I dropped my gaze. "But she chose to leave. Maybe that's the difference."

Dad looked away, clearing his throat as if his own pain still punctured his heart. I hadn't been the only one Mom chose death over. She'd left Dad, too.

How could she be so cruel?

We sat in tense silence for a few seconds.

"Anyway," I said a bit too loudly. "Watching this movie just made me think of the Wilds, that's all."

"Are you sure that's all?"

"What do you mean?"

"I mean, why are you so concerned about him? You haven't seen him in years. He's twenty-one now. He's not the kid you knew when you rode there."

"I know."

"How he's dealing with the death of his father isn't your concern."

I slouched, pulling a turquoise cushion onto my lap. "I can still worry about him."

Dad narrowed his eyes. "Look, all I'm saying is don't worry about things you can't change. He's living his life. You're living yours. That's all you need to focus on."

But that was the thing...I didn't want that separation.

I wanted friendship.

I wanted him to answer a stupid letter once in a while and prove that he saw me as someone valuable and not a nuisance.

That would never happen, but at least dreams were free. "Okay."

That response was pathetic. It made me look pathetic, sound pathetic, overall *pathetic*.

He stared at me for a second too long, perhaps reading my secrets that, despite practically being a stranger to Jacob, I was intrinsically tied to Cherry River in ways I couldn't explain.

Thanks to Dad, I was set for life. I had an income of my own. Contacts and offers and a career any young actress would kill for. But it couldn't change who I was at heart. And I was a girl insanely envious of a farm boy who woke with the dawn and worked with earth and sky all day.

It made no sense that the land called to me so strongly. Even though I was born a city girl, raised a city girl, and would most likely end up marrying a city boy, a piece of me didn't feel entirely safe unless it was on a sprawling estate with forests guarding every direction.

Dad somehow saw all that because I forgot to hide the truth.

He saw *me*.

The *real* me.

Not the rehearsed or scripted me.

And his face fell, understanding for the first time that I hadn't taken after him *or* Mom. I was a stranger pretending to be family.

I let him down. As an actress. As his daughter.

Slowly, he nodded as if we'd had an entirely different conversation. "You don't just miss the Wilds, do you? You miss their way of life."

I hugged the cushion to my chest, trying to ward off his uncanny revelation. "I'm sure it's just a case of the grass is greener on the other side."

His eyes tightened. "Yet...I don't think it is." He pinched the bridge of his nose, inching toward the edge of his chair. "All this time, I believed you enjoyed travelling with me. When your mom was happy, she adored living in exotic places, going to the best restaurants, and shopping in the priciest shops." He chuckled sadly. "I love to travel too. I'm good at my job because I enjoy slipping into the skin of another person, but only because it shows me how great my own life is when I come home…to you."

For some reason, tears prickled. I didn't know what to say or where I fit in thanks to Dad's strange epiphany.

"Who do you take after, Hope Jacinta Murphy? Who are you when horses and farms flow in your blood rather than Hollywood and make-believe?"

I shivered as his stare became too intense.

"You care more about things you've never experienced than the world you've been brought up in." He shook his head. "I thought, to begin with, it was just the novelty of horses that all little girls go through. But I'm too late. Too late to see that you're happier on the moor in mud than you are on the red carpet in a pretty dress." His chin fell, his gaze locked on the white rug on the hardwood floor. "How did I become so blind?"

The catch in his voice shot me off the couch so fast, the cushion and remote control slammed to the ground. Falling to my knees in front of him, I pressed my face against his trousers. "It's okay, Dad. You're overtired. You need to sleep—"

"What I *need* is to pay attention to my daughter who isn't ten anymore." His fingers pried under my chin, pulling my face upward. "You're seventeen. You're incredible. And you're lonely. That's what all this death stuff is about, isn't it? You're *lonely*. God, how long, Little Lace? How long have you been pretending to be happy for my sake?"

A tear rolled down my cheek, trickling over his knuckles at the wretched look in his gaze.

This was why I'd hid who I was. This was why I accepted minor parts he said I'd be good at and why I did my best to socialise with kids from the local school.

Because Dad had already lost so much.

And he couldn't afford to lose me too.

Why had he suddenly seen now? What had I shown to hurt him so badly?

"I'm not lonely, Dad." Even to my ears, the words were devoid of honesty.

He smiled sadly. "If that's the best you can do, you need better acting lessons."

I laughed at his joke, pulling my face from his touch. "Horse riding helps."

"But it's not just the horses, is it?" Dad cocked his head. "You're just as happy mucking out a stall with hay in your hair and manure on your boots as you are riding the damn creatures. What is it about being grubby and earning blisters that appeals to you so much?"

I looked away shyly. "I don't know."

When he huffed under his breath, slouching into the chair as if he didn't believe me, I rushed, "Honestly. I don't know. I have this…craving inside. A need to be dirty because I feel like I've done something to *deserve* something if that makes sense? I want to be outside. I want to take a seed and turn it into a plant. I want to watch something grow rather than remember someone die."

"Said like a true farmer's daughter." He smirked, making light of a heavy situation. "Perhaps the hospital gave me the wrong baby, huh? Maybe you're not mine, after all."

"I'm yours, Dad." I pointed at my green gaze, the identical colour of his. "I'm just…going through a phase, that's all."

"A phase?" He chuckled. "A phase doesn't last your whole life, Hope."

I shrugged, grinning back stupid tears and doing my best to assure my beloved father I was happy, content, and all his. "I'll be fine."

"I don't want you to be just *fine*. I want you to be happy."

I nodded, calling on all the acting lessons I'd tolerated for his sake to give the best performance I could. "I *am* happy. I'm sorry I made you worry."

With our eyes locked, he shook his head and stood. "I love you, Hope. But you truly are a terrible actress."

With a tight smile, he left me sitting on the couch with a boy holding an urn of ashes and a movie I should never have watched again.

Chapter Fifteen

JACOB
✶ ✶ ✶ ✶ ✶ ✶

Twenty-One Years Old

"YES, OF COURSE, Graham. She's welcome anytime."

I froze with my arms full of firewood, one boot planted on the doormat, and the other over the threshold to my mom's house.

I'd left for all of ten minutes to grab more fuel, and she gets on the phone to Graham goddamn Murphy.

"Mm-hm. I know," Mom murmured. "It's understandable she's lonely." Another pause. "Yes, it must be so hard. She's the odd one out. Privileged, so she's bullied. Free-spirited, so she's misunderstood."

What the hell was she talking about?

Obviously, I knew.

Even though I hoped I was wrong. There was only one person Mom and Graham would be talking about. Two, perhaps, if they had a death wish and discussed me.

However, I wasn't the subject today…Hope was.

Goddammit.

It'd been years since I'd had to stay on guard around her. Years since a letter. Years since she'd come to stay.

I thought I'd been in the clear.

"Next week? Yes, no problem. We don't have a horse camp on, but she's welcome to visit. Between Cassie and me, we'll make sure she rides a lot."

Oh, *hell* no.

The wood prickled my biceps as I squeezed the bark tight. I didn't want a trespasser on my farm. I had enough to do without babysitting.

Because that was what would happen.

I'd end up babysitting because Mom and Aunt Cassie would

say they were too busy with their rescues and charity work to play pony chaperone to a kid.

"Yep. I'll get Jacob to pick her up from the airport." A pause. "No. No problem at all. I know how busy you are over there. The TV show is great, by the way." Another pause. "We'll look after her, don't you worry. Okay then, uh-huh. Sure. Yep, will do. Talk soon."

She hung up and I had a good mind to turn around, drop the firewood, and go home. Screw making her the mushroom pesto pasta I'd planned. She'd just invited an enemy into our home.

Invited, yes. But Hope isn't here yet.

There was still time to prevent it from happening.

I glared at Mom as I stomped to the fireplace and the rattan basket for holding wood. Dumping the armful into it, I stood, brushed off bark pieces and small splinters, and crossed my arms. "No."

She mimicked me, crossing her arms and readying for battle. "Don't you 'no' me, Jacob Wild. Four p.m. on Wednesday. She's flying in from Edinburgh. She'll be jet-lagged, hungry, and expecting a friendly face. You *will* be that friendly face. You will drive her here. Help her settle and get over whatever grudge you have against her, got it?"

I opened my mouth to argue, but she hadn't finished.

"Oh, one other thing. You might as well know because I'd rather you get over your indignation before she arrives. I'm going to let her stay in your old room instead of the bunk beds for camp students. Graham said he's worried about her and wants her to have lots of company. She doesn't know he's set this up, and I expect it to be a good surprise for however long she stays."

Slowly, I unwound my arms, fisting my hands. "And how long will that be?"

Mom shrugged. "He didn't say, and I didn't ask." She bustled into the kitchen, deliberately busying herself with pulling ingredients from the fridge, including a bunch of fresh vegetables I'd grown in my garden.

My entire body boycotted the idea of visitors. My heart smoked with possession over my mother. I didn't want to share her with some kid who didn't deserve to be here. Let alone allow a girl to sleep in my room—a room I'd barely set foot in for four years.

But I knew when I was beaten, and after one too many early starts this week, I didn't have the energy to fight. "Why now?"

Mom pulled a cutting knife from the block, giving me a sad smile. "Because she's lost."

Kicking off my boots, I walked toward her. "That isn't our problem."

"I know." She stopped what she was doing. "But I was lost once. Ren was lost. Cassie was lost. Everyone is lost at some point in their lives." Her blue gaze seared into me. "Even you were lost until you started working the farm. It's not our problem if Hope is lost, but it *is* our obligation to help her find her true path—even if it's just by being her friend."

My temper faded.

I was older now, and rational arguments always took the sting out of my anger, leaving me low and lacking and very aware of how much I still had to learn. I pretended to be a good person, but in reality, I wasn't.

"Okay, Mom." I nodded. "I'll be nice."

"Thank you, Jacob."

I padded into the kitchen, nudging her out with a smile. "I'll cook dinner. Go sit down and relax."

"Okay." Standing on tiptoes, she dared kiss my cheek, and I schooled my need to rock backward out of her reach. Her soft lips stung rather than filled me with comfort, and my eyes shot to the blown-up photograph of Dad, Mom, and me when I was five.

The ghost I lived with shook its head.

The fear I carried clutched me closer.

Tearing my gaze from the perfect family moment, I sliced into a mushroom and shoved aside what I truly wanted to say, to admit, to confess.

Hope might be lost, but...so was I.

Still.

I'd always been lost.

I'd most likely *always* be lost.

And one lost person definitely wasn't qualified to help another.

Chapter Sixteen

HOPE

* * * * * *

MY EYESIGHT HADN'T changed.

My body was no different.

My heart exactly the same.

Yet as I stepped from security clearance, scanned the small crowd collecting loved ones, and noticed Jacob Ren Wild dressed in scruffy jeans, a black long-sleeve shirt, and a tanned, sweat-stained cowboy hat, I no longer felt like me.

My eyes *saw* differently.

My body reacted strangely.

My heart shed off its chrysalis and grew wings.

Wings that fluttered and tickled as I studied the man who'd replaced the boy I used to know.

Funny how I remembered what he looked like. Funny that I remembered his stubborn stares, surly sulks, and wary distress. But I hadn't *truly* remembered.

I hadn't truly seen.

Before, I'd seen him with a child's eyes. Eyes wide with wonderment for a boy older than me. A boy I believed had the answers to death and dying. A boy who had the lifestyle I wanted but could never hope to earn.

Today, as I pulled to a stop in front of him and our gazes locked and the world fell away, I didn't see him through the eyes of that little girl anymore. I saw him as a woman. I might still be young, and still hold romantic ideals with a soul full of loneliness, but I was awake, I was aware, I was knowing.

"Hello, Hope."

His voice held a deeper, more jaded quality to it.

His skin was slightly weathered from working outdoors.

His body stronger, eyes darker, his face a landscape of roughness, judgment, and warning.

But in his cool, unnerving stare, I found something I didn't know I'd lost. I earned something I'd misplaced. Retrieved something I'd walked away from.

He was the penny on the street you picked up for good luck. The four-leaf clover you tucked into the pages of a book for good fortune. The wish you made to the starry sky, believing there had to be more than this.

My suitcase was suddenly as heavy as the world. My fingers opened, releasing it.

And I did something.

Something unpermitted and uninvited but something I should've done many years ago.

Opening my arms, I crashed into him. My cheek pressed against his heart. My body to his body. I shivered at the scent of leather and horse and hay, nuzzling him, hugging his warm strength, digging nails into rigid muscles that flexed and flinched beneath my invasion.

For a second, time stopped.

The noisy airport faded. The anxious need to find something bigger than myself no longer hissed like static.

All that existed was us.

There.

Linked and joined and bound.

But then, it was over.

His fingers pried my elbows away, unwinding my arms and pushing me out of reach. His eyes blackened with torment. His jaw clenched with pain. And I understood that touch between us was something I needed, but something he would never tolerate.

All the boys in Scotland paled in comparison. Other kisses. Other dates. Other flirts. Nothing mattered; nothing was more real, more desirable, more unattainable than standing in front of Jacob Wild, begging him to notice me, all the while knowing he never would.

Letting me go, he gave me a harsh look, then ducked to collect my abandoned suitcase. His gaze travelled over me, from the top of my head to the toes of my new riding boots, and he swallowed.

Just once.

A swallow that spoke volumes to a girl who'd already made up her mind that pain was better than loneliness and she would do whatever it took to heal him.

* * * * *

I stared at the ceiling Jacob had no doubt stared at as a child. I stroked blue sheets he'd most likely slept in and listened to crickets and night silence that had serenaded him to sleep.

The drive to Cherry River had been a fairly silent one. Apart from the occasional question from me and the short answer from Jacob, we'd sat motionless as he drove us to the small town where he lived.

There, my welcome was much more heart-warming. Della intercepted us as Jacob pulled to a stop outside a lovely one-story house drenched in dusky pinks and the last threads of orange from sunset.

She gathered me in a motherly hug, kissed my cheek, made a fuss of my arrival.

Jacob had taken my suitcase inside, leaving me alone with his mother. Two seconds later, he reappeared, smiled at Della, tipped his hat at me, then hopped into the dinged-up truck and drove away.

My eyes tracked him, following the plume of dust as he made his way over a meadow, toward the treeline where a rustic cabin could barely be distinguished amongst the woods.

I worried that the moment he left me, I'd second-guess everything. I feared I'd become embarrassed by how I reacted seeing him again. That the urge to call my dad and request a rescue mission from his crazy surprise would swamp me.

But nothing happened.

I stayed present and focused and happy.

I still couldn't believe how I'd gone from being in school in Scotland to sleeping in Jacob Wild's bed. The day after Dad and I had our chat, I'd found an envelope with flight tickets on my dresser and a note that read, *'Be a farm girl for a few weeks. Try a new character on for size.'*

I'd tried to argue. I didn't want to leave him because I didn't want him to worry about me. But he'd been adamant.

So here I was.

Sleeping under the same roof as Della Wild. Replacing her son who no longer lived at home with a girl she would never have known if it wasn't for a book secretly published by her husband.

I didn't expect to sleep.

I fully expected to stay awake with racing thoughts.

But slowly, surely, my eyes closed, my heart quietened, and for the first time since I'd slept on my own in the stable at Cherry River, I found the place where safety and adventure collided.

Where hard work promised great rewards. Where dirt triumphed over clean.

And I slept.

* * * * *

"I was perfectly fine with toast, Mom. Stop your damn fussing."

I paused in the corridor, tugging on a grey sweater and yanking my ponytail from the neckline. No one had come to wake me, and the sun shone through the skylights and windows as if angry with me for wasting one moment of its brightness.

"I can fuss all I want. You've been working since five a.m. Toast isn't enough when you're pulling the hours you do. Now shut up, sit down, eat your eggs, and be grateful."

Once again, my skill at eavesdropping came in handy as I inched toward the end of the corridor and leaned against the wall. I couldn't see Jacob or Della, but thanks to the open plan space, they sounded so close.

A noise I'd never heard before and one that set fire to all my nerve endings rippled through the living room.

A laugh.

A carefree, indulgent, loving laugh.

Masculine and deep and pure.

I never knew Jacob could sound so…at ease. So content. So…*normal.*

"Always so bossy." He chuckled, his mouth full of whatever Della had cooked for him.

"Always a mom," she replied, pots and pans clanked loudly in the sink as she cleaned up. "If you're not careful, you'll starve."

"Believe me, I won't starve."

"You're right. Not while I'm around to feed you."

Another chuckle from Jacob, but this one was strained with the thread of pain I was familiar with. Did anyone else hear it? Did his family see how difficult he found being loved? Or was it just me and my fascination with death?

Because it was death that vibrated in Jacob.

Or at least…fear of death.

When I was going through my obsession after Mom passed, I couldn't stop watching YouTube and the strange and wonderful content people uploaded there. Extremely personal stuff like eulogies at family funerals, burials of beloved pets, and goodbye letters from loved ones.

I'd watched them to see if I could understand where a soul

went once it left its mortal shell. I studied each as if they held the answer on how to contact the afterlife and bring my mom back from the grave.

No such answers were revealed.

But an underlying theme existed.

Each video, every tear and hug and goodbye, resonated with the same mistrust of life, the same disillusionment of living—the same fear of loss because that loss would come again and again because we humans didn't just love one thing. We loved *countless* things, which meant countless ways of being hurt.

When Mom first killed herself, I felt that way too. I'd shy away when Dad tried to hug me. I'd pull back from a kiss, and close my heart to affection. I was terrified of loving Dad so much that he'd leave me like Mom did.

But that just added emptiness to my loneliness, and I threw myself into loving even harder. I fell in love with Keeko and Dad all over again and promised myself that no matter the pain, I would be strong enough to give them my heart, knowing they'd take a piece when they died.

Accepting that pain was the price of love.

I'd accepted it.

Jacob had not.

And standing in the corridor of the Wild's household, a firework of understanding crashed over my head, cascading me in compassion.

That was why he was so closed off. That was why he was so cold and short-tempered and prickly.

He had everything anyone could ever want. A loving family. A happy home. A successful business.

And it petrified him.

"Oh, Hope!" Della clutched her chest, blonde hair sailing over her shoulder as she slammed to a stop. "God, don't lurk like that, you'll give me a heart attack!" A dirty tea-towel dangled in her hands, ready for the laundry where she'd no doubt been heading.

"Sorry!" I ducked around her into the living room, moving out of her way. "I just had a shower. Didn't, um…want to interrupt."

"You're not interrupting." Della smiled, rubbing her chest a little before dropping the tea-towel onto a side table and turning toward the kitchen. She waved at me to follow. "Come and have breakfast, then we'll go for a ride. Sound good?" Before I could agree, she tugged me toward the breakfast bar where Jacob sat perched on a stool, his mostly empty plate showing remnants of mushrooms, an omelette, and spinach.

He tipped his chin in my direction. "Afternoon."

Della swatted him around the head. "It's nine a.m. Don't make her feel bad."

He'd already succeeded as I sat on the remaining stool and dangled my feet like a child. "I guess it was jetlag that made me sleep so late."

"Nine a.m. is not late, Hope." Della placed a plate of delicious looking goodness in front of me, then grabbed the salt and pepper grinders from the pantry. "Jacob just doesn't sleep, that's all."

Jacob smirked as if it was a super-power. "Being in bed annoys me."

I swallowed at the thought of him in bed. Did he sleep naked or in shorts? Did he lie spread-eagled on his back or curled into a ball on his side?

Why am I even thinking about this?

His mom was *right* there.

Tearing my gaze from his, I speared a mushroom and bit into it. The flavour exploded, earthy and salty and yum. "Wow, these are super good, Mrs Wild."

"Please." Della waved a clean tea-towel in my direction as she dried a frying pan. "Call me Della. And they're good, aren't they? Jacob grew them."

My eyes widened as I looked at her son. "You *grew* these? How do you even grow mushrooms?"

"Depends on the species." He finished his final mouthful, drained the rest of his orange juice, then stood. His height meant his eye level rose, looking down at me with cool assessment. "Google it."

Glancing at his mother, he gave her a rare smile. "Thanks for the second breakfast. I'll make dinner tonight to repay you."

"You don't have to repay me for every meal I make you, Wild One."

"I know." Grabbing his well-used cowboy hat from the end of the countertop, he positioned it just so over his dirty blond mess and bowed in my direction.

I couldn't tell if it was condescending or some strange goodbye, but his voice was deep and kind rather than chilly and mocking. "Have a good ride, Hope Jacinta Murphy. My mother will take great care of you."

And once again, like all my interactions with Jacob, he left well before I wanted him to.

* * * * *

"So…"

I squinted into the sun where Della sat framed by its golden glow atop a grey mare called Stardust.

"So?" I fisted both reins in one hand, shielding my eyes so I could see her better. "Did I do something wrong?"

"No." Della laughed softly. "Not at all. I was just going to ask how you're enjoying being home from Scotland."

"Oh." I nodded, dropping my hand and doing my best not to look down the hill to where the growl of a tractor occasionally found us on the breeze.

Jacob was down there.

He'd waved at us as we'd ridden from the stables and followed a well-used track around the perimeter of Cherry River.

I'd been given a bay gelding called Cody, and so far, he'd been grouchy about being woken from his midmorning nap and had strong opinions on traipsing up a hill with me on his back.

"Yeah, the weather is nicer for sure." I smiled. "The horses are fierier too. The highland ponies are pretty bombproof and unfazed by much."

Della nodded. "Yet you fell off and broke your arm, right? Was that pilot error or horse spook?"

I laughed before I could stop myself. How did she pick the *one* question I didn't have a straightforward answer to?

"What's so funny?"

Shaking my head, I stroked Cody's neck. "Nothing really. Or at least, nothing that will make sense."

"Try me." She pulled Stardust to a halt and turned to look down the gentle hill we'd climbed. Below us, Jacob was a miniature version of himself, sitting in the cab of a rusty red tractor as he dragged some contraption behind him, leaving a white residue on the grass.

"What's he doing?" I truly did want to know even though it was also an attempt to change the subject.

Della peered at her son, sighing with affection. "Staying busy and not learning how to relax."

"What do you mean?"

She gave me a strange look, her blue gaze almost as bright as the sky. "Nothing. It's lime. The earth is a little acidic and growing too many weeds. He's making it alkaline again." She ran her fingers through Stardust's mane. "The joys of having horses. Their manure isn't good for healthy grass."

"I had no idea."

She shrugged. "Why would you? Ground management and crop rotation aren't exactly a required degree when you're travelling the world acting."

I winced.

Yet another subject I didn't want to discuss. Somehow, Della had an uncanny way of cutting through the unimportant stuff and focusing on topics that made me cringe.

"Okay, that's two now." Della grinned, blonde hair curling around her shoulders. "Which one do you want to tell me first? Why you fell off and broke your arm, or the part where you flinched when I mentioned acting?"

Cody pawed the ground, jostling me in the saddle. I used the excuse of settling him to keep my eyes far away from Della's knowing ones.

Strange that I was brave enough to consider telling her about my lack of interest in acting when I'd yet to tell my own father. Then again, I wouldn't hurt her by admitting that his dreams weren't my own.

Sucking in a big breath, I rushed, "I don't want to act. I have no interest in saying lines or dressing up or making stories come alive on screen. I'm almost finished with my studies. I could quit now if I wanted, and Keeko is supplementing my education with university grade lessons, but I'm too afraid to stop because if I do, I don't know what that will mean. Will Dad expect me to get into acting full time? How will I say no to bigger parts when schoolwork is no longer my excuse?"

I inhaled again, plucking the soft material of my riding leggings and already regretting my honesty. "Please, keep that between us."

Dad and Della weren't close, but there was no telling if my being here was a ruse for me to tell her stuff so she could spy on his behalf.

She stayed quiet, the only sound the distant growl of Jacob's tractor and the soft inhale, exhale of our horses. Finally, she nodded. "Anything you tell me is strictly between us, Hope."

I flashed her a quick look. "Thanks."

"If you don't want to act, do you have something else in mind?"

I bit my lip, once again avoiding eye contact. "Yes."

"Want to tell me?"

For a second, I shook my head. Then I remembered that, out of anyone, she would understand the most. She was a writer, after all. She'd penned her personal tale—shared her world with strangers—allowing her love to be read and watched a thousand times over.

That was the sort of magic I wanted to create. The power to touch people through conjuring the story rather than delivering someone else's.

Sitting tall in my saddle, I admitted, "I want to be a scriptwriter."

Her eyes widened just a little. "That's interesting."

"What's interesting?"

It was her turn to look away. "When we first met at the movie premiere, I had a hunch you'd be a good storyteller."

"Oh, really?" A flash of heat and pride warmed me. To be acknowledged as something other than a child of Hollywood was wonderfully liberating.

"Yes." Della smiled. "You were very eloquent even as a ten-year-old. From the first moment you introduced yourself, you had a tale about the origins of your name. That's a skill."

"No, that's just talking too much."

"Wrong. That's fate already deciding who you'll be."

We fell quiet as the tractor turned off and Jacob leapt from the cab to fiddle with the contraption on the back. He was sure-footed and confident working with such heavy machinery.

Della turned Stardust away, nudging her into a walk. "And the reason you fell off?"

Damn, I thought I'd gotten off the hook.

Staring at her back, I encouraged Cody to follow, murmuring self-consciously, "It was because of Jacob."

Della tensed. "Oh? How come?"

"I remembered how he looked sailing over the fence with no bridle or saddle on Forrest that day he made me ride him. He made it look effortless. Like magic." My shoulders rolled, recalling my attempt at such skill on a creature I had no bond with. "When my instructor left the arena to grab her phone, I took off Polka's tack, scrambled on bareback, and kicked her toward a jump. She had no idea what I wanted, and I had no clue what I was doing. It ended in disaster."

Della looked over her shoulder, assessing me in that calm, all-seeing way. "My son is many things, and reckless is one of them."

"It wasn't reckless. It was awe-inspiring."

"No." Her eyes narrowed. "Jacob is kind, gentle, caring, and generous. But with good attributes comes bad, and one of his flaws is searching for freedom from things he doesn't want to face. He believes he's immortal. One day, he'll realise he's not."

I froze in my saddle, but Della wasn't finished. "Promise me you won't be reckless like him."

Our eyes locked, held, and sent messages I didn't fully comprehend.

Before I could reply, Della's gaze fell to the glint of silver around my throat. "Jacob might be reckless, but he also has good taste in jewellery." She smiled knowingly. "The locket suits you, Hope."

Leaning forward, she urged her mare into a gallop, leaving only wind for conversation and the pound of hooves as I chased her.

Chapter Seventeen

JACOB
* * * * * *

STANDING ON THE deck of my cabin at one a.m. usually meant I was alone in the world. The owls in the trees, crickets in the grass, and the vast, incomprehensible emptiness of the galaxies above my only company.

But not tonight.

Tonight, my sanctuary had once again been intruded upon.

I stiffened as my gaze trailed Cherry River from one end of its boundary far, far in the distance to the other. As I skimmed over my mom's house, Grandpa John's house, Aunt Cassie's, and the equestrian business, my attention landed on the candy pink and white stripes of a pyjama-clad girl with brown hair so dark it looked black and feet so bare they looked like white slippers.

What the hell is she doing out of bed?

Mom had kept her occupied all day with a long hack around the farm, saddle and bridle cleaning for the riding school after lunch, and then a visit to Aunt Cassie's to do God knew what.

When I'd finished work, I'd found them sharing freshly squeezed lemonade in the setting sun on Mom's porch, giggling over something I wasn't privy to. Despite my discomfort with how well Mom and Hope got along, I kept my promise and cooked dinner—bowing to the pointed glares to ensure there were three helpings, not two.

I'd stayed mostly quiet while we ate a simple meal of honey roasted ham, crisp green salad, and fresh buttery rolls, and made excuses to return to my own space the moment I'd helped with the dishes.

I'd done my best to relax at home—even going as far as turning on the TV and listening to the mindless drone of nonsense I didn't care about.

But I couldn't turn my brain off. Couldn't stop the possessive annoyance that Hope was in my space, hanging out in my room, and making my mother laugh when I'd failed in that level of companionship.

I'd gone to bed early, hoping sleep would be my salvation, but when the mattress refused to cradle me into unconsciousness, I'd given up.

So there I stood, nursing a mug of hot chocolate laced with whiskey—whiskey Mom didn't know I drank—and instead of finding peace surveying the empire I'd inherited, I spotted an enemy who didn't belong.

The world was hushed and heavy as if waiting for something to happen as Hope picked her way through the bottom meadow, crossed the small bridge Dad had made, and followed the path to the willow grotto.

Each footstep brought her closer. Each explore guided her unwanted presence to my door.

The thin navy T-shirt and linen pants I slept in didn't stop my skin from prickling with unease as Hope's head came up.

Our eyes tangled, locking together in a way that felt almost physical.

The silver moonlight obscured her face but didn't hide her sudden stillness. Sudden awareness. Sudden fear of discovery.

Neither of us moved for the longest moment.

Her as still and wary as prey. Me as coiled and on edge as a predator.

Finally, she raised her arm and waved, breaking the spell, sending a wash of something hot and angry down my spine.

Slugging back my cocktail of chocolate and liquor, I placed the empty mug on the wooden seat I'd carved and leapt off the deck.

Soft grass was the perfect carpet as I padded barefoot toward her. Silver light and flickering stars were our only witnesses to being out of bed when everyone else dreamed safely.

When I was close enough to whisper rather than shout, I murmured, "You shouldn't be out here."

Her head tilted, brown hair sliding over her shoulders like liquid silk. I hated that she no longer resembled a child. I despised the fullness of her chest beneath such girlish pyjamas and the way her hips filled out her riding gear.

It'd been a long time since I'd seen her, and this new woman in front of me didn't compute with the waifish girl I'd done my best to scare off.

"I couldn't sleep." She blinked with eyes too hooded to be innocent. She spoke with a voice too rich and feminine to belong to the annoying Hope Jacinta Murphy.

My hands curled, fighting away sick appreciation. For years, I hadn't bothered mingling with anyone other than family. Back when I'd attended school, the girls showed off their newly formed bodies and flaunted their sexual preference. Their obvious flirting turned me off rather than on. They all seemed so desperate to impress, so eager for a connection that would end up destroying them.

Hope, meanwhile, was none of those things.

She was shy beneath strength. Quiet beneath conversation. And when she'd hugged me?

God, she'd shown me pain had multiple levels.

A hug from family could sear and sting.

But a hug from her?

It drew blood.

"It isn't safe to wander around this late on your own." My hands balled, my voice thickened, and I did my best to keep my eyes on her face because there was no way I could look at her body. No way I could permit myself to see the change in her, the growth, the knowledge that she might drive me to rage and disturb my carefully perfected world, but she was the most beautiful creature I'd ever seen.

Soft but sharp. Trusting but careful. Fragile but brave.

All the things that drew out the best and worst in me. I wanted to be kind, so she was happy. I wanted to be cruel, so she'd leave.

I didn't have the strength to fight both instincts or convince myself I was content with being alone. My phobia of getting close to anyone ordered me to back up and point at Mom's house. "Go back, Hope."

She bit her lower lip, looking at where I pointed before capturing my stare again.

I didn't stand a chance with the way she studied me. The same way she'd watched me as a child with a certainty and calmness that made me fidget and bristle. Only now, a deeper element was there too. A terrifying welcome. A petrifying invitation that had nothing to do with the years we'd danced around each other and everything to do with this new torturous existence.

"I don't want to go back yet." Her voice whispered through

the grass, sounding part breeze, part shadow.

"What *do* you want?" My jaw clenched.

What the hell sort of question is that, and why did I ask it?

She cocked her head, hair tumbling, eyes searching. "To walk." Taking a hesitant step toward me, she smiled softly. "Want to walk with me?"

"What I want is for you to get off my property."

Her smile warmed instead of cooled. "Can I walk on it first? Then I'll get off it."

I couldn't understand her. Was she joking with me? Teasing? Being plain exasperating? Crossing my arms, I raised my chin. "Walking it would take hours. It's big."

A snicker fell under her breath. "Big, huh?"

I froze. Did the girl who'd screamed riding my horse just make a sexual innuendo? Then again, nothing was child-like about her anymore. Her youth had transformed into an elegance I didn't like.

I wanted to shut her up, to send her away, and forget about this odd encounter. Instead, I found myself dragged into the strangeness. "Oh, it's big. Bigger than you've seen."

Her cheeks pinked. Her gaze dropped to my mouth. "I like big."

The heavy air electrified with something I didn't like. Something that made my heart race and body tingle against my will.

I didn't appreciate her answer. How did she know she liked big? What exactly were we discussing here? The size of my cock or my farm? I wasn't adept at playing these games. I didn't *want* to play these games. I wanted her gone.

"Look—"

"I get it." Hope interrupted me, her voice losing its horrifying invitation and returning to simple acquaintance. "It's late, and you want to go back to bed. Don't mind me." Her lips twitched, unable to help herself. "Besides, if your farm is so *big*, surely you won't care if I walk a small piece of it? You won't even notice the areas I've explored."

"I can't leave knowing you're out here on your own."

"Why? Think I'm going to get abducted?"

"No." My hands curled into fists. "No one would dare trespass. I'm worried you'll trip and break your leg, and no one will be around to save you."

"So you're worried about me?"

I scowled. "I didn't say that."

"You said you're worried I'd trip and break a leg."

"Exactly." I nodded. "You're not to be trusted."

"I have walked before, you know."

"Yeah, on red carpets."

She stepped toward me purposely, planting bare feet into thick grass. "Wrong, I've walked on Scottish moors well past midnight after an ex dumped me. I've gotten lost in a thunderstorm after a picnic went wrong. I've—"

"Someone dumped you?" Once again, anger bubbled at something I shouldn't care about. She was dating already? She was only seventeen, for God's sake.

Her eyes flashed. "To be fair, I wanted to be dumped."

"Why?"

"Because I didn't want to give him my virginity." Her voice was level and honest, not in the least bit self-conscious discussing this sort of thing with me.

This girl had no limits. She openly talked about napping with her deceased mother and now fooling around with some boy.

"Are you always this forthcoming with personal stuff?"

She ducked to pluck a dandelion from the grass. "Not really." Holding out the orange weed to me, she said softly, "I find you easy to talk to. You're my friend. My *only* friend. And if you're my friend, that means you immediately qualify to hear stuff other people don't. I can joke with you about inappropriate things. I can tell you secrets. I can be honest…more honest than I've ever been with anyone."

I didn't take the proffered dandelion.

"No, you can't." Pushing her hand away until it fell to her side, I shook my head. "Friend isn't a word I'd use to describe me. I've told you that before."

"Why not?" She dropped the weed into the grass, her face gloomier than before. "What would you call this then?"

"An inconvenience."

She sucked in a breath before fire mingled with the green of her gaze, making them burn. "You know what? You're just as mean as you were when you were fourteen." Temper painted her cheeks a bright red. "Just because I make you uncomfortable doesn't mean you have to be cruel to me."

"Who said anything about you making me uncomfortable?"

She laughed icily. "Oh, come on. I see you. I understand you. I'm not asking for anything more than you can give, Jacob. I'm not asking you to go out with me or expecting you to kiss me or even believing you'll eventually tell me your secrets in return for mine. All I'm asking for—"

She cut herself off, pacing away with jerky steps. "Ugh, it doesn't matter. I'll go." Spinning in place, she stomped in the direction of Mom's house.

I watched her for a few seconds. I didn't move as her hair bounced and her stupid pink and white striped pyjamas made her look as young as when we'd first met.

I'd successfully gotten my wish. No more weird attempts at joking, no more awkward interactions, and no more bizarre chats at midnight when adults believed we were in bed.

I turned to go.

The wind picked up.

The guilt I always tried to outrun found me.

The prickle of disappointing the one person I missed more than life itself ghosted down my spine.

I groaned, looking at the galaxies above. *"Really?"*

Another gust of air.

"You're really gonna make me feel like shit over this, Dad?" I hissed into the night.

The breeze died away, leaving the air stagnant and stifling.

I knew the wind was just nature and nothing supernatural surrounded me, but I'd long since turned to a figment of my imagination for guidance. It'd become a habit. A crutch. Something I couldn't stop even if I wanted to.

I'd told Hope that I felt my father's praise and judgment.

I felt it now, and I wanted to tell him to back off. To yell at the phantom to leave me the hell alone. I was allowed to put a girl who meant nothing to me in her place. I was permitted to be honest about not wanting her friendship.

But even as I shouted silent thoughts into the sky, a wash of shame was my reply.

Thick, terrible shame because I knew why Hope was here. Her dad had sent her to us because she was lonely. And I'd just made it worse by not offering her sanctuary in the one place she hoped she was welcome.

"Wait!" I called, my voice slicing through the darkness and lashing a lasso around her waist.

She slammed to a stop, turning to face me as I jogged toward her. "What? What did I do now?"

"You didn't do anything." I pulled to a halt, raking fingers through my hair. "It was me. I'm…I'm sorry."

"You are?"

"Don't push it. You were right. I was cruel. That's all I'm apologising for."

She linked her fingers together in front of her. "Thank you."

"You're not welcome." I wanted to stay mad, but a half-smile curled against my control.

She grinned back. "You really are hard work. You know that, right?"

I brushed past her, my linen pants growing damp from dewy grass. "So I've been told."

She trotted to keep up, falling into pace with me. "Why do you do that?"

"Do what?"

"Act all pissy to keep people at a distance?"

I didn't look at her, fighting my temper to answer politely instead of commanding her to get on a plane and fly far, far away. "Why do you think it's an act?"

"Because no one wants to be alone—even those who go out of their way to scare everyone into hating them."

I ignored her, focusing on walking to the boundary fence in the distance.

Hope's breathing picked up with the exercise, but she didn't lag behind. After a couple of strained seconds, she muttered, "How about we make a deal?"

"What deal?" I flicked her a look, surprised she kept up with me. She kept breaking into a jog to cover the distance I did in one step.

"We agree to disagree."

"That makes no sense."

"It will if you let me explain."

I rolled my eyes. "Fine. Explain."

"I would if you stopped galloping across this paddock."

"I'm walking." I chuckled. "I'm doing what you asked. You said you wanted to walk. So walk."

She halted, her chest rising and falling, out of breath. "I see there are no grey areas with you. It's all black and white."

I turned to face her; the moon was no longer behind her, but shone directly on her, casting her face in liquid silver, making her look like a perfect statue. A forest goddess that pagans would've prayed to for good crops and bountiful seasons. With her hair wild and free, her breath fast, and eyes bigger than I'd ever seen, she truly was the prettiest thing.

And I despised her for it because pretty was an illusion just like love. An illusion that could cause pain the moment you coveted it.

Jamming hands into linen pockets, I rocked on my heels. "What are you getting at?"

Coming closer, she looked me up and down from feet to nose.

I shivered under her inspection as she lingered on my lower belly, my mouth, my eyes.

"What are you doing?" I backed up a step, prickling with awareness, on guard for an attack just from a single stare.

"I'm doing you a favour."

"I don't want any favours."

"I see that, but you're getting this one, and you're going to accept it because I'm sick of fighting with you."

"If you're so sick of fighting, you know where the exit is."

"Yes, and you know how to be nice even when you're being mean."

I opened my mouth to retaliate.

I had nothing.

Stalemate.

She crossed her arms. "Why does everything have to be an argument with you?"

"Not everything." I did my best to follow this new thread of conversation. "Just this thing that happens when you talk to me."

"I annoy you?"

"It's that obvious?"

That awkward silence again. Only this time, I didn't feel guilty. I hadn't delivered it in my usual scathing way. Humour had laced the question even though truth rang too.

Hope believed she'd had a breakthrough in understanding me.

I would gladly teach her about disappointment.

She hadn't figured me out; I'd just remembered my oath to my father about protecting those who needed protecting. It didn't matter if I liked her or not. She was our guest, and I would behave from here on out.

"You annoy me too." Her whisper caught me off guard. "Just saying."

I chuckled under my breath. "I already figured that."

"Good."

"Fine." I froze.

Shit.

What the hell?

I'd been raised hearing that flippant saying. Mom and Dad had trademarked it for saying 'I love you.'

It was a phrase that meant a lot to me.

And I *definitely* didn't just say 'I love you' to Hope.

"This walk is over." My voice turned cold and detached. "Go to bed, Hope." Turning my back on her, I traversed the meadow in the opposite direction.

Get it together, Wild.

There had to be a simple explanation for the moods Hope brought out in me. I was overtired, overworked, overstressed. She just played on those issues. That was all.

Hope appeared at my side, skipping and jumping over tussocks of thick, ready-to-cut grass. "What just happened?"

I didn't look at her, just kept walking.

When I didn't answer, she said, "You were thawing toward me. Then, all of a sudden, you iced me out again."

"I'm not a season. I don't thaw or ice."

She laughed cynically—far too old and jaded to come from such a young girl. "You're worse than a season. At least you know what you're gonna get with winter or summer."

"No, you don't." I rolled my eyes at her city stupidity. "The weather is the most temperamental thing on the planet."

"Wrong. *You* are." She ran ahead of me, planting herself in my path. Holding up her hand, she bumped my chest with her palm, forcing me to stop.

"Don't touch me." I growled.

She dropped her hand, leaving behind charcoal and ash from her unwelcome heat.

"The deal. You didn't let me tell you about our deal."

"There is no deal."

"There could be if you let me finish."

Inhaling hard, I crossed my arms and put a step between us. "Fine, if it will make you leave, tell me. Fast."

"Okay." She nodded, brushing back hair and standing as tall as she could with importance. "You don't like people getting too close. You don't like being touched, and you don't like losing those you love."

My eyes hooded in warning. "Where are you going with this, Hope?"

She held up her hand, begging for patience. "I don't have any people to get close to. I don't mind being touched, and I'm afraid of losing those I love but can handle it if it happens."

"What do you want? An award?"

"No, I want you to understand. We're opposites in that respect. We've both lost a parent, and it's changed us in different ways, but it doesn't have to be an issue between us."

"That's because there *is* no us."

"But there could be."

I laughed coldly. "No, there couldn't."

"Friends, Jacob. Everyone needs at least one. We're different, but we're the same too. We're both lonely."

I stormed around her, only to find her in front of me again. "I'm not lonely. Have you met my family? I have lots of company."

"I have met them, and they're all afraid of you."

"Afraid?" I flinched. "What the hell does that mean?"

"They all want to love you, Jacob, but you don't let them."

"This conversation is over." I cut to the side. If she kept blocking the way to my cabin, so be it. I'd just head to Forrest's paddock and sleep beneath the willow instead.

Hope didn't chase me, but her voice dug claws into my back, slamming me to a stop. "I give you my word, Jacob Wild. I will never ask for more than what you can give. I won't touch you. I won't hug you. I won't pry into your mind or demand to know more than what you tell me. I also promise not to like you very much. I'll be honest when you're being a jerk, and I'll be your friend even when you are my enemy. But for the rest of the time, I'll just be there. You can yell at me, talk to me, or ignore me completely, but at least you know you don't have to try with me. You'll be free to just hang out with no expectation or obligation. And then, when I go home to my dad, you won't have lost anything. You won't even care when I'm gone."

I couldn't breathe.

It took every drop of willpower to turn and face her.

She stood in shadows thanks to clouds obscuring the moon, and the meadow no longer looked magical. It looked like a wasteland, and she was some angel of death, giving me an offer that came with eternal damnation.

"I told you once, and I'll tell you again." I balled my hands until my nails dug into my palms. "I'm. Not. Lonely."

Very slowly, almost as if she floated rather than walked, she came toward me. "You might not be. I might have that completely wrong. But I am. Can't you see? Your letters hurt me, Jacob. Your indifference when all I wanted was someone to talk to made me feel like dirt."

"You want an apology for that too?" I sneered. "You didn't get the hint then, and you're not getting it now. I'm not looking for a friend."

"You're looking for something."

Everything inside me turned ice cold. "I'm done." I pointed for the second time at Mom's house. "Leave. I won't ask again."

"You're not asking now. You're ordering."

"Yet you're still here, so my orders aren't working."

"That's because you haven't given me an answer."

"Because there is no answer to give!"

She sighed as if her patience had run as thin as mine. "I'm not asking you to like me. I'm asking you to *accept* me. That's all."

"You're our guest. I've already agreed to be nice to you while you're here."

"Being nice is just another form of indifference. I want more."

"You just said you wouldn't ask for more." My eyes searched hers, trying to understand this strange creature. She was willing to have a friendship with someone who honestly couldn't cope with such a thing. "Why are you doing this?"

She smiled sadly. "Because ever since I saw you on set, I've wanted to know you. I'm not afraid of you, Jacob. And you need someone who isn't afraid of you."

"I don't need anyone."

"Are you honestly so sure about that?"

My heart pounded, making me shake with violence. "Deadly. Now get out of my way."

I no longer cared if she was out here until dawn.

I didn't worry she might get hurt.

All I cared about was getting the hell away from her.

Immediately.

Right now.

Before she pushed me too far, and I did something I'd regret.

Hurt her.

Kiss her.

Fall for her.

They were all as terrifying as the last, and none of them could be permitted.

I left Hope alone.

And with every step I took, the knowing, condemning breeze of my conscience chased me all the way home.

Chapter Eighteen

JACOB

* * * * * *

THE WEEK ONLY grew worse.

Hope's presence infiltrated every inch of the hundred acres I was responsible for, hounding me, judging me, punishing me.

I barely slept. I hardly ate. I existed on frustration, resentment, and rage.

For seven nights, I made excuses for why I couldn't go over to Mom's place to make dinner like I usually did. I stayed out on the tractor for far longer than normal, and when I dragged my weary ass into bed, my mind only raced faster, repeating everything Hope had said.

"I will never ask for more than what you can give."

"You won't even care when I'm gone."

Hope believed I was some shallow, cold-hearted bastard who destroyed anyone for getting close to him. She thought I didn't need their love. That I'd shut myself off from feeling. She wouldn't have been able to make such an offer if she didn't.

However, if she knew me, *truly* knew me, she'd understand that if I let her become my friend, there was no way I wouldn't care when she was gone. That I wouldn't miss her, want her, and be miserable in her absence.

I kept people at a distance because I loved *too much*, not too little.

I'd worshipped the ground my father walked on. I'd looked up to him, adored him, and tried to be him to make him proud. I was like any kid—totally infatuated with his idol—only to learn the hardest lesson a kid could learn.

Love—no matter how deeply it was felt—was not enough to stop death.

In the end, you were helpless.

Utterly, ridiculously helpless.

That was what I was afraid of.

Not love.

God, love for me? It was a drug I was addicted to. I'd grown up drunk on it with parents I adored. But the blind belief that my world would always be perfect was chipped away piece by piece every time Dad coughed until all that remained was a bleeding heart and the stark understanding that it was simply better not to care. Saner not to bother. Less agonising not to fall.

Just like an addict, I could handle being around the substance I wanted by not giving in to it. But Hope was there, offering me tiny morsels, lying to me that it wouldn't tear me apart if I partook, just a little.

But I knew better.

I knew if I bowed to her deal, I wouldn't be able to stop myself, and I'd tumble from a place of function into one that would be total, awful chaos.

So no.

Hope was not permitted.

Friendship was banned.

Mom and Aunt Cassie could keep her loneliness at bay, and I would protect all of us by staying far away.

And so, I kept going to work, kept living my life, kept keeping my promise all while Hope slept in my bedroom and borrowed my mother for her own.

For seven days, I grew more and more exhausted, fighting the desire to be part of whatever was going on in the house where I'd been raised and reminding myself all over again that I shouldn't care.

Until one day, the ramshackle world I lived in came crashing down, and Hope got her wish.

Chapter Nineteen

HOPE

* * * * * *

I COULDN'T BELIEVE I was about to admit it, but I could only do so much horse riding before I became itchy for other things.

Della had been beyond amazing to me—the true opposite of her short-tempered son. She'd shown me where all the tack lived, the horse feed and vitamins, the trails that were safe, and the perfect picnic spots to sit with a good book and enjoy.

Most mornings, she'd ride with me, but by the afternoon, she had her own life to attend to. Chores to complete, errands to run, and an extended family to take care of without worrying about some random actor's daughter.

I spoke to Dad every other day and had a few evening Skype sessions with Keeko to assure her I was completing the lessons she'd sent me via email.

All in all, life found a new rhythm, keeping me occupied and content at Cherry River Farm. The loneliness and searching for something other than the paparazzi-filled make-believe life I'd lived had paused, and even though I spent large chunks most days on my own, I wasn't sad like I'd been in Scotland.

The earth kept me company.

The sky was my friend.

The forest listened to my tales of woe, and the grass was a perfect mattress to nap in the golden glow of warm sunshine.

For seven days, I stayed away from Jacob. Not that that was hard. If I hadn't caught glimpses of him here and there, I would've thought he ran into the trees and never returned.

Most nights, I went for a walk once Della was asleep and I could sneak out unnoticed, but I didn't bump into him again.

His cabin remained dark.

His deck empty of night-time watchers.

Our fight lingered in the air, but I didn't let it chase me back inside. I'd become familiar with the grotto, creek, and even gone to see Forrest one evening.

I hadn't dared go into his paddock, but he'd come to investigate me hanging on his fence. I'd earned a hand sniff followed by a warning snort before he raised his tail and trotted off like any proud stallion.

His attitude reminded me a little of Jacob's. Bluster threaded with danger and full of warnings—a show of strength when, really, there was so much fragility beneath.

On the eighth day of being a guest of the Wilds, I waved goodbye to Della as she and Cassie hopped into the horse truck to collect more rescues and ensured I bathed Stardust and Cody who'd kindly taken us for a gallop that morning. I fed them, led them back to their paddock, and swept up the hay mess left in the stable.

Once I'd finished my tasks, I ambled home to Della's house, conscious and overly aware that I hadn't seen Jacob today. I hadn't heard the grumble of his tractor or caught a fleeting glance as he shot by on the quad.

I wasn't at ease not knowing if he was around or okay.

Entering the Wild's house, I headed to Jacob's room—that had swiftly become mine—and changed from my horse-hair-covered leggings and into a comfy pair of grey yoga pants. Slipping into a pink T-shirt with gold flecks, I braided my hair, used an elastic band I found on Jacob's dresser to secure it, and made my way to the kitchen.

There, I created a veggie sandwich with the leftover roasted vegetables from the night before, squirted a generous amount of mayonnaise, then tucked it into a bag along with a packet of salt and vinegar chips and a Mars bar I found in the pantry.

I remembered everything I did with explicit detail—more so than any other morning. It was as if I knew something was coming, and my brain was preparing itself by centring in the now, calming itself in the present, and existing in the serenity before the storm.

It took me fifteen minutes to hike up the gentle hill that overlooked Cherry River's houses and out-buildings. Another fifteen to cut across the ridge, weave around the apple orchard that Jacob's father planted (according to Della), and spread out the picnic blanket that I'd often used for my afternoon lunches alone.

I sat down.

I placed my sandwich, chips, and chocolate bar just so in

front of me.

I turned on my e-reader and prepared to lose myself in a world of villainous vampires and angelic witches, only for my entire body to shiver with fear.

Coldness. Dread. Panic.

Had someone died?

Was Dad okay?

Why did I suddenly—

I looked up at the sound of thundering hooves.

A blur of roan and grass and Jacob as Forrest shot from the woodland, galloping below me through wildflowers and meadow. There was no glint of bridle or sign of saddle and stirrups. No tack between horse and rider.

They moved effortlessly together.

Jacob leaned forward, and Forrest ran faster. Jacob tipped to the left, and Forrest followed in a sweeping arc as if he had wings.

Forgetting about my lunch, I stood on shaky legs as Jacob urged Forrest to fly quicker, straight toward a post and rail fence. A fence that wouldn't be forgiving if he messed up the stride or didn't clear it.

My eyes wanted to close as they approached the obstacle at breakneck speed, only to soar and leap, seamless in their perfection, landing softly and just as fast on the other side.

Jacob's seat was unmatched. He didn't bounce riding bareback. He didn't hang onto the mane or cling for purchase. His legs were his ballast. His back strong. Core engaged. He was utterly insane as he removed his fingers from the roan's neck and sat up tall. Spreading his arms wide, he gave all faith and existence to the horse who took his rider's trust and ran ever faster.

Faster and faster.

Nimble and quick and crazy.

A fallen tree that'd lain on the ground for years by the way nature had reclaimed it loomed in their path. The dead root system shot to the sky, the trunk itself weathered and massive.

Jacob kept his arms spread, making it seem as if he was part element himself—a man made of air with a sorcery over animal and land. His messy golden hair streamed behind him. His face resolute and determined.

And he kicked Forrest with an urgency that looked tangled up with the need to run, fear of life, and the weight of whatever madness he lived with.

It only took a second.

A brief second to watch the most horrifying thing.

Forrest reached the fallen tree.

Jacob leaned forward into jumping position, his arms still spread wide.

Forrest jumped.

His legs tucked. His body arched.

But it wasn't enough.

The horse's knees whacked against the root system, breaking twigs and debris, interrupting the flow of such a gigantic jump.

Forrest tripped mid-air, his feet kicking as if he could reconnect with earth, but it was too late. The horse somersaulted, throwing Jacob over his head, catapulting him into the thick grass.

I gasped, heart hammering, hands clamped over my mouth while I waited.

Waited for horse and rider to stand, brush off their catastrophe, and continue.

Only...the horse got up and not the rider.

The horse trotted around, tossing his head, telling the tree off for making him fall.

But Jacob didn't get up.

For four eternally long heartbeats, I waited.

Please, get up. Please, get up. Please!

Nothing.

I ran.

Chapter Twenty

HOPE

✱ ✱ ✱ ✱ ✱ ✱

"JACOB, CAN YOU hear me?"

I cradled his head on my lap, my fingers fluttering over his forehead like they had for the past five minutes since I'd slammed to my knees beside him.

He was breathing, but the angle of his back sent terror infecting my heart. I didn't want to move him. I'd heard the stories that you shouldn't move someone with suspected spinal issues. But as I'd kneeled next to him, he'd woken just long enough to try to sit up. With a tortured expression, he'd groaned and fought.

I'd caught him as he'd passed out again.

Even unconscious, his forehead furrowed and jaw knitted tight in pain.

"Come on. *Please*, wake up."

Forrest pranced around us, splitting my attention between his dangerous hooves getting too close to my patient and doing my best to keep that patient alive.

Why, oh *why*, didn't I bring my cell phone? Why did I have to be the one to witness such a disaster? How long would Della and Cassie be gone? Where were John and Chip and all the rest of the damn family living on this farm?

Bending over Jacob, I pressed my forehead to his, hoping he'd hear my thoughts if he couldn't hear my voice.

"Please wake up," I silently begged. *"I'm not equipped to deal with this. You can't die. You know I have issues with people dying, and I don't have enough answers about where souls go to let you leave. So…you have to stay."*

Pulling away, I searched his pained face for any clue he'd heard me.

"Come on, Jacob. Please, *please* wake up." I tapped his cheek lightly, earning another heart-wrenching groan. His body seized as he sucked in a gasp, his spine soaring upward.

"No! Don't move." I clamped my hands on his shoulders, keeping him as still as I could.

His eyes flew open. Wild and hazy, they danced over me, the sky, everything and nothing.

"You're okay. You fell off Forrest. But I've got you. Just don't move, okay? Just…get your bearings. That's it. Relax." I stroked his cheek with the back of my hand, heart racing for help.

His eyes hooded again as whatever blow to his head tried to drag him under for the third time.

"Hey!" I yelled. "Wake up. Helloooooo!" My stroking turned to tapping again, and his gaze shot wide. This time, they focused, locking onto mine.

A film of sweat covered his forehead. Sweat caused by injury, not by the sun. He must be in a lot of pain for his system to perspire so quickly.

My nerves skyrocketed. All I wanted was someone to come racing over to tell me what to do. To take responsibility. To fix what I didn't know how to fix.

"You're okay. Just…don't move and let me figure this out."

He winced as he disobeyed me and moved anyway. Just a shuffle in the grass, a wriggle on my lap but enough to send my heart scrambling out of my chest.

"Ca-can you feel everything?" I bit my lip, eyes zooming down the length of his body, skipping over his blue T-shirt, faded denim, and scuffed-up boots.

He nodded, frowning deeper. "Yeah." He moved his right leg, then his left. "See?"

"I don't think you should be doing—"

"Let me go, Hope." His gaze landed on my face, looking up at me from where I had his head cradled in my lap.

"You should probably stay where you are."

"I'm not lying like a cripple in the grass."

"You're not a cripple."

"You're right. So let me up, dammit."

I removed my hold on his head, allowing him to sit up slowly. I tried to help, pushing his shoulders gently, but he gave me a glower, and his silence was all I needed to back off.

For a minute or two, we sat surrounded by crushed grass, Forrest snorting and pacing as if feeding off his owner's agony, and the birds chattering away uncaring.

Jacob stayed slouched like a broken puppet, his hands massaging his lower vertebrae.

"D-do you want me to do that?" I shuffled closer.

"No chance." He didn't bother looking over his shoulder, continuing to unkink muscles and hopefully do the correct thing and not mess himself up even more.

Finally, he stretched slowly, arching his neck left and right, wincing and hissing between his teeth before planting his hands on the ground and hoisting himself awkwardly up.

"Wait!" I shot to my feet, dashing in front of him. "Honestly, you should stay where you are. Do you have a phone on you? Let me call your mom or aunt or even a damn ambulance. You should be checked out."

His face blackened. "You're not calling an ambulance."

"Your mom then."

"Her either."

"But you need help."

He smirked wryly. "That's why you're here."

"But I don't know what I'm doing."

"Just do what I tell you, and everything will be fine."

I clamped hands on my hips. "Look, you flew off a speed demon and crashed at warp velocity into the ground. You probably have a concussion, not to mention a tweaked back. Even if you can walk now, I've heard that—"

"Hope." Jacob held up his hand, stumbling a little to the side. "Just...quit it. Okay? I'm alive. That's all that matters."

"But your mom—"

"Would lose her ever loving mind if she knew I'd been hurt."

"I agree. So you shouldn't have been so reckless."

He groaned. "God, don't you start. You've been hanging around her too much."

"She's right, though. You shouldn't be jumping without tack. It's stupid."

"Wrong." He leaned toward me. "It's the only thing I have where I'm free."

I froze.

I'd said something similar to him years ago. And what was worse, I understood exactly what he meant. I didn't like it, but I nodded and backed down. "Okay. We'll do this your way."

"Gee, thanks."

I narrowed my eyes. "Just because you're hurt doesn't mean you get to be nasty. I'm willing to do what you want, so the least you can do is be grateful."

For a second, we glared at each other. I was close to

apologising and admitting that seeing him in pain wasn't good for my sanity and I'd do whatever he wanted, but slowly, he nodded.

"You're right. I'm sorry." He gave a lopsided smile. "I keep having to apologise to you. It's becoming a habit."

"Perhaps be nicer in the first place, and then you wouldn't have to."

"That would probably fix the problem." He took a hesitant step forward. He wobbled, hissed between his teeth, almost fell.

I didn't think.

Just acted.

Rushing to his side, I ducked under his arm and became the crutch he needed but would never ask for.

He stiffened as my arm looped around his considerable bulk, my fingers locking on his hipbone.

For a second, we didn't move. I expected him to push me away. To remove all traces of me touching him. To demand I get as far back as possible. However, it was a testament to his injury because he merely cleared his throat and gingerly put his arm over my shoulders.

I did my best to hide the kick my heart made. The leap of happiness that he'd accepted my help. The tingle of connection after wanting to touch him for so long.

Did this classify as a hug?

Not really.

But it was contact, and that was all that mattered.

"This means nothing and is never to be discussed again, got it?" He growled under his breath.

"I understand."

"Good." He tripped forward, dragging me with him and putting a little, but not a lot, of his weight on me.

I didn't tell him to lean on me more. I didn't want to give him any reason to stop accepting my help. A tiny bit was better than nothing.

Slowly, ever so slowly, we inched across the paddock toward his cabin.

Jacob whistled, halting Forrest's manic pacing, bringing the stressed-out gelding into a calm plod behind us.

"You're kind of a horse whisperer, you know?" I said quietly, moving with him when he moved, and pausing with him when he caught his breath.

"Nah. It's just about building that bond."

"You have a bond with every horse here."

"It might seem that way but no. I just listen, that's all. I listen, and the horse then trusts it can speak to me, and I won't ignore it."

"That's kind of the definition of a horse whisperer."

He stumbled, flinching with a wash of heat so warm it seeped into me, making me sweat. "Are you trying to be annoying or just distract me?"

"A bit of both." I smiled shyly. "Is it working?"

"Depends."

"On what?"

"On if you're more interested in being annoying or distracting." He gave me a wry smile I was beginning to recognise as his version of armour against connection. He used quips and sarcasm to deflect deeper subjects and prevent anyone from getting too close.

"If I wanted to be annoying, I'd say you should really call your mother."

"And I'd say you're an idiot if you think I'm going to tell her about this."

"Wait, what?" I pulled to a stop, making him twist in ways he probably shouldn't.

"Goddammit, Hope." He rubbed his lower back.

"You have to tell her. There's no way you can hide the fact you can barely walk."

"I've hidden worse." He bashed his temple with his palm as if attempting to clear the fuzz from his mind.

"You have?"

He lumbered back into walking. "This isn't the first time I've fallen off."

"But why do you keep it from her?"

He rolled his eyes as if I was the stupidest person alive. "I'll spell it out for you, shall I?"

The way he caught my gaze warned I wouldn't like his explanation. "It's okay. You don't have—"

"My father passed out in that meadow the day I was born."

Goosebumps shot down my arms. "The one you fell in?"

He nodded, jaw tight and eyes strained. "Mom called an ambulance all while in labour with me. She didn't stop taking care of him until he woke in the ER and gave her the very bed he'd been lying in."

"Wow."

"It was a long time ago, but I see her looking at that meadow now and again, and I know she remembers. How could she not? It was the beginning of the end, really. Dad lasted far longer than anyone predicted, but eventually, he still died. She still lost him, and I made a promise never to cause her the same pain." Jacob's hair fell over his forehead as he struggled to walk faster. "So you see? She must never know because I've already disappointed my dad by hurting myself. I can't hurt her too."

I stayed quiet as we began the gentle slope up to his cabin. Forrest came with us, his soft breath puffing close to my ear.

"That might seem noble in your mind, but it's not. She'll find out. Eventually. And then be furious you kept it from her."

Jacob was quiet, his breathing laboured and sweat rolling from his hairline as we finally reached the decking around his cabin.

I hadn't come up here. I hadn't been invited or permitted. But now, he clutched me closer, placing more weight than he had before as he attempted to climb the first step of three.

Nuzzling into him, I braced myself so he had something firm and strong and not weak and wobbly.

When he'd climbed the decking steps and released a haggard groan, he shook his head and dragged me toward the sliding glass doors to his home. "Once again, you have it wrong."

"Believe me, in this, I know I'm right."

Letting me go, he braced himself on the glass.

I missed his heat, even if he was burning up with pain. Looking over his shoulder, he spoke calmly to the gelding. "You're free, Forrest. Hope will take you home in a bit."

The horse nickered and promptly ambled off to eat grass. Luckily, the massive veggie garden, just to the left of Jacob's deck was fenced off because the carrot tops looked mighty tempting.

I shook my head in awe. Either the horse spoke English or Jacob had some magical powers I desperately wanted to learn. Every horse I'd ridden had tolerated me, but none of them loved me like Forrest loved Jacob.

Pushing open the slider, Jacob hobbled inside.

I stayed where I was, unsure if I was supposed to follow or go.

He turned slowly, resting his hand on a wooden table that looked as if it'd been carted from the forest, given legs, and left in all its natural glory. "You're wrong, and I'll tell you why. My mother loves me almost as much as she loved my father."

"What?" I crossed the threshold, stepping into Jacob's private world. "Don't be absurd. She loves you just as much."

"Stop interrupting." He glowered. "She loves me *almost* as much, but it's still enough to break her if I died too. Just a simple cut and she loses it. I made a promise to a ghost that I would do everything necessary to protect and look after her, and this is me keeping that promise."

Pointing at the kitchen which was drenched in sun thanks to the skylight directly over the large black sink, he added, "Get me some painkillers. They're in the pantry. If you feel inclined, make us some lunch. I'm hungry. And then, you and me are going to sit here quietly while my body mends."

"Ever heard of please?"

"Not really."

"Well, you should learn."

"And you should learn to mind your own business."

I opened my mouth to retort, but he smirked. "You're my excuse if Mom comes asking why I haven't finished raking the west paddock. I'm finally being a good host and hanging out with you."

"I don't know about this." I tiptoed toward the kitchen, feeling as if I trespassed on his privacy just by breathing in his home. Heading into the walk-in pantry, I scanned the neat shelves of tins, packets, and sauces before finding a tower of anti-inflammatories and pain relievers.

Grabbing a box, I moved back to him. "Use these a lot, do you? Got a pretty decent stash."

He waited for me to pop two from the blister packet before cocking his head. "Come on, Hope. Two won't cut it. Four, *please.*"

"*Four?*"

He nodded as if I was a simpleton.

"You can't have four."

"I can. I do. Now gimme. I even said please."

Reluctantly, I popped another two into his palm. He didn't even wait for me to get a glass of water before he swallowed them dry with a flick of his head.

"Experienced in self-administering pain relief, huh? I'm beginning to think your mother is right when she calls you reckless." I tutted like a frustrated nurse. "Then again, she probably knows more than you give her credit for."

Jacob grinned, hobbling toward the comfy-looking tanned couch and sitting down carefully. It took a while for his spine to roll and go from standing to resting. Once he was in position and breathing hard from fresh agony, he patted the couch beside him. "None of your business or concern. All you need to worry about is being a convincing liar."

"I'm not lying to your mother." I sniffed, sitting primly.

"Acting then. You know how to do that." He slipped deeper into the furniture, his skin whiter than I'd seen. "Either way, Hope, what happened today is our little secret. Got it?" He pinned me with a livid stare, delivered with dark gaze and darker promise.

Slowly, I reclined, keeping his stare and committing myself to this crime. "Okay, Jacob. Our little secret."

I didn't bother telling him that I was a terrible actress.

He sighed as if he'd needed my agreement more than he let on. His eyes fluttered closed, and on the softest breath, he murmured, "Thanks."

Chapter Twenty-One

JACOB

* * * * * *

"KNOCK, KNOCK. JACOB?"

I rolled my eyes, giving Hope an exasperated look. "It's open, Mom. You don't need to say 'knock, knock.' Just come in."

Mom stepped hesitantly through the open glass doors into my simple but cosy living room. She eyed me suspiciously.

I'd deliberately sprawled on the couch—even though it hurt my lower back—and her sharp gaze took in the remnants of cheese toasties and curly fries that Hope had made for lunch on the coffee table.

"What's going on?" Her eyes danced from me to Hope sitting lotus-style next to me, her eyebrows rising. "I noticed the west paddock hasn't been raked." Her face didn't know if it wanted to settle into annoyed or worried. "Any reason why?"

I didn't like the way she studied me, but I didn't have the mobility to move and hide. My head pounded like a bastard, my vision flickered sometimes, and my lower back was hot and achy. Pins and needles occasionally shot through my hands, making me very aware I might've tweaked a nerve or two in my spine.

"Decided to take the day off." I motioned to Hope with my chin while grabbing the TV remote and making a big display of pausing the movie. A movie Hope had chosen on Netflix, but something I hadn't been paying attention to.

My thoughts had been on my fall. Reliving the rush of galloping Forrest as fast as he could over the tree trunk. Cringing under the memory of tumbling over his head as the horse cartwheeled one way and I went the other.

I didn't feel the ground; everything was just black.

I hadn't seen it coming, and I couldn't do a damn thing to stop it.

If Hope hadn't been there…well, I might still be in agony in the very same meadow where Dad almost died.

Rather convenient she'd set up a picnic spot not far from where I'd almost killed myself. I'd eyed her when she told me where she'd been—not quite believing her. *Especially* seeing as she had a habit of eavesdropping and following me around when she thought I didn't notice.

After lunch, I'd made Hope inspect Forrest from nose to tail to ensure he didn't have any swelling or cuts from our shared accident.

She'd touched him gingerly while I sat on the bench on the deck. She wasn't afraid of him per se, just very aware that he was a moody bugger and could cause her injury in a single second.

Luckily, it was just me with the wounds, and Forrest returned to eating grass around my home, mowing a haphazard path as he followed his nose to sweeter shoots.

"It was my fault, Della." Hope smiled innocently. "After our ride together, I saw Jacob heading to work. I asked him to give me a tour."

"A *tour*?" Mom frowned, not believing that I'd suddenly become an amiable guide.

"Mm-hm." Hope nodded, biting her lower lip before adding in a rush, "He didn't want to, of course. But I..."

Her green gaze caught mine, full of conspiracies to keep my secret hidden. For an actress, she wasn't very good at telling a convincing story.

Inhaling quick, she finished, "I didn't take no for an answer. He kindly showed me around, then I offered to make lunch and chill for a bit."

"Right." Mom crossed her arms. "Say I believe this highly unlikely tale, what exactly is Forrest doing out of his paddock and eating our soon-to-be cut baleage?"

I cleared my throat, smirking. "He's allowed a day off too, Mom. Don't you think?"

"Humph." She tapped her foot, looking me up and down. "What's really going on? Are you hurt again? What did you do this time?"

My heart picked up. I never knew how she did that, but she always seemed to know if I was injured. Gritting my teeth, I pushed upward, forcing my body through its aches and bruises to stand.

The world went black for a second while I waited for blood flow to restore my vision. When I could see again, I spread my arms, TV remote still in hand. "Not hurt. See?"

Mom came closer, only for Hope to shoot up and intercept her. "Do you want help with dinner? It's late, and I'm getting hungry again. I'll walk back with you to the house if you want?"

Mom's stern worry for me melted in soft affection for Hope. "Sure, that would be lovely. Be nice to have some company." Her eyes flashed to mine, making sure I got her message—that I hadn't been around much this week, and I'd let her down. "You'll come too, right, Wild One?"

I shrugged. "Nah, think I'll crash actually. Big day tomorrow. Early start and all. You know how it is."

Mom couldn't hide her flinch. "Oh, okay. Fair enough."

Hope once again smashed through the tension by looping her arm through my mother's lax one. "Great. Girls' night. I really fancied watching a chick flick, but Jacob wouldn't let me. I'd be happy to watch them all with you, Della." She smiled, her acting much better. In fact, a little too good as a glisten of tears shone before she blinked them away. "It would mean a lot to me."

Mom's heart didn't stand a chance against a broken girl asking to spend time with her. A girl who didn't have a mother and was effectively reaching out to mine in a way she hadn't done before.

I didn't know if it was part of the pantomime, or if Hope truly did enjoy hanging out with her. Either way, it worked because Mom patted Hope's hand and gave me a weary look. "Okay, Jacob. Guess we'll see you tomorrow."

"Definitely." I tapped my temple, moving from the couch to be a gentleman and walk them out but unable to hide the hiss of pain as another prickle of pins and needles shot up my spine, over my shoulder, and down my arm.

Mom froze.

Hope gasped.

I stayed exactly where I was, drowning in pain.

Once again, Hope came to my rescue. "Congratulations, Jacob. You finally get your house back."

I gritted my teeth, doing my best to sound normal. "Nothing has sounded so good."

Her eyes narrowed. "I know it was a chore for you to spend the day with me, but thank you just the same."

I should thank her too. I owed her huge for this—for protecting my mother with her lies. For walking me back here. For making me lunch.

But being grateful and showing it were two very different things.

I merely nodded and let my silence fill in the blanks.

With our eyes locked—mine full of threats not to tell Mom and hers full of concern for leaving me alone—she led my mother out of my house and left.

* * * * *

"What do you do when you fall?"

"You get back up." I chuckled. "Duh."

"And what do you do if you get hurt?"

"You ask for help and get better."

"And what do you do if you're in danger?"

"Be brave and face it head-on." I grinned, feeling pretty good about myself for having such a great answer.

"Wrong, smartass." Dad laughed, his dark eyes full of mirth. "You don't put yourself in danger to begin with."

"That's no fun." I pouted, my eight-year-old hands busy building Legos even while talking to my idol.

"You can have fun if it's safe."

"But what if I want to jump Binky, and Mom doesn't want me to?"

"Then you listen to her." Dad coughed, his hand covering his mouth, his body wracking.

My ears rang.

My eyes watered.

I couldn't be there while he had an attack.

Bolting from my bedroom, scattering Legos in my rush, I bowled into Mom carrying freshly folded laundry down the hall. Socks and T-shirts went flying as she grabbed me, yanking me into her arms and holding me as Dad finished coughing in my room. "It's okay. He's okay. Everything is okay."

Her lies were getting less and less believable.

I trembled, peeking out from her embrace as Dad came toward me and leaned down until he was eye level. "Please, Wild One. Don't be afraid of me." His calloused fingers tucked my blond mess behind my ear. "It's just a cough. It can't hurt you."

Tears trickled down my cheeks. "But it hurts you."

Mom flinched, her own trembles matching mine as I hugged her back, desperate for someone to convince me that we would all stick together, no matter what.

Dad ducked to his haunches, opening his arms wide. "Come here. Both of you."

Mom fell to her knees with me in her hold, dragging me down with her. In a huddle in the hallway, Dad crushed us to him, kissing the tops of our heads, trembling with us. A trio of shaking while we were all punished by love. Dad might've been scolding me for back-flipping into the pond and hurting my wrist again, but really, he should scold me for loving him.

Because love...that was the most dangerous thing a person could do.

I didn't need to be eight or eighty to understand that.

It was engrained on my psyche, forever imprinted on my soul.

"Okay, then." *Dad pulled away, his eyes strained with pain I recognised.* "How about we go for a walk, huh? Get some fresh—"

I shot upright as a lacerating knife sliced into my lower back.

My dream—more like a nightmare—shattered, leaving me alone, broken-hearted, and in emotional as well as physical agony.

"Goddammit, *ow.*" I twisted on my bed, doing my best to seek a position that would stop the unbearable shooting pains. Sweat dampened my sheets, and my breathing sounded raspy and loud in the silence.

Unable to find a better spot, I fell still, staring through one of the four glass walls surrounding my bed. There didn't seem to be a moon tonight, and the stars were gloomy too. Only the ghostly silhouettes of grey trees against midnight sky could be seen.

Another knife dug into my back, making me groan.

Painkillers.

I need more painkillers.

And of course, the box was on the kitchen counter.

"Ah, shit." This was the problem of living on your own and not wanting anyone to get close. It left you terribly alone when things went wrong.

Thanks to my dream, Dad felt even closer tonight—as if he hovered around me like some fictitious angel, making sure I recovered from my accident. "You know, if you truly are watching me, make yourself useful and bring me drugs, 'kay?"

Nothing replied. No breeze. No creak. No shiver.

"Fine." Digging my fingers into the mattress, I inched to my feet, my back as stiff as concrete, my legs unwilling to swing smoothly to the floor. It took every effort and then some, leaving my heart thundering and sweat decorating my bare chest.

My black boxer-briefs were the only thing I wore as I hesitantly wobbled upright, lost sight for a second or so, then shuffled from my bedroom. One arm stayed outstretched, dragging my fingers along the smooth white walls for balance while the other massaged my lower back, desperate to find some relief.

My living room was the same as when Hope left. Our dishes still on the coffee table, and the TV on standby mode after being paused for so long. After she'd gone, I'd given up pretending that I wasn't in some serious trouble, popped more drugs, then soaked in the bath hoping that would ease the tweaks before crawling into bed and passing out.

Talking of passing out, I grew tired. So, *so* tired as I skirted around the dining room table and into the kitchen.

My fingers shook as I grabbed the painkiller box and ripped out a strip of white tablets encased in silver foil.

Relief would be found in about twenty minutes.

All I needed to do was pop these suckers and—

The world was spinning.

The ground was rushing.

The blackness welcomed me back.

* * * * *

"Come on. This is your last chance. If you don't open your eyes this very second, I'm calling your mother *and* an ambulance, Jacob Wild."

Something prodded me.

Something soft covered me.

Something warm and gentle stroked my forehead.

"Last warning. One…two…"

I opened my eyes, squinting against the sun streaming through the skylight I'd installed over the sink.

"Oh, thank everything holy."

I tried to speak, but my throat was dry, and my jaw bruised for some reason. Waggling my mouth left and right, I cringed against yet another ache.

"You hit your chin on the counter, I think. When you fainted."

Fainted?

I didn't faint. Men didn't *faint*.

I looked up into eyes that were becoming far too familiar in this position. My head was once again on Hope Jacinta Murphy's lap, only, instead of grass cushioning my body, I was on the cold tiles of my kitchen floor with the comforter from my bed thrown over me.

Her legs were my pillow, soft but unable to stop the sudden drumming in my skull. My hand came up to press against my temple, doing my best to add pressure to the pain and push it out of my mind.

"Don't do that." Hope's fingers lashed around my wrist, pulling my palm away.

Swallowing against the throbbing in my jaw, I croaked, "Why exactly are you in my house?"

"I came to see how you were."

"In the middle of the night?"

"It's eight a.m., Jacob. See?" She nudged her chin at the pooling golden light everywhere. "Please tell me you can see that. What's your name? Where are we? How many fingers am I holding up?" She shoved three in my face, her breath minty fresh and hair laced with coffee.

Pushing her hand away, I muttered, "Three. Now, let me up."

She only pressed my shoulders deeper into her lap. "I'm not letting you up until you promise me something."

My temper spiked, helping drown out my pains. "Promise me you won't break into my house uninvited again, and you have a deal."

"The door wasn't locked, so I didn't break in. And besides" —her eyes tightened— "if I hadn't come to check on you, you'd be a lot worse off. Believe me." Her hands rubbed my shoulders, tucking the comforter tighter around me. "You were unconscious. Your skin was like ice, and you've cut the inside of your lip. God only knows how long you've been lying here."

"I could've managed."

"Yeah, managed by getting hypothermia and dying."

"It's summer. It's not cold enough to get hypothermia."

"Now is not the time to argue with me. I'm mad at you." Her eyes glittered, mouth pinched, fire crackled all around her. She was definitely mad. But she had no right to be.

Preparing myself for a bolt of agony, I jack-knifed off her lap.

"Hey!" She scrambled after me.

I groaned, regretting my decision as the room swam, and I very nearly threw up. My body tried to retch, but I flatly refused to be sick in front of Hope. I'd already embarrassed myself enough, thank you very much.

Rocking forward, I tried to clear the thick clouds in my head. The painkillers I'd attempted to take last night lay like little enemies in their packet within grabbing distance.

Snatching them, I managed to pop two before Hope stole the foil, almost slicing my thumb as she yanked it from my hand. "You get two. And only because you can barely move, and you need to move. Right now."

"I do?" I tossed the pills back, lodging them low in my belly to work their magic. I wished it was instantaneous. "How come?"

Hope stood, brushing off floor crumbs and odd pieces of grass I'd trekked in and hadn't bothered to sweep up. "Come on." Leaning down, she opened her arms for me to...what? Hug her? Hold her as she hauled my ass up?

No way.

Waving her back, I growled. "I can get myself up."

"How? The same way you fell?"

My eyes narrowed to slits. "Your annoyance level has just gone up a thousand percent."

"I don't care if I'm annoying if it gets you better."

"How is driving me crazy going to fix me?"

"Well, for one thing. You have a choice."

"Oh, great. Another choice. Is this like the deal you tried to offer me? The one where you want to be my friend but expect me not to care when you're gone?"

She froze.

I froze.

I looked at the stainless steel toaster refracting sunlight around the kitchen. "Look, I—"

"Don't. It's fine." She straightened, standing over me with a sad expression. She paced away for a second, thoughts racing before she selected one and strode back. "I know where I stand with you, Jacob. I know you don't want a friend, and I know I upset you. But please...let me help you."

I studied her, searched her face, tasted the loneliness she thought she kept hidden, and understood the drive to find answers to a world she didn't belong.

We were more alike than I would ever admit.

The only difference being, she could tolerate being hurt by love.

And I could not.

Taking a deep breath, I reached up and clutched the cutlery drawer handle. Using it as a crutch, I slowly, very slowly, hauled myself up.

Pins and needles once again tortured my hand, but I stood without wobbling, my vision clear and full of Hope. "You can help. Today only."

Her gaze locked on my half-naked form, skimming over my boxers. The scars I'd earned from working the land. The muscles I'd formed from hard labour. Nothing was soft or pretty about me these days, but Hope didn't look as if my weathered, well-used body offended her.

If anything, the way she stared made my heart chug harder and not from pain.

Everywhere she looked, it felt as if she touched me. She bit her lip, her fingers coming far too close, wanting to trace a particularly nasty slash across my left peck that'd earned twenty stitches when I was eighteen.

I'd picked a fight with a piece of fencing wire. I'd been tightening the spool, cranking too tight, when the metal decided to crack into me, shredding flesh from muscle.

That injury I hadn't been able to hide from Mom. The torrent of blood and torn T-shirt hinted I wasn't exactly in great condition.

Hope's attention dropped lower, lingering on the only piece of clothing I wore, drawing far too much heat and need to that area.

My vision greyed on the edges as things between my legs tightened against my will.

Rocking backward out of her reach, I cleared my throat. "Uh, Hope…"

My voice broke her trance, slamming her back into reality.

"Sorry. Um, today?" She shook her head. "No, I'll help you for however long you're injured."

Her tone was papery, full of the same shivery heartbeats pounding in my chest.

I supposed I should be flattered that she found me attractive. I didn't need to be skilled in dating and flirting to know the depth in her gaze wasn't because she'd found me lying on my kitchen floor like an idiot. She looked at me with eyes that said she wanted more than friendship.

A hell of a lot more.

And that could never be permitted.

Turning my back on her, I hid the groan of moving too fast and placed a hand in front of my suddenly uncomfortably tight boxer-briefs.

Hope cleared her throat, sounding more like the opinionated, chatty girl I knew rather than the needy, hungry one.

"I'll keep helping you until you're better."

"I'll be fine by tomorrow."

"If that's the case, then okay. I'll stop bugging you tomorrow."

I stiffened as another wash of pain rushed down my spine. Even I knew I wouldn't get over this by tomorrow. That meant I'd have to put up with her for a lot longer than I wanted…than I could handle.

"Now, about that choice." A rustle sounded as she placed hands on her hips like any strict nurse, eradicating the sexual tension between us. "Choice number one, and the one I want you to take—we call Della, tell her the truth, and let the adults decide how to fix you."

I held up my hand, turning back to face her. "You already know the answer to that. It's a hard no."

She sighed. "In that case, where are your car keys and please tell me you drive an automatic."

"It's a stick, and they're in my jeans pocket, which are on my bedroom floor."

Hope nodded as if she'd been drafted into battle and didn't know a damn thing about warfare. "Wait here."

I didn't have time to reply as she flew through my living room and disappeared into my bedroom. The sound of drawers and my wardrobe opening and closing made my possessive temper flare.

What the hell is she doing in there?

Finally, she came out with a grey T-shirt, clean pair of jeans, black socks, and my trusty steel caps. Placing everything on the countertop, she forced her eyes to stay on mine and not linger on my half-naked body. "Put those on. We're leaving."

"Leaving?" I fisted the T-shirt, throwing it over my head and feeling marginally more comfortable and not so exposed. "Where are we going?"

"To the hospital."

"Whoa. Yeah, no way in hell we are."

Hope stepped right into my personal space, popping it, infecting me, hurting me far worse than any trapped nerve in my back. "Listen here, Jacob Wild. You're hurt. You don't want your mother to know, and I'm not equipped to deal with this. I can't drive, but I'm going to learn just so I can take your sorry butt to see a professional who can tell us if this is serious or something time will heal. If you don't like that, then I can leave. But if I leave, I return with Della, and you can see if you'll win a fight with her …which I doubt, by the way."

I glowered.

The bruise on my jaw ached as I clenched my teeth. "You truly are the most annoying person I have ever met."

"Bite me."

"Oh, I'd like to do more than that, believe me."

Her eyes flared, her cheeks pinked, but then her anger was back in force.

She stomped to the door and snapped her fingers as if I was some belligerent pet. "Get in the car. Now."

Chapter Twenty-Two

JACOB

* * * * * *

"YOU'RE GONNA STALL again—"

"Shut up."

"I'm just sayin', feed the gas with your right foot. Otherwise—"

"When I want you to talk to me, you don't. And when I want you to be quiet, you're suddenly the most talkative person on the planet." Hope threw me a glare as she stalled my ancient hand-me-down truck that used to be my dad's and brushed chocolate hair away from her eyes. "Ugh, this is going to take days to get there."

I held back my laughter.

Her pout was rather adorable—especially as she'd actually done quite well. Better than I thought she would for a total beginner. It'd helped that my house was on a hill and the roads through Cherry River were on a gentle decline right to the road. She'd struggled to get it into first gear, but after that, her coordination with changing gears and steering wasn't too bad.

Equestrians usually had good hand-eye coordination and picked up complex tasks quickly, thanks to a hobby of riding creatures that could kill you at any moment.

But now, we were on the main road, and the small town's only traffic light had broken her momentum and created havoc with her trying to roll forward smoothly rather than bounce in a bunny hop.

"Look, I'll drive." Unhooking my seatbelt, I couldn't hide the hiss of pain as I twisted in my seat to open the door.

"You can't drive."

"I can drive better than you."

"You're hurt."

"I can still drive."

"No, you can't."

"Don't tell me what I can and can't do, Hope."

She huffed impatiently. "It took you ten minutes to climb into this thing. You're not getting out of that seat."

"Yeah, see, this is the point where your worried routine becomes a bossy routine, and I don't take orders from girls—"

"You don't take orders from anyone."

"Exactly." I nodded, cracking open the door and bracing myself for yet more torture. "Now swap."

"Don't move." Clamping a hand on the steering wheel that was far too big and ancient for her dainty hands, she faced me with a quick corkscrew of her body. "Don't you think I can tell how much pain you're in? You're sweating, and it's not that warm today."

I tensed. "You don't know me, Hope. Don't pretend you do."

"I know enough to see when you're being stubborn and stupid."

"Did you just call me *stupid?*" My voice fell deathly quiet. "I'd be careful if—"

"Oh, please. I'm not afraid of you, Jacob Wild." Her forehead furrowed in concentration as she turned away from me and attempted to drive off again. "Close your damn door." The crunch of old gears made me wince, and the roar of the accelerator being stomped to the floor made the engine squeal.

Her heavy foot worked, giving enough juice to the decrepit engine to prod it back into life. We leapt through the air in a lurch of machinery and diesel, the senior gearbox complaining as Hope redlined before clunking into a higher gear.

She didn't look at me as she death-gripped the steering wheel, doing her best to navigate pedestrians and traffic law.

I pulled my door shut, looking at her from the corner of my eye.

Who *was* this girl?

Multiple versions of Hope lived inside my head. The timid, ice-cream-loving chatterbox at the movies, the shy morbid-questioning kid from her first ride, the nervous, apologetic girl who thanked me for talking about death, a letter-writing fiend who came across as desperate for a friend, and now *this* version.

A girl, who at the start, came to us as a refugee for a home-grown family rather than Hollywood fakery and seemed to be polite and sweet and quiet. Had that all been an act, or was this new Hope the imposter?

Because nothing was sweet about her when she was being so damn pushy and dictatorial. Instead of giving me sympathy for my pains, she barked at me like I was a pain in *her* ass. She snapped her fingers and treated me like some underling. As if she could *control* me.

It didn't matter that she was right. At least the part about me driving. I could've driven but not all that well. The shooting pains were in my legs now and just sitting in the car's uncomfortable seats put pressure on areas that screamed in displeasure.

I kept watching her as we drove through town, trying to figure out who she truly was. I didn't like not understanding people because I didn't like being surprised. I thought I had her nailed as the try-hard horse-obsessed girl who might giggle and attempt friendship but was a pushover and could easily be told to leave me alone.

This new Hope—or perhaps the *real* Hope—wasn't so easily swayed.

"Which way?" she muttered, downshifting as she came to a stop sign.

"Left." I ignored the urge to massage my spine, cursing the constant pins and needles.

With her tongue trapped between her lips in concentration, she slowed, looked both ways, then turned left and managed to keep the engine idling high enough to switch back into gear and gather speed.

Grudging respect filled me. "You said you've never driven before?"

She nodded once, eyes locked on the road. "Never."

"Not even on your dad's knee?"

"Not once." She swiped at a strand of hair tickling her jaw. "He drives the latest model something or other. Most of them drive themselves these days, anyway."

"Yeah, I saw that there's a car that'll parallel park for you. Taking away yet more skills and making humans ever more stupid."

She threw me a look. "What other skills have we lost?"

"Map reading for one." I winced as I shuffled, unable to find a comfortable position. "No one reads paper maps anymore. It's all GPS on their phones."

Her eyebrow rose. "You're saying you still read paper maps? I didn't even think they still printed them."

I scowled.

Hope's attention waned as the hulking, ugly hospital came into view. It squatted on the horizon, intimidating and fear-inducing with its prison-like windows, faded red and white paint, and aura of cemetery rather than healing.

I tried for the fiftieth time to get her to change her mind. "Let me make an appointment with my doctor. Honestly, I know you kind of have me as your hostage right now, but the hospital is completely unnecessary."

Hope slapped on the indicator, pulling left into the car park and casting us in the shadow of the chipped and underfunded medical institution. "A doctor will just refer you to X-rays. You need them now, not in a few days." Following the signs for A&E, she added, "Besides, your doctor might be sworn to secrecy to keep what happened from your mom, but there will still be a record of your appointment."

"Huh." I crossed my arms, studying her closely. "You really are showing your true colours."

"What colours?" She pulled into a bay of three parks, nosing the wide truck into the middle one, going over the white lines. She should reverse and straighten up. Instead, she unclipped her belt, gave me a chilly look before slipping from the vehicle, and reappeared on my side.

My door swung open as she stood there, foot tapping, impatience bright in her green gaze. "What colours?" she asked again.

"You're sneaky."

"I'm practical."

"You're tyrannical."

"I haven't even started." She smiled thinly. "Just try refusing to go inside, and then you'll see tyrannical."

My heart skipped a beat as she licked her lips, her body shifting as if preparing for a fight.

A physical fight.

With me.

The thought of her manhandling me from the car and dragging me into the hospital made laughter bubble but also a strange sort of other need bubbled too. A need to fight back. A desire to touch her and have her touch me, which was so against everything I stood for that the strange need switched into common nausea, eradicating whatever had sprung between us.

Tearing my eyes from hers, I did my best to hide my nerves. "Does your dad know you're this overbearing?"

"I'm not overbearing."

"Oh, really?" I chuckled, hollow-voiced and extremely aware

of how this visit would tax me. "You're like a headmistress."

"And I'm sure you'd know all about being told off by the headmistress."

"Are you telling me off now?" I used her as a distraction from the living, breathing monster we were about to enter.

"I will if you keep stalling and don't get out of the car."

"Not stalling."

"I say you are."

"And I say you should quit badgering me before I stop behaving." Swinging one leg toward the door, I glanced at the hospital behind her. Already, my heart raced with denial.

How could I willingly step into that place of sickness?

Memories of Dad flickered and filled me with dread. It wasn't often that I went with him for his treatments, but occasionally, I'd keep him company. I'd clutch his hand as we walked down sterile corridors and past rooms full of the terminally ill.

The beeping of machines keeping the unlucky alive. The scent of medicine fighting a losing battle for patients like my dad.

People would be coughing in there.

Loved ones would be crying.

Death would be cloying.

Life could not survive in such a place.

Goddammit.

Air was suddenly hard to come by as my throat closed in panic.

"Oh, for goodness' sake, Jacob." Hope squashed against me, leaning over me in a whip of movement. Her body pressed against mine. Her stomach on my thighs, her breasts on my crotch. Her long hair tumbled over her shoulder, landing in my lap.

"What are you—" My breath vanished. My voice disappeared. I gulped.

She'd successfully stunned me stupid as her tiny hand found my belt and unclicked the buckle.

Her heat was vibrant and warm and alive.

So, *so* alive.

She woke up the cold parts of me. She called forth the dormant pieces of me.

She made blood spring into unpermitted places and hunger unfurl at an alarming rate.

She made me feel *real*. More real than I'd ever felt. More noticed. More wanted. Just *more*.

My panic attack faded, bowing to fresh fear caused by her

proximity.

She'd successfully made me curse something other than that doomed hospital all while we sat in the car park of a mortuary.

Her eyes met mine, her arm still slung over my lap.

My heart crashed and collided with so many new emotions. My fingertips burned to touch her cheek and brush aside that strand of hair all before burying a fist in the rest.

She licked her lips, a hitch in her breath causing my stomach to twist.

But then a wheelchair rolled past with a sick patient and grieving spouse, and the brief absurdity of whatever I felt toward Hope vanished.

The hospital grew bigger.

My panic swelled thicker.

And I remembered why I hated everything Hope stood for.

She was lying to me. She was hurting me more than anyone had in years.

She lied and said the hospital saved people, but really, it severed marriages, separated families, and I couldn't do it.

I couldn't trust that Hope was young and invincible because death took even those who seemed immortal.

I couldn't *do* this.

Rage replaced my hunger. Rage at being forced to recognise that this life of keeping people at arm's length hurt me just as much as it hurt those who cared for me.

Maybe more.

"Get. Off. Me." My hiss licked around the truck, sending goosebumps over her forearms. Looking through the windshield, I kept my attention on a crow preening its feathers on a skeletal tree. "Now."

I struggled to suck in a breath as Hope slowly arched up and removed her touch.

She moved too slowly.

She needed to be gone immediately.

My hand lashed out. I hastened her journey.

I pushed as gently as I could. She still stumbled a little.

"Don't touch me. Ever."

Her eyes flashed green fury. "Well, stop making this so difficult."

Difficult?

She didn't know the word difficult.

She didn't have triggers.

She didn't have broken pieces that had the power to take bravery and turn it into sheer, mindless terror.

Her fury morphed into something else. Something I couldn't quite recognise. Her head tilted like the finches I fed on my deck, her gaze flying from me to the hospital and back again.

And then, there it was.

The worst thing she could do.

Compassion.

Empathy.

Pity.

I wanted to be sick.

"Oh." Her shoulders fell as genuine regret smothered her. "I get it now. I'm so, *so* sorry, Jacob." She sighed softly, nervousness making her that much more annoying and pretty. She caught my eye, beseeching and kind. "It's just a building. It's...it's okay. I don't like hospitals either, but it's just four walls and a roof with doctors inside. They'll make you better."

The pain she'd caused my heart was finally stronger than the pain in my back.

She'd granted me a miracle.

A miracle where I no longer felt anything other than panic as I slid from the car, brushed past her, and stalk-shuffled toward the lumbering, disgusting building without a backward glance.

Chapter Twenty-Three

HOPE

* * * * * *

"DID YOU SEE? Jacob Wild is here."

I froze, the magazine I'd been mindlessly flicking through forgotten on my lap. For three hours, Jacob and I had waited in the ER. He wasn't considered a top priority, and we'd sat side by side, butts aching in hard chairs, stony silence wrapping us in our own painful little world.

Fifty minutes ago, his name had been called on a crackly intercom, and he'd left on stiff legs and stiffer spine, not saying a word to me.

No 'goodbye.' No 'I'll see you soon.' No 'You can come with me, if you want.'

Nothing but his back and the awful feeling I'd done something unforgivable.

What was I supposed to do?

I'd headed to his house this morning, hoping to find him either in the fields or at least not too sore from his accident the day before. I'd planned on tagging along while he worked or asking for another forced day of hanging out together.

But that was before I'd knocked, peered through the glass sliders, and seen him sprawled unconscious on the kitchen floor.

I didn't really remember much after that.

I'd shut down my terror and focused on doing whatever I could to help. I'd tried calling his mother. Only, his phone had a screen lock, and I didn't know Della's number. I'd contemplated calling an ambulance but knew the trouble I'd be in when he woke.

My only option was to stay with Jacob and try to wake him up or leave him alone and rush back to Della's, all the while hoping she and Cassie were still around and not on some new errand or chore.

In the end, he'd opened his eyes, drenching me in residual

jitters and a rush of adrenaline. I needed him better. And if that meant I was stroppy with him, then so be it. No one ordered him around these days, and that was part of the problem. They let him get away with too much. They walked on eggshells.

To be fair, his attitude made me want to do the same.

But the fear of pissing him off was mysteriously absent under the anger I now harboured. Anger because he didn't look after himself, and I vowed I'd do it for him if he wouldn't.

But there was also pity.

So much pity because the terror and grief in his eyes before marching into the hospital shattered my stupid heart. I'd pushed him without thinking. I'd been cruel and bossy.

"I know. It must be pretty serious for him to enter a hospital. After what happened with his father and all."

I stiffened, eavesdropping when I shouldn't.

"Yeah, I remember what happened after the funeral. You?"

Every inch of me wanted to spin in my orange plastic seat and stare at the gossipers who spoke about Jacob as if he were nothing more than town prattle and not a living, breathing, hurting…*friend*.

"Didn't he ride his horse to the hospital a week or so after? Tied the thing up right outside by the ambulance bay."

"You're right. He marched in with hay trailing after him and demanded to see his father."

"His dead father."

"Such a sad day," the older woman murmured. "My friend who works as a receptionist here said he wouldn't leave. He was adamant his dad was still alive and the hospital was hiding him."

Oh, God.

My heart squeezed and dropped lifelessly into my stomach.

Jacob had come here as a ten-year-old on Binky looking for his dad?

Tears sprang to my eyes at the thought.

"Took three staff to get him home."

"So terrible. Least he didn't do that again. But the coughing thing, Gladys."

Gladys made an agreeing noise. "I know. So tragic."

The younger woman tutted under her breath. "I was in line at the supermarket one day, a year or so after his father's death. Jacob and his mother were in front of us, and Jacob had a total breakdown when my husband coughed. Wasn't Neville's fault. He had the flu, but the Wild boy turned catatonic."

"Yep. He needed therapy then, and he probably needs therapy now."

Their gossiping lowered to a whisper, "Well, he must've had some. Otherwise, no way he'd be here. Guess that'll make the girls happy, seeing as he's the richest unmarried boy in this town. If he's not crazy anymore, that'll give them all a fighting chance to be the next Mrs Wild."

A long pause followed by a shuffle of person and squeak of plastic as the two ladies committed deeper to their tattling. "Do you think he's crazy from his daddy dying or from the rumour that his parents were brother and sister?"

"Ah, Lorraine, that Mclary court case cleared up there was no incest. You don't still believe they were siblings, do you?"

"It would explain a lot, though, wouldn't it?"

Another pause while my temper steadily rose.

How *dare* these women discuss Jacob as if he were some outcast of society? As if any of his behaviour was his fault? He'd been a boy who didn't know how to deal with his grief, and they'd laughed at him instead of given sympathy. No wonder Jacob iced everyone out. I'd do the same if such rumours circulated about me.

I'd had a fair share of stories made up about my life. The online articles that said my mother was really Carlyn Clark who played Della in *The Boy & His Ribbon* and not a woman I looked very similar too called Jacinta Murphy who'd died by her own hand.

Every week, some blogger stated Dad had married some Scottish waitress or abandoned me in some equally ridiculous tale.

Rumours came with the territory of movies and TV.

But Jacob lived in a small-knit town that should have his back. Not suspect his origins, discuss his bank account, or talk nastily about the deceased.

"I always thought Ren Wild landed on his feet. Came from nothing, yet the Wilsons gave him part of their farm." Lorraine sniffed. "If I knew a bit of hardship in my life would mean I could be a millionaire and a landowner in my thirties, then sign me up."

"I know. Easy way to get rich, that's for sure."

Easy?

Right.

I'd had enough.

I couldn't listen to another second of this.

Slapping my magazine onto the chair next to me, the loud

thwack reverberated around the waiting room, making people in different states of injury flinch.

Spinning around, I found two women—one older with grey speckled hair and another younger with reddish blonde—sitting with their heads together and a conspiratorial look on their faces.

The younger woman, Lorraine, held a tea-towel around her hand where a small stain of blood hinted at a kitchen accident.

For a second, my anger spluttered. She was hurt. She was in the hospital. I should—

I should stand up for Jacob.

God knew how often he'd been talked about behind his back.

Pointing a finger at both women, I said coldly, "You should be ashamed of yourselves."

"Excuse me?" Gladys startled, her watery eyes growing wide. "Who are you?"

"I'm the girl who brought Jacob Wild to the hospital. I'm also the girl who can't sit and listen to any more of your nonsense." More pairs of eyes landed on me as I stood. This new drama was far more entertaining than two-year-old magazines.

"You were eavesdropping on our conversation?" Lorraine's nose reached the ceiling. "You know what they say about listening to things that don't concern you."

"See, that's where you're wrong. It *does* concern me. It concerns me a great deal because you're utterly heartless to laugh at a boy's inability to move on after his father—*his father*—died. You're cruel to gossip about one of your own. A son of this town who is a hard worker and a loyal friend."

My voice shook as more fury layered it. "And you're a freaking moron if you think Ren Wild had it easy. Did you not see the movie? Did you not hear what that Mclary farmer did to him? What they tried to do to their own daughter? You think Ren would've chosen that life, knowing he'd find some happiness all before he died anyway?"

Furious tears glittered, blurring the two women I wanted to slander and shame. "Do you think he wanted to die by coughing? Do you think he wouldn't trade being wealthy if it meant he got to live a lifetime with his wife and son?"

The waiting room no longer existed. Patients and blood and a building full of pain no longer mattered as I leaned toward the two women and saw nothing more than stupidity. "Do you not think he'd give up *all of it* for one more day with the boy you're laughing so callously about?"

Something hard and bruising latched around my upper arm.

And then I was moving, dragged toward the exit by the very same boy I'd been defending. He showed no signs of being in pain. No halted gait or tweaked spine. The strength in his fingers commanded me not to say a single word. Not a peep. Otherwise, I wouldn't like the consequences.

"Jac—"

"Don't." His face shimmered with outrage—a visible emotion with strains of hatred, resentment, and violence etching lines around his eyes and tension around his jaw.

I bit my lip as he hauled me from the hospital and practically threw me through the doors.

Stumbling from his force, I tripped down the steps and spun to face him as he winced and slowed, unable to descend the stairs as effortlessly as he'd evicted me from the waiting room.

"Keys." He held out his hand.

I fumbled in my pocket even as I whispered, "You can't drive."

His dark eyes, once again a malicious gleaming black, dared me, just *dared* me to stop him. He didn't have to say a word. His stare was reprimand enough.

I dropped the car keys into his outstretched palm, flinching as he clutched them with brutal fingers. He strode off with rage fluttering in his wake.

Trailing him, I glanced back at the hospital, expecting to see a line-up of gossip-loving townsfolk, taking photos, jotting down what I'd said and how this ended. Ready to sell my mistake to the highest bidder.

But there was no one.

Just me and a boy who hated me.

God, what would Dad say if he knew I'd picked a fight with women in a hospital of all places? How on earth would I sit in a truck next to Jacob when his temper was so frayed even the car park wasn't big enough for the two of us?

More tears came, but these weren't born from anger. They were created from fear. Fear of going too far. Fear of ruining our friendship before it had even begun.

"Jacob, I'm…I'm sorry."

His shoulders came up, barricading my apology.

"Please, I wasn't intruding. I was—"

He slammed to a stop. His voice strangled. "Grandpa. Wh-what are you doing here?"

And just like that, I was no longer the worst part of Jacob's day.

I skidded to a halt a few steps behind him, locked in place as the gruff, larger-than-life man climbed wearily from an old Land Rover. "Ah, Jakey. What are *you* doing here?"

Jacob's rage found a new victim. The slight shake in his tone hinted at the mess his insides had become. "I asked you first." His hands balled by his sides, the glint of keys digging into his fist. "Why are you here?"

The old man, who'd been nothing but kind to me whenever I'd run into him on the farm, scratched his white beard as if searching for a lie. Only, no lie came, and he hung his head. "Can we talk about this at home? Get your mom around, and we'll have dinner together, okay?"

"No." Jacob backed up, bumping into me in his haste. "Tell me now. What the fuck is going on?"

His grandfather didn't reprimand for the curse. Instead, his eyes welled with grief. "I don't want to do this to you, Jacob. Not here." He moved toward Jacob, only for his grandson to feint to the side, a hiss of agony revealing his back wasn't coping.

"Are you dying?" I expected Jacob's voice to be strained and suffocated. However, it was strangely cold and remote, as if he'd already slammed up walls between him and the hardship of death.

John shook his head. "All of us are, Jakey. Some faster than others."

"That doesn't answer my question." Jacob bit. "Oncology is here. You know that as well as I do. That's where you're going, isn't it? *Isn't it?*"

"Jacob, listen to me." John held up his hands in surrender. "It's not something I can say in a parking lot. Let's just go home."

Jacob laughed coldly. "Can't go home until you've finished your treatment, Grandpa. You know how strict they are about keeping your appointment. Dad never missed one, but it didn't help him, did it?"

I didn't know what to say. Should I stay out of this? Try to touch Jacob? Be on John's side?

But Jacob decided for me, stalking toward his grandfather with a slight limp. "How long, huh? How long until you die?"

John's huge frame slumped in defeat. "A year or so."

"Of course." Jacob chuckled in a chilling, heart-breaking way that sent knives down my spine. "I knew it. I just fucking *knew* it."

He looked at the sky, a haggard groan escaping as if he

wanted to scream but didn't have the strength.

Then he was gone, bolting stiffly toward his car.

And I did the most cowardly thing of my life.

I let him haul himself painfully into the driver's seat.

I didn't move as he slammed the truck into reverse and shot from the parking lot as if the flames of damnation were already licking at his feet.

I stood frozen to the concrete as the squeal of an ancient engine stole him away and vanished around the corner.

A large, comforting hand landed on my shoulder, hugging the entire joint and part of my collarbone and bicep too.

John Wilson was so big and strong and...sick.

Looking up, I rubbed fingers under my eyes to remove any trace of tears. "Hello, Mr. Wilson."

"Bah, John. Please." The old man squeezed me. "You okay?"

"I will be." I nodded. "Will you?"

His hand dropped. "Not now he knows. No."

"I'm sorry."

Sorry for whatever you've been fighting. Sorry for the limited time on earth. Sorry for life in general.

"He had to find out sooner rather than later." He sniffed. Silence fell between us for a long moment. Finally, he asked, "Anything I should know about? Why was Jacob here?"

I rolled my shoulders, looking at the painted lines on the concrete. "He fell off Forrest. Hurt his back."

"Ah."

My eyes met his. "Please don't tell Della. He made me promise."

John smiled sadly. "Sometimes promises shouldn't be kept."

"If it's bad, I'll tell her. I'll find out tonight what the doctor said."

He grinned. "You're a brave girl, standing up to him."

I cracked a smile. "Or just stupid."

"Stupid is sometimes mistaken as bravery, but in this case, I don't think it is." He shuffled around me, another sigh shaking his big frame. "I've got to go. Can't be late." Tossing me his keys, he added, "If you can wait an hour, I'll drive you home. Just hang in the car or go to the hospital cafeteria and grab some lunch. You got any money?"

I shook my head, feeling like a leech who'd stumbled into family drama and had no idea how to get out of it.

Pulling a scuffed leather wallet from his back pocket, John

gave me a handful of bills. "Grab a drink. Looks like you need one. And then, we'll talk on the drive home. Deal?"

He didn't wait for my reply.

Just like his grandson, he left without a goodbye.

Chapter Twenty-Four

JACOB

✶ ✶ ✶ ✶ ✶ ✶

DRIVING THROUGH CHERRY River, I clutched the steering wheel. Partly from pain and partly from hoping I wouldn't be noticed.

Please don't let anyone be around.

Of course, that wish went unanswered as I turned the corner by the stables and almost ran Aunt Cassie over.

She had a biscuit of hay under one arm and a box of worming syringes in the other. In the paddock beyond, Mom had a bony yearling tied up, grooming him, doing her best to break the cycle of abuse and fear.

Aunt Cassie stopped. Mom looked up and smiled distractedly in my direction.

I didn't wave, hoping they'd just go about their business.

I wasn't in luck.

Mom went back to cooing and cuddling the rescue colt, but Aunt Cassie waved the worming syringes as if they were a stop sign, flagging me down.

"Goddammit."

Shifting my leg from the accelerator to brake, I hid the wince from yet more pins and needles. The extra-strength painkillers the doctor gave me hadn't done crap, and all I wanted was a hot bath and to be horizontal as soon as possible.

I slowed to a stop as Aunt Cassie came toward the driver's side and waited for me to roll down the window. The second I did, she shot me a grin. A normal grin that said she didn't know about my fall or subsequent hospital visit.

Well, good. At least Hope had done one thing right.

She'd kept my secret.

Then again, it was the *only* thing she'd done right. What the *hell* had she been thinking, talking about my father that way? Why had she been yelling at those women?

I'd done my best to stop my thoughts straying to Hope on the drive home, mainly because the moment they did, they'd skip to Grandpa John.

The shock on his face.

The dismay in his eyes.

The lies he'd spun for years unravelling by his feet.

Did Aunt Cassie know? Did Mom?

How long had they been in on his illness without telling me?

"Hey, Jacob." Aunt Cassie squinted in the sun.

"Hey." I swallowed, wiping away the sweat beaded on my upper lip from the pain of driving home and the agony of knowing Grandpa John would be gone sooner than I could bear. "What's up?"

Her eyes twinkled with mischief. "Saw Hope driving this old relic with you as co-pilot this morning. Care to explain?"

"Why do I need to explain?"

"'Cause you never let anyone drive this rust bucket." She leaned closer, a meddling glint on her face. "What made her so special?"

I stiffened. "Maybe she just asked nicely."

"Or maybe something's going on between you two."

I narrowed my eyes. "What are you implying?"

She rested her hand on my door. "Not implying anything. I'm asking straight up if something's going on between you and Hope."

I sat in icy silence, hoping the visible disgust on my face would warn her to back the hell off.

Instead, her grin became a smirk. "Ah, so something *is* going on."

"I'd quit before—"

"Before what? Before you admit you have feelings for her?"

I sniffed, indignant. "No feelings. Nothing's going on. Nobody is interested in anybody."

"Ah, see that's where you're wrong. *She* has feelings for *you*."

My back blazed fresh agony as I sat bolt upright.

That revelation wasn't new. I'd sensed such a thing myself.

But to have others know?

Shit.

Just shit.

"I have to go." I kept my temper, barely. "Work is calling." I hated to admit it, but I wouldn't be working today. I might be forced to take a week off at this rate. My back wasn't going to heal overnight—as much as I'd argued with the doctor.

"Ugh, work. Take the day off. You deserve some fun. Fall in love. Fool around. Be *young*, Jacob."

"Did you get into the cherry liquor early this year, Aunt Cassie?"

She snickered. "Ha ha. No. I just want you to be happy—"

"Enough."

Her smile faded as seriousness I didn't want shadowed her. "I'm worried about you, Jacob. You're twenty-one years old. You should have sneaked out and been with a few girls by now."

"What the hell is this? Why are you suddenly so interested in my love life?"

"You don't have a love life. That's my point."

"Wow." I barked a laugh. "Are there no boundaries within this family anymore?" I fumbled for the gearstick, wishing the old truck was a rocket ship and could launch me into outer space. "I'm done. This is the part where I leave." Shoving the engine into first, I stomped on the accelerator.

She clutched my door, moving with the roll of my tyres. "Jacob—"

I paused. I couldn't exactly drive off with her holding on to my truck. "Let go, Aunt Cassie."

"Not until I've finished." She looked away, her cheeks pinking. "I know Della most likely had the 'chat' with you, but if you ever want a refresher or just want to ask an embarrassing question that isn't 'Mom appropriate' you know you can come to me? Right?"

I shuddered at the thought of asking Aunt Cassie for sex advice. What the hell would she know? She was married with a daughter a few years older than me. I doubted she even kissed Chip these days, let alone got naked with the guy.

"I know this subject is awkward..." Cassie shifted a little uncomfortably. "But sex doesn't have to mean anything if you're not looking for an emotional connection. You can just be physical—"

"Stop." I wiped my mouth with my hand. "Seriously. Please stop."

"You don't have to be a monk just because you don't like getting close to people."

"Oh, my God. Drop it."

"You know that, though, right? You know about condoms and—"

"Shit, yes. Okay!" My cheeks turned into an inferno. "I know the mechanics. I'm well equipped, believe me." My voice lowered, mingling with embarrassment and sorrow. "Dad told me all I need to know."

"He did?" Her eyes widened. "But you...you would've been so young."

"He said he wished someone would've told him that stuff when he was young."

Her cheeks pinked. "Fair enough. In that case..." She let go of my door. "I love you, Jacob. We all love you. We just want you to be happy."

Her love was tangible—just like my mom's, Uncle Chip's, and Grandpa John's. I felt it in every stare, smile, and conversation.

The pain in my back relocated to my heart.

"Thanks." I smiled as much as I was able. "Truly. I still think you're drunk...but you're sweet for attempting to have the worst sex talk of my life with me."

"Welcome." She laughed and blew me a kiss. "Go find that girl of yours. Get a real kiss—"

"And you just had to ruin it again. Stay off the booze." I didn't roll this time. I shot forward, kicking up gravel in my haste.

I glanced in my rear-view mirror.

She laughed harder, blew me another kiss, and continued across the drive to Mom and the rescues.

She said everyone loved me.

And I knew that. Of course, I did.

Yet they'd all kept secrets from me.

Grandpa John was dying.

His impending demise was unforgivable, and the fact that no one told me was equally inexcusable. I might not be as touchy-feely as the rest of my family, but that didn't mean secrets could be kept from me.

How could Aunt Cassie joke about hooking up with someone when her dad was dying?

I'd lived that particular tragedy myself.

It wasn't something you could forget—even while they were still alive beside you.

Pressing harder on the gas, I left my aunt and mother behind and headed toward an empty cabin, lonely couch, and desolate existence.

A *safe* existence.

The only existence I could cope with.

Chapter Twenty-Five

JACOB

✶ ✶ ✶ ✶ ✶ ✶

"JACOB. JACOB. *JAKE.*"

My eyes flew wide, locking onto a darker shadow hovering over me in the night-shrouded room.

Self-preservation kicked in, and I jack-knifed up. Agony lanced down my spine, and thunder exploded in my head. Despite the pins and needles and woozy vision, my hands curled, ready to punch the intruder or run for the rifle I kept for equine catastrophes.

Soft hands touched my fists as I raised them, cursing the quaking in my body. "Hey, it's just me. Hope. You *do* remember me, right? The fall didn't wipe out your short-term memory?"

I groaned, shaking off her touch and inching myself back down to the pillows. "Believe me, if my concussion *had* wiped out my short-term memory, I'd still know who you are. You're in my long-term, Hope Jacinta Murphy, and that is not a good thing."

I deliberately used her full name, reminding her that I was fourteen when she first made an awkward impression on me and seven years definitely didn't classify as short term.

"That's true." She sat down without asking, pressing herself against my thighs wrapped beneath the quilt. My eyes narrowed as she made herself comfortable, encroaching on my personal space, and not having the decency to get off my damn bed.

Her legs came up, sitting cross-legged, her hair loose and sleek over her right shoulder. Stars glittered strong tonight, casting my glass-box bedroom in silvery, shadowy light.

So many things were wrong with this picture. What the hell was she doing in my bedroom? Why did she think we had the sort of relationship where sitting on my bed uninvited was acceptable?

Giving her a glare, I shuffled higher, shoving my pillows behind me, so I sat up too. My spine had something nasty to say about the new position, but there was no way I could lie down with Hope beside me. It made me feel weak, vulnerable, and unwanted heat travelled into places I never intended to use. "What are you doing here?"

"I wanted to check on you."

"You could've come during daylight hours like a normal person." Then again, I was thankful I'd had no visitors today. Even Mom had stayed away, which meant I'd been able to spend all afternoon in bed.

She plucked at my blankets. "I-I didn't want to come too soon. Thought it might be best if I let your temper cool."

I rubbed my face, shoving away the last tendrils of sleep. Not that my brain was much help at the moment. According to the doctor, I had a fairly severe concussion. He'd put me on anti-inflammatories with strict instructions to rest. He said I couldn't even think as thinking was an activity.

He obviously didn't know what running a farm entailed.

But I didn't need to think to know why Hope avoided me. I also knew I'd been rough with her, dragging her from the hospital and trying to kill her with a single stare.

I owed her another apology, but at the same time, she owed me.

As if she heard my thoughts, she blurted, "I'm *so* sorry for discussing your father with those busybodies. I shouldn't have gotten upset, but they were talking about you and saying such silly things that I couldn't stop myself." She shrugged shyly. "I thought I was defending you, but I know it could've looked like I was meddling."

Damn.

I never had a chance at staying pissed when a sincere apology was given. Regret glossed her eyes as nervousness that she'd severely upset me etched her face. She might be wearing pyjamas, but she hadn't been to sleep yet, and the thought of her tossing and turning, worried about my reaction...well, it stole the final threads of my rage and made me sag into the pillows.

"I'm sorry, too."

She rubbed her arm where I'd grabbed her, smiling softly. "It's fine."

Sitting up with a hiss, I reached for her bicep. "Did I hurt you?"

She froze, pulling back a bit. "No, don't be—"

"I did. I hurt you." Running a fingertip over the pink and white cotton, I wished her arm was visible to assess how badly I'd screwed up. She winced a little as I put pressure on where my fingers had been.

I'd bruised her.

Shit.

Leaning back, I groaned. I'd done so many things wrong lately. "I didn't mean to hurt you."

"I know you didn't."

"It just…it gets to me when I hear people talk about him, you know?"

"I'm the same. When the paparazzi spread lies about my mother's death, I get super possessive and want to take their cameras and notepads and shove them down their throats."

I half-smiled. "Violent little creature."

"When those I love are threatened, yes, definitely."

My heart stopped beating. "Yet, I'm not someone you love, so why defend me?"

Her cheeks glowed an interesting peach before she dropped her gaze and found my navy blanket fascinating. "Because I have a feeling you've had to put up with that sort of nonsense for a while, and I know how draining it can be."

"This isn't Hollywood, Hope. I don't have rumours spread daily about me like you actors do."

"No, you have it worse."

I cocked my head. "How do you figure? I don't see my name on a magazine cover with a made-up scandal just to sell copies. They're vicious in your world."

"Yeah, but those close to us—those who truly matter—know it's all just lies. We know the truth, so we don't care what others say." She looked at me, her gaze going far deeper than I wanted. "You, on the other hand, know the people whispering behind your back. A small town should be supportive of its own—not treat you as gossip."

I feigned disinterest. "Nothing new. Even while my dad was alive, they talked about me."

"Because they think you're a product of incest?"

Everything inside me stilled. My voice turned short and sharp. "I just remembered you know far too much about my family thanks to that god-awful movie."

I expected her to argue, to assure me that she didn't know everything. Instead, she nodded, her face apologetic. "You're right. I do know more than I should."

Our eyes tangled together.

That awful pressure in my chest returned, whispering lies that I could handle one touch, one kiss, one dose of connection.

Tearing my attention away, I cleared my throat. "Yeah, well, I don't like it."

"I know." She shrugged. "Not much I can do about it, though."

The sadness in her tone irritated me. I didn't have the patience to deal with her or myself tonight. "Look, I need to rest."

"What did the doctor say about your injuries?"

"Nothing. I'm fine."

She laughed under her breath. "Yeah, right."

"Don't push me, Hope. It's late. I'm tired. Go back to my mother's house."

She fell silent, her gaze dancing around my bedroom. I waited for the questions of why I slept in a glass box, but she nibbled on her bottom lip. "You moved up here so young. Della still really misses you, you know."

My hands curled in quickly building anger. "Don't try to guilt me for moving out like any kid does."

She locked eyes with me, a direct challenge. "If you didn't already feel guilty, there's no way I could make you suffer it."

Another wave of blistering heat crested through me. Goddammit, she drove me crazy. I wanted to curse and kiss her, all at once.

This damn girl.

This aggravating, irritating, *troublesome* girl. "Once again, you've successfully annoyed me to the point of insanity."

"Well, if you stopped being so short-tempered, perhaps you wouldn't find me so annoying."

"You're saying I'm the one with the problem?"

She sniffed. "Seems like you're the one apologising all the time."

"Only because you're my guest, and I promised I'd be civil."

"If this is you being civil, I don't want to know what you're like when you're being rude."

"Hang around and you'll find out."

"Maybe I will." She crossed her arms, the opinionated girl wrapped up in candy pink and white stripes. "Perhaps I'll have better luck making you accept my help if I never leave."

"If you never leave, I might end up doing something we'll both regret."

She sucked in a breath.

My tone had betrayed me. It'd thickened with something other than frustration. A hint of lust. A droplet of attraction. It only pissed me off more. "You don't belong here, Hope. Take the hint and go back to where you came from."

Her chin came up as if I'd physically struck her. "I belong here more than I belong there."

"As if that's true." I laughed coldly. "You wouldn't last a day working the land. You think running a farm is just about riding and having picnics in the sun."

Tears glittered in her eyes but not from sadness. They were pure vexation and temper.

The same cocktail burned in my chest.

"I know it's not. I want *more* than that. I'm bored with being a guest. I want to work."

I shook my head condescendingly. "You'd last one day."

"I'd last forever if you gave me a chance."

Silence slammed down like a velvet curtain around us. Blanketing our stupid argument, pausing our hot rage.

Forever?

She wanted this life—*my life*—forever?

But…she couldn't.

She had to go back to the glitz she was born into.

This was *my* space.

My sanctuary.

I couldn't deal with another person I had to avoid to protect myself. I needed her gone for my survival, not just my peace of mind.

"This isn't your home, Hope," I murmured, my voice gentle but tight with warning. "My mother is not your mother. My family is not your family. And my land is not your land. Got it?"

A tear rolled down her cheek, glittering with matching fury in her gaze. "Oh, I get it. You don't ever let me forget it. But guess what, Jacob Wild. That mother of yours? That family of yours? They're not yours either because you never *accept* them as yours. You're afraid to. You think by staying up here in your lonely cabin, you won't get hurt when they—"

"Out." The room spun. My heart hurt. I felt sick. "Get out. *Now.*"

"Be my pleasure." Hope shot off my bed, shook her head as if she wanted to continue fighting, then spun around and vanished from my bedroom.

I just wished she'd vanish from my mind as easily.

Chapter Twenty-Six

JACOB

✶ ✶ ✶ ✶ ✶ ✶

FOUR A.M. AND I couldn't get back to sleep.

Hope had left a few hours ago, leaving me tormented and tortured. My mind wouldn't stop replaying our argument, throwing better comebacks I should've said, coming up with better warnings I should've uttered.

I was doing the opposite of what the doctor suggested with a concussion, but it wasn't my fault.

It was hers.

How dare she imply she wanted to stay longer than a week or two? How dare she hint that she belonged here more than I did?

Goddammit, she'd stolen any rest I might've snatched tonight and made it impossible to stay in bed.

Hauling my aching ass up, I wobbled for a second as the room went black, then grabbed a pair of grey sweatpants from the floor. Bending over to pull them on hurt like a bitch, making me crave more painkillers. I'd do what I did earlier today—yet another thing against doctor's orders—and chase the pills with a healthy swig of whiskey.

They didn't work as well without the extra help from medicinal liquor.

Padding my way down the corridor toward my living room and kitchen, I massaged my temples, doing my best to eradicate the constant headache. A headache made worse by Hope's unwanted midnight visit.

I didn't bother turning on any lights thanks to the moonshine coming through the skylight. Dawn wasn't that far away, and typically, I'd be sleeping until five a.m. when the lightening sky would nudge me to begin a new day.

That wouldn't be happening today.

As much as I wanted to—craved to—I wouldn't be able to lug heavy farm parts or lumber around on a cranky tractor.

How much longer could I hide my pain from my mother? The fields needed tending, and the many chores needed completing.

Mom knew me as a workaholic. I didn't even take afternoons off.

Three days in a row was bound to shove her headfirst from suspicions into hysteria.

The kitchen tiles were cold on my feet as I passed the spot where Hope had found me passed out and headed to the pantry. There, I found the bottle of whiskey that I'd bought a few months ago. The town might gossip about me but there were a few people on my side.

One of those people being the elderly, almost blind Mr. Dunback who ran the local bottle shop.

Even when I wasn't legal drinking age, he went along as I handed him cash and kindly wrapped up the amber goodness in a brown paper bag.

It wasn't like I drank to get drunk or to run from my life in a haze of alcohol. I drank because I liked the taste, and it was something of my own. Something no one else knew I indulged in now and again.

Pulling a glass from the cupboard, I splashed a healthy amount of whiskey into it, then opened the box of drugs prescribed by the doctor. Popping two out, doing my best not to take four like usual, I placed them on my tongue and swigged them back with a large mouthful of searing, spicy liquor.

I gasped, blinking away the sudden eye water and taking another sip for good measure.

"Oh, my God. Are you *drinking*?" A blur of movement dashed from the couch toward me.

My heart rate exploded, once again on high alert for a serial killer there to murder me.

But no.

It was just Hope.

Goddamn Hope who didn't get the clue that she was not welcome.

Clutching my half-empty glass, I growled. "I thought I told you to leave."

"And I told you I came to check on you."

"Yeah, by waking me up and arguing with me. I'm pretty sure you established I was coherent enough to hold a conversation."

She crossed her arms, her cheek showing indents of the lacy

cushion Mom had thrown on my bare couch as homey decoration.

Wait, did she *nap* on my couch?

"I found you passed out yesterday morning. Did you honestly think I'd be able to sleep not knowing if the same would happen today?"

My toes dug into the tiles as my body tensed. "You took me to the hospital, remember? Against my wishes, I might add. I'm fine."

She leaned forward, trying to snatch my whiskey. "Obviously, you're not fine if you're drinking." Her prim sniff made annoyed amusement gather.

"My home. My rules." I smirked. "Get over it or, better yet, *leave.*"

"I'm sure drinking is against the doctor's orders."

I groaned under my breath. "I'm not going to do this again." I didn't have the energy for another war. "You've seen that I'm still standing. You know where the door is. Goodbye." Raising the glass to my lips, I barely earned a sip before she snatched it from my hold and tossed the entire thing into the sink.

The glass shattered. The whiskey spilled. I stood there gobsmacked.

Silence once again thickened as I gawked at the mess, then back at her. "I can't decide if you're deliberately trying to drive me insane or if it's just a by-product of whatever spoiled world you've grown up in." My voice vibrated with temper. "Just because you're used to getting your own way all the time doesn't mean you can manipulate, guilt, and berate me into doing things—"

"Shut up, Jacob." She held up her hand, her patience as frayed as mine. "Just, please…shut up. I don't want to keep fighting with you. I don't want to argue. I'm just worried about you, and since you've sworn me to secrecy, it's on me to take care of you."

"It's not on you at all. Did I *ask* you to play nursemaid?"

"That's the thing." Her face softened. "You don't have to ask."

"And you don't get it. I didn't ask because I don't need someone lurking over me."

"I'm not lurking."

"Oh, you're definitely lurking." Grabbing some paper towels from under the sink, I scooped up the glass shards and tossed the mess into the trash. "I'm tired, Hope. I'm in pain. I agree that I don't want to fight, so please, just leave me alone."

Her shoulders fell as darkness gathered her close. If it hadn't been for the stray stars picking up strands of copper and chocolate from her hair, it would've almost disappeared into the night. "If that's truly what you want, I'll go."

"Great." I perked up, the promise of a Hope free morning allowing me to be generous. "Thanks. I appreciate it."

She licked her lips. "I'll go, but first, I need to ask two questions."

"Oh, for God's sake." I stiffened, already sensing that this eviction would take longer than I planned. "What part of—"

"I didn't say it would take long. They're short. I promise."

"If they're short, then they're not important and can wait."

"They're important. And if you answer them" —her eyes narrowed to a green glare— "politely and calmly, I'll tell you what your grandfather told me in the car ride back home. Unless you forgot you drove off without me, leaving me like some unwanted stray. I had to depend on the kindness of an old man who pities me just because I attempt to talk to you."

I didn't rise to her bait or let the fact that Grandpa John liked Hope enough to pity her entice me into another battle. Instead, I claimed a fresh glass, looked her dead in the eyes as I poured a generous splash of whiskey, then carried my drink to the dining room table.

I sat stiffly, cursing my shirtless back as the cold wood of the chair hurt my spine and dared, just *dared*, Hope to take my second drink away.

Her gaze never left my glass as I held it to my lips and drank deeply.

She sighed, moving toward me and sagging in the opposite chair.

I expected her to scold me again for my choice of hydration, but she merely whispered as if afraid of my answer, "What did the doctor say is wrong with you? Is...is it fixable?"

Taking another sip, mainly to vex her as well as keep the fiery taste on my tongue, I replied, "Of course, it's fixable."

"So, you haven't broken your back?"

"*What?* That's crazy. Would I be walking if I had?"

She nodded. "I've been Googling your symptoms. A lot of sites say you can still walk with a fractured back. If you have pins and needles and trouble peeing, then it's a possibility."

"I'm not discussing if I'm having peeing issues with you."

"But are you?"

"Holy hell, *no*. Okay?"

She flinched. "Okay, then. So…what's wrong?"

"Nothing."

"It's not nothing."

I looked at the ceiling for strength. "The X-rays and MRI indicate I have swelling in a couple of discs in my spine, which are pressing on my nerves. And a concussion. That's all."

"That's *all?*" she asked with an incredulous raise of her eyebrows. "That's not nothing, Jake."

My fingers curled tight around my glass. "That's three times now."

"Three times what?" Her forehead furrowed.

"That you've called me Jake instead of Jacob."

"Oh." Her gaze kept mine prisoner, trying to read me. "And you don't like that, I'm guessing."

"My name is Jacob. That's what I like."

"Or Wild One."

I shot another mouthful down my throat. "That's for family only."

"Just like Little Lace is for my dad's use only." Her fingers strayed to the locket I'd bought her, peeking out from her nightwear.

"Exactly." We continued staring at each other, aware that there was a lot unsaid between us. History. Complications. Things that didn't have a place because we *had* no history or complications. We were practically strangers. Two strangers too stubborn and opinionated to get along smoothly.

A bad match, through and through.

Changing the subject, she asked gently, "And the concussion? Are there any recommended treatments to speed up your recovery?"

Her gentleness made answering even harder. "Rest, which I can't afford. And anti-inflammatories to help with the swelling."

"Okay." She settled deeper into her chair; her features distracted as if mulling over ideas. "That will work."

"What will work?"

"My offer."

"I don't want any offer."

"Just hear me out." Leaning forward, she smiled in a way that made her eyes greener and cheeks pinker. Everything about her seemed so goddamn pretty, it reached into my lungs and stole my breath.

Somehow, she commanded every shred of awareness in one heartbeat. My living room vanished. The chair beneath me was no more. The dawn was utterly inconsequential.

Nothing else existed but her.

What the ever living *hell?*

I slugged back the rest of my whiskey, coughing a little on the burn.

I decided there and then I preferred her when she was picking a fight with me. I could handle argumentative Hope because anger became my shield. It was easier to lie when nothing but aggravation grew inside me.

Having her so calm and quiet soothed my jangled nerves too much, leaving space for all new issues. Issues I couldn't ignore the longer we stared at each other across the table.

Her eyes skittered from mine to my naked chest more times than she could control.

That hungry look from yesterday returned. A look far older than her seventeen years but so tentative too, as if she wasn't used to such a feeling.

My own gaze dropped lower, dancing over the collar of her pyjamas to the white and pink stripes of her full chest. She was well endowed for a girl of her height. It made her look like some erotic doll that dirty men would play with instead of eager kids.

And what the hell was I doing comparing her to a doll?

Was I the dirty old man in this scenario?

Not that I want to play with her.

Holy shit, *what?*

I wanted her out of my house and my life.

Clearing my throat, I tore my eyes away, wishing my heart beat for an entirely different reason to the real one. The one that made me feel twitchy and tingly and wrong.

I shifted in my chair, my hand disappearing under the table to readjust the sudden tightness that wouldn't stop swelling, no matter how much I commanded it to.

Hope at least distracted me from my impossible dilemma. "So…about my offer."

"The offer I don't want."

She half-smiled. "You truly are hard work. You know that, right? I bet you don't really want to argue all the time. You're probably thinking something else entirely."

The fact that her comment was far too close to the truth made heat travel up my neck.

Nudging my empty glass, I wished I had more whiskey. I glanced at the abandoned bottle in the kitchen but decided against getting more—not just because the thought of standing was too much to bear but because I didn't want to destroy this kind-of-truce we'd formed.

Plus, the part of me that was turning my life into a nightmare was hard and aching and in no fit state to be seen by a girl—especially one who drove me insane and was unchaperoned in my house at daybreak.

She might see me as a pervert…or worse, a guy issuing an invitation.

She might *touch* me.

Kiss me.

And I'd break.

Like a fucking coward.

Raking fingers through my hair, I shook away images of kissing someone for the first time, of finding out how wet and soft her tongue was. To peel her clothes off and taste—

I gave up brushing my hair back and squeezed the bridge of my nose instead. It activated my headache, helping me ignore things like naked bodies and hot kisses.

Sure, I'd noticed girls at school. I'd had wet dreams. I'd come by my own hand.

But my fear of touch wasn't superficial. It wasn't something I could over-ride.

My need to stay apart from everyone had grown into a non-negotiable law that ensured I chose celibacy over connection because I was weak enough to admit I could never sleep with someone and not care for them.

The heart that'd cursed me to never heal from my father's death had condemned me to a life of singledom because I wasn't like the guys in my town. The guys who fucked girls and didn't call them. The guys who spoke about their conquests as if they were toys.

Those bastards didn't have hearts.

But I had a broken one.

And I could never experience sex.

I wasn't prepared to suffer the level of sorrow my parents did on the night of my tenth birthday. I wasn't capable of enduring tear-filled goodbyes, bloody and soul-shattered for eternity.

"Jacob…" Hope murmured, her chair creaking a little as she reached across the table to touch my arm. "Are you okay? Your

215

headache bad?"

I dropped my fingers, moving away from her. "Yeah, headache. Uh-huh."

I was gutless.

I would never tell her the truth.

The truth that I needed her to stay mad at me if I had any chance of surviving her.

"Did you want to go back to bed?"

Bed was the last place I wanted to be. I was in enough physical and sexual pain without staring at a mattress that could be used for pleasure, granting relief to my current agony and opening the trapdoor to a lifetime of torture.

Daring to meet her gaze, I shook my head. "No. Get it over with. Tell me your offer and then I'm kicking you out of my house so I can rest."

"You're saying my company isn't restful?"

I chuckled despite myself. "I'm saying your company is *stressful*."

"I don't mean it to be." She swallowed, fiddling with her fingers again, linking and unlinking, looping and unlooping. A habit. A nervous habit that I'd become familiar with, and I hated that I knew that. That we were building a relationship even though I fought against such a dangerous thing. "I'm sorry I'm so annoying. I'm just...I'm worried about you."

"Don't be. It's not your job."

Her eyes caught mine again, snaring me with concern and complications.

I looked away, wiping my mouth with a suddenly shaky hand. "Look..."

"The actor who played you in the movie didn't show what you went through as a kid adequately."

"Excuse me?"

"Before I left Scotland, I kind of watched *The Boy & His Ribbon*." She noticed my scowl, rushing, "I know what you're going to say, and to be honest, I don't like watching the flicks my dad acts in, but he *is* rather talented, and he made me forget he's my dad, and I only saw *your* dad. Not that that's any better, of course, but it's a beautiful thing, Jacob, to watch a real-life love story. To know that age couldn't keep them apart. That circumstances and judgments and monsters couldn't stop them from falling in love and living happily ever after."

She flinched. "Well, not happily ever after but happily just the same."

"The ten years that I had him weren't exactly happy, Hope. He struggled. He died slowly. If that's the sort of movie you like watching, then you're sadistic."

Her chin came up, her readiness to fight brewing. "I'm not sadistic. I'm a stupid romantic. Anyway, that's not my point. My point is, the more time I spend with you, the more worried I am that you've forgotten how to let go...to be free."

"Freedom is a relative term."

"Freedom is *love*."

We glared at each other. "Keep going down this path, and your welcome will expire forever."

She tucked hair behind a delicate ear. "Why can't you just...I dunno, accept me as a confidant if not a friend. I'm only trying to help you."

"No, you're pushing me. And I don't like to be pushed."

"Maybe you need to be pushed. Maybe that's my purpose."

I stood on aching legs. "Maybe it's time for you to leave."

She stood too, her temper clashing with mine. "Maybe if you let yourself care about others, you'd see you don't have to be so alone."

"Don't go there, Hope." I balled my hands. "Not tonight."

"Well, when can I go there, Jacob? Because someone really needs to make you face your issues. Being afraid of love isn't healthy. It will end up killing you. You have to be able to see that."

"Leave." I marched toward the glass slider and wrenched it open, ignoring the slash of pain in my spine. Muggy summer morning tiptoed in as if sensing my home was full of animosity.

"But I haven't told you what John said in the car on the way home."

"Not interested. It's probably all lies anyway."

"It's not. You should talk to him, Jacob. He wants to tell you what's going on."

"Too late. He's dying. That's all I need to know." I crossed my arms. "Now, are you leaving, or am I?"

"Just...let's calm down again, okay? There's something I want to suggest, and I need you rational in order to do it."

I laughed coldly. "You're saying I'm not rational?"

"Not when it comes to family, no. You're completely *ir*rational."

"Right. Good to know." Stalking to the couch where my jacket lay thrown to the side as if Hope had used it as a blanket while she slept uninvited, I shrugged into it with a hiss, shook out the pins and needles in my hands, then headed to the door.

I didn't bother with shoes. My feet were used to trekking through forest and field. "When I return, I expect you to be gone."

Slipping into the dawn, I vanished from old pain, new pain, and frustrating girls who thought they could fix me.

Chapter Twenty-Seven

HOPE

✶ ✶ ✶ ✶ ✶ ✶

I SCREWED UP.

I knew that.

I'd pushed too hard.

I'd annoyed him too much.

Jacob hadn't talked to me in two days.

Then again, he hadn't talked to anyone.

Because he wasn't here.

The next night, when I went to check on him and ensure he wasn't passed out like last time, all I found was an empty cabin and unmade bed. I flew around, checking the bathroom, the deck, the spare bedroom, terrified I'd find him unconscious or worse.

When I found no signs of him, I'd had no choice but to blurt my fears to Della.

Her reaction wasn't what I expected.

I'd braced myself for a worried tirade. However, she merely patted my hand and smiled with a knowing mother's smile and said her son had too much of his father in him, and sometimes, he couldn't ignore the call of the forest.

He'd gone camping, apparently.

Gone camping with a swollen spine and a concussion.

Out there on his own with no one to check on him, tend to him, help him. Probably drinking when he shouldn't be drinking and ignoring the recommended dose on painkillers.

What about the farm? What about the hot days coaxing the ground to sprout grass so fast, it visibly grew between one morning and the next?

Della just shrugged and said they had local contractors who could help if Jacob stayed away longer than normal. She acted as if it wasn't a big deal. That the lost revenue by having a third party do the work didn't matter.

But it mattered a great deal to me.

I wanted to work the land.

I wanted to know what it felt like to drive a tractor and watch lush grass fall to the ground and turn into golden hay. I wanted to be dirty and sunburned and thirsty and so, so proud of being a fundamental piece of the seasons and nature itself.

I wanted it so bad, I silently hated Jacob for running before I'd been able to deliver my proposal. A proposal I doubted he'd take, but I would risk asking anyway.

By the third day of Jacob vanishing into the thick forest surrounding Cherry River, the sun was determined to bake the land and turn me into a roast chicken. Instead of riding, Della loaned me a black and pink bikini, pressed a fresh beach towel into my arms, a bag with cold lemonade and pasta salad, and told me to spend the day swimming in the large pond.

I guessed I'd overstepped yet another welcome, driving her mad with my hovering and constant enquires on when her son would return. Although, she hadn't asked when I would be leaving, and when Dad called, he didn't push me to go home.

So that was something.

I didn't want to go back yet, and luckily, the adults didn't pressure me to give up this wonderful existence, even if Jacob turned it into an occasional nightmare.

So there I sat, bikini hiding the important bits, sun cream protecting my skin from crisping, a delicious, untouched lunch, and my e-reader full of books. I'd returned for it after tending to Jacob, but instead of reading, my attention stayed locked on the horizon, waiting for a glimpse of the wayward wanderer to return.

For an hour, I daydreamed of Jacob appearing, walking proud and tall from the trees. I indulged in a fantasy where he'd stride straight toward me as if he knew I'd been waiting for him, drink in my half-naked body, and stop being so afraid of the chemistry rapidly growing hotter between us.

He wouldn't try to push me away or scare me off.

He'd slink his arms around my waist, grab a handful of my hair, and kiss me.

Truly, *truly* kiss me.

Not the teenage experiments I'd experienced with Brian. Not the in-the-dark fumbling where un-educated fingers pinched my nipples far too hard.

I hadn't gone far in my sexual exploration. Brian taught me how to squeeze and coax him to an orgasm. And he'd promised to make me feel good with his fingers in my body.

However, it hadn't felt good.

I hadn't come.

He'd gotten mad.

It'd left me feeling mostly empty.

My experience lacked any spark or magic, leaving me disillusioned with the lust part of being in love. If being touched and made love to was so great, why hadn't I managed to find a hint of it yet?

I scowled into the sunshine.

You're lying to yourself.

Out of all my intrepid excursions into growing up and figuring out sex, I could list on one hand how many times I'd earned butterflies.

And not just butterflies, but cannon-exploding, powdery-wing-confetti butterflies.

And they all centred on Jacob.

A kiss from Brian was nothing, *nothing* compared to a stare from Jacob.

A single stare from the boy who wanted nothing to do with me managed to hijack my entire nervous system leaving me hot and cold, brave and jittery, dry-mouthed and wet-pantied.

My heartbeat quickened as I fell deeper into my fantasy. A fantasy where Jacob would kiss me until my legs collapsed and my mind turned blank. Where he scooped me up like any gallant hero and carried me back to his place. Where he stripped me naked, licked the sweat from my skin, and bit me in punishment for making him crave me as much as I craved him.

I shivered in the hot afternoon, goosebumps scattering over my arms as nipples tingled and lips throbbed for such a thing.

What would it be like to see him naked? To feel his body on mine, *in* mine?

A full flush made me very aware I was breaking some unspoken rule by having such daydreams about Jacob Wild.

Standing, I abandoned my lunch and e-reader. Moving closer to the pond, I padded down the small jetty someone had built. My pulse was erratic, my breathing shallow. I needed to expend my nervous energy in some way.

A swim would hopefully help.

In icy water to douse my needy thirst.

Spreading my arms, I leapt into the lily-pad decorated pond.

I expected a refreshing chill, but what I got was a tepid, sun-warmed bath.

Breaking the surface, I cursed my overly explicit imagination. My skin still sparkled for touch. My tummy clenching for something I hadn't experienced before.

But none of that mattered as I twisted in the liquid, brushed back wet hair, and squinted once again at the trees acting as sentries around Cherry River.

And unlike before when the horizon had been empty of people, now, it held a solitary figure.

A boy.

A man moving stiffly, slowly with a small backpack on his bruised spine and a weathered cowboy hat on his concussed head.

Chapter Twenty-Eight

HOPE

* * * * * *

I MOVED FAST but not *too* fast.

After all, I didn't want to seem desperate.

Hoisting myself from pond to jetty, I flew to where I'd laid my frangipani-flowered towel and quickly wrapped it around my dripping body. Looking over my shoulder to make sure Jacob was still there, I scooped up the lunch Della had packed and slipped my feet into glittery flip-flops.

Armed with a peace offering and barely dressed, I made my way out of the willow grotto and toward Jacob who laboured toward his house a paddock away.

He hadn't seen me—either too focused on his pain or deliberately blocking everything out. Either way, it gave me time to delete some distance between us before I called, "Jacob. Hi."

He stopped, his shoulders rolled under his backpack, his hands shoved deep into jeans pockets. He didn't turn to face me, just waited for me to catch up.

I broke into a jog, moving around him with my arm outstretched with the pasta and lemonade. "A peace offering."

The second I caught sight of his face, the sunshine—that had been pretty a heartbeat ago—became absolutely breath-taking. The gorgeous weather was no longer just sun and sky; it was utterly sublime. Everything seemed brighter, sharper, more *real* now he was back.

A five o'clock shadow covered his throat and jaw, a leaf clung to his dirty blond strands, and a smudge of earth contoured his cheekbone.

He looked wild and rugged and full of warning like any forest creature that didn't do well with humans. The hardened edges he kept sharp and shiny were somewhat duller, though—as if he'd found what he needed in the trees, and exhaustion had found him in return.

"Hi," I whispered again, unashamedly drinking him in from his dirt-stained T-shirt, faded well-used boots and everything in between.

I had the privilege of witnessing his jaded, weary eyes flare as I blocked his path. No doubt he'd expected me to be in clothes and not a bikini. Thanks to my jog over here, the towel had slipped to my waist, revealing the lycra-covered breasts Dad tried to deny his young daughter had and the curves that would make me a perfect double for some 1920s pin-up.

"Why are you mostly naked?" His voice was charcoal and ash as if he hadn't spoken in days, which was probably true from camping in the woods on his own.

Unless he talked to owls and mice.

Or ghosts.

"I've been swimming." I grinned, squinting in the brightness, thankful for the beads of water trickling from my hair. The droplets kept me cool while Jacob's face shone with sweat. I had so many questions. So many worries. So many everythings.

But I swallowed them all back, reminding myself for the millionth time since I'd found him missing that I wouldn't push so hard. That I'd be kinder in my approach and not rise to his anger. I would be soft and understanding, and if he got mad at me, so be it.

I wouldn't enter another argument.

Or at least…I hope I won't.

Smiling as if we were best friends, I offered the pasta again. "You must be hungry."

His tongue darted between his lips, leaving them wet. I did my best to ignore the answering squeeze deep in my belly. His gaze fought to stay on my face, but he lost the battle—just like I lost whenever I saw him shirtless—his dark eyes hooded and turned smoky, trailing down my water-speckled skin.

I breathed harder as his stare burned me like a candle held too close, flickering over the triangles hiding my breasts and the towel hanging precariously low on my hips.

His jaw tightened, his body tensed, and he stepped away as if I'd done something wrong.

Keeping my smile genuine and wide, I sank into the thick grass with its pink, purple, and yellow flowers, looking up at the tall boy who carried such pain.

Pain he thought he masked with temper and rage, but pain I glimpsed regardless. Whether it was a moment in a fight or this moment in quietness, he couldn't hide from me, and he knew that.

He sensed that.

He felt what I did and that made me a threat.

And in a way, I liked that I threatened him. It meant I made him *feel*. He couldn't look at me with the same barriers in place. He couldn't talk to me with walls firm and firearms ready. I forced him to come out from behind those shields, and I had to remember that with that power came a huge responsibility of care.

Dad taught me that.

He'd been at the brunt of Mom's disappointment and constantly craving nature for years. Her unhappiness at having all her dreams come true didn't make sense, but she was empty inside, eaten away to a rotten core, unable to be grateful for even the simplest things.

She didn't care we had more than most.

She didn't sit in awe at what she and Dad had created.

She just set her goals higher, strove for bigger, fought for better, slowly killing herself with the impossible.

Dad would just stand and weather her violent mood swings, never once shouting back or striking her when she struck him. He stayed calm and cuddled her close when the storm had passed, and Mom was herself again.

He'd caught me spying on a massive fight the night after some red carpet party. I'd dashed to my bed and hidden beneath the covers still in my pretty lemon dress. But he'd pulled back the blankets and explained that Mom didn't mean what she said. She loved us really. She just couldn't see how lucky she was.

I'd asked Dad why he put up with abuse—because it was emotional and physical abuse. And he'd said it was our job to be the carers of those who carry the pain. Pain could manifest in many ways, and it wasn't up to us to point out how hurtful and cruel such pain could be.

We had to be brave and show the hurting that they could share their agony or deliver their agony. Either way, there would be no judgment or condemnation.

Only love.

For the longest minute, I feared Jacob would just continue walking to his home and leave me sitting in the field alone. But then the clouds in his eyes dispersed and the tiredness in his body increased, and he all but collapsed beside me.

As he reached up to shrug out of his backpack, a gentle hiss escaped his lips, tugging on my desire to help him be free of the equipment but knowing better than to touch him.

I waited for him to shove the bag aside, then smiled in triumph as he fell backward into lush green grass. He groaned long and low as his hands spread to the sides and his eyes closed and a look of almost-peace softened his handsome face.

There was still pain—so, so much pain—but at least his exhaustion took the edge off and gave him a small reprieve.

I wanted to know what he'd done in the forest. Had he slept in a tent or open air? Did he swim in a river and cook on a cheery flame? Or had he just rested beneath a tree, allowing his body to knit itself together and his mind to quieten?

Instead of ruining the silence with my queries, I fell back and lay beside him.

He flinched a little as I sighed at the blissful sensation of springy grass beneath and blue skies above.

But he didn't move away. He didn't get up to run.

And we lay there, side by side, not saying a word.

And in that silence, somehow, we became friends.

* * * * *

I woke to Jacob sitting beside me, his jaw working and throat swallowing, eating the pasta his mom had made for me. The sun had slipped farther in the sky and my skin was a little tight with UV exposure as I sat up and hugged my knees to my chest.

Jacob glanced at me from the corner of his eyes, giving me a single nod before stabbing another mouthful of pasta. That nod could've meant anything, but I decided to interpret it as a simple hello and a peace treaty that we could do this sort of thing. This normal sort of thing—just hanging out with no agendas or arguments.

The creamy bacon and mushroom smelled good, and my stomach grumbled.

I hugged my knees tighter, doing my best to hush up my appetite. Jacob deserved it. Who knew when his last meal was?

Unfortunately, he'd heard, and a smirk danced on his lips as he finished a few more mouthfuls, then passed the mostly empty container to me. "Finish it."

I wanted to say no, but I didn't want to start another war. Instead, I smiled and nodded, taking the Tupperware and fork.

The same fork that'd been in his mouth.

My heart pounded as I harpooned a piece of penne and wrapped my lips around the utensil. Was it wrong to prefer his taste over the creamy mushroom? Was it immoral to have belly flutters and body flushes at the thought of having some part of him in my mouth?

He didn't help my wayward thoughts as his eyes locked on my lips, not looking away even as I selected another bite and placed it as delicately and as prettily as I could on my tongue.

I wished I'd snuck into more actresses trailers as they prepared for sex scenes. They practiced their orgasm faces and oh-my-goodness-yes-right-there gazes in the mirror before the cameras rolled. I'd spotted Carlyn Clark practicing once, running her tongue along her bottom lip with a hazy, dreamy look on her perfect features.

I'd tried to mimic that night and ended up embarrassing myself when Dad found me flirting with my hand mirror and contemplating if I should make out with it.

There was no mirror here in the sun-dappled meadow, but there was a boy who I'd been fantasising about making out with for longer than I could remember.

Hot silence prickled with intensity the longer Jacob stared at my mouth.

The fork in my hand began to shake. My body took control, pebbling my nipples, making them visible beneath the flimsy triangles of my bikini. My tongue licked my lower lip without my permission as if these signals were ingrained in biology, not flirtation.

Jacob's nostrils flared, he tensed, and for a second—just a micro second—he swayed toward me as if totally bewitched and unable to stop himself from claiming what I so blatantly said he could have.

But then a horse nickered in the background, and the silence became awash with insects buzzing and a breeze rustling and laughter from his family somewhere by the farmhouse.

The moment was crushed by noise and reality.

And I was no longer hungry.

Pushing the last few mouthfuls toward him, I muttered, "Here, you have it. I'm not hungry, after all."

His hand wrapped automatically around the container, but his brow furrowed as his attention fell on the fork.

The fork we'd both tasted and sucked.

I hoped he thought the same things I had. The same deliciously naughty things about licking me instead of the pasta. Goosebumps spread over my arms as he bit his lower lip, concentration furrowing deeper tracks in his forehead.

For a second, I thought he'd toss the rest of the pasta into the grass—anything to avoid a touch of mine, but I froze as he stabbed the lone pieces of penne into one bundle and raised the fork to his mouth.

I stopped breathing.

So close.

If he used the fork, we might as well have kissed. His saliva with mine. Our tongues together. Our—

With a bone-deep sigh, he shook his head, cracked his wrist like he held a whip and shot the penne off the fork and into the greenery. Instantly, sparrows dive-bombed the unsuspecting pasta, squabbling over who got what.

So much for that stupid idea.

I slouched in my towel, plucking a long piece of grass and twirling it in my fingers. He couldn't even bring himself to eat off the same implement as me. The chances of him ever being comfortable enough to kiss me?

Yeah, I might as well give up now.

I should've given up years ago—around the time I started dating boys to do exactly that—to forget about Jacob Ren Wild and find a boy who *actually* wanted be touched.

A wash of soul-crushing sadness filled me.

Not for me, but for *him.*

How awful an existence it must be to be so afraid of touch.

How terrifyingly lonely a life to prefer aloneness than company.

I sighed, stripping my long piece of grass into green noodles.

Placing the Tupperware into the bag, Jacob pulled free the homemade lemonade and swigged half back in a few gulps. Pulling the bottle away from his lips, he wiped the top with his shirt hem, then with a bashful look, he gave it to me.

I hid my pain and stupid fantasies and nodded sweetly. "Thanks."

He flinched as if he hadn't expected me to talk. As if the farmyard chatter was better than speaking with me.

Ignoring yet more hurt, I drank the refreshingly tart liquid. This time, I didn't bother to save him any and drank until all the citrus drops were gone. Afterward, I passed the bottle back to him where he capped it and placed it with the empty Tupperware.

With a soft groan, he pulled up his knees and drove his fingers through his hair. The leaf that'd been tangled there fluttered to the grass, only to be scooped up by me.

Oak.

A baby leaf.

Probably miles from its family, depending on how far Jacob had travelled.

"Thanks for the lunch," he muttered, his hands still buried in his thick, unruly blond mess.

"No problem."

"I'm sorry I got angry with you again the other night."

"No worries."

"And I'm sorry for any and all future fights we'll end up having."

My heart skipped a beat at the thought of spending enough time with Jacob to warrant such interaction. "It's fine."

He huffed, his eyes still squeezed together and head bowed. His forehead pressed against his knees as if he was so exhausted, he barely had the effort to sit.

I squirmed beside him as my mind ran riot with things I shouldn't say, promises to help him, oaths to protect him. He'd hate any sign that I cared.

I'd tried the forward game and only pushed him further away. I no longer strove for a relationship that could be considered normal with fondles and giggles and kisses.

Jacob wasn't that type of guy, and really...I wasn't that type of girl. I *wanted* to be, but death still stalked me. Blackness still crouched in my mind. Morbid questions still demanded an answer. Questions that kept me firmly in reality, and I understood why Jacob feared dying because of the very same reasons I didn't. Death was coming for *all of us*—regardless of how we lived our lives.

It could tap us on the shoulder tomorrow or slam into us four decades from now.

No one could predict when.

And the thing that made it so scary wasn't the fact that it was *going* to happen. But the fact that we suffered while waiting. And that suffering was caused entirely by us resisting the inevitable.

Jacob had to stop resisting.

Resisting life and love and happiness.

If he could do that, then his suffering would end.

He'd accept.

He'd relax.

He'd be *free*.

Twisting my knees under me so I propped myself up a little

higher, I cleared my throat. "I have something to say."

His shoulders stiffened. "What is it this time?"

"I hadn't planned on bringing this up." I shrugged. "Well, not until you'd had a good night's rest and a decent shower. But…"

His eyes narrowed with suspicion. "But?"

"You're tired. You're calmer than I've ever seen you. Exhaustion makes you easier to deal with, so I'll get it out now. After all, tomorrow is another day."

He huffed. "And just because you've lived on my farm for a week, you're suddenly Scarlett O'Hara?"

"Almost two weeks, actually. And wait…" My mouth popped wide. "You know *Gone with the Wind*?"

He rolled his eyes. "Seriously? It's a classic. One of Mom's favourites."

I paused, my heart aching a little. "But…it's not a happy ending. Rhett leaves her."

"Just like my dad left my mom." Jacob smiled cynically. "I think she likes the movie because Scarlett keeps going. It reminds her to be strong."

I fell quiet for a moment.

I didn't think that was the reason at all. "I think she likes it because it ends with the hope of them working it out," I whispered. "As the onlooker, you believe they'll get back together off-screen. You can't accept anything else."

"Yeah, but the chances of them ever seeing each other again are slim."

"You don't know that."

"Kinda do. That's just life."

"Some people find each other again against all the odds."

Jacob narrowed his eyes. "Are we still talking about the movie here?"

I bit my lip, looking at the grass.

I'd always felt sorry for Della losing her husband, but it hadn't pierced my heart as truthfully as it did sitting beside her son in that meadow. There I was, pretending I could be Jacob's cure—that I was like him with my lack of parent and acquaintance with death—but in reality…I was an imposter.

I didn't know such heartbreak. I couldn't watch *Gone with the Wind* without clutching my chest when Rhett walked out the door. I'd always made up an alternative ending where they were together again.

Was that how Della survived each morning? Believing one

day she'd see Ren again?

Wow.

The pain.

The faith in the impossible and improbable.

Blinking, I swallowed back my stupidity. I wasn't some magical girl to put Jacob back together again. I wasn't there to repair him or teach him that love wasn't something to be feared because even death couldn't sever it.

Yes, I knew loss. But I didn't know true agony. And Jacob's agony? I'd never understand because I wasn't *capable* of understanding.

The belief and hope I'd hugged for so long suddenly vanished, and Scotland with its fake actors and scripts and make-believe seemed so much safer than here in the meadow with a boy who'd lived a far worse tragedy than me.

I'd overstayed my welcome.

I didn't want to intrude any longer.

I want to leave.

"Hope?" The unusual softness in Jacob's voice made me wince. "What's going on in that mind of yours?"

"Nothing."

"It's something."

"No." I shook my head. "It's not."

He pursed his lips, letting a couple of seconds tick past. "What did you want to talk to me about?"

"It doesn't matter now." I shifted to stand, but he lashed out, his fingers spreading over my hand.

We froze.

Two statues locked in disbelief.

His fingers pressed into mine for the barest of moments before he ripped them away and wiped them on the grass.

My skin seared, forever branded and greedy for more.

"You're leaving," he stated in a detached, icy voice; the polar opposite to the softness of before.

"How did you know?" I asked, petal soft and just as fragile.

"Just do." Planting his hands into the earth, he grunted in pain as he pushed up slowly, standing like an old man and not a young farmer. He wobbled a little, shaking his head and blinking.

I unfolded my legs and met him on two feet. "You should be happy I'm going."

"I am." He brushed past me, swiping the backpack from the grass as he did. "See ya round."

His march had a slight limp, his hips not as limber, his back not as supple. He was hurting, and I'd just somehow made it worse.

All selfish reasons for wanting to leave vanished, and once again, I had the undeniable desire to *help*.

Pulling the towel around my breasts, I knotted it in place, then jogged after him. "Wait."

"Nothing to wait for."

"What I was going to say before—"

"Isn't important."

"Just, stop, will you?" I slammed to my heels. "Does your mom know you're still injured?"

He stopped, turning around like a hunter. "Why? What does it matter to you?"

"Does she or not? Just answer the question."

He crossed his arms, his full height making me tip my chin to meet his eyes. "No. Unless you've told her."

"I didn't."

"Good, then she doesn't know."

"But you have an entire farm to run while you're hurt. Otherwise, she's gonna find out."

He shrugged as if he didn't care. "I'll figure it out."

Daring to step closer, I breathed, "*I've* figured it out."

His eyebrows rose. "You have, have you? What did you figure?"

"I'll help you."

His face went blank, then a vicious chuckle fell from his lips. "*You?* You want to help *me?*"

"Very much."

"You think you can drive the tractor, raker, baler, hoist hay onto trailers, stack it in sheds, run new fence lines, fertilize—"

"I can do whatever you can do." My spine straightened. "I can't explain it. I know you think I don't belong here but something about the land says I do. I want to get dirty. I want to work hard. I want you to show me."

He leaned closer, anger building. "I'm not playing babysitter, not when I already need help with my back screwed."

"Exactly. Show me and I'll help you. I'll do it all."

He laughed coldly. "You'd last five minutes."

"You said that before, yet you don't know that." I stepped into his personal space. The smell of sun-warmed skin, leather, and pine sap filled my nose. "Give me a go."

He rocked back, trying to put space between us but unwilling to concede defeat by backing away. "No way."

"Give me a chance to learn."

"Nope."

"I can *help* you."

"You'd be a hindrance." His lips curled, baring his teeth. "A hindrance who I thought was leaving."

"Yeah, and you didn't look all that happy about me leaving a second ago."

He laughed once. "Oh, don't flatter yourself, Hope. I was happy. Believe me."

"Okay then…how about a deal?"

"Another one?" He rolled his eyes. "What's with you and deals?"

"You never let me announce the last one. And besides, they're a bargaining chip. Makes dealing with you easier."

His jaw clenched. "You're not exactly Miss Easy-to-get-along-with either, you know."

"Only because you bring out the worst in me."

He swallowed a growl. "Fine, what's your deal?"

"Show me." I sniffed. "Let me work for you, and if I can't cope with the workload or I'm not doing it to a standard you expect, then fire me."

"*Fire* you? I'm not going to pay you, so why would I fire you? You're not my employee."

"You're right. I'm not. I'm your friend."

"There's that nasty word again."

I wanted to stamp my foot in frustration. "Fine. Ask me to leave."

His face blackened. "Okay then, leave."

"I didn't mean right now."

He threw his hands up. "I can't win with you. You tell me to do something, yet when I do, you ignore me anyway."

"I meant I'll leave if you ask me to go *after* you've seen if I'm a help or a hindrance."

"God, you're complicated." He rubbed his mouth with a dirty hand. "Why does everything have to be so damn difficult with you?"

"This is simple, Jacob. Exceedingly simple. You need someone to help you with the fields. You need to keep your injury a secret. If you let me work with you, Della will think you're being nice and showing me what I've wanted to do since I arrived on your stupid farm, and you get a free labourer who knows how to hold her tongue."

He went to interrupt, but I held up my finger. "*And* if it's not working and you genuinely think I'm failing as a farmhand, then ask me to leave, and I'll leave. No arguments. No bargaining. Just a packed suitcase and a flight back to Scotland."

Silence sounded as loud as my thrumming heartbeat as he studied me.

His breath was torn, his hands fisted, yet another fight that I'd promised wouldn't happen lashed around us like lightning.

Finally, he asked in a harsh voice, "You swear on your mother's soul that you'll leave if I've had enough?"

I hid my flinch and nodded. "I swear."

"You'll go if I say I can't do this anymore?"

"I promise."

"And you'll do everything I say without question?"

I nodded again, tasting victory. "Definitely."

He looked over my head at the horizon beyond. At the overgrown grass, afternoon sunshine, and horses painting a perfect postcard of his empire. His eyes darted left and right, assessing workload, cataloguing timeframes and requirements.

And slowly, he nodded.

He accepted.

He agreed.

"One week, then we'll reassess." His dark gaze landed on mine.

"I can live with that."

"Good."

I should've just smiled.

I should've walked away with a smug sway of my hips and hid my victory grin. But my mind was still full of his parents' love story. The inner depth of *The Boy & His Ribbon* and the many phrases that became so heavy with meaning and affection.

And I couldn't help myself.

Sweeping up on tiptoes, I pressed my lips to his stubble-covered cheek.

I kissed him.

I claimed him.

And all I whispered was, "Fine."

Chapter Twenty-Nine

JACOB

* * * * * *

WARM WATER CASCADED over me.

The shower was supposed to wash away the dirt of camping, the pain of falling, and the god-awful sensation of Hope's lips on my cheek.

It wasn't working.

I'd shaved my stubble. I'd soaped my face. I'd done all I could to remove any trace of her kiss, yet my skin burned as if she'd poisoned me.

And what the hell was she doing saying 'fine' in that breathy, intoxicating whisper? Did she know what that word meant to my family? Did she say it deliberately?

Of *course* she did.

Her dad had played mine.

She'd witnessed the lines, she'd read the script. She'd probably laughed with her father over the silly habits and sacred phrases of my parents.

Goddammit.

My fist drove into the tiles, hard enough to bruise but not hard enough to break. Hope didn't deserve that sort of power over me. I wouldn't bow to her mind games. I wouldn't succumb to whatever plan she thought she'd set in motion by working with me.

But that kiss…

Fucking hell.

No matter what road my thoughts chased, they always ended at the same dead-end of her lips on my cheek and her scent of lilies, sunshine, and lemonade in my nose.

I should never have left the forest. I should never have believed I was safe enough in her company to let down my guard. And I should never have permitted my body to react. To stand, two hours later, under a stream of scalding water, doing my best to get my need under control.

The viciously hungry greed for another kiss, another touch, another *something* to grant peace from the snarling, clawing desire in my belly.

My hand brushed the hardness between my legs, my blood begging for a release all while the thought sickened me. Because the reality was, I didn't just want a release.

I wanted Hope to be the one to deliver it.

And that was the most petrifying admission I'd ever had. I *wanted* her to touch me. I wanted her to *kiss* me.

I wanted her to stay as far away from me as possible.

She was dangerous.

She was gorgeous and annoying and brave and sexy and driving me out of my goddamn mind.

How the hell had this happened?

Which argument switched my anger into want?

And how the *hell* did I stop it?

* * * * *

"You're late."

I narrowed my gaze through the dark gloom of sunrise. I'd slept like the dead last night after succumbing to my disgusting needs of jerking off in the shower.

I'd done my best to keep my mind blank and sterile as I pumped ruthlessly and clinically to an orgasm. It wasn't about pleasure. It was about salvation. And I hated, *hated* that images of Hope had managed to crawl into my mind, and I now had fantasies of her on her knees before me, her lips wet, her body naked, her hands around my—

"It's dawn. You're just an overachiever," I muttered, moving stiffly toward the light switch in the barn where the tractor and attachments lived. I'd also slept well thanks to four painkillers, a slug of whiskey, and the fact I hadn't been at all comfortable in the forest for the past three nights. "What are you even doing up yet, anyway?"

"Your mom told me five a.m. is your typical start."

"Just like she told you where to find me, I'm guessing?"

Hope smiled with perfect teeth and her damn perfect face. "Yep."

"Wonderful." My sarcasm was as dark as the dawn.

Pressing the switch, a wash of warm electrical light chased away shadows and spiders, granting false day to the otherwise still fast asleep farm.

Hope sat bold and unwanted in my tractor. Her hair twisted into a ponytail, the long, glossy brown sticking through the back of a beige baseball cap I vaguely recalled was my mother's. She wore a white singlet with a pink bra peeking by the straps, jeans far too clean for field work, and one of my old shirts with a torn elbow and tatty collar the same colour as golden hay.

"What are you doing wearing my stuff?" I moved around, staying busy so I didn't look at her and remember what I did last night.

"Your mom lent it to me." Hope plucked the cuff, pushing it up her skinny forearm. "I think it suits me."

"It looks ridiculous."

"I'll take that as a compliment." She beamed, leaping down from the old cab and standing by a rugged tractor wheel far bigger than she was. "How are you this morning?" Without waiting for my reply, she launched into another conversation that reminded me of the morning starlings outside my bedroom. "I'm *so* happy you agreed to let me help you, Jacob. I'm so excited; I can't tell you how excited I am. I mean, I can tell you. Obviously, I speak, and you listen, but I don't think you truly get what this means to me." Her eyes glittered with joy that tried to infect me but was just as insidious as a disease.

Spinning around, she pranced toward the old shelving where tins held old nails, new screws, odds and ends, and rusty tools wanting to play their part but semi-retired in their decrepit age. "I want to know how everything works. I want to know what seeds to plant and how you keep weeds out and about irrigation and what you do in case of a bug infestation."

She clutched a pipe bender to her chest, skipping back toward me as if it was a Golden Globe or whatever award she could win in her Hollywood world. "What does this do? Is it hard to use? Should you teach me now or is it not important?"

I rolled my eyes, forcing a yawn and layering boredom thick. "Unless you're planning on becoming a plumber, you don't need to know what a pipe bender does."

"Ah, okay." She grinned, placing it back amongst the relics. The same relics Dad had claimed from the farmer who'd hurt him. The police had appeared one day with a box of stuff and said it was his if he wanted it. They'd kept the brand, though. The cattle mark that had been seared into all the children Mclary had bought.

"...so yeah. That's what I think."

I hadn't been paying attention to whatever Hope prattled about. Continuing to ignore her, I climbed onto the tread of the tractor to check the fuel gauge.

Half full.

Better take a gas can with us to top up rather than returning to the barn. We stockpiled diesel at low prices, filling up large tanks buried underground.

It wouldn't take long to fill a canister or two.

Twisting to leap off the tractor, I miscalculated the jump. My back tweaked, my head sloshed, and I fell forward, completely missing my footing.

I braced myself for a hard, painful landing.

Only, something soft and delicate intercepted, wedging her shoulder against my chest, taking my entire weight for a second before she toppled to the ground with me on one knee and a hand speared to the concrete beside her.

My palm slapped by her face for balance, my body poised over hers while she landed on her back with hay in her ponytail and dirt smudging her cheek.

I stopped breathing as my body once again reacted.

Reacted way too fast and utterly out of my control.

She sucked in a breath as I shifted, pain lashing down my spine and my fingers tangling in her hair on the floor.

Her eyes lost its infectious lime joy, turning forest green with sick invitation. She shifted a little, her legs falling apart in a way that made me think she didn't know she'd done it. Her desire hijacked her control, just like an erection had hijacked mine.

Our bodies understood whatever was going on between us.

The basicness of sex seemed so utterly simple.

My hips screamed to come down and slot between hers. My back didn't give a damn if such a position would kill. All I needed was her flush against me so I had something to hold and press against and *goddammit*—

Breathing hard, I scrambled upright, doing my best to hide the tightness of my jeans. "You okay?"

Hope sucked in a breath, her legs scissoring together as if she'd only just realised what she'd done. "Yeah, you didn't hurt me." On the floor with her baseball cap askew, lips plump from no kiss and eyes wild from no touch, she didn't look seventeen.

She looked a damn sight older and scarily younger all at the same time.

My chest physically hurt as my heart played some awful

version of Jenga with my ribcage, tugging on each bone, trying to see which rib would cause the rest to come crashing down so it would be free to go to her.

"That's good." I rubbed the back of my neck. "You should've just let me fall." My voice sounded thick and strange to my ears, gravelly with self-denial and frustration.

Climbing easily to her feet, she brushed off cobwebs and barn muck. "It was instinctual to help. Sorry." She smiled softly. "To be honest, I'm more worried about your concussion than your back. Your balance seems off."

I turned away, striding as smoothly as I could to the stack of red diesel canisters in the shadows. "I'm fine."

"I know." She followed me, grabbing a can without me asking. "Just making observations."

"Well, don't."

"Okay, Jacob." She looked me up and down, her gaze lingering on places I wished it wouldn't. "I won't." Tossing the canister into the tractor's small storage box, she clapped her hands together, uncaring about the dust, and grinned. "The sun is waking up. Let's go meet her on the fields."

* * * * *

I would never admit this out loud.

Even under pain of death.

Never.

I'd take this secret to my grave.

But Hope...I'd completely misjudged her.

She might've been born to stardom; she might've been raised by nannies, taught by scholars, and lived in mansions, but she'd merely tolerated such an existence.

The Hope who had a sunburned nose, three chipped nails, and a grubby white singlet revealing way too much pink bra was not the girl who'd arrived here, lonely and confused, seeking meaning to her life a couple of weeks ago.

She was right.

Plain and simple.

She *did* belong to the land, and the land belonged to her. I'd never seen something so...*right*...or so strange. In five hours, Hope had lost her tentative seeking and fully embraced her place in this world.

Her path had forked. Her future amended. And it was all because of the very same thing that had healed and hurt me. Confused and consoled me. Trapped and tempted me.

Land.

"Like this?" she asked, the sun doing its best to turn brown hair blonde with its overly hot rays. She kept shoving the long strands off her shoulder as she bent over the back of the tractor where we needed to change the mower for the raker attachment.

"Nah, the lynchpin first, then the coupling."

"Ah." She nodded as if she understood. What made it doubly annoying was she *did* understand. Everything I told her cemented itself into her brain as if she already knew this stuff.

With a quick tug on the well-greased pin, she unlocked the mowing blades and looked up to where I sat in the tractor. Giving me a thumbs up, she grinned into the brightness. "All good."

Trusting her, even though instinct commanded I slip to the ground and check, I lowered the large contraption until it fell the rest of the way to the grass. It clunked as the coupling came loose, ready to be removed.

Normally, I'd head down and do what was needed, but with my back being so tetchy…well, Hope had proven her worth.

I couldn't have done this without her. As the day wore on and the sun burned hotter, my headache grew more intense, making my balance unreliable.

And just because Hope stopped pointing out when I grew dizzy didn't mean she didn't stop noticing. Almost every time, she'd be there with a bottle of water and a painkiller.

She never smirked or made me feel like a patient. She just delivered what I needed and walked away, leaving me to my own issues at being taken care of.

Tearing my eyes from hers, I pulled forward at a snail's pace, then ambled over to where the raker sat in the tree shadows. Hope trailed on foot, her tiny frame bouncy and high on life in my rear-view mirror.

Her step was springy, her smile so wide it caused premature wrinkles by her eyes. She glowed with joy. Literally *glowed* with it as if she were some woodland creature that'd slipped into a human skin for a day and marvelled at a brand new existence.

She didn't try to hide how happy today made her. She didn't apologise for laughing for the sake of it or for skipping for no reason.

She was pure ecstasy, and her freedom in such wonder and delight caused painful shards in my chest. She hurt me because I hadn't been around such carefree happiness before. If my mom smiled, it held a tinge of grief. If my aunt laughed, it shadowed with sadness. If my grandpa grinned, it tinkled with memories of lives taken far too soon.

Cherry River might look like the ideal place to live but buried in the wind and trees and grass was permanent heartache.

Only Hope was free from such afflictions.

Only Hope could look at the forest where we'd scattered Dad's ashes and see heaven and not a ghost.

Only Hope could twirl in the wildflowers and grin at the sky rather than feel guilty for being so happy.

Watching her made me feel wrong.

I wanted to tell her to be respectful of those who could no longer be here with us. To tell her the dead were watching, and it wasn't fair to have such a good time when they had run out of time completely.

But how could I snatch away her joy when she'd fought so hard to find it? How could I tell her to leave this place when it would be like kicking her from a home she'd wholeheartedly claimed?

"Hey, Jacob! You've driven right past it!"

Goddammit.

I pulled back on the accelerator, shaking my head from gloomy thoughts. The urge to apologise to Dad—to look at the trees and say, *'I'm sorry she's so happy when you're gone and can't be happy anymore,'* overwhelmed me.

Doing my best to ignore such things and convince myself that Hope's glee wouldn't reflect poorly on me with my dead father, I scowled, reversed, and lined up for the rake.

The nasty looking implement could take out an eye, lung, or leg with the row upon row of sharp spikes ready to gather cut grass and place it neatly into heaped lines to dry.

"Watch yourself," I commanded as Hope fiddled with the coupling, looking a bit lost. I couldn't in good conscience make her fumble with something so dangerous. "Back away."

"I can do it."

"Hope." I growled. "Back away. I'll do it. You drive."

"Really?" Her eyes turned wide.

All day, I hadn't let her drive. I'd explained what I was doing as I shifted gears and pulled levers to set the mower down and pressed pedals to add torque, but I hadn't let her into the captain's seat.

Gritting my teeth, I grabbed the rail and steering wheel and twisted to climb the two steps to the ground.

My right leg threatened to give out on me, my knee unlocking for a second as I reached earth. I teetered with balance, but then Hope was there. Her body pressed against mine, her arm wrapped tight around my waist.

I sucked in a breath, my heart charging faster than Forrest in full gallop; my mouth dry and body hard and blood craving, *craving* something it couldn't have.

She'd taken far too many liberties, and I'd been far too weak for letting her.

"Let go of me," I hissed when Hope gave no sign of stepping away.

She licked her lips, nodding in submission but not going anywhere. Her forehead pressed against my shoulder, nuzzling into me before a tiny moan escaped her, and she tore herself away.

That little moan echoed like a gunshot in my ears, making me lightheaded for all new reasons.

I couldn't remember what the hell I was supposed to be doing. I stood like an idiot as she climbed the tractor and plopped like an excited child in the chipped and weathered seat.

"Did I say you could get up there?"

She frowned. "You *just* said I could drive." Grabbing the wheel, she leaned down, searching my face shadowed beneath my cowboy hat. "You do remember…right?"

I frowned, flipping through memories—

Something about Dad and skipping and the rake.

Ah. Yeah, I did say she could drive.

Damn, this concussion was stealing tiny chunks of my day and turning me into a moron.

"Fine. Don't touch anything." Taking my hat off to swipe sweat-damp hair, I shoved the leather back onto my head, then moved to the rear of the machine. My fingers weren't as agile, and my spine ached like a bitch as I bent over to angle the coupling into the right position.

The tractor connector needed to come down. Seeing as Hope wasn't exactly an expert in farming shorthand, I moved toward the side and tapped the tread to get her attention.

Her eyes stayed locked on the horizon where Forrest ran with a large herd of rescues; someone had decided to go for a hoon because a flock of four-legged beasts flew in formation effortlessly up the hill, tails streaming, manes dancing, hooves thundering.

"Hey." I thumped the step, once again angry at the sheer bliss on her face. The absolute contentedness of this country moment to a city girl like her. I didn't like that she looked as if she'd fallen in love. I didn't like the way she melted and sighed and—

"*Oi!*" I grabbed her boot that was no longer box-fresh and new but covered in dirt with a scratch or two.

"Oh, sorry!" She snapped out of her trance, smiling with pink cheeks. "I was caught up."

"You can say that again."

"Jacob...this place." She opened her arms wide as if she could embrace all of Cherry River. "How do you get anything done out here? It's spectacular. It's amazing. It's the best place on earth."

"It's just a farm."

Her eyes turned sharp. "It's not just a farm. It's so much more than that, and you know it."

I glowered, daring her to say only good things happened here when bad things did on a regular basis.

Ignoring my look, Hope breathed, "Knowing you're a part of it? That you're linked somehow?" She shivered. "It's the best thing I've ever experienced. *This* is what I want. I don't know how I could ever go back to a city after this. How do people live in high-rises? How do they cram into trains or eat in crowded restaurants when this...*this*—" She once again followed the wave of horses as they slowed from a canter to a trot. "This is where souls live. This is real. This is—"

"This isn't yours," I snapped. "Don't fall too deep, Hope. Only heartbreak follows."

I hated that she felt the same way I did. I despised that she understood the loathing for society and the unwillingness to become close to others. She'd shared my world for two minutes—she wasn't *allowed* to understand.

She would go back to those cities and eat in those crowded places and travel on congested transport because she wasn't welcome here.

She upset my simple balance.

She made me wonder what life as free as her, as happy as her could be like and, in turn, threatened everything fundamental about me.

She stilled.

A cold breeze snapped from nowhere, licking around us. A breeze I'd always associated with my father but now just believed was coincidence.

My dad was gone.

He wasn't watching us. If he were, he'd be torn apart with how callously Hope paraded her life and health in his face.

Hope leaned over me, her tongue wetting her lower lip. "What if it's already too late?"

"What?" My heart stopped beating. "*What* did you say?"

"What if I've fallen, and there's no place else for me?"

Nausea filled my gut. "Then I guess you better discuss adoption with my mother. I know Dad always wanted a daughter. Suppose you'd do."

She flinched. "I know you're being deliberately cruel, but I see right through you."

Everything inside went cold. "You see nothing."

"I see everything."

"You're a child."

"No." She shook her head, hair spilling from her baseball cap. "I'm your friend."

That fucking word.

It drew blood.

It was a knife digging deep in my chest.

Ever so slowly, I reached out to grab the two handrails. "Stop saying that." With a painful hiss, I hauled myself up so I wasn't so beneath her. So she wasn't so above me. So we were on even ground.

Hope slipped off the tractor's seat, kneeling on the dusty, dirty floor where the pedals waited for commands. Her fingers dug into the rubber matting as she locked eyes with me, ferocity and fight equal to mine. "I see your fear. I see your anger. I see how you want to run but don't. I see you love but wish you didn't. I see how deeply you *feel*, Jacob, all the while begging you were heartless." Her hand came up; her fingertips kissed my cheek.

It physically hurt worse than any hug, touch, or smile.

"Don't." Everything inside me raged. I tore my face from her reach. "I've told you before. Don't touch me."

"And I say you need to be touched."

"I don't need anything."

"Oh, really?" Her gaze dropped to my mouth. "You don't need *something*? You don't lie in bed at night wanting—"

"Never."

Her eyes hooded. "Liar. I think you're hungry…just like me."

"I'm not like you."

"I think we're more alike than you'll admit."

I forced a laugh. "Why? Just because you want me, you think

I want you in return?"

She sucked in a breath. For a second, she arched away, but then her body softened. "I know I'm pushing you. I know I'm driving you crazy. And I know I'm breaking all my promises, but Jacob...you're right. I do want you. I want to *help* you."

"That's all you want? To help? Now who's the liar?"

Her voice turned feathery and windswept. "Fine. I want you in other ways. I want—"

"Stop." This had gone on long enough. "Get off my tractor." *Get out of my goddamn life.*

I gave orders to my fingers to unlock so I could drop to the ground, but they only squeezed tighter, hauled me higher, brought me closer.

"No." Her eyes flashed.

"Yes," I hissed.

"Not yet. We're finally getting somewhere."

"We're going around in circles."

"Only because you're too afraid to admit you feel what I do."

"I feel nothing."

"You feel *everything*. You're *alive*...you just wished you weren't."

"Shut up, Hope."

"No. Not until you accept that you're lying to yourself."

"*I'm* lying?" I bared my teeth. "*You're* the one lying. The one *believing* in lies. I don't want your help. I don't want you on my farm. I don't want anything from you." My breathing roughened as my lips tingled to smash on hers. To kiss her. To be normal and no longer be so goddamn afraid of finding something so precious only to be suicidal when it was lost. "I definitely don't want you."

"Once again, you're lying." Her chest rose and fell. "You're thinking about it. You've wondered."

"Never."

"I have. I've wondered what it would be like to kiss you."

Everything locked down. My cock swelled. Pain manifested in every cell. "Find something else to wonder about."

"That's impossible."

"Why?"

"Because when it comes to you...I can't think about anything else."

"Hope..." Breathing was a struggle. Everything was a goddamn struggle. Her voice was a trap, her eyes a cage. I was caught, drawn against my will to feel, to want, to crave. "Don't push me."

I can't do this.

Please, don't make me do this.

"Jacob..." Her eyelashes painted spidery shadows on pretty cheeks. A piece of grass hitched a ride in the valley of her sun-tinted breasts.

I was losing.

Losing myself.

Losing to her.

I shuddered as she came closer, crawling to me. "You don't have to be afraid of me."

"I'm not afraid."

"I think you are."

"*You* should be afraid. Afraid of what I'll do if you keep pushing me."

She smiled sadly. "I am. I'm afraid *for* you." Once again, she touched my cheek, branding me with venomous fingertips. "I know I shouldn't. I promised myself I'd stop, but today has shown me just how incredible life is. This place. This afternoon. *You.* You live in paradise, Jacob, but your mind ensures you live in hell. Please..."

She didn't continue, her cheeks pink and eyes imploring, full of desire and temptation.

I'd never had someone stand up to me this way.

Never had someone fight with me, killing me word by word.

She was my greatest nemesis.

She was my cruellest foe.

"Jacob...please just let me show you. Show you that you can have—"

I snatched her wrist, yanking her fingers from my face. "Have what? Love? Sex? What my parents had?"

She nodded. "Yes."

"You think I want those things with you?"

She flinched. "If you don't, then at least I've pushed you into admitting you want them with someone."

"Who *are* you?" My fingers tightened around her wrist.

"I'm you. I'm your opposite. I'm what you need."

"You're infuriating."

"That too." She rocked her wrist in my hold, activating hunter instincts, my heart racing to keep her captive.

I squeezed her harder. "You're ruining everything."

"Maybe." She sucked in a breath with a blood-heating hitch.

"Or maybe I'm fixing everything."

"Don't fool yourself."

"Stop *lying* to yourself."

"Stop being so goddamn stubborn."

"Kiss me and stop avoiding the truth."

Heat became a forest fire as we locked in a war.

I wanted to *kill* her.

I wanted to kiss her.

I wanted to be left the hell alone. "Enough." I forced myself to let her go. "I'm done with this."

"Don't." Her hand soared to my cheek again, her thumb tracing my bottom lip. "Don't run."

My cock left the realm of hard and turned into concrete. Concrete threatening to crack and splinter if it didn't have a tiny taste of whatever bristled between us.

She leaned closer, her gaze no longer temper-focused but hazed with need.

My mouth went dry. My heart stopped beating. The earth fissured beneath me, sending me into pits of despair.

"Kiss me…" Her command could barely be heard, snatched by the breeze. The same breeze that licked around us, cocooning us, fighting us.

"No."

"Please, Jacob."

I needed to get away.

Now.

But she had me snared, gutted, broken.

I had no free will anymore.

No earthly way of removing myself from this nightmare.

My back bellowed. My mind ran crazy with lust. It took all my willpower to meet her eyes and hiss, "*Leave.* You're fired."

The desire on her face flickered. Her stubbornness faltered for a second. A blissful second where my heart scrambled for fresh air.

"You can't fire a friend."

"You're not my friend."

"I am."

"You're my enemy."

She shook her head. "I'm not, can't you see?"

"Get off my land."

"No."

"I'll physically throw you out if you don't leave."

Her chin came up, her cajoling switching to anger. "Go ahead. But you'd have to touch me first. Touch me, Jacob. See if you're immune as you say you are when I'm seconds away from losing everything."

There was no fresh air because she'd stolen it. Every breath I inhaled Hope. I inhaled sunshine and lemonade and lust.

I wasn't just lost.

I was dead.

Murdered by the one thing I never wanted to feel.

"Hope...just stop." I was willing to concede defeat if she just left me the hell alone. I needed to run. To remember how to live in a world of love when I couldn't have any of it.

"I'm so sorry, Jacob." Her eyes glittered. "So sorry I'm hurting you."

"Then stop. Stop all of this."

"I can't."

"You mean, you won't."

She nodded, tears welling.

Something about this argument was different. It scratched me, scared me, scarred me.

Fucking *terrified* me.

Beneath my anger, beneath the attempt at a truce and the truth of pain, the broken kid inside me got on his knees for help.

I wasn't equipped for this. I was used to family accepting my desire to be left alone. I was conditioned to earn peace by pushing away those who cared.

Hope didn't give me those rewards.

She didn't slink away when I growled.

She didn't stop pushing me.

Pushing and pushing, always goddamn pushing.

"Leave."

"Like I said, you'll have to touch me first."

"If I touched you again, Hope Jacinta Murphy, you'd wish you'd run when I gave you the chance." My voice blistered the sky.

She froze, a thread of wariness decorated her face. "Try me."

"Get off my tractor."

"Make me."

"Get out of my life."

"Bite me." She snapped her teeth together. "I'm not going anywhere. Not yet. Not until—"

"You're leaving. Today."

"Only if you physically make me. Otherwise, I'm going to

stay. Today and tomorrow and all the days in the future. I'm in love with your land, Jacob Wild. I'm in love with your mother and your family and your horses, and I'm even falling for yo—"

"Fuck, stop. Stop. Just fucking *stop*." I lashed out, grabbing her wrist and jerking her toward me. I meant to yank her from the tractor. My mind was full of images of tossing her to the soft grass, leaping onto the machine, and driving away to somewhere I could find sanity.

But the second I touched her again…*shit*.

That was my first mistake.

Pulling her closer until we were nose to nose was my second.

She froze as we almost bumped foreheads. I waited for her to arch back, to give me room, to get out of my personal space, but she just hovered there. Her green eyes as vibrant and as unforgiving as some emerald river, her button nose pink and cheeks shiny with temper.

My fingers wrapped tighter around her wrist.

And this time, I couldn't let her go.

I'd run out of strength.

She'd drained me, ruined me.

She'd won.

I forgot why I needed to keep my distance.

I forgot why being happy was a sin.

I forgot why I had promises that kept me locked here and why I didn't let people get close.

I forgot about all of it.

All I saw was Hope.

Her eyelashes, her chin, her mouth.

And I did something I'd never done before.

A twenty-one-year-old guy, who cursed his own species and swore an oath of celibacy to avoid the agony of broken love, chose that moment to condemn himself.

I blamed the concussion.

I blamed the sun and meadow and Hope.

Oh, I blamed Hope.

Definitely, *definitely* Hope.

This was her fault.

All of this.

Especially this.

This.

Kiss.

I swooped up before I could change my mind.

Our lips smashed together.

Hope cried out.

I groaned.

Pain bruised between us followed by mind-shattering relief.

Relief to touch and not fight it.

Relief to feel contact and not fear it.

Relief to find a tiny taste of the pleasure I'd been battling ever since Hope arrived and was no longer a timid ten-year-old but a feisty seventeen-year-old who wouldn't take no for an answer.

Her fingers dove into my hair, dislodging my cowboy hat to tumble down my back. Her lips parted beneath mine, her tongue eager and brave, darting into my mouth before I could comprehend exactly what I'd done.

The silky slipperiness of her, the faint lemonade taste, the heat that rivalled the sun.

I snapped.

Dragging her toward me by her wrist, I grabbed her around the waist and half fell, half lowered her to the ground. Our lips never unlocked, messy and fast, hungry and unschooled.

My hands splayed over her hips as I pushed her against the huge tractor wheel, trapping her in place. My back bellowed as I leaned against her, weighing her down from mouth to toes.

She shivered. A deep moan escaped her, filling my lungs as my hardness found the welcome parting of her thighs.

Her kiss switched from wild to frantic.

My hands cupped her head.

Hers squeezed my ass.

I wanted to punish her for pushing me.

I wanted to curse her, climb into her, get her naked, and never let her go again.

She was maddening and frightening and everything I'd always avoided.

Yet having her in my arms, I was free.

Free to suck her tongue and bite her lip and squeeze her close. So fucking close we both struggled to breathe, fighting a physical war rather than one filled with words. Our teeth clacked as our kiss deepened, our heads danced, and tongues tangled.

What the hell was this...this *insanity*?

Nothing else mattered but this.

Nothing else entered my mind but this.

I would happily *die* in this.

Die in this kiss.

Kill for this kiss.

I needed more.

I needed everything.

She squirmed in my arms, brushing hard things and sending violence ripping through me.

"You're killing me." I kissed her with all the aggression she'd caused. "What the fuck did you do?" My cock begged for touch—*her* touch.

I wanted to goddamn cry that I'd prevented myself from feeling such things, all while my heart shot itself because it knew it would never be whole after this.

It was cursed.

For always.

"Jake—" Her teeth caught my bottom lip, followed by a lick and a kiss.

I lost all control.

She *made* me lose control.

My height meant I had to duck to gather her close. I hugged her delicious body against mine, pressing my excruciating ache into her.

Years of strict rules and self-preservation tactics all dissolved with the desire for more.

I fell to my knees, dragging her down with me.

She pushed me into the thick grass, straddling me.

Not once did we stop kissing.

We weren't human anymore.

We were blood and bone and bruising, brutal desperation.

I didn't know if my eyes were open or closed. All I saw was darkness, hunger, need. She didn't push me away as I pressed her deeper into my lap. She didn't tell me to stop as my fingers slid up her belly and found her breasts.

She encouraged me.

She spurred me on, fighting to get closer, pushing me down as if she wanted to lock me against the very same earth she'd fallen in love with.

I couldn't catch my breath as we fought. Messy and out of control with lips burning and tongues licking and hands claiming every inch of each other.

There was no first anymore.

No first kiss or first touch or first flirt.

We'd demolished every law, and I wanted, *begged* to finish every other first.

Her hand dove between us, fingers rubbing hard against the steel in my jeans.

I nipped her in approval, grabbing her wrist and pressing her palm over me. Fingers weren't enough. I wanted her entire hand.

Fumbling for her singlet, I wrenched it halfway up her belly. Our mouths were wet and hot, our breathing haggard.

Nothing had ever felt so good, so intoxicating, so *right*.

I couldn't stop kissing her long enough to pull the fabric over her head.

But it didn't matter anyway.

Because thundering hooves echoed in the land beneath us like a war drum.

Closer and closer.

A terrified call from a mother who was overprotective and fought against death every day like me.

And the world came smashing back.

And I remembered why I could never do this sort of thing.

I pulled away.

Hope launched to her feet.

I flopped onto my back.

And the consequences of what I'd done broke me.

Chapter Thirty

HOPE

* * * * * *

IT WAS MORTIFYING.

Absolutely, tummy-churning *mortifying*.

What had I been *thinking?*

I had to have been drunk. Drunk on life, on farming, on everything that tingled in my blood. I'd just been so *happy*. So light and giddy and caught up in the magic of a dream come true.

But that wondrous joy had made me loose-lipped and stupidly courageous.

I should *never* have said those things to Jacob.

I should *never* have been so idiotic to push him into kissing me.

God!

That person goading him wasn't me. That person kissing him had been a crazy, reckless girl who put everything on the line in one insanely tense fight.

A week had passed since then.

A week since I'd almost broken Jacob, destroyed myself, and somehow enjoyed the exquisite sensation of his lips on mine, his tongue tangling with mine, his body pressed against mine.

I still couldn't believe it was real.

It had to be a dream, right?

A kiss from Jacob wasn't something I'd ever earn in reality. And certainly not the kiss we'd both tripped head first into. The kiss that changed me as a person, woke up my soul, and shot alive my heart in ways I never believed possible.

But it *had* happened because the mortification was still there.

The shame and horror when Della caught me clinging and kiss-drunk on top of her son within viewing distance of her house. When Jacob had kissed me, I didn't think about who might see. When the touch and taste of his lips met mine, my thinking capacity was done.

Finished.

I became a creature of lust. I wasn't responsible for my actions. I think back now and blush at the force and speed things escalated.

All because of *me*.

I'd attacked him—pure and simple.

First with words and then with touch.

I'd done *everything* I said I wouldn't, and I'd made Jacob hate me even more.

But the crazy thing was?

He'd attacked me back.

He'd kissed *me*.

Yanking the brush through my hair, I tugged a little too hard. My cheeks pinked in the mirror, relieving the angst and sickening guilt when Della halted her galloping horse, threw the reins away, and leapt to our side.

God, I was her *guest*.

I slept under her roof, ate her food, and lived in luxury thanks to her hospitality. And what had I done? I'd pushed her son into the grass, mauled him, and who knew what would've happened if she hadn't arrived.

That was the power Jacob had over me.

He turned me into a girl I didn't really like. A girl who did things she promised she wouldn't do. The urge to help him, heal him, *love* him overwhelmed me to the point where I was no longer in control.

And what made it even worse?

Della didn't *care* we'd practically been tearing each other's clothes off. She didn't even look at me as I turned scarlet and tugged my singlet down as fast as I could.

She'd merely thrown herself at Jacob and grabbed him as if certain he was dead. She'd shaken him, glowered at him, and demanded to know if he needed an ambulance.

And the whole story came out.

Della had experienced a terrible case of déjà vu. The meadow wasn't helping her nerves as it continued to gather a ledger of incidents. First, Ren collapsed from his condition after leaping off a tractor, then she saw her son tumble from the very same tractor his father had.

Thanks to her husband passing out in that meadow, Della didn't think. She didn't see me. She only saw another loved one being claimed by death far too early.

That made me doubly guilty because it was *me* who'd pushed Jacob to the ground.

Me who'd straddled him into the dirt. Me who—

Argh!

I yanked the brush harder, trying to shut up my thoughts.

It was over.

Della was okay. Jacob said he was fine. And he'd barely looked at me since.

Life had fallen into a taut rhythm where I still helped Jacob with his work, but whatever chemistry existed between us had been locked behind a fireproof door, and Jacob had become immune.

My heart kicked unhappily as I slipped a black T-shirt over my lacy white bra and clutched my silver locket. The lace from my mother and the jewellery from my lover.

Lover?

You kissed one *time.*

You've been working together for a week, and he's barely spoken two words to you since.

He's hardly your lover.

Giving my reflection the bird, I hauled on a pair of jeans and left the bathroom.

I could usually bypass Della at this time of the morning, but today, she caught me.

She stepped from her bedroom wing as I exited the bathroom.

I smiled shyly. "Oh, morning, Della."

We'd cleared the air a few nights ago when we'd had dinner, just the two of us, and I'd explained my role in what'd happened.

I'd told her how I pushed him. How I said things. How I did stuff I probably shouldn't have.

Instead of scolding me, she'd apologised profusely for jumping to conclusions and ruining our moment. There were no awkward warnings not to get involved with her son. No 'you're both too young' conversation or request for me to leave.

She'd been so understanding and sad at the same time. Sad because she knew what I knew.

Jacob was never going to forgive me for what I'd done.

I might as well leave because whatever friendship we'd managed to conjure was now dead.

She smiled, lack of sleep and age-old grief shadowing pretty blue eyes. "Morning, Hope. Much planned today?"

"Not sure." I shrugged. "I think Jacob said we're baling the back paddock. Something about hundreds of bales that need storing before the dew settles."

"Ah, you're in for a late one then. Take a pair of thick gloves. You'll need them." Heading toward the kitchen, she added, "We'll all help you load them onto the trailer and into the barn. You can't be expected to lift so many bales on your own, and Jacob definitely isn't lifting any. Not with his bad back."

"Wait? You know about that?"

She tapped her nose. "I always know."

I snickered. "I had a feeling you would. I did tell him to tell you."

"Good luck telling him to do anything."

I sighed. "I'm beginning to understand that."

"You'll win him round again, you'll see." She poured water into the kettle. "He can't hold a grudge forever."

"You sure about that?"

We shared a smile before she shrugged. "Not really. But if anyone can get into Jacob's head, you can."

What about getting into his heart?

"Guess I'll see you later?" I asked, my pulse already racing at seeing her son and spending yet another stressful day with him.

"Wouldn't miss it." She blew me a kiss as I headed to the door as if this was my house, and she was my family, and this was the life I'd always lived.

Something was inherently odd that I was so at home here with dirt under my nails while fighting with a farm boy. Odd that I didn't miss my old life, raised by nannies and daughter of a famous actor.

Odd that I'd left that world so easily.

Yet to leave this one…it killed me just thinking about.

* * * * *

"You shouldn't be lifting that."

Jacob ignored me, his shirtless back rippling with tanned sinew and muscle as he hauled a perfectly formed hay bale from earth to trailer.

Tugging my overly big gloves back into position, I moved to stand in front of him. "I know you're mad at me, but your back, Jake. You can't lift—"

"I'm not mad." He swiped his forearm over his chin, removing a stray piece of hay. "I'm furious. And don't call me Jake."

I blinked. "Furious at me?"

"No. At me." He sighed heavily. "I should never have kissed you last week."

I froze.

We hadn't brought up that subject.

It was totally off-limits, despite working ten-hour shifts together every day. I'd respected his coldness and desire to forget it ever happened, and honestly, I'd been too afraid to bring it up in case he asked me to leave.

I'd *loved* kissing him. I'd loved touching him. I desperately wanted more. But if he asked me to go...*God.*

Glancing toward the horizon where the sun made its lazy way to bed in a wash of pink and gold, I forced myself to be brave. He'd brought it up. We had to talk about it sometime or later.

Avoiding looking at the way sweat trickled down his stomach or the tense way his shoulders bunched, I whispered, "Kissing you was one of the best things I've ever done."

He flinched. "Yet it was one of my worst."

Ouch.

I rubbed at the hole he'd punctured in my chest. Pacing away, I kicked at some hay that the baler had missed. We'd worked eleven hours straight, turning two huge fields from rowed grass into perfect square bales wrapped up with twine.

We needed to get those bales into storage before the evening dew settled. We didn't have time to discuss our lack of a love story.

"I'm sorry, Hope. That wasn't fair." Jacob slouched against the rim of the large trailer. "What I meant was...I let our fight turn into something it shouldn't. That's all."

"Our fight was about how we felt about each other. It made sense it would lead to something like that."

His head whipped up, eyes dark. "How we *felt* about each other?"

"Oh, come on. I like you, Jacob. You must know that by now."

His jaw clenched. "Doesn't change anything."

"It could." My throat threatened to close. "If you wanted it to."

"I don't."

I nodded, unable to find the strength to reply.

We stood in painful silence for the longest heartbeat before he kicked off from the trailer and came toward me. "I don't want to hurt you, Hope. I've been going over how to tell you this without coming across as a heartless asshole, but…" He swallowed before forcing himself to continue. "I know you think I'm just being stubborn when I say I'm not looking for a friend. But…the honest to God truth is I'm not."

I tripped back a step, unable to ignore the urge to flee. "Oh, that's—"

"Don't say it's fine because I know it's not. I'm doing my best to stay calm to show you how serious I am about this. I know you think I'm some charity case who needs help. I know you think I need taken care of but—"

"I don't think that. I'm not pushing you out of charity."

"Either way, I'm grateful for what you've done for me. Your hard work has been much appreciated, but…" He sighed long and harsh.

"There's that but again."

He gave me a tight smile.

I gulped. "But…you want me to leave? Like you asked before we kissed?" My voice was the size of a field mouse.

He tensed. Our eyes tangled. And in that stare, I saw everything he didn't want to say. Everything he would *never* say. The fact that he *did* feel something for me. Felt something that terrified him enough to stay far away.

"That was said in anger, forget it. I'm not asking you to go." He ran a hand over his face, smearing a streak of dirt. "I'm just asking for…space."

"Space?"

"For the time being, yes."

"Can I still work with you?"

"Yes."

"Can I still talk to you?"

"Of course."

"What about hanging out with your mother and family?"

"I *want* you to hang out with them. They're amazing people."

"Then…" My heart had never hurt so much. "How is that not a friendship, Jacob? How can we spend all those hours together and not be bound in some sort of connection?"

"I don't know." He shrugged as if it grieved him to have people love him. As if he already mourned the love that could be stolen. "I just know I can't care for you the way you want me to. I don't like how it scrambles me up inside. I don't like being so mean to you. That isn't me and it sucks that I keep being cruel when you're only trying to be kind."

I pocketed those sentences. I bottled up that pain. I saved them for the day I'd walk away from Jacob Wild and entertain a proper job—a job I was more suited to than playing a farmer's hired hand.

I didn't know what to say.

Jacob scuffed his boot into the earth. "I've been thinking about this all week. It's been driving me insane. I can't lie and say that kiss wasn't amazing. It was. It caught me off guard. It showed me...how easy it could be to—" He shook his head. "Anyway, I hope...I hope I haven't hurt you. I'm sorry I've been so rude to you. It's just...I can't cope with closeness the way other people can." His ebony eyes met mine. "Can...can you understand that?"

I gritted my teeth, doing my best not to show how badly he'd decimated me. The belief I'd held since we were kids slowly dissolved, fading away like smoke.

He'd finally been honest with me and instead of appreciating that, I wanted to hurt him back.

I wanted to yell, *'Please love me!'* Instead, I forced myself to be better than the broken anger inside me. Dropping my gaze, I whispered, "I'll always be your...um, not-friend. For as long as you let me stay."

I had no backbone but only because he'd stolen it. Just like he'd stolen my lungs, my heart, my soul. He'd stolen them so many years ago, yet he didn't want them. He'd never asked for them or given his in return. And although I ached for a heart and begged for a soul and wished for a backbone, I had no idea how to claim them back.

"I'll be a good host to you from now on. I promise." He smiled. "I won't be so...argumentative."

"Oh, well, that's a relief." I did my best to laugh when all I wanted to do was cry.

I'd lost.

I'd failed.

It was over.

"Guess we better get back to work." He gave me a haphazard, half-hearted grin before turning and striding toward the trailer. His shoulders came up, a curse falling from his lips. "Ah, shit."

I moved to follow him, my instinct to help still strong, but then I caught sight of what he had.

At the real reason he'd cursed.

And it wasn't because of me.

Della, Cassie, John, Chip, Nina, and even my dad made their way through the gate and toward us in the field.

What on earth?

Della had said she'd come help, but I hadn't expected the entire family. And I definitely didn't expect my father. When had he arrived? What was he doing here?

Please, don't be here to take me home.

Even though it made sense to leave. Even though it would probably be for the best, the thought of no longer living at Cherry River snaked terror around my heart.

I wasn't ready to go. I would *never* be ready to go.

Even if Jacob and I forever remained nothing more than neighbours, I loved this place too much to turn my back on it.

"He didn't say he was coming." I slipped to Jacob's side, waving at the workforce coming to aid us. "He's not exactly dressed for this kind of work. He won't last ten bales."

Jacob gave me a strained smile. "You sound more and more like me every day." With a soft chuckle, he added, "You're getting possessive of the land, thinking others can't care for it as well as you, wanting to protect it."

I eyed him. "Is that why you didn't want me working with you?"

His gaze slid to the horizon and the endless heavens above. "One of the reasons."

I desperately wanted to ask what the other reasons where. But I couldn't handle more bitter honesty tonight.

Jacob sucked in a breath and strode forward, welcoming the new labourers.

And I followed him, patching up my broken pieces, being the brave little actress I was born to be.

Chapter Thirty-One

JACOB

* * * * * *

"SO YOU'VE BEEN keeping Hope busy, I take it?"

I looked up from stabbing the roast chicken Grandpa John had made. Hope's dad sat amongst my family for dinner, thinking he belonged but definitely didn't.

Last night, we hadn't finished bucking hay until well after midnight. The pizzas Mom had delivered to the barn kept us going until the last trailer load, then we'd all crashed into our respective beds, with Graham in the hotel he'd booked under an alias (no way was he sleeping in my mom's house).

I'd been jealous of the relieved groans upon finishing. The achy muscles and tired waves goodbye.

That should've been me.

I wanted the bruises and blisters.

I wanted the sweat and blissful sensation of a cold shower after such hot, hard work. Instead, Mom and Grandpa John had ganged up on me, threatening to tie me to the TV for a week of forced rehabilitation if I didn't drive the tractor while they had the fun job.

It unmanned me.

It made me feel lacking and argumentative and unneeded.

I hated that they'd known about my injury all along.

Couple that with the stress of telling Hope I couldn't be what she wanted me to be...yeah, I hadn't slept.

Then again, I hadn't slept since I kissed her.

"Busy in what way?" I asked coldly. "We've both been very busy." I meant to sound indifferent, but the sentence reeked of a challenge. As if I'd hinted Hope and I had been busy doing *other* things.

Goddammit.

I couldn't trust myself anymore.

I couldn't even speak without second-guessing everything I said.

Hope's face heated beside her father as she gave me a small shake of her head. "I've been helping Jacob do some chores, that's all."

"That's not all," Mom cut in. "She's been working so hard. Look at those biceps. If I didn't know she came from Hollywood, I would've said she'd always been a farmer's girl."

Graham narrowed his eyes. "I said the same thing to her last night." He gave me a glare. "As long as she's a girl who farms and isn't a *farmer's* girl, it's great."

Hope shrank deeper into her seat.

I knew what Graham was hinting at.

And God, the temptation to claim she was mine, to announce we'd made out like animals danced on my tongue.

But I was no longer that guy. I'd done my utmost to be civil to her yesterday and I refused to continue making her life difficult.

Our fights only drew painful emotion from me when all I wanted was to treat her just like any hired help—safe and distant.

She wasn't mine.

She would never be mine.

That was the way I wanted it.

The way I *needed* it.

With a quick glance at Hope, I said, "She's whatever she wants to be."

Hope flinched, her gaze welling with all the agony I'd painted her with yesterday. I hadn't wanted to hurt her. In a way, she'd hurt herself. Not once did I encourage her crush on me. I'd done the opposite. I'd been cruel and short-tempered, and really, this mess was her fault.

However, it didn't stop the fact that I'd been in hell ever since our kiss.

Literal, physical *hell.*

Fighting myself, my heart, my body's need for connection. Her taste still tainted my tongue. Her breathy moans. Her eager fingers. Her sweet tongue.

I could barely function.

I obsessed over her.

I broke because of her.

She'd shown me how easy it would be to fall. Way, *way* too easy to allow my heart to kill me.

The week we'd worked side by side in silence, I'd beaten

myself up for the way I'd treated her. I'd relived every fight and replayed our kiss over and over and *over* until all I could think about was her.

And that was the worst thing I could ever do.

I couldn't *stop* thinking about her.

I couldn't stop the hunger.

It drove me insane, and I lost myself to it.

I'd known I couldn't tolerate one drop of affection without breaking, and I'd been right. A single dose of togetherness and I was willing to cut open my chest and tell Hope to take whatever she goddamn wanted because it was all useless anyway.

But then the nightmares started.

The living breathing torments of her coughing, her dying, her gone.

And it hurt.

So fucking much.

And I wasn't strong enough.

For any of it.

So I'd plotted my way out of purgatory and shut down such needy desires. I locked away that compulsion for human connection and remembered that love became loss, weddings became funerals, families became dust.

That helped me yesterday when I finally got up the balls to tell her that I would be polite from now on. I would be helpful and gracious and do whatever it took to make her stay the best it could be.

But that was all I could offer her.

No more arguments.

No more kisses.

Just civil, meaningless interaction where neither of us got hurt.

Graham turned to his daughter. "And what do you want to be, Little Lace?"

She gulped, pretending cutting a piece of broccoli was way more involved than reality. "Um, not sure."

I hated that I knew she had no other family. That it was just her and her dad. No grandparents, no uncles or aunts.

I was the loner yet I had a family that didn't let me stay alone. Whereas she was the quintessential family lover with only one.

"She wants to work the land," I murmured, unable to tear my eyes from Hope. "She's good at it too. You should buy her a hobby farm and let her do whatever she wants with it."

Graham stiffened. "She could buy her own. She has her own income." Looking at his daughter with pride, he said, "You know, Steve has been asking when you'll be back. He has a role in a crime show he thinks would be perfect for you. The lead."

I couldn't stop watching Hope, and I didn't miss the way she tensed but grinned as bright as the stars. "That sounds great. Thanks."

"Want me to tell him you'll audition for it?"

"Um…" Hope placed the broccoli on her tongue, giving herself time to reply. After she'd chewed for far longer than necessary, she said quietly, "Can I, um, think about it? There's still so much to do here, and…and I'd like to stay a bit longer, if that's okay?"

Graham jerked as if he wasn't expecting such a reply. But then he nodded sadly. "You don't want to come home."

Everyone stilled.

Hope stared at her plate. "It's not that. I'm beyond grateful you came to see me. That you helped us last night. It's amazing to see you, and I love you so much, but…eh—" Her gaze shot to my mother's, begging her for help.

A strange kind of possessiveness clawed me. She looked at Mom for help. She'd accepted my desire to stay distant and didn't expect me to fight her battles.

Goddammit, that hurt.

How did I stop it from hurting?

How did I turn off emotions when they were the worst thing in the world?

Mom cleared her throat. "It's not that she doesn't want to go home, Graham. She's just too kind-hearted to leave in the middle of a busy summer." Her attempt at damage control couldn't hide the stares father and daughter gave each other. The admittance from Hope that she wasn't into acting. And the disappointment from Graham for finally seeing what he'd ignored all along.

"Besides, Jacob hurt his back. He's healing, but Hope has been invaluable. It's fine if she stays with us," Mom murmured. "For however long she wants."

Graham looked up, smiling gently. "That's very kind of you, Ribbon."

Wait…what the—?

Gasps sounded around the table.

My hands fisted around my knife and fork.

Ribbon was my father's nickname.

Ribbon was full of love and marriage and history.

Ribbon was a name *no one* else was allowed to use.

It was buried, just like he was.

What the hell was this jackass doing, using something that wasn't his to use? That would *never* be his?

Mom shot me a worried glance. John reached over and planted his big paw over my shaking fist. Aunt Cassie hushed up Nina, and Chip took a swig of beer.

But it was Graham who stopped me from launching across the table and punching him.

"Sorry." He held up his hands. "I didn't mean to use that. It came out. Habit from the movie, I'm afraid." He bowed his head, true contrition in his gaze. "Sorry, Della. I know what that nickname means, and it wasn't my intention to—"

"It's fine." Mom grinned, not doing a very good job at hiding the faint gleam of tears. "Been a long time since I've heard that. It's…it's just a shock, that's all."

Graham hunched. "My mistake. I won't do it again."

He was right because after this dinner—a dinner thanking everyone for their help hauling last night—Graham was going back to Hollywood, and I wished he'd take his daughter with him.

I wanted my farm back.

I wanted my life back.

I wanted an end to this pain.

Chapter Thirty-Two

HOPE

* * * * * *

"LET ME CARRY that."

I shook my head, walking away from Jacob with the heavy sack of horse feed in my arms. "Nuh-uh, I can manage."

Ever since Dad left three days ago, Jacob and I had fallen into a different rhythm. Trying on new personas to see which would cause the least amount of friction, while pretending we were okay with whatever mess existed between us.

There were so many things we hadn't addressed—topics that were banished to a coffin of unmentionables, just like my questions on death. Life had moved on, pretending to be simple but really paving a treacherous road over complicated.

I'd seen him watching me as I'd kissed Dad goodbye.

I'd kept watching him as Dad kissed me in return.

His body clamped up, his lips thinned, his eyes became unreadable.

But I could read him.

He saw so many kisses.

He saw so much affection.

He saw endless ways to be hurt.

And he'd shut down even more.

His withdrawal made me miss my dad a lot.

I wanted advice. I wanted acceptance. Working beside my father until well past midnight the other day—laughing at his city ways and doting on his exhaustion of hauling hay—all reminded me that love wasn't something to be fought.

It was something to be valued, appreciated, *protected*.

But once again, I'd hurt him just like I'd hurt Jacob.

I'd hurt two men just by being myself.

I wasn't my father's Little Lace anymore. And I wasn't leaving like Jacob wanted.

All in all, I was a disappointment to everyone.

How sad was that? So sad that neither men could understand I didn't *intentionally* cause them pain.

I was just being *me*.

I was growing into who *I* wanted to be.

If others didn't like that…where did that leave me?

Alone?

Not wanted?

Forever having to fake who I was to please them?

Jacob huffed. "It weighs as much as you do."

"As if you know how much I weigh."

He stalked toward me, eyeing me up and down. Before I could get out of his way, he scooped me from the ground and held me *and* the sack of feed. "Yep, just as I suspected. Same as the grain."

"Hey, put me down." I wriggled in his embrace, making him stiffen.

He dropped me to my feet, then plucked the feed from my grip without any effort. Meanwhile, my body tingled from where he'd touched me, and I felt a hundred times heavier with need.

I could stay at Cherry River my entire life. I could hang around with Jacob until I was old and grey and a total spinster with a hundred cats, yet he still wouldn't drop his guard for anything more than polite acquaintances.

However, the fact he'd just willingly touched me in a public place was shocking. But then again, the reason he had wasn't.

He was old-fashioned; raised with a gentleman's code even if it was a little outdated. Now his back was on the mend, he didn't let me do any heavy lifting. If he deemed me too fragile for a task, he grew gruff and bossy until I let him do it.

To start with, I'd fought for equality.

In the end, I'd given up.

It wasn't worth the argument even though I was more than capable.

Crossing my arms, standing in the middle of the massive warehouse where tractor parts, fence equipment, veterinary supplies, and stock feed loomed high on industrial shelving, I narrowed my eyes. "If you've taken yet another job from me, what exactly is there left to do before we go home?"

Home.

Cherry River was only a ten-minute drive away, but I missed it already.

I missed its open spaces and blue skies and peaceful serenity.

The local township wasn't big, but it still held concrete and glass and people. People who smiled friendly-like but couldn't hide their edge whenever they looked at Jacob.

"If you're so willing to be of service, head inside and grab some powdered mag and Epsom salts."

"Powdered what now?"

"Magnesium."

"For...?"

"For the horses who get crazy from grass. And before you ask, the Epsom salts are in case any of the herd brews an abscess or two."

"Right." Nodding with importance, I gave him a smile. "I can do that."

"Good." Jacob winced as if already afraid of the word I could say in response.

The word that opened old wounds and prevented scars from forming over age-old pain.

I swallowed it down, whispering it to myself instead.

Fine.

"What's next after this?" I asked, deliberately changing the subject and allowing Jacob's tension to unravel.

He studied me with narrowed eyes before muttering, "I suppose we could go eat before returning to Cherry River."

"Eat, as in eat in a *restaurant?*"

He rolled his eyes. "Yes, in a restaurant. That a problem?"

I hid the bubbly joy working its way through my bloodstream. "No problem. I haven't had a burger and fries in forever."

I swallowed more words I knew he wouldn't approve of.

I've never been out in public with you before.

I never thought you'd take me out.

Could this be classified as a date?

Could lunch between two people who'd known each other forever, worked together every day, and shared a kiss mean something other than just 'getting food?'

Don't be ridiculous, Hope.

There is nothing, and there will never be anything more between you.

"Yeah, well. A burger would be good. I'm starving." Jacob gave me another strange look. "Go grab the mag and salt. I'll come find you once I've put this in the truck."

"Okey-dokey."

Jacob rolled his eyes. "Why are you so chipper all the time?

It's annoying." Not waiting for my reply, he hoisted the feed onto his shoulder and strode toward his already loaded truck while I traversed the large warehouse to the attached building where smaller, more valuable things were stored.

Cooler air wafted over me as the sliding doors welcomed then closed behind me, hushing up the sounds of old farmers and forklifts.

Shelves upon shelves of drenching, stock vitamins, wet weather clothing, and milking supplies created a maze.

Where on earth will I find mag and salt?

"Hi, you look a little lost." A soft chuckle whipped my head to the left where a guy about my age smiled. He wore scruffy Wranglers with a red shirt depicting him as staff. His hair matched mine in colour but he had blue eyes, not green.

He was cute, and I blushed as he studied me a little too closely.

"Um, actually, I'm looking for powdered mag and Epsom salts."

"Horsey chick, huh?"

I puffed up with pride. "Yup."

"I used to ride when I was younger. Fell off, though, and never got back on."

"That sucks. They do say you should get back on after a fall. Otherwise, you might never."

The guy laughed. "Well, maybe you could convince me to give it another go sometime."

I froze. Did he…did he just ask me out, or was this small-town flirting?

"Yeah, maybe." I smiled brightly so I wouldn't hurt his feelings. "So, can you, eh, show me where to go?"

He swiped a hand through his hair. "I'll do you one better. I'll escort you there myself." Striding forward, he looked over his shoulder for me to follow. "Come on."

"Okaaay." With a hesitant look behind me, mainly to see if Jacob had finished stockpiling, I chased after the red-shirted guy.

He guided me around a few shelves before stopping in the middle of one with a sign saying equine supplements. Tapping his lower lip with his finger, he scanned the bags of different minerals and vitamins before selecting two and handing them to me. "There you go. All sorted."

"Cool. Thanks so much." I opened my arms to take the bags. "Right, then. I guess I'll go pay." I scanned the store for the checkout.

Before I could leave, the guy asked, "You new in town?"

"Um, kind of."

"Moved here or just visiting?"

His smile was eager and eyes approving. The fact he didn't know who I was, who my father was, and most likely had never read a tabloid or gossip magazine in his life was refreshing. I wasn't used to being flirted with. Brian, back in Scotland, had been the only one to approach me, and I suspected only because he thought he could marry into money.

I'd never been normal enough or left un-chaperoned by my father or Keeko to be at the mercy of flirty shopkeepers.

I blushed. It was nice to be appreciated. To be *noticed*.

To be liked for just being *me*.

"Just visiting, but if I had my way, I'd move here in a heartbeat."

"Move to a small town like this?" He shrugged. "Why?"

"Why not? It has everything you need. A cinema, small shopping mall, restaurants. And miles upon miles of open spaces. It's heaven."

"I guess." He rubbed the back of his neck. "So you've seen the local sights then? Someone's shown you Clover Waterfall and taken you to Sock Gully?"

"No, not yet."

He perked up. "You should. They're awesome. The waterfall has some great swimming holes farther downriver, and in the gully, someone has created a walkway in the treetops. You have to strap on a harness so you don't fall, but the adrenaline rush is awesome."

"Sounds great."

Why had Jacob never told me about those places?

The guy held out his hand. "I'm Carter."

Awkwardly, I shifted the two bags into one arm and reached out to shake his hand. "I'm Hope."

He squeezed me with warm, strong fingers. "Nice to meet you, Hope."

My cheeks heated as he held on for a little too long before letting me go.

He glanced at the ground before catching my gaze with determination mixed with worry.

I knew that concoction well. I approached Jacob that way most of the time. Brave enough to want something from him but fearful enough of the consequences.

"You're really pretty, Hope."

Shock and embarrassment ripped a stupid giggle from my lips. "Um, thanks."

"You're welcome." He grinned, growing a little more confident. "I'd love to take you out sometime. You know...if you're keen? I don't have a horse, but I do have a car, so I can take you some places and show you around."

"Wow, that's—" I stiffened. Prickles danced down my back, and I knew, just *knew* we were no longer alone.

Jacob was watching me.

Jacob was listening.

And I didn't know how that made me feel, knowing the boy I'd chased for far too long was watching another boy chase me.

Was that karma?

Or merely a recipe for disaster?

In all honesty, I wasn't looking for more complications with dating or making new friends here. But the fact that Carter liked me after only knowing me for a few minutes made me a tiny bit vindictive.

"You know what? That sounds nice. Thank you."

Carter's boyish face blazed with happy disbelief. "Wow, really? You'll go out with me?"

A fuming presence appeared at the top of the row, cowboy hat shielding his gaze, fists clenched by his sides. Other customers dispersed, leaving us in a pocket of silence.

Jacob moved slowly. So slowly it was as if he stalked me, hunted me, knew I had nowhere to run and would take his time mauling me.

Carter was oblivious as Jacob arrived beside him and tipped his chin so his midnight eyes locked onto mine.

There, I saw things I'd been desperate to see for months.

Possession.

Connection.

Want.

And all my silly ideals of agreeing to date a boy who could never replace the one I truly wanted evaporated.

"You finished here?" Jacob said icily, carefully putting his hands in his pockets as if to prevent him from punching Carter.

"Yeah, almost." Trying to keep the peace, I added, "Carter, you know Jacob Wild, right?"

Carter flinched. "Eh, yeah. Hey, man. You went to school

with my older brother, Yan."

Jacob nodded stiffly.

"Carter kindly offered to show me Clover Waterfall and Sock Gully. Want to come with us?" I kept my tone light and carefree, ignoring the challenge of testosterone flying around.

Carter's shoulders fell as he looked at me. "Oh, you want to go out in a group?"

I swallowed, keeping a careful eye on Jacob. "If that's okay? I'm staying with Jacob's family. They're my hosts. It'd be rude not to invite him."

"It would be *very* rude." Jacob looked me up and down as if I'd done something unforgivable and he was seconds away from throwing Carter into the horse vitamins.

"Exactly. That's why I'm inviting you." I sniffed.

Jacob looked threateningly at Carter. "She has it wrong, by the way. She's staying with *me*, not my family. She's working for me. She's my employee, and I say if she has free time to go gallivanting around town."

"*Gallivanting* around?" I snickered. "There'll be no gallivanting, Jake. It's just spending the day outdoors."

His eyes flashed to mine, heat mixed with annoyance. I knew his irritation was because I'd called him Jake again.

He scowled. "I don't remember agreeing to give you days off."

My temper pinched to respond. "I don't remember signing some slave contract saying I couldn't."

Jacob stepped toward me, his heat and electricity frying my senses. "You kinda did when you agreed to work for me until I fired you."

I matched his step with one of my own, bringing our chests to almost touching. "You're saying you'll fire me if I go out with Carter?"

"I'm saying try it and find out."

"You're so pig-headed."

"You're so naïve."

"You don't control me, *Jake*."

"You're my responsibility, *Hope*." He pointed at Carter. "Waterfalls can wait. Feeding a mob of hungry horses can't."

"Why can't you just admit you—"

"I won't admit anything." Jacob lowered his head, his brow shadowing turbulent eyes. "Why can't you stop being so damn—"

"Um, this is nice and all." Carter backed away, hands raised in surrender. "But I've got to go." Throwing me an apologetic look, he said, "Nice meeting you, Hope. I'll, um, be in touch. Catch you guys around." He spun on his heel, practically bolting toward another customer for shelter.

"Ugh, now look what you did." I planted hands on my hips. "You scared him off. He didn't even get my number."

"You're lucky that's all I did."

"He was just being nice, Jacob."

"No, he wasn't, *Hope*." He bit my name like last time. "His older brother is one of those assholes I told you about who promised girls the world just to get into their pants and then dumped them. He'd do the same."

I shrugged, feeling stupidly bold. "And if I just wanted him to get into my pants?"

Jacob's face blackened to ash. "Then I'd have to break a few of his fingers for daring to touch you."

Moving toward him, I sucked in a breath against the sheer intensity he pulsed with. The immense power he had over my body. The undeniable attraction and connection we shared. "You don't scare me. You wouldn't hurt anyone without cause."

He leaned toward me. "Oh, he'd give me cause."

My stupid heart kicked in a flurry. He was laying claim to me. Making me believe he wanted me and there was something worth fighting for between us.

He couldn't do that.

He couldn't lead me on that way.

I wanted to hurt him.

I wanted this over.

My fight tangled with sad resignation. "You can't have this both ways, you know."

He sucked in a breath. "Excuse me?"

"You know what I mean." I waved my hand. "You've told me time and time again that you don't want me. That there will never be anything more between us than acquaintances."

"Your point?"

My eyes widened. "My point is…you can't stop me from finding friendship with other people if you're not willing to provide it."

"I'm not stopping you."

"Yes, you are. You chased him away like a puppy."

"He *is* a puppy. A puppy that hasn't been neutered."

"What are you doing? You shouldn't care—"

"I don't." His jaw worked.

"Then why are you—"

"I've already told you. I'm *protecting* you. He comes from a family of assholes. You want to be used and hurt by him? Then, by all means, I'll back off." His voice lost its heat, slipping back into collected ice. "Is that what you want?"

What I want is for you to want me the way Carter does.

My shoulders slouched; my hands fell from my hips. "I don't know what I want anymore."

"What is that supposed to mean?"

"I guess it means you're driving me insane." Hugging the bags of horse minerals, I brushed past him and stormed down the aisle—he could figure out about paying.

He stalked me, every step I made he chased me with an identical one until we left the store and I made the mistake of spinning to face him by his truck.

Sunshine beamed down on us, cloaking him in golden softness. His hat shadowed his face, making his eyes black and cheekbones so sharp my fingers tingled to trace them.

The second I caught his gaze, he sighed and pinched the bridge of his nose. For a moment, my entire body throbbed to hug him. I wanted to crush him close and tell him it was okay to like me...even just a little bit. It wasn't a death sentence.

But I knew better than to try.

Rolling his shoulders, he forced himself to speak. "Look, I'm sorry. I didn't mean to do that."

I froze. An apology was the last thing I expected.

"I just...I don't want you getting hurt. If you want to go out with someone while you're here, I'll, um, I'll think about which guys I went to school with and let you know who isn't a womanizing bastard."

I couldn't stop my shocked laugh. "Wait, you're saying you'll play *matchmaker* now?"

"I'm saying I'd rather protect you than let you get hurt."

Goosebumps sprang over my arms despite the sunny heat. How could this hurt so much? Why did the thought of Jacob willingly setting me up on a date crush me right beneath his muddy boot?

He was trying to be nice.

To be *civil*...just like he promised.

Rubbing my arms, I looked at the ground. "It's okay, Jacob. I don't want to date anyone."

"But you just agreed to go out with—"

"Only because the waterfall and gully sounded cool. Not because of him in particular." I forced myself to smile as if he hadn't just ripped out my heart for the billionth time. "It's fine. Don't worry about it."

"If you need a friend, Hope, then the least I can do is help you find one."

There he went again, creating hurt on top of hurt. "Your mom is my friend. Cassie. Nina. I have enough. Truly."

He squeezed the back of his neck. "Then why do I feel so fucking guilty for what I just did?"

I shrugged. "Nothing to feel guilty about."

His gaze fell to my locket. The locket he'd bought me. The locket that'd touched my skin every day for years because I couldn't stop thinking about him. "I know...I know I'm not easy. I didn't mean to—"

"Stop." My voice threaded with temper. "It's fine. Let's just go home. I'm suddenly not hungry after all."

I reached for the passenger door, but Jacob just stood there. Tall and unmovable, strict and unlovable. "That goddamn kiss ruined everything."

My fingers clamped on the door handle. "What?"

"Things were okay before. There wasn't this...*mess* between us."

My hand slowly fell away, curling into a fist. "This *mess*?"

"Yeah. This. Whatever this is."

"And whose fault is that?"

He looked at the sky, a morbid chuckle on his lips. "Yours. Most definitely yours."

"How do you figure?"

"You're the one who invited yourself to my farm. You're the one who pushed me. You're the one who *kissed* me."

My jaw fell open. "I think you'll find *you* kissed *me*."

"A momentary lapse of concentration." He prowled toward me, hands shoved deep into his pockets. "Something I wish I could take back."

I struggled to keep eye contact as tears welled and sadness crept up my spine. "Oh, don't worry. You're not the only one. I wish I could take it back too. I wish I could go back in time and never have met you."

His eyes hardened to glittering gemstones. "That would definitely make life a lot simpler."

"And simple is acceptable to you, isn't it? Nothing complicated. Nothing *messy*. No relationship of any kind."

"Exactly." He nodded sharply.

"Well, too bad. I've ruined your simple."

"Yeah, you did. But I'm dealing with it."

"Ha! You're not dealing with it at all!" Running hands through my hair, I laughed coldly. "You know what? You want space? Fine, I'll give you space. I'm done pining over you. I'm done being so stupidly hopeful that one day you'll wake up and realise that friendship isn't something to despise. I've liked you for years. Years! What a waste. Though, the way you just acted with Carter makes me think a part of you *does* like me. That a tiny piece of your heart is open to the idea of getting close to someone, but that's a lie, isn't it? And I keep falling for it every damn time. But you can't have it both ways, Jacob. You can't say you want to protect me when you don't even care about me. You can't act as if I'm yours when you've made it abundantly clear I will never be. So just stop, okay? I've gotten the message. *Finally.* I'll leave you to your simple. But just because you're not happy doesn't mean I don't want to be. So stop scaring away those who try when you're too afraid to do the same."

My voice cracked, and I had nothing more to say.

I hadn't even planned to say that.

But it'd spilled from a place that held a lot of hurt, and I was done.

I couldn't take it back.

And right now, I didn't really care what happened.

"Here." Shoving the plastic bags of horse minerals against his chest, I hissed, "Pay for those. I'm going to walk back to Cherry River. I'll see you later."

He bowed his head as if I'd cut him with a thousand knives.

And maybe I had.

But I was done worrying about his feelings.

He wanted to prove he had none?

He'd just succeeded.

"Goodbye, *Jake*."

This time, it was my turn to leave and not look back.

* * * * *

Lying on my back in a freshly baled field, the stars above were my friends.

Wisps of clouds formed grey ribbons over glittery orbs, soaking up my frustration and pain.

I'd been out here for an hour. The muggy summer air had cooled, and my thin pyjamas didn't protect me from a slight chill. The prickly stalks of harvested grass weren't nearly as comfortable as lush meadow.

But I didn't want to be in bed. Definitely not in *his* bed.

I couldn't sleep.

I hadn't seen him since I'd walked back from the feed store, taking my time to meander down local streets and cut across another farmer's land who raised alpacas. The funny animals had mobbed me, searching my pockets for snacks, all while their woolly coats gave me something to hold onto while I tortured myself with memories of what'd happened.

Why had I said what I did?

Would he ask me to leave?

Was having him love me more important than staying at Cherry River?

Who am I kidding?

It wasn't as though I could stay here indefinitely. This wasn't my home as much as I liked to pretend it was. I didn't belong here. I didn't belong anywhere. But I'd trespassed enough, and time waited for no one.

Regardless if I left tomorrow or next year, I would leave eventually.

There was no other conclusion to contemplate.

"Hope."

I flinched as my eyes left the patchwork galaxy above and focused on the blonde-haired shadow beside me.

My heart raced as I propped myself up on my elbows. "Della. Um, what are you doing out here?"

"I could ask you the same thing."

"Couldn't sleep."

"Me either." She smiled. "Do you mind?"

I shook my head, scooting into a sitting position. "Not at all."

With a small nod, she lowered herself beside me, sighing as the ribbony clouds dissolved, giving a glimpse of a crescent moon.

For the longest while, we didn't speak. Our silence was companionable and soothing. I guessed our minds were on similar things. The love she'd lost and the love I'd yet to find.

Finally, with her arms wrapped around her knees and silver starlight making her look more my age than my dad's, she said, "You're very brave to love him, you know."

I stiffened.

Words escaped me, and I shivered, not knowing how to respond. Stupid tears welled for no other reason than my affection for this woman. This wonderful woman who'd taken me in, shown me what it would've been like to have a mother who actually wanted a daughter, and cared for me as kindly as she cared for her son.

She hadn't judged me, ridiculed me, or scolded me for making Jacob's life harder. She'd stayed out of the way, her comforting presence there but not prying.

She glanced at me, tucking blonde waves behind her ear. "He's too much like his father." She smiled with a sad shrug. "And I'm sorry for that. I'm sorry he's hurting you."

I sighed, plucking a piece of stalky grass. "He doesn't mean to hurt me. He's just…"

"Stubborn." Della smiled.

"Yeah." I nodded, sighing again.

"Just like Ren, he's a loner at heart, but he has so much love to give to the right person."

"Are you sure?" I didn't have the guts to ask if I was the right person or not.

"Am I sure?" She raised an eyebrow. "What do you mean?"

I daren't look at her. "Are you sure he's *capable* of loving? I mean…he seems pretty adamant that he's not."

She shook her head sadly. "Ah." Looking at the moon, she murmured, "I'm afraid that's my fault. *Our* fault."

"Yours?"

"Ren and me."

I waited for her to elaborate, but when she merely kept staring at the spider web of stars above, I understood there was nothing more to be said.

I spoke instead. "He knows how I feel about him. But he refuses to admit he feels something, too." It wasn't awkward discussing this with Della. She'd become my friend over the past weeks. Besides, her sad calmness and loving hopefulness spoke to something smarting inside me. "He refuses to see the truth."

"And he'll continue to refuse."

My heart sank to the dirt below. "Forever?"

She shrugged, never taking her eyes off the dark horizon. "Depends."

"On what?"

"On how much pain you're willing to go through until he does."

"And if I don't know if I'm strong enough?"

She turned to face me, her blue gaze wise and understanding. "Then that's Jacob's loss." Reaching out, her soft touch grazed my cheek. "If he can't see how brave and beautiful you are, then he doesn't deserve you. I'm not talking ill of my son. I love him more than I can bear, but seeing him push away happiness, all because we stupidly taught him that happiness causes so much suffering, breaks my heart. Don't let him break yours too, Hope."

Her hand dropped away as she pushed upward and stood over me, blocking out the moon and stars. "I meant what I said to your father. You're welcome here, for however long you want. With Jacob or without. I hope you know that."

My heart fisted around a nucleus of agony, but I nodded gratefully. "Thank you. That means a lot to me."

"The fact that you're trying to help my son means the world to me. It's the least I can do." She laughed softly. "Besides, the past has a funny way of repeating itself. I was once in love with a boy who didn't love me the same way, and it was the hardest thing I've ever done to make him see otherwise. But it was worth it in the end. You're a wonderful girl, Hope. If anyone can put up with Jacob, it's you. You're the best daughter anyone could ask for."

I blushed, choking on a sudden wash of tears. Tears for a mother I never truly knew. Tears for a father who was so far away. Tears for true love broken by stubbornness.

Della smiled, hearing what I couldn't say. Knowing how much she meant to me. How much *all* of this meant to me.

"Goodnight, Hope." Blowing me a kiss, she headed back to the house where soul-mates had lived, death had visited, and heartbreak continued to haunt them.

Jacob had moved from that ghost-filled house, but his heart still carried them regardless.

I didn't belong in either home.

So I stayed in the field.

Neutral territory.

An island of confusion.

A girl blanketed by midnight.

Chapter Thirty-Three

JACOB

✶ ✶ ✶ ✶ ✶ ✶

"YOU'RE HURTING EVERYONE, Wild One. Didn't I teach you to be better than that?"

I hung my head, slipping back into the child I'd been when I lost my father. The child who still dictated a lot of my fear. The child petrified of love.

Dad moved around the small clearing where trees canopied and protected us. The trunk I'd carved Dad's tattoo and our initials into was already so much higher than that awful day of his funeral.

Funny that I knew this was a dream.

Funny that I knew he was dead and this was just a figment of my sleeping unconsciousness.

Funny that none of that mattered.

I was still being scolded. Judged. Condemned.

Dad moved to sit on the log in front of me. The fire that was always the heart of our campsite blazed with orange flames.

"Didn't I tell you to look after her? Didn't I tell you to keep her happy?"

I nodded, thinking of Mom and how I'd hurt her, thinking of Hope and how I'd broken her, thinking of my family and how I'd only caused them pain. With heavy regret and burning anguish, I dragged a stick through ash and cinders. *"You did."*

"Didn't I tell you not to be afraid? That death isn't the end? That nothing ever truly dies?"

"You did."

"Then why are you resisting, Wild One? Why can't you give into life? Into love?"

"Because...you lied." I dared look up. Dared stare into the eyes of my imagination and study the father who was no longer real. He looked healthier than I'd ever seen him. Bronze hair glowing, dark eyes knowing, a face full of immortality.

"How did I lie?"

"You lied when you said true love never dies."

"I didn't lie."

"Tell that to Mom. She's dying every day without you."

Dad shook his head sadly. "She's not dying. She's waiting."

"Waiting to die."

"Perhaps. Or waiting for another to make her live. Or waiting for you to be happy."

"I am happy. I don't need love to be happy."

He scoffed, throwing me a beer that magically appeared in his hand. Icy cold, dew decorated, and straight from the hands of a ghost. "You're saying you're happy?"

"I'm saying I have everything I need."

"That wasn't what I asked."

My eyes narrowed as I twisted the lid off the beer and swigged the cold liquid. "I'm keeping your promise. I'm watching over her. I'm keeping her safe. I promised I would never leave her, and I won't. What more do you want?"

Dad drank from his own beer, his throat working as he swallowed. "I was wrong to ask such a thing of you. Consider this an ending of that promise. You're free to do whatever you need."

"I don't need anything." I glowered, getting angry with the one person I never should.

"Wrong." He grinned with annoying fatherly wisdom. "You need her. The girl who's fighting for you."

Hope.

My fingers clenched around the beer bottle. "I need nothing."

"If that were true, your subconscious wouldn't be trying to convince you otherwise."

"You're saying I'm choreographing this dream?"

He laughed. "If that isn't the case, then are you willing to concede I might be talking to you from the grave, and I was right all along?" He leaned toward me, smelling of wood-smoke and childhood and loss. "That even gone, I'm still here. That there is no end."

"I don't know what to believe anymore."

"That's a start." He stood, and the fire swirled into dust, drenching us in darkness. "Give in, Wild One. Just give a little and see where your heart guides you. Perhaps that compass was meant to lead you to Hope all along. Now wake up. Wake up and—"

I soared upright.

Sweat drenched my back. My lungs couldn't catch a proper breath. My heart pumped manic blood through terrified veins.

Shit, that felt so real.

So strange and crazy and *real*.

And the strangest part was, I knew what Dad was about to say before I woke. His voice rang in my ears as if he spoke in the quiet stillness of my room.

"Wake up and apologise. Wake up and be brave. Wake up and accept life in all its gifts and glories, all its sadness and suffering."

If I had scripted that entire illusion, then I was seeking absolution from my promise—searching for a way to be free of looking after my mother—which made me an awful, terrible son.

But then again, I'd descended into an awful, terrible person.

I led Hope on by growling at Carter, refusing to let her find joy with anyone else, and trying my hardest to make her as miserable as me.

I couldn't handle the feelings she invoked in me.

I couldn't handle the dominating desire when she spoke to other guys or the gut-sinking realisation that *I* wanted to be the one to take her to the waterfall.

Why the hell was I so screwed up?

Why couldn't I get past this?

Why couldn't I just do what Dad said and let my heart guide me instead of my mind ruling me all the goddamn time?

Dad was right. My dream was right. *I* was right.

This was no way to live.

I couldn't keep doing this anymore.

But I didn't know how to break free.

Round and round my thoughts went, fighting a heart that was brave and cursing a soul that was pitifully fearful.

I wasn't ten anymore.

I'd survived death. I had a family who loved me. I had a girl who put up with my bullshit even though I went out of my way to be cruel.

I didn't deserve them.

I'd *never* deserved them.

And this wasn't the man I was meant to become.

I was supposed to be better than this.

I *wanted* to be better than this.

I just didn't know how.

How did I stop fighting life?

How did I stop battling everything that made me human?

The answer?

Give in.

The simplest notion.
The hardest thing.
Give in.
Accept.
Trust.
And…apologise.

* * * * *

I left them letters.

I used a tip from my old man and penned letters to my loved ones.

One to Aunt Cassie, Uncle Chip, and Cousin Nina.

One to Grandpa John.

One to Mom.

I hadn't figured out how to be the son Dad expected me to be, but my dream had slapped me awake enough to see the error of my ways. So what if I struggled? I shouldn't take it out on those who cared for me.

I wasn't strong enough to say it face to face. Words stuck in my throat at the very thought of admitting I loved them. Just the image of such a thing made me want to run into the forest and never come back.

But letters I could do.

Letters could be my starting point. The first step in my rehabilitation to being normal.

However, just as words strangled my throat, they clogged up my pen too.

I sat for hours, searching for the right ones to apologise for my coldness, my remoteness, my lack of love. I sat in the glittery golds of dawn and wrote the shortest but hardest letters of my life.

I didn't want to push them away anymore.

I needed their help if I stood any chance of solving the riddle in my heart and finding the courage to be vulnerable.

Vulnerable to their sickness and suffering.

Defenceless to their eventual death and burial.

Life would mess me up and leave me with yet more scars, but I would no longer be this freak who couldn't afford the cost of love.

Before they were out of bed, I dressed in my jeans, steel caps, and a green T-shirt, and snuck into their respective houses. A letter was left on the table in Aunt Cassie's place, and one was left on the kitchen bench in Grandpa John's.

Was it weak to let written words do my apologising for me or brave to leave such permanency on paper? I couldn't take this back. I couldn't pretend I hadn't woken with a new determination and the undeniable need to be *more*.

I needed their accountability to ensure I didn't slink behind well-constructed walls and gates.

Crossing the paddock between my grandfather's home and my mother's, my head whipped up as the front door opened and Hope appeared. Freshly showered, brown hair wet and glossy, she stretched out her spine before stooping to slip on well-used, dirty boots.

I broke into a jog.

She couldn't leave.

Not yet.

"Hope, wait."

She stilled as her eyes flew up, catching mine. The sun already painted her in a buttery softness that made my heart kick and body twist and all manner of courage evaporate.

"Jacob. Wha-what are you doing here?" She scooped her long hair back, pulling an elastic from her wrist and securing it around her ponytail. "I was heading to the barn. Didn't you say we're selling the extra hay we don't need? What time will people arrive?"

My boots sounded loud and punishing as I climbed the steps to stand before her. "They won't be here for another hour or so." She never looked away. The anger she nursed for me. The hunger she cursed for me. The messy complications between us. My skin prickled with nerves as I looked at her mouth and swallowed hard. "Can you, eh, wait here? I just have to do something, but then I'll be back."

Her gaze widened. "Wait where? On the deck?"

"Or in the meadow. I don't mind. Just…don't go anywhere too far."

"Okay…" She frowned as I brushed past her and darted into the house. I held her stare as I closed the door, sucking in a breath and doing my best to calm my panicked heartbeat.

Hope would be the last person I would apologise to, but first…there was someone else of utmost importance.

Striding through the family home that filled me with such comfort and tragedy, I slipped down the corridor to my parents' room.

I found Mom making her bed, curtains open to sunshine, life beginning a new day. She fluffed a final pillow, smiling as I entered. "Jacob, what a lovely surprise." Moving around the neat bed, she came toward me but stopped before giving me a hug. Even though every part of her screamed to be affectionate, she respected my differences.

One of these days, I'd be strong enough to yank her into a hug without thinking. But today, it took everything I had just to stand there.

Clenching my hands, I said, "I had a dream last night. About Dad."

Her eyes traded her clear motherly look and shadowed into a lost widow. "Oh?"

"He told me to get my head out of my ass basically."

She laughed. "Sounds about right."

"He told me to apologise."

"There's nothing to apologise for."

"There is, and we both know it." I jammed hands into my pockets, curling the letter I'd written for her. "I'm sick of being so afraid. I'm sick of pushing you guys away. I *miss* you. I miss how it used to be before..." I looked away. "Before he died. I miss thinking everything would be okay. We lived in miracles back then. He kept surviving, and we kept loving, and I thought it would be that way forever. It's time I grew up and realised that there is no forever, and that's...that's okay."

Mom came toward me, resting her hand on my forearm. Even that small amount of contact threatened to break me. "It's okay, Wild One. It's okay not to want to accept such grief."

"You're saying you accept it?"

"No." She shook her head. "I'll never accept that he's gone. But I can accept that nothing I do will change that, and I'm only hurting myself by resisting the truth."

"I love you, Mom. You know that, right?"

She squeezed my arm. "Of course, I know that. I'll *always* know that, no matter if you moved across the world and never spoke to me again. And I love you, too, Jacob. Forever. And I can say forever because I believe what your father does. There is no end. There is only a pause. Life is too precious just to finish and not transform into something else."

I nodded even as a crest of pity crushed me.

Pity for her.

Pity for my mother and her steadfast beliefs that she'd see my father again.

Despite my new conviction to be kinder to the living, I still believed death was final. Dad might watch us; I might have dreams about him, and sometimes indulge in the thought he was out there…somewhere, but where Mom believed love joined them for eternity, I couldn't handle that sort of hope.

I couldn't stomach the promise of something else because how utterly soul-destroying would it be to look forward to death, only to find out it was nothing but…well, *nothing*.

An end.

A true termination.

I was doing my best to come to terms with the fact that nothing was permanent in this world all while my mother believed in new beginnings.

Gritting my teeth, I reached out and hugged her. Hard and fast.

With her fragile form in my arms, I committed all over again to my promise. This woman was everything I had in the world; I would not forsake her by being too weak to care.

I would uphold my vow to my father. I would make her happy. I would stay by her side until the end.

With a kiss on her cheek, I pulled away, fighting the whispers in my blood to keep my distance. "Thank you. For everything."

I turned and walked swiftly away before it got awkward. Yanking the letter from my pocket, I left it on her dresser as I made my way from the house.

I was drained and tired and a jangled mess of nerves, but I had another apology to make.

Hope.

And somehow, I knew she'd be my hardest.

* * * * *

"I can't find the ledger book." Hope looked up as I stepped into the small office off the tack room. The rainbow of ribbons Aunt Cassie had won over the years being a professional equestrian decorated the walls, and her riding photos took up the tiny free space between shelves holding everything a farm could ever need.

Nodding, I strode to the rusty filing cabinet and pulled out the second drawer. I selected the current year's ledger and passed it to her.

She huffed. "Thanks."

"Welcome."

"Cassie told me it was in the desk drawer."

I shrugged. "I had a sort-out a few months ago. My farm. My filing decisions."

"Fair enough." She blew hair from her gaze, hugging the ledger as if it was bullet-proof. "So…"

I rocked on my heels. "So."

"Um." She looked at the floor before catching my gaze again. "What did you want to talk to me about?"

"You didn't wait for me like I asked."

She bit her lip. "Yeah, sorry. I needed to move. I woke with a lot of nervous energy and couldn't stay on the deck. I didn't know how long you'd be, so figured I might as well be useful."

I smiled, genuinely, kindly. There hadn't been enough of that in my dealings with her. "You've been very useful since you've been here. I don't think I've said thank you." My voice deepened with serenity. "Truly, Hope. You've been an amazing help."

Her eyes widened. "Oh, well, you're welcome. Thank you for letting me be a nuisance and hang around."

"You were never a nuisance."

She cocked her head. "All right, who are you and what have you done with Jacob Wild?"

I spread my hands. "I'm right here, and the asshole version of me is gone. I owe you an apology. Multiple apologies."

Slowly, she put the ledger onto the cluttered desk. "Gone? I-I don't understand."

I crossed the small space between us. "What I said that day we baled hay—about not wanting to be close, about needing space—I was a jerk. About all of it. I'm doing my best not to be that person anymore."

She backed away as if my sudden change of heart was more terrifying than my previous surly ways. "Is this about the other day in the feed store?" She sighed. "You don't owe me an apology, Jacob. I was deliberately pushing your buttons. It was my fault. If anything, I owe you an apology for what I said."

"It's not about that. You were right to call me out on my bullshit."

"No, I've been too pushy. Way, *way* too pushy."

"Perhaps, but you were right to push me. I needed to be pushed. I, eh…" I cleared my throat. "I needed you."

She froze. A tiny noise escaped her. "Well, thanks…I guess. That's very sweet."

"Sweet?" Reaching out, I brushed aside a strand of glossy chocolate hair that'd come loose from her ponytail. I tried to ignore the way my heart stopped pounding and once again rattled demonically at my ribcage. It wanted out. It wanted her. It wanted a different kind of life. "I'm many things, but I'm not sweet."

"Jacob, I…" Her green gaze latched onto my lips. She licked her own, ensuring my body reacted in all the wrong and horribly right ways. "I'm not sure what's going on."

I dropped my hand. "Let's just say I woke up with new morals."

"And these new morals mean what exactly?"

"That I'm done being such a loner."

She scowled. "You can't just switch off something like that."

"I can if it's hurting those I care about."

I can try at least.

Her entire body froze. "Don't do this. Don't do what you did at the feed store."

"Do what?"

"Make me believe you actually have feelings when you were pretty successful at proving you didn't."

I sighed, hating the way my body shook. Hating the weakness she caused me. The regret she gifted me. "I do have feelings, Hope. They're just not easy to deal with."

"Feelings for me?" She winced as if she hadn't meant to say that out loud. "I mean—"

"Feelings for everyone." I paced in front of her, needing to move before I exploded with the itchy, irritable sensation of allowing emotions to control me. I was so used to switching it off, pushing it away, pretending I felt nothing.

Standing in that office, I drowned in *everything*.

It was the hardest thing I'd ever done.

Rubbing my throat, I strangled, "Look, it was wrong to chase Carter away. I know that." My jaw clenched, unwilling to voice my next sentence. "I-I can get his number for you. If you want. Go out with him. I want you to be happy, Hope. Despite what you think."

She laughed under her breath. A cynical, cold little laugh. "You still don't get it, do you?"

I raked a hand through my hair. "I get that I'm still hurting you, and I'm doing my best not to."

Her eyes glittered for a second before she nodded sharply. "Sorry. Ignore me. I appreciate your offer, Jacob, but no. I don't want his number."

"What do you want?" I breathed.

Hope stiffened. I froze. The room became half the size, filling to the roof with tension.

Shit, I shouldn't have asked that.

She smiled sadly. "I don't think you want an answer to that question."

I didn't know how to reply.

I'd come here hoping this would be easy. But Hope scrambled me up. She made me sweat. Made me churn.

Emotions were cyanide, and distance was the cure.

Cold-hearted cruelty the only antidote.

A single dream about Dad telling me off couldn't prevent the triggers that'd governed my life since he died. A nudge from my unconsciousness couldn't *fix* me.

As much as I wished it could.

I sighed, kicking the leg of the dinged-up table.

What the hell was I thinking?

I'd stupidly woken with the idiotic thought I could be the man Hope wanted. That I could attempt—just attempt—a...*relationship* with her.

A physical, emotional relationship that would shatter me into smithereens.

But standing there, on the precipice of changing my world forever, I couldn't do it.

I wasn't brave enough.

I wasn't man enough to fall.

Every time she smiled my way or helped with a chore, I desperately wanted to be sane enough to love her.

What wasn't there to love?

She was a farm girl. A *farmer's* girl. A diligent worker who didn't care about mess and mud and mayhem.

She was perfect.

She was kind and gorgeous and a huge part of my family already.

It should be so *easy* to love her.

So why was it so fucking hard?

Caskets, cremations, and crying littered my mind, trapping my feelings, caging my love, preventing me from breaking the chains I'd lived within since childhood.

Maybe, I had it wrong.

Instead of being afraid of love...maybe I truly was incapable.

Impotent against the end.

Powerless against forever.

Death was always just around the corner. Slithering in the shadows, selecting its next victim.

I wished I'd known then what was about to happen.

I wished I'd understood how simple this complicated moment was when faced with what my future had in store.

But I didn't.

And I struggled like a coward, giving up the fight as I settled back into my familiar.

Clamping both hands on my head, I looked at the ceiling and exhaled hard.

Silence fell for an eternal moment before I let my arms tumble to my side and faced Hope with an apology instead of bravery. "There's something I want to ask you."

She didn't know the war I'd just fought. Didn't understand the conclusions that'd caused bloodshed.

All she knew was I was a master at causing her pain.

"Okay." Her green gaze travelled to my mouth, hypnotising me with the way she stared. The connection between us lashed tighter than any rope, and I would've given anything to grab her. To kiss her again. To pretend I was cured and normal and capable of affection like so many others.

I couldn't be with her the way she wanted me to be.

But I could offer a better scenario to our current situation.

I could be brave enough to do that.

Please...let me.

Spreading my hands in surrender, I murmured, "I said I didn't need one, but it turns out...I do."

"Need what?"

"Someone to call me out on my mess. Someone who's stubborn and feisty and not afraid of me."

She smiled softly. "I'm guessing that someone is me?"

"No one else fits that criteria."

She laughed under her breath, her eyes warming in ways that made knives puncture my chest. "What do you need from me?"

"Something I said I'd never need."

Her body stilled. "Tell me."

I swallowed.

And swallowed again.

I couldn't take this back once I'd said it.

I'd have to find a way to honour it, savour it, not be afraid of it. "A friend. I need a friend."

"A friend?" She snapped upright.

I nodded firmly. "Yes."

She couldn't hide her shock. "I thought you hated that word."

"I hate what it represents."

"What does it represent?"

I shrugged, searching for an answer that would make sense but, in the end, just settled on one word. "Pain."

Her gaze darkened with compassion I hated. "You think being friends with me is going to hurt?"

"I don't think. I know."

"Why?"

I sighed. "Because I'll care for you. I'll like you. I'll get used to having you around."

"And that's a bad thing?"

"Terrible."

She fell quiet for a moment before murmuring, "Then why put yourself through it?"

"Because I'm sick of pushing people away."

"Oh."

"I love my family, but they don't see me like you do. They don't drive me crazy like you."

She smirked. "I do have a good talent at that."

"You do." I half-chuckled. "So...do you agree?"

"To be your friend?"

"To be my friend."

She nudged her boot into the dirt, thoughts racing over her face. "And when I go back home? What then?"

Something hot and sharp dug talons directly into my heart. The harsh possessiveness to keep those I cared about close so I could protect them from everything—prevent them from death— killed me already. "Then I'll miss you. I'll hurt. But life moves on and...and well, nothing is permanent. Not life, not love, and not friendship."

Hope frowned. "Life might not be permanent, but the other two things are."

"No. They're not." Pacing away, I found an old pair of baling gloves on the desk and pulled them on, ready to sell hay to city folk. "When it comes to this argument, you won't win. Love and friendship are fleeting things. Some last years. Some last days. But in the end, they all *end*. I've struggled with this my whole life. Don't try to ruin my acceptance when I'm still not sure I can."

Hope bit her lip. Her tiny boots brought her closer to me. "Can I ask one question, and then I'll shut up about all of this."

"Fine. What is it?"

A pink blush worked its way over her cheeks, transforming

her from pretty to breath-taking. I wanted so, so much to kiss her. But this was as far as I could go. I knew my limits.

"This friendship…could it eventually be…more?"

The clock ticked loudly in the dusty corner while I worked out the best way to reply. While I worked out how to tell the truth, all while wishing it was a lie. "No."

"Okay." She sniffed but nodded bravely. "I just needed to ask."

"Friends. That's all."

"I get it."

"No, I don't think you do. But that's okay." I moved forward and took her pipsqueak hand in my huge glove. "Friends is already asking a lot of me. I don't want to hurt you worse by failing at giving you more."

Her smile was understanding and pure. "I understand, Jacob."

"Thank you." I squeezed her hand, switching it into a slightly awkward handshake. "Friends?"

She squeezed me back. "Friends."

Chapter Thirty-Four

HOPE

* * * * * *

A MONTH.

One glorious month where life was full of perfect, wondrous, brilliant moments.

A month when I grew up, learned about hard work, basked in the joy of diving into the pond after a long sweaty day, and swelling with pride of growing my own vegetables. Not to mention the indescribable honour of Jacob Wild accepting me.

My friend.

He liked me for me.

He'd let down a wall…for *me*.

My previous weeks at Cherry River were nothing, *nothing* compared to that month. To be honest, I didn't believe Jacob could switch overnight and trade snappish temper with calm rationality.

But…he did.

I'd catch him a couple of times with locked jaw and grinding teeth as he held back retorts no longer welcome. I caught glimpses of hurting eyes and worried soul as he fought the urge to run, but through it all, he remained true to his promise to be my friend.

And not just I benefited.

His entire family did.

Nina was encouraged to come hang out with us and became a friend I would happily stay in touch with when I left.

Della was invited to Jacob's house for dinner more often.

John and Chip weren't kept at arm's length, and I'd often hear the rumble of masculine laughter coming from the tractor shed as the men did their best to fix broken engines.

Summer had been kind to Cherry River with endless long, warm, sunny days, and somehow, with Jacob's smile, the proverbial cloud lifted from this place, and a new chapter began.

One that I hoped wouldn't just last for one book but for

always. This place needed true happiness. The veil of perpetual grief needed to be shredded.

It wasn't that I didn't understand or honour the hole left by Ren's death, but this place couldn't continue to be a graveyard. Della had to remember how to laugh without tears. Jacob had to learn how to live without fear. And everyone else had to be free to be joyful without drowning in guilt.

A little piece of healing happened.

Life wasn't as painful.

Or at least, it wasn't for the Wilds.

For me, though?

The pain only grew worse.

Jacob.

He treated me with such kindness now. His smiles were genuine and his gratefulness true and that made my life that much harder. I had no arguments left to keep my heart safe behind a fence.

There was nothing bad to focus on; only the good to uncover.

Without intending to, Jacob revealed what sort of man was hiding beneath that broken exterior, and I fell hopelessly in love with him.

The day he asked to be my friend, he kept throwing me thankful stares as we worked in the barn together, tossing down hay for customers who came to fill up their own sheds for the winter. It was a long day with blisters on fingers from hauling and blisters on brains from arithmetic and totalling up sales. After the last truck drove away, I fully expected Jacob to leave as he usually did without a backward glance. Him to his place, and me to Della's. No interaction again until daybreak.

That day, though, he cocked his head and guided me toward the stables where Forrest and a chestnut mare called Gingernut were tied up, waiting for us.

I'd ridden Gingernut before, and out of all the horses here, she was the one I had the best bond with.

I hadn't told Jacob that. I hadn't told anyone. Yet he'd chosen that particular horse for me.

He'd read me silently. Knew me intimately. He'd bulldozed past the remaining barriers I had and crushed me into rubble.

That was the first hint of the pain I was about to endure.

The first taste of trouble.

When we tacked up and mounted horses in a splash-perfect

pink and tangerine sunset, we didn't have to speak as Jacob urged Forrest into a gallop and I followed.

We rode for two hours.

He guided me on trails I hadn't seen and led me through areas of the woods that were horse friendly. Deep dusk decorated tree trunks into skeletal shadows while owls hooted above our heads.

While I rode in a saddle and bridle, Jacob rode in just a halter.

And that symbolism kept me awake that night after we'd put our horses to rest, and I struggled to sleep in his bed. All this time, I'd believed Jacob was too afraid to get close, so he wrapped himself up with barbwire.

But really...he was the most vulnerable.

Just like he was vulnerable when he rode Forrest with no tack. He was vulnerable in life because he had no tricks to protect himself. He couldn't pretend. He didn't hide his wounds or deceive those around him into thinking he was anything more than who he could be.

He was honest, raw, and open.

There was nothing counterfeit about him.

And that became obvious as we worked side by side, living in the present rather than the past or future.

A week after our friendship began, Jacob looked at the sky on a scorching summer's day and turned off the tractor. We'd been patrolling the fence lines, spraying Roundup to kill the weeds creeping high over wire and post.

We weren't done.

But Jacob merely took my hand and guided me to the pond where I'd watched him stumble from the forest with a concussion.

That seemed an eon ago.

A *lifetime* ago.

"Ready?" He smirked.

"Ready for what?"

"To swim." Scooping me up, he threw me jeans-clad and T-shirt wearing into the pond, then cannon-balled after me.

I came up spluttering while he laughed. A happy, deep laugh that made a home in my ears and set up a shrine in my heart.

Droplets danced on my eyelashes as the sun shone on him, turning his dark blond hair honey and distrusting midnight eyes a mystical grey.

He seemed lighter these days too. Not just in mood but in colouring.

As if the shadows that'd hurt him for so long were losing their strenuous grip.

We swam for an hour, slowly peeling off clothes until we were just in our underwear.

When he threw his soaking jeans onto the bank, and his shirtless chest bunched to toss his T-shirt, I sank beneath the surface and screamed.

Screamed for the unfairness and the rightness of it all.

Unfairness because I'd found the man who fit me above all others.

And rightness because we were *friends*, and if my only purpose was to help Jacob remember how to have a companion, then I was doing everything he needed.

My wish of helping him was coming true.

He was learning to trust me.

He was learning to *like* me.

And I wouldn't do anything to jeopardise that.

I wouldn't swim over and touch him.

I wouldn't hug him from behind and plaster my wet bra to his back.

I definitely wouldn't try to kiss his gorgeous face with hair messy and five o'clock shadow framing the most perfect lips.

Because that would be about me, not him.

And I was done being selfish.

Instead, I tucked up the heartbeats of my pain and stored them deep in an aching chest. I did my best to keep love from my eyes and desire from my voice and stayed perfectly platonic.

The rest of the day was as idyllic as the morning.

Our clothes dried, thanks to the hot sun, and we dressed, his eyes carefully away from my body while mine couldn't stop roaming over his. Damp but refreshed, we continued weed maintenance in ease and contentedness.

Later that night, we arrived home to a delicious barbecue that John had put together.

Fresh bread, cool coleslaw, smoky sausages, and fried onions, along with salads and chicken wings and icy soda.

Everyone joined in, milling together around the old picnic table overlooking the willow grotto.

It was one of the best moments of my life to be surrounded by family and love, but it was also one of the saddest not to be surrounded by my own mother and father.

As much as I cared for these people, they weren't mine.

They'd never *be* mine. I was just a visitor, a girl passing through, a side character who would be gone soon and forgotten.

As the evening wore on, I stood slightly apart, smiling in happiness to see Jacob's family not tensing before they talked to him or flinching if they brought up Ren. The stiffness between them softened, and John pushed his luck by touching his grandson more than anyone.

I hadn't asked, but I didn't think John had told Jacob his diagnosis yet. He probably didn't want to ruin this wonderful summer moment when his grandson was willing to laugh and be a part of his family instead of a loner locked in a cabin on the hill.

Della found me when the strawberry shortcake was passed around.

We stood quietly beneath a tree with sparrows roosting loudly above us. Her presence was once again comforting; a medicine to the illness her son caused.

We ate the sugary dessert in silence, watching Jacob as he discussed turning the back meadow into a full orchard with peaches, plums, and apples with John.

As the sun set on such a brilliantly flawless day, Della turned to hug me.

And I buried my face in her neck, shuddering with the unbearable need to tell her how much I'd fallen for her son. How much he meant to me. How much his happiness cost me because I could never jeopardise this new Jacob. I could never tell him how I felt because all he asked for was friendship and friends were all we'd ever be.

But I didn't need to tell her because she knew.

Her touch told me she understood the agony of unrequited affection.

Her kiss told me to be brave, to be patient, to weather the suffering because…who knew…perhaps one day, I'd get my happily ever after.

Maybe one day, Jacob would fall for me, and then it would be me begging death not to take him. Me fighting the fear of losing him. I'd regress to that tiny kid who'd clutched a stupid piece of lace after her mother committed suicide.

A silly, pushy girl who wasn't *worthy* of being loved.

A girl who wasn't allowed longevity of such a thing.

That night, I went to bed exhausted and in more pain than ever.

And it wasn't the only night of agony.

There were so many exquisite moments of togetherness. Working with Jacob was my favourite place to be, but hanging out with him at the dinner table, hearing his husky, melodic laughter, seeing him be so gentle with the horses, watching him tend the land as if it were a much-loved family member—it all chipped away at my defences.

By day, I behaved perfectly. I'd smile but not too broad. I'd laugh but not flirt. I'd keep my eyes above his belt and my desire hidden.

But I couldn't stop my physical reaction.

Couldn't stop the quickened heartbeats or hitched breath if he came too close; the tingling over my skin or the prickles along my scalp when he gave me a lopsided smile goodbye and tipped his cowboy hat.

I didn't know how much longer I could love him and not tell him.

The days were bearable (just), but the nights were intolerable. I never went to his cabin uninvited now. I stayed in his bed at Della's house and fought with fantasies of what it would be like to be more than friends.

I drove myself mad with illusions.

At the end of the month, Jacob surprised me by showing up at dawn outside his old bedroom door. On his back rested a backpack full of things, and in his hands rested another slightly smaller bag, but just as stuffed with belongings.

Luckily, I'd become an early riser and already had a shower. Crossing the room to let him in, I finished pulling the brush through my damp hair and repositioned my locket to glitter over my white T-shirt instead of growing hot against my skin. "Jacob…what are you doing here?"

"It's Sunday."

"So?"

"So no work today."

"We've worked Sundays before."

He grinned, shoving the smaller backpack into my arms. "Not this one." Not waiting for me, he leapt off the deck with a move so light-hearted and free, it made him look like a rebellious teenager and not a weathered farmer. "I want to show you something."

Shrugging the backpack on, I found my boots tossed in the corner and shoved them on my feet. "Show me what?"

"You'll see." Holding out his hand, he waited as I tied my

laces and closed the glass sliders.

With a soft breath, I shoved down another rush of besotted affection, commanding myself to stay calm as I placed my palm in his.

Unfortunately, his touch was fireworks and dynamite. Electricity pulsed up my arm, defibrillating my heart with pain, pain, *pain*.

With a wince, I tugged my fingers from his, shaking out the tingles. "Where are we going?"

Jacob frowned at my withdrawn hand. "Forest."

I smiled. "I'm assuming you mean the place with trees and not your horse?"

"You assumed correctly." He struck off into a ground-covering stride, expecting me to keep up.

I trotted after him, looping my fingers under the backpack straps and wishing I'd had a glass of water. If he kept up this pace, I was in for some hard exercise. "What's so urgent to see in the forest?"

"Nothing." He gave me a grin. "Just want to make use of the day, that's all."

"Della know we're leaving?"

"She doesn't need to know everything we do. Besides, she knows where I go if I leave for a few days. I take after my father, after all."

"Wait." My breath came a little faster, but I was fitter than I was a couple of months ago. "We're spending the *night* there?"

"You saying you're chicken?"

I scowled. "I'm not chicken."

"In that case, yes." He smirked. "We're spending the night there."

* * * * *

For three hours, we hiked.

My thighs and calf muscles grumbled for the first hour or so, then started whinging on the second hour, and by the final stretch, they howled their displeasure.

Every part of me ached.

Jacob, meanwhile, showed no adverse effects. His concussion no longer affected his balance, and beneath the weight of the backpack his spine was strong and straight.

No signs of his painful fall off Forrest lingered, and I was glad. Beyond glad there hadn't been any long-term damage.

"This is the spot." Jacob stopped in the middle of a small

clearing. Trees soared heavenward while bracken and bushes thickened the undergrowth, ringing us in foliage protection. The ground wasn't as leaf-littered as I expected, and a circle of ash-covered rocks hinted a camper had been here not long ago and lit a fire or two.

"Is this where you came when you disappeared those few days?"

He nodded, letting his backpack slip from his shoulders and bounce against the earth. "Uh-huh."

"You walked all that way with a busted back?"

He gave me a careful look. "I did, but it didn't take three hours. It took much longer."

"Why travel so far?" I moved around the quaint campsite, loving the niches made by woodland creatures and the obvious human tampering with a carving or two in tree bark and a couple of logs strategically placed for fire gazing.

Jacob shrugged. "Not sure. Anywhere in the forest would've done. Then again, this was the first spot Dad brought me, so it's kinda special. It's far enough away to make you glad when you arrive and close enough to home if anything goes wrong. Plus, the farther away from human habitation you go, the purer the river is and the easier the game is to hunt."

I stiffened. "Please tell me we don't have to kill something for dinner tonight. I'll happily starve if that's the case."

He laughed. "I should make you gut a rabbit just to show you the reality behind eating meat."

"Why on earth would you want me to do something so gruesome?"

"Because you're blind. You're used to meat coming in pretty plastic wrapping. You've been desensitised to seeing an animal give up its life for you to have lunch."

"If you're trying to make me a vegetarian, it's working."

He laughed again, kicking aside weeds as he dropped to his haunches to brush unburned twigs into the fire pit. "Nah, just showing you real life. You're different from most people, Hope. You weren't born to this life, yet you're happier here than the locals. You're strong, quick thinking, and not afraid to get your hands dirty."

I flushed with pride.

I hadn't worked my butt off for Jacob to be proud of me. I'd done it because it'd made me proud of *myself*. But I also couldn't deny I liked him looking at me this way—full of awe and friendship and…affection.

But then the look was gone as he cleared his throat and moved toward his discarded backpack, his hands blackened with soot. "It does make me wonder, though."

"Wonder what?" My boots crunched as I followed.

"Wonder if Cherry River had been a farm that raised stock for slaughter, would have accepted this world so easily."

I froze. "I-I never thought about that."

He pulled out a large nylon tent and shook it open. "Don't you find it funny that all we farm is grass and keep rescues?"

"No. Because like I said, I didn't think about it."

"There's plenty of money in grass, don't get me wrong. We ship up and down the country. But there's money in meat too. But Grandpa John has never been in the business of killing. I think it was my grandmother Patricia who said he could never raise animals if they were destined for a plate."

Taking off my own bag, I went to help Jacob spread out the tent on a flattened section of earth beneath a tree with bushy branches. "I like the sound of this Patricia."

"Yeah, me too." His eyes grew soft. "She died. Like everyone does." His gaze flashed dark as he forced himself to stay present and not slip into grim memories. "Did you know your grandparents…before they died in that car crash?"

"How did you know they died?"

He snorted. "Google."

"Ah." I rolled my eyes. "So you'll also know Dad sold me as a concubine to a big-shot director for a role?"

"There was a lot of bullshit about you online, that's true."

"Meh, I don't care." Answering his previous question, I said softly, "I didn't meet my grandparents before they died. It's just been Dad and me for a very long time."

"Do you miss your mother?"

Even though I'd grown used to Jacob asking me questions about myself over the past few weeks and the intense way he pocketed my answers—as if he kept all trivia about me for safe-keeping—I flinched at that one.

My fingers found their way to wrap around my locket where the remaining piece of her lace lived.

His gaze followed, but he stayed silent.

"I think I miss the *idea* of her more than I miss her." I glanced away, hating myself, but for the first time, I was ready to be honest. Brutally honest. "Dad loved her. I know that. But I don't know if she loved him the same way. My memories are starting to fade, leaving only the loudest moments, and unfortunately, those moments were of her screaming at Dad about petty things." I glanced at the dirt under my nails from harrowing yesterday. "I-I don't like that I look like her. I don't want to be that cruel to anyone or that unhappy with life."

Jacob stopped moving, giving me his full concentration. "You're not cruel."

"I know." I nodded. "But sometimes, I have to work extra hard not to be ungrateful like she was. She had everything in the world. Everything society said she should want anyway—rich and famous with a cute daughter and a handsome husband—but it wasn't enough. That greed to find something that *would* make her happy is what killed her in the end."

Jacob released the tent and came slowly toward me.

I sucked in a breath as he cupped my hand locked around my locket. His grip was dry and warm and protective. His eyes danced over mine. His height shadowed me from the dappling light around us.

For the longest moment, he stared. Stared deep, deep into me, giving me no place to hide. I felt judged and studied and *known*. And when his fingers tugged the chain around my neck, I moved like liquid into him.

There were no bones left in my body, only malleable willingness to go wherever he wanted because he didn't see a girl born to acting royalty, or a starlet who had money and a career just waiting to unfold at her feet. He saw me grubby and slightly sweaty in the middle of a forest and knew I wasn't lying.

Knew I wasn't lying when I said this—this place, this *magical* place—made me content.

And that made me happy because it meant I wasn't like my mother at all. Not even a little bit. Because every day the sun woke me up, I was grateful. Every night I went to bed, I was thankful.

I didn't need anything more.

All I needed was this very moment where Jacob kept me prisoner with my necklace and the forest cradled us from civilisation.

My heart pounded as Jacob licked his lower lip.

"You are the simplest, most sweetest person I've ever met," he whispered. "You are… fascination and fearlessness all wrapped up in gratitude."

I swallowed hard as his body brushed against mine.

"If you were anything like your mother, Hope Jacinta Murphy, then I would still be afraid to try. Too shit terrified to be your friend. You don't love possessions or money or superficial things. What you love is *life*. You love the one thing that can be taken away so damn easily, and that makes you the bravest person I know."

I wanted to reply.

To burst into tears.

My chest swelled with so, *so* much emotion. So many feelings that had no words or descriptions. Jacob had stripped me bare and kept me safe all at the same time, and I no longer just loved him.

I *needed* him.

I needed him to be free like me.

His head bowed, and the faintest graze of his nose on mine zigzagged a lightning bolt deep into my belly. His grip on the chain around my throat tightened, pulling me closer against him.

I swayed into him, parting my lips, offering up everything.

And I waited.

I waited and prayed and got on my knees for him to accept what I was ready to give him, but he just sighed torturedly, smiled tormentedly, and pulled away. Letting my locket go, he gave me a look born from heartache and hope.

Hope.

Like me.

There was hope he might one day love me…even if it was the tiniest speck.

But even if he could…his heartache would rule him forever.

"Sorry." He cleared his throat from sand and ash and turned away.

* * * * *

"You did well today," Jacob said, breaking the silence that'd kept us company along with the crackling fire, occasional scurry of something furry in the bushes, and an owl hoot or two.

"Thanks. It was fun." I snuggled deeper into the sleeping bags we'd spread on the yoga mats close, but not too close, to the fire.

All day, I'd locked down the desire he'd invoked by clutching my locket. I kept my eyes far from his, threw myself into camp tasks, and pretended I wasn't a shaking mess every time he came near.

Even the chore of gathering firewood with him sent goosebumps decorating me. A guided tour of this piece of paradise made my stomach clench. A simple dinner of packet pasta and squished blueberry muffins made my heart swoon at the domesticated bliss.

I fell into the daydream that we were a couple, and the tent we set up didn't require the two separate nests on either side of the central pod.

That we'd sleep in one.

Together.

Touching.

Kissing.

Confessing that this friendship wasn't enough anymore…for either of us.

But that hallucination was dashed as Jacob finished erecting the tent with ease and practice, then stepped inside the three-room shelter. The air changed, his back stiffened, and his attention locked on the right wing as if it were a portal to hell.

He froze in the gathering twilight, seeing monsters I couldn't imagine.

Ice slithered down my spine.

Had this tent belonged to his parents'? It was too big for a solitary traveller, but it was well used.

Used by a family perhaps.

A trio who'd become a duo.

I backed up, climbing over the zipper door, leaving Jacob to his ghosts and horrors.

Whatever had happened in that tent had irrevocably changed him, but I didn't know how.

Curiosity chewed at me, although our tentative connection whispered I had no right to ask.

I didn't say a word when Jacob decided to put our mats and sleeping bags by the fire instead of in the tent, and we skirted the topic of death with fire-roasted marshmallows until my fingers were sticky and sugar dusted my lips.

Jacob interrupted my thoughts. "Reckon you could survive a night out here on your own?"

His voice, rough and gravelly at this time of night, threatened to tear my secret from my chest.

I love you.

Shaking my head clear, I clutched my hands together for support. "Not without someone preparing a backpack for me with everything I need."

He laughed quietly, his eyes mirroring burning flames.

Why did he have to be so handsome? So brilliant? So wild?

My heart physically hurt. It wrapped itself up in a blanket of thorns, bleeding with need just to tell him.

To say *thank you.*

I love you.

Don't be afraid.

Ugh.

I glared at the sky where gleaming stars mocked me from above.

"You adapted well enough."

"I had a good teacher."

He cleared his throat. "You're a good student."

My body locked down, the sleeping bag unable to eradicate the chill in my bones for denying what I most needed.

I needed his arms around me.

His lips on mine.

Get a grip, Hope.

You are his friend.

F.r.i.e.n.d.

Friend.

"It's so quiet out here." My tone was waspish and loud as if the wooded serenity was an inconvenience and not a privilege.

"Yeah. The silence has a way of making your thoughts unavoidable." He shifted beside me, his forehead furrowing.

I wanted to agree, but I daren't admit my thoughts were all about him. His were most likely on dead fathers and dying grandfathers while mine were on more trivial things.

Things like unrequited love.

Trivial because they were pointless and only hurting myself.

Silence fell.

A shooting star ripped up the inky vastness in blazing suicide.

Jacob's voice once again crept into my ears, making my heart quicken. "What do you want from life?" He kept his eyes firmly on the masterpiece above us, but his hands fisted on his sleeping bag.

For a while, I struggled with an answer.

It was a question that could seem blasé, but in that infinite moment, alone and linked with the cosmos, it was the most important thing I'd ever been asked.

My cheeks warmed for no other reason than honesty. "Everything that everyone else wants, I suppose."

Don't do this, Hope.

Secrets like this shouldn't be shared while alone in the forest.

"And what exactly is that?"

I pressed my lips together, fighting the urge. But I was weak. I was pushy. I couldn't help myself. "Family...someone to love. A best friend to laugh with. A house. A *home*." I squirmed, embarrassment and fear skipping down my skin. "Those kind of things."

If you took away wealth and hierarchies, in the end, that was all anyone ever wanted. The general consensus of life: two-legged, four-legged, feathered or scaled.

A mate.

A hearth.

A belonging.

Jacob sighed. His voice barely audible with charred edges, as if the fire had scorched his throat. "I don't know if I do."

I stiffened, doing my best to seem unaffected.

"I've tried really hard the past month," he whispered. "Really damn hard. I'm glad I've made my mother smile more, and Grandpa John feels he can touch me without me ripping his hand off. But..."

He slung an arm over his eyes, blocking his face from view. "I'm still so goddamn afraid. I was hoping that fear would go away, but it's only grown worse." His voice blackened with coal. "I'm sick of being so fucking screwed up."

I didn't know if he expected a response or if this was purely to ease the bleeding of his soul. Taking a gamble, I breathed, "It's okay to be afraid. You've been blessed with the best family in the world. It's unthinkable to lose something so precious. You're so aware they can be gone in an instant."

He groaned under his breath. "Death shouldn't have scarred me this permanently. You lost a parent, too, but I don't see you breaking because of it."

"That's different."

He stiffened. "No, it's not. The fact is, you're much stronger than I am. I keep letting everyone down. I keep waiting for the pain to go, for the fear of loss to vanish so I can be brave enough to care. But it just...never happens. I still picture them dead. I still steel myself against their touch. Pieces of me lock down whenever I try to love them. I-I can't control it."

I couldn't handle his rawness, his openness. I didn't know what I'd done to deserve it, but he'd shown me every dark, haemorrhaging secret, and I couldn't lie there without touching him.

Crawling from my sleeping bag, I slotted my body along his. "It's okay. We're all different. It's not something you—"

"Shut up, Hope." He sucked in a harsh breath, his entire form locking down. "I don't even know why I told you. Just...forget it."

He didn't push me away but his entire body bellowed for me to back off.

I should let him go.

I should give him space.

Instead, I slung my arm over his waist and nuzzled into his chest.

His temper sizzled, making my hair stand on end.

"Let me go."

"No." I shook my head, inhaling the leather and sweet smell of hay and sunshine clinging to him. "Talk to me. Get it out. I won't tell anyone. I swear on my mother's grave, whatever you tell me stays out here, just between us."

"I've said everything I shouldn't."

"Well, I'm here if you want to say more."

"I don't."

"We have all night."

He jack-knifed upright. "Wrong." Shoving the sleeping bag off him, he stood over me, silhouetted by fire and starlight, and for a second, I was afraid.

Afraid of him, his anger, his damaged, screwed-up soul.

But then his shoulders slouched, and the night air washed the fear away. "I'm eh...going for a walk." With one hand buried in his hair, he gave me a look full of eternal misery. "I'm sorry...for what I said."

"Stop apologising."

"Just...go to sleep."

I sat up, hugging my knees to my chest. "I'll wait until you get back."

He smiled sadly. "You might be waiting a while."

I cocked my head, wishing he'd finally see that when it came to him, I was already committed to waiting. I'd wait for the rest of my life. I'd wait until my heart stopped beating. "I don't mind."

"You don't mind if you have to wait all night?" He raised an eyebrow almost condescendingly.

I merely nodded with conviction and utmost truth. "A single night is nothing. You're worth a millennium of nights."

He sucked in a grunt as if I'd punched him in the chest.

Giving me one last look, this one full of confusion and uncertainty, he turned around and vanished into the tree-hidden darkness.

* * * * *

I had a dream.

A dream about a girl and a boy and a shadow.

A shadow that refused to let the boy care for the living, because the dead already owned him.

In my dream, I offered the boy an ice-cream. I tried to coax him back into happiness. But the shadow wouldn't let him go. It whispered lies. It said I would die and leave him. It spoke of genocide and homicide and death, death, *death*.

And the little boy nodded.

He agreed with the darkness and accepted its black, black cloak, then turned his back on me.

He accepted a life of loneliness as payment to never endure loss again.

And the little girl just stood there…waiting.

* * * * *

I opened my eyes to dawn.

A silvery, ashy dawn that barely made it from treetops to forest floor.

I'd waited for as long as I could. Well past midnight when creatures grew bold and the sensation of being watched by predators and prey chased me into the tent.

I sat in my sleeping bag, ears pricked for Jacob's footsteps and not some hungry beast. But my eyes had steadily grown heavier, my mind fuzzy, until my body tumbled into sleep.

And I'd been harassed by dream snippets and nightmare wisps until a twig snapped, wrenching me upright.

He's back.

Crawling from the tent, I swallowed hard as Jacob covered the dying fire with a kick of dirt and turned away from curling smoke. With a quick look at me, he nodded, then grabbed his backpack and began dismantling our night in the woods.

Without a word, I went to help him.

Like usual, we worked harmoniously, him focusing on one chore and me on another. A dance really. A choreographed routine that said we were used to working side by side, even if we weren't used to talking.

Once the tent was back in its nylon carrier and the sleeping bags rolled up, we headed from the clearing and back on the overgrown path.

Jacob handed me a muesli bar, his fingers grazing mine as I took it.

We flinched.

He gritted his teeth.

I swallowed a moan.

Our morning as strained as last night.

But neither of us knew how to fix it, and it wasn't until Cherry River came into view that I finally found the courage to whisper, "Nothing happened. Nothing was said. You have my word."

He paused, his dark eyes lingering on the empire he toiled over. "I didn't mean to say those things. I love my family. I don't want you thinking I don't."

"I know you love them."

He stood taller. "I'm lucky. Very lucky to have them."

"You are."

Catching my gaze, he murmured, "Summer is almost over."

And in those four words, I knew what he was saying.

He'd agreed to let me help over summer.

Soon, he wouldn't need that help.

Autumn was coming.

And when it arrived, he expected me to be gone.

Chapter Thirty-Five

JACOB
✳ ✳ ✳ ✳ ✳ ✳

"I'M PROUD OF you, Jacob. Immensely proud."

I placed the chipped coffee mug in front of Grandpa John—no coaster required on this dinged-up, well-used family dining table. The steaming hot chocolate smelled overly sweet, and I craved a splash of whiskey to put in mine.

I'd need it.

I already wanted to bolt from the farmhouse and pretend this conversation never existed.

I wasn't mentally prepared for this. I was still messed up from camping with Hope two days ago. I hadn't slept. I'd forgotten what it felt like to live a normal life where my heart didn't skip a beat whenever I saw Hope or my stomach didn't plummet whenever I admitted I was falling in ways I couldn't.

It pissed me off.

It *petrified* me.

On a minutely basis, I cursed my idea of being friends with her.

Why the hell did I take her camping?

At least before that night, I'd been able to pretend things were survivable.

Now, I could barely speak without wanting to attack her. The violence in my blood was confused. It wanted to kiss her, but it also wanted to strike her.

To hurt her so she left and never came back.

Gulping a mouthful of chocolate and focusing on my grandfather instead of my torment, I asked, "Why are you proud? Because we made more money this season than any other, or because I've helped Cassie break in three extra horses?"

He chuckled. "Both."

"You can thank Hope for the grass return."

And then you can say goodbye because she's leaving soon.

I was glad at the thought of her gone.

I was eager to see her go.

I was suicidal to admit I'd miss her.

So fucking much.

"I have." He grinned. "She's been an asset to this place. I'm so glad you two have been getting along so well."

"Yeah." I stared into my drink, wanting to talk about anything other than Hope.

I'd stupidly thought by eliminating the stress between us and becoming friends, we'd be able to work in peace. That my body wouldn't have such highs and lows of irritation and affection.

I'd thought I could handle a friend.

That I would find comfort in company.

But no.

I'd only condemned myself to a living hell.

A hell that didn't stop, that tortured me with images of her alive in my bed and then dead at my feet. The devil mocked me with a future of her by my side, sharing the care of Cherry River, and being family instead of just a friend, but in the same breath, he tore her away, delivered that undoubted pain, and crushed me beneath certain despair.

I hurt.

All the goddamn time.

"I'm also so proud of the way you've let us be closer to you. That letter you gave me was much appreciated." Grandpa John leaned forward, his intensity searing into me. "We've missed you, Jakey. I was worried. Very worried. Ren wouldn't have liked seeing you so closed off."

I tore my eyes away, staring at the melting marshmallow in my mug.

I supposed I should say the customary thank you, but there was nothing to be proud of.

What he saw were lies.

Only I knew the truth.

The bitter, brutal truth.

Before, I'd been honest with my pain.

But now, I lied and hid it.

I was worse.

So, so much worse.

Grandpa John cleared his throat, changing the subject as if he sensed my unravelling. "So, have you decided to go ahead with your plan for the orchard expansion?"

My muscles clenched. I appreciated his olive branch, but I wasn't there to talk about trivial stuff. He'd asked me here to discuss his illness. The subject we'd been avoiding since that fateful day at the hospital. My back was healed. My concussion no more. Yet Grandpa's sickness hadn't gone. It was still there, eating him alive. "You're seriously going to talk about the farm?"

"I'll talk about whatever interests me."

"You're only wasting time. Skirting the real topic."

"No." He shook his head. "I'm easing into it. Is that a crime?"

"It is when it's taking everything I have to sit here and pretend nothing is wrong."

He sighed, his beard fluttering with breath. "There's nothing wrong, Jacob. Everything is how it should be."

"Oh, don't give me that crap." I slouched, crossing my arms. "I don't need to hear about God's plan or life cycles. You're not well. It's shit. Don't pretend it's any better just because you're *okay* with it."

"I *am* okay with it."

"Well, I'm not. So spit it out. Tell me how long I have to be mad at you."

He laughed at my morbid humour. "Chances are, I'll outlive you, my boy. Hope told me why you were at the hospital that day. Jumping that crazy animal without tack is just asking for an early grave."

"That crazy animal has my back."

"Kick you in the back, more like."

"I've never understood why you all hate on him so much. I've had him for years now. He's proven he's trustworthy."

He nodded. "You're right. It's not fair. We're holding onto an old bias."

"I'll tell him you apologised."

He chuckled, sipping his hot chocolate.

In the time it took him to swallow, the air switched from strained to outright sinister. The silence hissed about disease, and I stiffened until I was as wooden as the seat I sat on. "So…how long?"

His face lost any hint of humour. "I told you in the car park. A year or so."

"That's nothing."

"I agree. That's why I'm pleased to announce it's more like two or three, possibly even five years. The treatments have worked. Bought me more time."

Neither of us said it, but our thoughts were on Dad. About how he kept chiselling away at time. Just a little more. Just a little more.

Until there was no more.

Taking a sip of my drink, I dared meet the intense gaze of the wizened old wizard I called family. "We'll find another treatment. Buy you even more."

"I won't chase miracles. I'm at peace with that timeframe."

"So you're giving up?" I bared my teeth. "Didn't figure you for a quitter."

He reached for my hand, but I slipped it off the table and into my lap.

He sighed. "I'm not quitting. I'm accepting. And besides, I've had a wonderful life. I've loved the most amazing people. And if I'm honest, I'm tired. I'm ready to see what else is out there."

His eyes drifted to a sun-bleached photo of the grandmother I never met. A woman with kind eyes and red hair and a lemon-printed apron carrying a steaming casserole. "I miss Pat. She was the life of my heart. When she went, she took most of me with her. I didn't wish away the extra time I've had with you guys, but I'm also not going to fight to stay."

"Wow." I narrowed my eyes. "What a shit thing to say. What about Mom? What about Cassie, Liam, Adam, Chip and Nina? Don't they get a say in this?"

"What about *you*?" Grandpa John placed his elbows on the table, studying me. "You're so worried how others will cope, but I'm more worried about you."

"What the hell does that mean?"

"It means you never got over Ren's death. You can't stand hearing someone cough. You—"

"We all have faults."

He shook his head. "Those aren't faults, Jakey. They're phobias."

"You're saying I need therapy? Like the rest of the people in this town?"

"No, I'm saying life isn't black and white, alive and dead, happy and sad. It's a blend. The only guarantee is today. Not tomorrow or next year. It's good to plan for the future, but at the end of the day, you have to be content with what you have right now. Otherwise, you'll never live."

Anger worked its way down my spine. "I didn't come here for

a lecture."

"Perhaps you need one."

"What I *need* is for you to tell me what's wrong."

John leaned back in his chair, crossing his arms over his considerable bulk. "When I asked you over here, I intended to tell you anything you wanted to know. To list how it will happen. What to expect. To put your overactive imagination to rest. But..."

I sat taller, prickling with unease. *"But?"*

"I'm not going to."

"You're not going to tell me how you're going to die?"

"Nope." He stood, taking his empty mug to the sink. "I'm not. Because that isn't the part that matters." Striding back toward me, he stood over me, dwarfing me, driving me deeper into the chair like a headmaster telling off a delinquent student. "Listen to me, Jacob Wild, and listen well. I'm alive. Right now. I'm happy. *Right now.* I'm going to battle for however long I can, and I'm going to love you for always. The end hasn't changed. It was always going to end with me dead, just like your story will end when you're dead. Who cares how it happens? It's not important. What *is* important is what you do with the days you have *right now.*"

Patting my shoulder, he squeezed me tight.

Normally, I'd allow him the liberty.

Normally, I'd bite my tongue and swallow my pain and pretend I enjoyed the contact.

Not this time.

Not after he hid his illness.

Not after he dare scold me like an idiot.

He wanted to be honest?

Fine, I could be honest.

Soaring to my feet, I shoved his hand off me. "You want me to live *right now*? How the hell can I, huh, when all I can think about is attending your funeral? I already feel that pain. Already know what it's going to be like without you around. How am I supposed to accept *right now*, when I'd much rather have yesterday? At least yesterday isn't a surprise. At least the past can't hurt."

"The past is what's hurting you the most."

"Wrong. The future is."

John's face fell. "That's not normal, Jake—"

"It's a fact of life. You just said it so yourself."

"*Death* is a fact of life, but it shouldn't be in your daily thoughts, for God's sake."

"How can it not when it's taken so much from me?"

"It's taken nothing more than it's taken from other people."

"And maybe they're not coping, either. Maybe they're all screwed up like me."

John stood to his towering height. "You're forgetting I've lost two people who I loved with all my heart. My wife and then my son. Ren might not have been blood, but he *was* my son. To bury your partner is one thing, but to bury your child? It sucks, Jacob. It fucking sucks. But you grieve, you remember, and then you move on."

"You make it sound so easy."

"It's not. It's the hardest thing in the world."

"Then why bother? Why put yourself through it?"

John laughed sadly. A laugh full of the same heartache I lived with. "Because the world wouldn't be the same without love. Humanity wouldn't exist. The cycle of life wouldn't exist. *Nothing* would exist."

The thought of a barren wasteland was an image I'd imagined before. A world where animals lived singular and humans never paired.

It was one of the saddest things imaginable but perhaps the safest too.

"You shouldn't block yourself from caring because you already live with the pain of them gone," John said. "That's a sure-fire way to drive yourself crazy."

"Maybe I'm already crazy."

"Maybe. But it doesn't make me love you any less." John reached for me, aiming to pull me into his signature bear hug. "Come here."

"Hell no." I dived out of his reach, breathing hard, heart rate pounding against the sky. "Don't touch me."

"Someone should touch you. Remind you to stay with the living."

"I don't need reminding."

"I think you do. What about Hope? She wants to care for you. She's a stubborn, patient little thing. Let her care."

A full-body shudder took me hostage.

Hope.

Goddamn Hope.

She'd snuggled up to me two nights ago when I'd stupidly admitted how I felt. She'd crawled from her sleeping bag to lie against me, and I'd almost broken.

I'd already broken by clutching her locket and pulling her close a few hours before. But having her touch me in return was yet another laceration on a heart already flayed into ribbons.

She'd weakened me, but she hadn't fixed me.

God, why couldn't she fix me?

I couldn't be here anymore.

I couldn't listen to John or fight with myself.

I needed peace before I went out of my goddamn mind.

Backing away, I beelined for the door.

"Hey. Where do you think you're going?" John asked. "We haven't finished."

"I'm done."

"Jakey, don't run away from the first frank conversation we've had."

Wrenching open the door, I threw him a look I hoped was full of love as well frustration. "I'm not running."

He scowled. "You'll come back? We'll finish this?"

Probably not.

Definitely not.

"Maybe." Slipping from the house, I leaped from the stoop and ran.

* * * * *

Whiskey made everything better.

The smarting, cutting pain from talking to Grandpa John was now a mellow memory as I sat in an empty stable and nursed yet another tumbler of fire.

I hadn't intended to get drunk.

I'd planned on going for a ride with Forrest and then crashing into the sleep I hadn't been able to snatch since camping with Hope, but that was before I'd walked through a lonely cabin, stared into a bare fridge, and felt the unnatural breeze of my dead father judging me that I'd had the *unbearable* desire to run and never come back.

My muscles physically screamed to flee.

To break my promise to Dad. To disappear without a goodbye.

The urge was too strong. Too incessant. Whispering its nasty promises that if I made everyone hate me, then I'd be free from the agony they caused.

I wanted so badly to give in.

To vanish.

But…I couldn't leave.

I couldn't hurt those I adored. I would *never* be that selfish.

But I did need help, and that help came in the form of alcohol.

And that was how I found myself patrolling Cherry River with a rapidly dwindling whiskey bottle before finding refuge with hay and mice, tucked in the stable where no one would disturb me.

"Jacob?"

Fuck.

Of course, *she* would disturb me.

She would look for me, find me, critique me.

Dragging my knees up, I rested my forearms on them, dangling my drink in loose fingers. There was no point in running. She'd already caught me, and I was too hazy to care.

As I took a healthy swig of burning liquid, Hope's chocolate-haired head appeared over the stable door. Her eyes scanned the shadowy space before locking onto me in the corner.

I tensed for reprimands. I gritted my teeth against arguments.

But she merely sighed, opened the door, and entered. Without a word, she slid down the wall beside me, crossing her legs and glaring at the almost-empty bottle in my hands.

We sat there for ages.

Silent and strained.

Her thoughts were loud enough to encroach on the fog from my booze, but she didn't bother me with conversation.

Thirty minutes or so passed before my ass started to ache and my whiskey was no more. The empty bottle mocked me, and I left the realm of fog and slid into blurry exhaustion.

Hope chose that moment to speak. "You're a farmer, Jacob Wild. You know what that means, right?"

I raised an eyebrow, biting my lip against a world slightly off axis. "No." I twisted a little to stare at her, our shoulders kissing, our hips touching. She was warm and solid and my friend. It made me want to break down and cry and hurt her all at the same time.

"You are life and death itself." Her eyes stayed on the opposite stable wall. An unnatural redness on her cheeks made her glow. A slight rasp to her otherwise melodic voice made her wise. "You are a farmer. You plant seeds, so you give life. You cut the grass, so you take life. You rescue horses that need a second chance, yet you put creatures in pain out of their misery." She twisted to face me, her hand landing on my knee.

I froze, but she didn't stop touching me. "So you see, Jacob Wild, if you are afraid of death, then be afraid of yourself too. Be afraid of everyone, not just those you love. Be afraid of animals and seasons and calendars and oceans."

Her fingers dug into my kneecap, imploring me to follow her down this narrow and twisted road. "Do you see? Do you understand? The *world* is life and death. Every breath is life and death. Every dream. Every afternoon. Every breeze and falling raindrop. You have to accept that. You have to finally give in to *life* because you've already given in to death. We are *all* givers of life and granters of death—accept that you can't change that...and you're free."

My heart pounded.

The whiskey made me nauseous.

Her touch made me reckless.

Hope watched me as if she was there to break me from my prison and believed words could be the key. But I watched her from that prison, cloaked in darkness that'd been brewing inside me for months. A darkness that came from passion and rage, not life or death.

A passion that stirred and heated and infected my bloodstream the longer she touched me.

Anger added to the sickening mix.

Anger at my fear, my entrapment, my repetitive thoughts.

She made it sound so goddamn easy.

Accept it and you're free.

It wasn't that simple.

"Just accept, Jacob," she whispered, adding another layer of fuel to my already burning temper. "Just accept...*me*."

I lost it.

The whiskey thought for me. The alcohol removed my rules. And my hand swooped up to cup her throat.

She gasped as I curled my fingers tighter around the delicate column of her neck. She said I was life and death, and she was right. I could take her life so easily. No one would know or stop me.

Her pulse jumped erratically beneath my thumb. Her skin hot and soft and fragile.

The chain from her locket tickled my fingertips as I pulled her closer.

Her gaze dropped to my mouth, and something ricocheted through me. Something powerful and desperate and greedy...

Yanking her into me, I smashed my lips on hers. The faint taste of blood tainted the kiss as our teeth clacked, and her mouth parted in welcome.

I did what she asked me to do.

I gave in.

I let the liquor cut my morals as I jerked her onto my lap. Our kiss turned hard, deep, fast. Her body lost its stiffness, liquefying. Her lips slipped against mine, and her breath caught as her hands swooped to dig nails into my scalp.

I no longer saw or breathed or existed.

I was merely *there.*

An inconsequential piece of life, giving in to the natural symmetry of mating...surviving.

My thoughts collided and tangled as her tongue licked mine and her moan encouraged me to take more.

I lost all sense of where I was.

What I was.

Who I was.

Thanks to the whiskey, I did what Grandpa told me and lived *right now.*

I came *alive* in Hope's arms.

No half-life. No cursed life.

Just *life.*

I slid against the wall, taking her with me, letting gravity feed her to the floor where I sprawled on top of her.

Her legs spread, her breath catching as I slotted between them.

Our kiss turned wild and careless. Nips of teeth and curls of tongues.

I was drunk on her as well as whiskey.

Her fingernails scratched either side of my spine, dragging me deeper into her.

And, instead of fighting, I let her control me.

I shoved aside everything else.

All thoughts.

All phobias and pains.

There was nothing.

Just Hope.

"Fuck." I fisted a handful of her hair, deliberately drowning in her. And she welcomed me to swim deeper, to dive into her heart and sink to the bottom where I would never be alone.

Her hands roamed down my back, dropping to my jeans pockets and squeezing my ass, tugging me forward and into her. Her delicious heat short-circuited everything that made me human.

Her slender strength turned me on. Her fight and stubbornness made me hard.

My body sank lower, crushing her to cobbles and thrusting my vicious need against her. My thoughts scattered even further, leaving me love-starving and chaos-free. It was as if, in her embrace, death couldn't find me.

Our tongues danced faster.

Our hands groped harder.

There was no finesse or permissions.

Just raw, basic need.

But then fate intervened.

Fate decided to remind me I would *never* be free.

Mid-kiss, Hope coughed.

And I levitated off her in a single heartbeat.

She coughed again, wincing as she did her best to stop.

Each inhale and cough, she twined electrical wire around my heart and electrocuted me.
Defibrillating the useless muscle until there was no more whiskey, no more desire in my blood.

Just stark, terrified horror.

"Are you sick?" I tripped away, stumbling in my haste.

A cough.

Memories of hospitals and racking fits and medicines that couldn't cure slithered into my mind.

Threading both hands into my hair, I pulled hard, wishing I could crack open my skull and stop the past.

Hope scrambled to her feet, her lips red and hand reaching for me, imploring me to stay with her. "I'm not sick."

"Why the hell did you cough then?" I paced the small stable, growing crazed with claustrophobia.

"It's just…um…" Her eyes flew around the space. "Hay dust."

Everything shut down.

How many times had I heard such lies?

Don't worry, Wild One, it's just allergies.

That cough? Oh, it's nothing, just pollen.

Sore throat, that's all, kiddo.

Stop fretting, it's just a cold.

Lies.

Lies.

Lies.

"Jacob. Don't. It's nothing. I promise." Hope came toward

me, placing soft fingers on my forearm. "Please."

I shook her off. "Don't lie to me."

"I'm not. Truly." Her green gaze glittered.

Was it from fever? Was that why her cheeks were redder than normal and her voice scratchy?

I narrowed my eyes. "You're hiding something."

"No." She crossed her arms. "You're just projecting onto me." She sighed. "Look…can we talk about this? Talk about what happened here? Discuss everything when you're not drunk?"

"I'm not drunk."

She sneered. "I'm drunk just from kissing you with the whiskey on your lips."

I stiffened. "I didn't ask for company."

"And I didn't ask to be attacked."

We glowered at each other.

Slowly, her spine relaxed, and she spread her hands in surrender. "I'm your friend, Jacob. You asked for one, remember? And I wouldn't be your friend if I didn't offer a shoulder to cry on."

"I've always hated that figure of expression."

"Okay then…a sounding board. A—"

"Therapist?"

She squirmed. "If that's what you want." Another tiny cough escaped her. She flinched as I automatically shifted toward the exit. I was powerless against that trigger.

A cough equalled running.

The override button was missing.

"I don't need a therapist." I forced myself to stay in the stable, begging her not to cough again so I didn't embarrass myself further. My argument about not needing therapy wasn't holding up with the way I currently acted.

God, I wanted more whiskey.

"Tomorrow." She came slowly toward me, her boots gathering pieces of hay on her journey. "Please? If you don't want to talk, then perhaps we can try kissing again. Next time, maybe we'll be a bit more controlled, unlike the past two attempts."

I pinched the bridge of my nose, the world swimming. "There won't be a next time. This was another mistake."

She sucked in a breath but nodded. "Okay. But at least…we're still friends. And friends talk. I'm willing to listen to whatever you want." Moving toward the exit, she opened it before turning to face me. "I'm sorry, Jacob. Sorry for coughing and ruining tonight. I won't do it again."

I wanted to be normal.

To laugh at my idiosyncrasies and apologise for *my* behaviour, not hers.

She had nothing to apologise for.

Coughing was a part of life—just like so many elements I couldn't seem to handle.

But she slinked from the stable before I could find my tongue.

And I was back to being miserable and alone.

Chapter Thirty-Six

HOPE

* * * * * *

I LIED TO Jacob yesterday.

I stared directly into his eyes and lied.

He'd sprung me with a kiss. He'd taken my heart and left me ruined.

And in return, I'd probably given him the same virus currently taking over my immune system.

The flu.

I didn't know if sleeping outside when camping had chipped away at my defences or if the early morning starts had drained me, but yesterday, I'd woken with a stuffy head and scratchy throat, and today, I fought a fever with an ever-growing chesty cough.

I'd gone looking for Jacob last night to say I needed a couple of days off before I got worse.

I wasn't going to tell him I was sick…just that I needed to catch up on my studies with Keeko.

But that was before I'd found him drunk and drowning, and I couldn't keep my distance. I'd known the risk that I might cough. I'd battled the aches and fever as I'd done my best to talk. I'd tensed each time he studied me too closely and tried not to sniff back the sickness swiftly taking over my control.

And then what had I done?

In a moment of kissing insanity, I'd coughed and then requested we talk. I'd badgered him into accepting a date. With me. *Today.*

A date, or more like a counselling session, that I couldn't attend because I was so, so much sicker than before.

I'd woken this morning with congested sinuses, heaving coughs, and a temperature that made every muscle beg for relief.

Della had kindly given me some cold and flu meds, made me gargle with salt water, plied me with lozenges, then put me back to bed. She said she'd tell Jacob I wouldn't be working today and stood in my doorway with the saddest expression. "You know you can't be around him sounding like that, don't you?"

My shoulders rolled, slouching into the pillows. "I know."

"He won't react well."

I nodded.

I'd seen how he reacted in the diner.

I'd watched *The Boy & His Ribbon* and understood a cough was not just a cough to Jacob.

I covered my mouth as I hacked, wet and long. "I probably made him sick."

"I doubt it. He has a robust immune system." Della smiled.

My cheeks heated for other reasons than fever. "I, eh...he kissed me last night."

Her eyebrows rose. "Did you kiss him back?"

I bit my lip, nodding. "I asked to see him tonight. To talk about...what happened."

She pushed off the doorframe, coming to sit on the edge of my bed—of her son's bed. "You won't be better by tonight, Hope."

"I know."

"You'll have to stay away until you are. Otherwise, whatever progress you've made this summer will be for nothing." Patting my hand, she sighed. "I can't tell you what it means to me that he's accepted you as a friend. I've always wanted him to have someone. And I'm glad it's you. Glad he has someone looking after him when I'm not able to. It gives me peace knowing you're there for him."

My eyes watered, and I blew my nose.

She stood, brushing a piece of lint from her jeans. "Now, get some rest. Heal fast, so he doesn't have to know."

"Okay."

Waving, she left the room, leaving me to a head full of cotton and a throat full of knives.

Staring at the ceiling, I made a request to whatever all-seeing power was out there.

Please, please keep Jacob away until I'm better.

Don't let him realise I'm not immortal like he needs.

Closing my eyes, I wished and prayed that Jacob would hate me enough from the kiss to stay away for a few days. Because if he didn't. If he *heard* me...I had a bone-chilling knowledge that everything between us would end.

That our friendship would be over.

Our connection destroyed.
He'd cut me out.
He'd send me away.
For good.

Chapter Thirty-Seven

JACOB

* * * * * *

"JACOB? YOU IN here?"

I looked up, shielding my eyes from the sun's glare as Mom strode into the greenhouse where I'd planted some apple seedlings. I was deadly serious about dabbling in orchard growing.

There was money to be made in stone fruits, as well as berries—if I could figure out a way to grow them consistently.

"Yeah." I used the rag from my pocket to wipe the sweat from my forehead.

I wasn't in a good mood. Hell, I couldn't remember the last time I'd been in a good mood. Once again, it was Hope's fault.

That kiss.

That goddamn kiss would forever be linked to the fiery taste of whiskey.

And that cough that echoed in my nightmares.

At least she'd kept her distance. Mom had delivered Hope's excuses about needing to study with her tutor via Skype, but I reckoned she'd finally realised that kissing me was a mistake and was as pissed off about it as I was.

She needed space, just like me.

Thank God.

"Jacob…are you listening to me?"

I focused on Mom. "Sorry. Yeah. What did you say?"

"I said I've been looking all over for you."

"Well, you found me." I didn't have time for this. I wanted to be left alone.

Brushing past her, I grabbed a tray of baby peaches and carried them toward the potting table.

"You know, your father and I lived on an orchard for a couple of months as fruit pickers." Mom followed me, stroking the leaves of an infant plant with a wistful smile. "We stayed in a shack and worked every hour possible, but it was one of the happiest times of our lives."

It wasn't often Mom brought him up this nonchalantly, and my heart definitely wasn't strong enough for her tales today.

Clearing my throat, I said, "Don't you have more rescues to pick up?"

She narrowed her eyes, reading me too well. "I do. But not for another hour or so."

"Ah."

I wouldn't be getting rid of her anytime soon then.

Silence fell as I pulled a seedling from its tray and placed it into a bigger pot. Mom watched me work, her presence not nearly as annoying as Hope's.

After I'd transferred four plants and bedded them in with new dirt, she moved. Her hand went into her back pocket before slipping forward to place a small box on the earth covered bench before me.

The second I saw at it, I knew. "What the hell are you doing?"

The package was identical to the one she'd given me on my graduation in the diner.

Green wrapping.

Purchased by a ghost and given by a dead man.

"I don't want it." I backed up, slamming into a trestle with yet more baby fruit trees.

Mom bowed her head, staring at the gift. "I've been wondering when the right time would be to give you this. I've been watching you and Hope. Not knowing if I could. If she was the one for you. But...she told me you kissed her yesterday. And...I just had to."

"She *told* you?"

What the fuck?

Nudging the box toward the edge of the table, she murmured, "Ren told me to give this to you when you found the girl you were going to marry. I don't know if you'll end up marrying Hope, but in my opinion, she's the most important girl who will come into your life. You guys might break up, you might settle with different people, but without Hope, you wouldn't be ready to love anyone. And that is why I'm giving this to you now."

Our eyes met.

Mine frantic, hers resolute in grief. "Open it, Wild One."

"I-I can't."

"You have to."

"He wouldn't want me to have it yet. I don't deserve it."

"You do, and he would because he would've loved Hope, and you know it."

I clenched my jaw.

Goddammit, why did he have to do this? Why did he have to give Mom the same number of packages he gave me? Why did he keep making life so fucking hard?

"I'll go. Open it on your own." Skirting scattered soil, she came toward me. Standing on tiptoes, she dared kiss my cheek. "I love you. And I think she does too. Don't be afraid of that. *Never* be afraid of that."

I didn't say a word as she left. The greenhouse door squeaked as she opened and closed it behind her, leaving me in sweltering soup.

My eyes zeroed in on the green wrapping. It blended so well in here with bright leaves and glowing sunshine. It almost looked alive, as if it shimmered with Dad's energy, granting him a small portal in which to interact.

"You're a pain in the ass," I muttered. "Why can't you leave me alone?"

No reply.

No air to circulate. No trees to rustle.

Just hot, sticky oxygen.

Gritting my teeth, I snatched the box. It wasn't big. Barely palm size. It only took a second to tear at the paper and lift the lid.

I'd expected another tool. Something in the theme of a Swiss Army knife or compass.

Instead, I found something that stole the strength from my knees and buckled me against the table.

A note fluttered to the dirty concrete.

My hands shook as I ducked and unfolded it, recognising my father's scrawl.

Hi Jacob,

By now, the girl you've fallen in love with will be jealous of Della's blue ribbon. Any pretty girl should wear a ribbon. So give this to yours. Tell her it's from someone who's incredibly grateful she's fallen in love with his son. Tell her I know she's chosen well because once she's claimed the heart of a Wild, she'll never be alone again.

Love you, Wild One.

Dad.

Tipping the box, I glowered as a lacy cream ribbon unspooled. Elegant and old-worldly, the gift was as intricate and delicate as the lace Hope kept tucked tight in her locket.

Out of all the things.

Out of all the ribbons.

He had to buy a piece of lace for the girl nicknamed after it.

Chills scattered down my back. Was there no divide between this world and the next?

There couldn't be because in that terrifying moment, I stood on the edge of its never-ending vastness.

I heard my goddamn father chuckle for shocking me so completely.

I couldn't deal with this right now.

If he intended to make me slip further into crazy, it'd worked.

Plucking the ribbon from the floor, I shook the filigree fabric free from soil and snaked it back into the box.

The lid went on.

The presence of my father vanished.

And I stormed from the greenhouse for fresh air and sanity.

Forrest was waiting for me.

He understood.

And together, we flew away where no ghost or human could find us.

* * * * *

I was alone.

I'd always been alone.

A single entity in a big, black forever.

But slowly, a pinprick of light appeared, then another and another and another, spreading out like a giant clock and I was the centre dial.

Faces appeared.

Dad.

Patricia.

John.

Mom.

Nina.

Chip.

Hope.

Everyone I had ever loved or known morphed into being. Spotlights on all of them, faces shining but bodies barely visible.

I wanted to go to someone.

But who?

They were all spread out, scattered on the timepiece of life, separate and alone.

A compass appeared in my hand.

A compass given to me with an inscription in the metal telling me to find my true path. I clutched it tight, begging it to show me the way.

But it started spinning.

Faster and faster, blurring the outside world.

The faces were no more, just a blend of features as they spun like a vortex around me.

I grew dizzy.

I closed my eyes.

The compass whirred like a living thing in my hand.

It stopped.

I opened my eyes.

Everyone was gone.

Only a single figure stood before me.

The compass needle honed directly on her.

A girl bathed in a spider-web of light.

A lace-loving girl with hope in her eyes and love in her heart.

The compass warmed, nudging me that this was the right choice. This was my correct and chosen path.

I trusted it.

I stepped toward her.

But then, in a bang as deafening as a gunshot, she fell.

Her eyes closed.

Her body crumpled.

And all that was left was my compass pointing at a corpse.

I woke up drenched in panic.

My hands fumbled as I shot from my wet sheets and struggled to turn on my bedside light. I needed illumination. I needed to delete the sight of Hope dead on the floor by my feet.

The second the light clicked on, I launched out of bed.

Nausea bubbled. Dizziness made me stumble. I grappled with the wall as I tripped into my walk-in wardrobe and fell to my knees where I'd hidden Dad's gifts.

I tipped the plastic bag upside down and counted the tiny parcels.

One, two, three.

Three more to give to my mother.

Three more requests from my dead father.

All of them centred around the girl I was destined to fall in love with. Marry. Have children with.

Things that would never be feasible.

I didn't want those things.

I *couldn't* have those things.

Therefore, none of those events would come to pass.

Which meant Mom would never have the gifts selected for her by her deceased husband.

They'd rot in their pretty wrapping, never to be given.

No.

It couldn't happen.

I wouldn't be the cause of such tragedy.

I no longer wanted the obligation of being custodian.

I wanted them gone.

They were Mom's.

They were Dad's.

It was time she had them.

Chapter Thirty-Eight

JACOB

* * * * * *

"HAVE YOU SEEN Mom?" I asked Aunt Cassie as she carried a bucket of feed toward her chosen riding horse of the day. A cute dapple called Romy.

"Nope. Not since yesterday when we collected the two rescues." Her face fell, the cloudy sky softening the darkness of her brown hair. "God, Jacob. That place? Those poor things were chained to a tree with no food or water. They're all skin and bone. I officially hate people."

I jammed one hand into my jeans pocket while the other clutched the plastic bag holding Dad's gifts. "Glad you guys saved them."

"It's gonna take a long time to get their trust, poor things. Any sudden moves and they're explosive."

"I'll keep that in mind when I go see them later."

"Good." Aunt Cassie nodded distractedly. She looked me up and down. "Your grandpa told me what happened with you two the other day."

"Oh, yeah? He tell you that he's sick?"

Her face fell. "Yes. But he's doing much better with his new prognosis."

"What's wrong with him?"

She smiled sadly. "Not gonna work. He told me he's refused to tell you. I've been sworn to secrecy."

I scowled. "You don't think that's totally unfair?"

"Maybe." She shrugged. "But it doesn't really matter in the scheme of things. Worrying about it won't change it."

"No, but perhaps I could research and find a better treatment. I could ask around. Get a second opinion—"

"Stop." She swiped her forehead with the back of her hand. "He's had enough opinions, Jacob. He's very much like Ren in this matter and only willing to accept help so long as it doesn't interfere with his life with us. Don't get obsessed with fixing him."

What could I say to that?

They acted as if it was so wrong to try to fight sickness.

I didn't understand it at all.

Looking away, I scanned the fields, searching for someone else who was missing.

Not only was my mother MIA but Hope, too.

Her disappearance made me dark with unease.

"Anyway, see ya round." I gave Aunt Cassie a nod, repositioned my cowboy hat on my head, and strode off in the direction of my mother's house.

Normally, Hope would be jumping at my heels like an eager puppy ready to work.

She hadn't gone this long without making my life a living hell, and as much as I didn't want to face her after yet another violent kiss, I'd been raised better than that. I couldn't let my manners fail by not giving an apology and clearing the air.

She was right. I'd attacked her. That kiss was entirely my fault.

I had to make it right.

The second I'd given Mom her gifts, I'd stalk Hope for a change and tell her to get over it. What happened to friends and forgiveness? The weeks' chores were long, and I'd grown used to her help, goddammit.

Opening the gate that led toward the smaller paddocks, I scowled at the grass. Already, it'd sprouted to shin height even from our harvest last month. Soon, it would require another cut, not waiting for anyone to have a personal crisis or relationship complication.

See, this is why I'm better off alone.

I didn't do well reading into people's actions. I overthought. I wasn't equipped.

A whinny sounded, dragging my attention upward. At least luck had delivered one person I was looking for.

Mom patted the nose of a skinny palomino with sores on her hips and spine. Her ribcage looked as if it'd morphed from her flesh to be bone-white and visible in the daylight.

My heart clenched at the malnutrition. At the way the horse hung there in its halter, so used to being tied and accepting a hopeless situation. A bucket of food waited by her head, untouched as if she'd forgotten how to eat.

Aunt Cassie was right.

People were jackasses to do that to a creature.

I hope they rot in hell.

Mom noticed me crossing the meadow as she left the head of the barely alive palomino and skirted around the back of a blue roan with slightly more meat on his bones but a gnarly scar along his belly as if someone had tried to disembowel him and never stitched him together again.

I waved in greeting, a flush of love finding its way through my broken heart. Grateful that Mom was so caring to donate her money and time to these lost causes. They might not survive, but at least they'd have the best care, food, and attention. They'd know they were loved before their end came.

Mom smiled, raising her hand in return.

And that was when it happened.

An ending.

Time slowed as if it wanted me to know the exact sequence of events. To be sure I had crystal clarity to replay the horror over and over again for years to come.

It was my fault.

All my fucking fault.

I should never have waved.

Mom's arm came up. Her smile widened. Her love for me as bright as the golden sun.

And the blue roan saw her as a threat.

He saw a raised hand. Tasted more punishment, more pain, more torture.

He wasn't as broken as the palomino. He still had fight. Self-preservation.

So…he did what was natural.

He tried to protect himself.

His rump shot up, his hind legs gathered, and he double barrelled my mother in the chest.

"Shit!" I was running before she hit the ground.

The blue roan reared, his head tossing as he fought the rope tying him in place. The halter snapped as well as his mind. There was only panic left. He screamed and shot backward, his hooves landing on my mother's stomach.

She cried out as the heavy animal sank into soft flesh before he spied freedom and took off at a mad gallop, lead rope and broken halter dangling after him.

He would run into a fence and break his legs.

He would die by his own force or mine for what he'd done.

Breath caught in my throat as I skidded to a stop and kneeled beside the only blood family I had left. "It's okay. I've got you."

The bag full of Dad's gifts scattered as I tossed it to the side. Blue wrapped packages rolled into the grass, little dots of sky amongst green. They were utterly unimportant as I touched her face and assessed the damage.

My fingers itched to grab my phone from my back pocket, but Mom clutched my hand, her grip sweaty and tight. "Jacob—" Her spine bowed as pain shock-waved through her.

Blood oozed from her mouth, making my heart shut down. "Don't talk. It's all right."

I shouldn't move her. She could have a broken back or worse.

But she writhed in the dirt. Her blonde hair turned dusty, her blue ribbon falling from the golden strands as if it already tasted death was near.

Traitor.

I scooped up the ribbon as well as my mother and held her close. "It's all right. Just try not to move."

With one arm supporting her, I pulled my hand free from hers and dove into my pocket for my phone.

"Jacob—" She groaned, more blood pooling over her lips.

"Hush. It's fine." Adrenaline injected trembles into my veins, making it impossible to punch the numbers for an ambulance.

"Something isn't…right." Mom panted. "It-it hurts."

"I'll fix it. I promise." Brushing back her dirty hair, I almost passed out as a female operator barked down the phone.

"Fire, police, or ambulance?"

"Ambulance."

"One moment, please."

Mom squirmed, her legs kicking as she tried to hide from the pain. Goddammit, I'd do anything I could to help her. I'd trade places with her. I'd—

"Ambulance. What's the address?"

My voice caught as I commanded, "Cherry River. Cassie Collins will show you the field. A horse kicked my mother in her chest. It's serious. Get here. Now."

Mom moaned as I disconnected the call, doing my best to stay calm and collected but swiftly losing the battle to the quaking stampede of terror.

"Wild One." Her face scrunched up as a cough bubbled blood. Not red like before, but pink tinged and frothy.

Shit.

Shit.

Shit.

"Don't talk. Don't move. Don't do a damn thing until the ambulance gets here."

She cried out again, tears leaking from her eyes as she clawed at her chest. "Can't...breathe."

"What can I do?" What a stupid question. What an idiotic, *inconceivable* question. Resting her head on my lap, I dared drag my hand down her chest. Her cream shirt had pearl buttons in the shape of sunbursts, and I didn't have time to undo them.

With a quick rip, I pulled her shirt apart, revealing black bra and bruises.

So many goddamn bruises.

There were two almost perfect hoof prints directly above her breasts and two more trampling her upper stomach.

Tears burned my eyes. But it wasn't from the wounds given by a condemned horse.

I cried because of the oozing, spreading blood creeping beneath her skin.

I shuddered because of the white tip of bone sticking from her side.

I wanted to scream because of the rattle and wheeze that I knew so, so well from a father who'd struggled to breathe and suffocated his way into death.

The horse had punctured her lung.

And the gathering blood from other internal injuries added pressure and agony, slowly killing her.

"Fuck." I gathered her close, rocking, hating that my caustic tears splashed on her broken body but unable to stop them.

I should be braver. I should pick her up and carry her to the house. I should run into town and drive the fucking ambulance myself.

But I didn't do any of it.

Because I knew it was already too late.

Mom's blue gaze met mine, locking onto me in a way that blocked out the rest of the world. It shut down time, location, and life itself, sucking us into a bubble where nothing else existed but us.

There.

Right now.

Just like Grandpa wanted.

"Don't...cry." She sucked in a useless breath, pink bubbly blood painting her lips. "Please...*please* don't cry."

I nodded, biting my lip and hugging her closer. "I won't."

"Don't...miss me."

I convulsed. She wasn't just comforting me. She was saying goodbye.

Shaking my head, I rubbed at her cheek where a tear escaped her. "I won't have to miss you because you're not going anywhere."

Her smile turned into a bloody grimace. For a second, all she could do was focus on breathing. Her abdomen steadily turning crimson-black from spreading trauma.

"Promise me...Wild...One."

I couldn't reply. Words clutched brutal, bruising fingers around my throat, preventing me from speaking. Preventing me from curses. Preventing me from pleading for this to be a joke.

Why the fuck did I wave?

Why hadn't she been more careful?

She knew how unpredictable rescue horses were.

She knew *better*.

Rage heated me. I wanted to scold her. Shake her.

But her breathless pant made me squeeze my eyes so I wouldn't have to look death in the face as it took my mother away from me.

Anything but this.

Anything.

Please, God, anything.

"Jacob..." Mom's eyes glowed blue with fierceness even as they glossed with tears. "I need you...to promise me...something."

"Just rest. Help is on the way."

She sighed with a blood-bubbly cough. "I'll rest...soon. First...promise me."

My chest cracked in two. My ribs wanted to puncture my lung in her place. My heart wanted to sacrifice itself so she could live.

I shook my head, not strong enough to have a last conversation with my mother. But her body seized, and her eyes closed, and I hated myself to the pits of Hades.

I was making this harder for her. She wanted me to promise something.

I'd made a promise to a dying father.

Now, I'd make one to a dying mother.

That was my only purpose.

To be the good son—the son who loved his parents even if it

killed him.

Hope had tried to make me accept this. To accept that death was a part of life and it was only by accepting that I could be free.

She was wrong.

This could've been prevented.

This was *my* fault.

I'd murdered my mother, and now, I had the punishment of watching her fade away in my arms.

Joy was a myth.

Grief was my reality.

"Okay, Mom." Sitting taller, I swiped at my tears and swallowed back my rage. She needed me to do this for her. It would aid in her goodbye.

"Anything." I forced with gruff bite. "Whatever it is. I'll do it."

Regrets. Wishes. Pain.

All of it squashed my heart, suffocating me, taking me in her place.

She smiled, relieved. I was the ever-frustrating son, driving her mad until her dying day. "You are...so like... him. Sometimes too...like him."

For once, I didn't want to talk about my father. "Stop. Just breathe. Hold on."

She shook her head. "I'm...leaving...Jacob."

"No."

"Yes." Her fingers wrapped into fists on her belly, another wash of agony enveloping her. The sight of her bone puncturing her side seared my brain with nightmares.

I would always see that.

I would forever remember her this way and not the years of togetherness we'd shared.

I hated that.

I cursed that.

I wanted to pretend this wasn't happening and *run*.

"You...have a...wanderer's heart. Listen to...it."

"I don't need to wander to know I'm happy here."

"Your promise...kept you...here." She soared off my lap again, trying to curl into a ball around her pain.

I soothed her, cradling her close, not caring blood stained my jeans and T-shirt. Not noticing her tears and life force painted my fingers.

I didn't need to ask what promise.

She'd known all along what I'd vowed to Dad.

And I'd made her feel awful instead of protecting her.

I'd grown short-tempered when she wanted to spend time with me. I'd argued with her over trivial things. I hadn't let her touch or hug me. I'd held my love hostage and didn't look after her the way Dad would've wanted.

Fuck.

I'd give anything to be back in the greenhouse yesterday. Safe and breathing clear. Appreciating every moment I had with her.

Tears swam in my eyes, turning me blind. "I'm so, so sorry. I should've been better. I'm sorry I—"

"Never...be sorry." Her fingers sought mine, squeezing in a sudden burst of strength. "Go wander." She inhaled as deep as she could. "Take Hope...explore, visit, learn...but don't just be...like Ren and travel...the forests. Travel the oceans. Cross...the seas. Find...peace."

I sniffed back sorrow. "Peace is here."

"No." She kissed the back of my hand. "Torment...is."

My head bowed, praying to her.

I hated that she was right.

I hated that she knew me.

I hated that after today, I'd have no choice but to leave.

I would never be able to look at this land again without remembering the parents it had buried. Never be able to take in a rescue without wanting to kill it for what it had killed in return.

If I stayed, the final pieces of me would perish.

My sanity would slip into madness.

I would be nothing but hate and heartbreak.

A morbid laugh fell with torn tears. "He asked me to stay. Yet you ask me to leave."

She smiled with blood-tainted teeth. "We ask...only what you're...capable of."

"I'm not capable of anything."

"Yes...you are." She gasped, her mouth wide and anguish bright. "You're capable...of love. You just...need to trust..."

I didn't want to argue.

Not now.

My entire body convulsed as I swallowed despair-riddled fury and vowed upon her soul. "I'll leave, Mom. You have my word. I'll travel the world. I'll chase the seas. I'll explore it all...for you."

She nodded, accepting my pledge. "Take...Hope. She'll be there...for you...now that I can't."

No.

From this day forward, I am alone.

Single.

Solitary.

Slain.

But her blue eyes implored me, and I told a lie to comfort her. "Okay. I'll take her." I didn't think of the costs of lying to a dying parent. I didn't care I'd just sold my soul to purgatory.

"Good." Her eyes burned into mine, waiting for the eternal goodbye.

I gritted my teeth, knowing what she wanted. My throat closed up. Tears burned. And it took every power inside me to whisper, "Fine."

Fine, I love you.

Fine.

Fuck, none of this is fine.

She smiled, teeth no longer porcelain and lips sketched in red. "I…love you…Jacob." Her breath turned louder, wetter, thicker.

My heart pumped louder, wetter, thicker.

Tears lodged in my throat as I nodded. "I know."

"I…don't…have…to wait…anymore." Her skin lost the colour of living, slipping into blue as her lungs filled with blood. "I'll…find…him…now."

"Okay, Mom." My voice was muddied with suffering. "Go find him."

Her eyes turned hazy, looking at me but not really.

Already seeing through the veil that separated us from them.

Alive from dead.

I hoped for her sake, Dad was waiting.

I begged with all my being that the second her life ended in my arms, she'd awaken in a new one in his.

It didn't matter if I didn't believe in it.

I just wanted it to be true so she wouldn't just un-exist. That she'd be out there…with Dad, watching me screw up again and again, pitying me until my own dying day.

I rocked her, hugging her in ways I'd never been able to do before.

Her body didn't feel right.

It felt cold and lifeless and…empty.

"*God—*"

The sounds of an ambulance screeched through the air, the squeal of tyres on gravel hinting they tore down the driveway.

Their rushing noise only compounded my depression.

I didn't bother telling Mom to hold on.

I didn't look up or yell for Aunt Cassie to guide them.

Help was not needed.

It was already pointless.

"Goodbye, Mom." I ended my embrace, staring deep into the eyes of my beautiful mother, hidden beneath blood and bone.

She'd slipped away silently.

There'd been no last-minute farewells or whispered affections.

She'd said what she needed to.

I'd vowed what she wanted me to.

She was done waiting and had gone.

I nodded at the finality of it.

I no longer held my mother but a shell.

A corpse just like my compass dream had shown.

"Dad, if you truly are out there...if you're watching...I hope to God you've found her."

The thought of her alone, surrounded by black, lonely forever?

Fuck, it broke my goddamn heart.

Voices and shouts sounded.

Aunt Cassie's scream ripped through the heavy air, and a breeze erupted from nowhere.

Hurricane power and just as rogue, ripping over the field, tangling in my mother's hair, soaring to the wooded boundary and shaking the boughs of trees.

Was that my father?

His reply?

Or was it Mom, flying to find him like she said?

Or maybe it was both of them, finally together?

Either way, they were gone.

With trembling bloody hands, I gathered a small section of her hair and tied the blue ribbon back into the strands.

She couldn't go to the afterlife without her namesake.

She'd never opened the gifts from Dad, and the little blue boxes were trampled into the ground as people surrounded me. Paramedics, Grandpa John, and Aunt Cassie.

Before, I'd sat in aching sadness. Now, there were seized solutions and frenzied attempts at resuscitation.

Someone pushed me out of the way, pulling Mom from my arms and laying her on her back. Rough hands ripped her shirt wider. An oxygen mask was placed over her mouth. One man blew air while another pumped her heart, jiggling her chest with each compression, making the bone in her side appear and reappear with each false breath.

I was forgotten.

Not seen.

Not needed.

I couldn't watch anymore.

Turning around, I crawled on all fours and threw up.

The taste of grave dirt and cremated ash coated my throat as sour bile splashed on the ground.

No one tried to console me.

No one noticed.

The living was obsessed with the dead, surrounding her as if she were on a pyre about to burst into flames.

Grandpa John sobbed over his surrogate daughter.

Aunt Cassie wept over her deceased sister.

Strangers in uniforms tried to grant a miracle.

And I...I stumbled to my feet and walked away.

I swallowed back mourning, wrapped arms around wretchedness, and put one foot in front of the other with my mother's blood baptising me, urging me to keep a promise, commanding me to run.

My legs were too weak to fly.

My body shaking and full of shock, but I never stopped walking.

I walked past Forrest's paddock without a goodbye.

I walked past Hope as she appeared by the wooden gate, eyes wild and hands plastered over her mouth.

I walked away from all of it.

Everyone.

Everything.

I'd kept one promise for eleven years.

Now, I had another one to keep.

Stay.

Go.

I was their son, an orphan, free.

I didn't stop until I vanished into the trees.

Chapter Thirty-Nine

HOPE

✶ ✶ ✶ ✶ ✶ ✶

"DAD?" I coughed around snotty tears.

"What is it, Little Lace?" His voice instantly went on high alert, the protective father, the kind parent. His love made me cry even harder.

My head bowed as I stood in the kitchen of a woman who no longer existed.

A woman who'd been so kind and wonderful.

A woman who'd been alive this morning and now…was gone.

How was that possible?

How could this be?

"Hope? You there? What happened?"

My tears came faster, my coughs came thicker as I broke down in a way I hadn't been able to when standing on the outskirts of the paramedics as they tried to bring Della back.

I sank to the tiled floor, leaning against cabinetry its owner no longer needed.

"Dad…"

"Stop crying for one second, Hope. I need to know what's going on. Are you hurt? Injured? What can I do?"

"She's…gone."

"*Who's* gone?"

I sobbed harder, flashes of Della laughing as we rode together, snippets of Della beside me on the couch as we watched TV. Memories of her hugging me and soothing me when her son had made my life a nightmare.

"Hope, tell me right now. Do you need me to come there?"

The thought of him being here.

To have his comforting presence beside me at the funeral.

I wanted that more than I could say.

Jacob was missing.

No one knew where he'd gone.

I hadn't been there for him. I'd been too weak to stay healthy, and I'd let him down by hiding myself away with this *stupid* flu.

He had no one.

And everyone else on this farm had lost just as much.

They were wrapped up in their own grief.

Cherry River had shut down the moment Della's body was carted away in the ambulance.

I was alone.

I didn't want to be alone anymore.

Sucking in a sob, I coughed. "Della died, Dad. She's dead."

Silence answered me before Dad let out a low groan. "Christ. I'm jumping on a plane this afternoon. Don't move."

He hung up.

I wished he hadn't hung up.

I wanted someone to tell me that it would be okay.

That the two women in my life who I'd loved as a mother hadn't truly left me.

That it wasn't my fault they had died.

"Dad?" I whispered into the empty phone. "Dad? Please...come fix this."

Cradling the phone, I slipped into a foetal position on the kitchen floor.

And cried.

* * * * *

"Oh, sweetie." A soft hand landed on my shoulder, rousing me.

I opened gritty, tear-swollen eyes, meeting the gaze of Cassie.

Her hair was tangled and unruly. Cheeks splotchy and clothes hanging lank off a grieving body.

"Ho-how are you?" I asked around another cough, fighting the cold kitchen floor to creep upward against the cabinets.

"How am I? I think I need to ask you that." Cassie smiled gently. "How long have you been down there?"

I blinked at the night-filled house. Dusk had descended, followed by evening. I'd lost track of time, drifting off into sadness.

"I don't know." With her help, I clambered to my feet. I coughed again, needing to blow my nose and breathe.

This awful flu wasn't giving me any reprieve.

And now, I had no one to pop me painkillers with a motherly smile.

Another burn of tears threatened to drown me.

Rubbing my nose, I stared at the toaster, doing my best not to sob.

"I'm sorry no one came for you, Hope."

I shook my head quickly. "Don't apologise. Please, *please* don't apologise. I'm the one who should. I'm so sorry about De…" I couldn't say it. I couldn't make it so real.

We stood in terrible tension, hearts beating with sorrow. I rubbed my nose again, hating the tickle of sickness when bleakness was enough of a curse. "Where's Jacob?"

"No one has seen him since—" Her breath hitched, and fresh tears spilled down her face. "Since Della passed away." Shaking her head, she let me go and busied herself by turning on the lights and pouring a glass of water. "He's probably gone into the forest. He'll be okay."

She was most likely right about the forest but not right about being okay.

If I weren't so sick, I'd go after him.

I'd tramp through the forest in the dead of night and find him. He needed to know he wasn't alone. If someone didn't find him soon, he'd disappear in every way possible.

I knew that in the depth of my being.

Jacob needed someone to reach out and pull him back from the abyss.

To *hug* him.

If no one did, he'd shut down, and it would be too late.

It was probably *already* too late.

My chest ached as more tears welled, this time not just for Della but for Jacob.

I'd failed both of them.

I'd hidden from Jacob after an incredible kiss. I'd loved his mother like she was my own. I'd overstepped, over-pushed, and overstayed on every occasion. And Della had said it gave her peace knowing I was there for Jacob when she couldn't be.

I'd earned her trust.

She'd only been gone a few hours, and I'd already let her down.

God, the thought of her in some astral plane, watching her son break down while I curled up on her kitchen floor hurt so, so much.

"Have you eaten?" Cassie asked. Before I could answer, she laughed tightly. "What am I saying? Of course, you haven't."

Brushing her hands on her jeans, she cocked her chin. "Come on. You're sleeping at my place tonight."

"I need to find Jacob."

"It's past midnight, Hope. You're not going into the forest in the dark."

"But he needs us."

"He needs to be alone right now. To process everything."

I bit my lip. I didn't want to argue with Jacob's aunt—after all, she knew him better than me—but the creeping dread filling my stomach said otherwise.

Jacob was almost out of our reach.

"Come on." Cassie moved wearily toward the door. "Let's go."

"But—"

"No buts, Hope. Not tonight." Her eyes flashed, followed by more tears. "Please. Let's just…rest. After all, tomorrow is another day."

My heart clenched. I'd quoted the same thing.

Gone with the Wind.

At least in that tale, Scarlett and Rhett were still alive. In this one, both were dead.

All my strength vanished.

I had no power to argue, run into the forest, or even to head to Jacob's old room and grab a pair of pyjamas.

I was literally depleted and almost collapsed back onto the kitchen floor.

Cassie held out her hand, and I took it with a wash of fresh tears.

I cried for Jacob and Della, but I also cried for me.

I'd lost them both before I'd ever truly had them, and the thought of no longer being in this crypt of a house was a welcome one.

I didn't look back as Cassie squeezed my fingers and guided me outside.

My back stiffened as she closed the door behind us, the click all too final.

All too loud on an ending of someone's life.

Della would never walk over that threshold again.

I just hoped Jacob would.

Tomorrow is another day.

I'd find him.

I wouldn't let him disappear.

Standing on the deck, Cassie and I breathed in night air, fighting misery.

"Where...where is she?" I dared ask, keeping my gaze on the deck beneath my sneakered feet.

"At the hospital." Cassie sniffed, shaking her head as tears glittered on her cheeks. "She had her funeral plan already arranged. She'll be cremated, and we'll hold a simple funeral in two days."

"So soon?"

"It's what she wanted. Her wishes stated if she could no longer be with us and Jacob, she wanted to be with Ren as soon as possible." A sob caught in her throat. "She'll be scattered in the same place he was."

Fresh tears stung my eyes as they cascaded unbidden.

How much could one person cry?

I didn't remember crying this much when my own mother committed suicide.

And that made me wretched because how dare I mourn a woman who wasn't mine more than my own flesh and blood?

But Della had been there for me. She'd cared for me. She'd *wanted* to spend time with me.

And...I loved her for that.

Now, I missed her more than anything.

* * * * *

"Ah, Little Lace."

I looked up from the rocker where I'd sat since three a.m. The rocker where John Wilson smoked a pipe sometimes, surveying Cherry River and its lovely rolling meadows and perfect pony paddocks.

After a midnight snack of scrambled eggs on toast, Cassie made up the spare room for me. I'd smiled gratefully and closed the door, blocking the sound of other people's tears so I could indulge in my own.

But I couldn't sleep.

I couldn't close my eyes because every time I did, I saw Jacob out there, alone, covered in dirt and blood, his face vacant of humanity, his heart shattered into irreparable pieces.

I'd crept outside, intending to chase after him.

I'd stood on the deck and tried to visualise the path he'd taken me to go camping.

But as I'd pulled on sneakers and wrapped a jacket around my never-ending chill, utter exhaustion added lead to my legs.

Sorrow slammed into me like a wrecking ball, smashing my

knees, sending me tumbling into the rocker.

I promised myself I'd rest for just a few minutes.

I coughed and sneezed and bargained with my health that any second now I would be cured enough to gallop through the forest after Jacob.

They were lies.

My eyes closed on their gritty grief, and sleep dragged me under.

But now, it was dawn, and I was no longer alone.

Dad was here.

I thought I'd cried every drop.

I was liquid deficient from a day's worth of tears, but the second I saw my father, I broke.

I opened my arms, and he bent to scoop me into his embrace. He picked me up like I was a child again, cradling me tight as I buried my face into his neck.

I cried for Della and Jacob.

I cried for the horses she'd rescued and the family she'd left behind.

I cried for all of it.

And Dad didn't let me go, murmuring sweet things, stroking my hair with tenderness, holding my pieces together while I came undone.

By the time, I pulled away to blow my nose, his grey shirt was soaked and his face tired. The aura of airplane and travel hung over him, making him stoop under fatigue.

"What about work?" I asked softly.

He was always so reliable. The directors loved him for his commitment to a project. His trustworthiness to production timelines.

He shrugged. "Not important."

"But—"

"Stop." He smiled gently. "I'm here for you. And for Della. I'm so sorry, Little Lace."

I bit my lip, stemming more tears. "It still doesn't seem real."

"Are you okay?"

I shook my head.

"That's understandable. You had a great bond with her."

"I loved her." My eyes narrowed, daring him to argue.

He nodded. "I can see that. And Jacob? How is he?"

"He's vanished." I cursed as yet more water welled in my eyes.

When would it end?

How much more would I cry?

"Oh." Dad let me go, moving toward the edge of the deck and sitting wearily on the steps. "I guess we'll have to find him then, won't we?"

I gasped. "You…you'd do that? You'd go looking for him?"

He frowned. "Of course, I would. His mother just died. It's not good for him to be alone."

How lucky was I to have a father like him?

Rushing over, I threw myself at him. "Thank you. I've been so worried about him. Can we go now?"

Stroking my hair, he pulled away. "How about we have a shower and something to eat, and then we'll go find him."

Another delay, but a sensible one.

"Okay."

I could wait a little longer.

We'd find Jacob.

I'd tell him I was in love with him.

I'd care for him, protect him.

Just like Della would've wanted me to.

Chapter Forty

JACOB

* * * * * *

I WATCHED THEM from the treeline.

I hugged the hunger in my belly and wiped at the dirt on my cheek as they invaded my forest.

My parents' forest.

The cemetery.

I knew they'd come.

I didn't know when, but I knew it would end here.

Where I'd stood as a ten-year-old and said goodbye to the ashes of a man I missed more than anything. That day, Mom had hugged me and told me it wasn't him in that urn—that he was free and all around us.

Had she lied?

I supposed she was about to find out for herself.

The procession was small and intimate.

Family and close friends only.

At the back of the crowd walked Hope with her father.

He had no right to be here.

Thanks to him, I had my dad's cough repeating in my head in two different styles. I'd watched him die twice. And I'd had to deal with his daughter who disturbed and hurt me in the strangest, horrifying way.

We hadn't spoken since that god-awful kiss.

If I had my way, we'd never speak again.

Hope's eyes were never still, searching the fields, the shadows, the trees.

Looking for me.

I should feel guilty for running off without any explanation. I should stride from the woods and meet my family with an apology.

But when Mom died, most of me died with her.

I couldn't pretend I was okay or soothe the grief of others.

I was done with the living.

For two days, I'd fended for myself in the barest way possible. I still wore the clothes stained with my mother's blood. I'd stayed alive with a few drinks from the river and a handful of local berries, but that was all I'd foraged for. I couldn't hunt because I couldn't stand the thought of more blood and bone. I couldn't watch another life be taken.

My hands shook as humanity came closer.

I wanted to bare my teeth and run.

Soon.

Soon, I would disappear for good.

Once this funeral was over...I would exist no more.

Their hushed voices met me, weaving around tree trunks and whispering in the leaves. Grandpa John and Aunt Cassie led the sad procession, a black lacquered urn wrapped with a blue ribbon in Aunt Cassie's arms.

My heart twisted into knots.

But no tears fell.

I hadn't cried since.

I didn't know if I ever could again.

Something had locked inside me. Painful and thick, the barrier fortified with barbwire, imprisoning me in solitary.

I couldn't process what'd happened.

I couldn't *accept.*

All I knew was...nothing was worth this type of pain.

Nothing.

"How can we do this without him?" Aunt Cassie asked Grandpa John as they arrived in the clearing where the soft breeze was never still.

"He'll come. I know he will." Grandpa squeezed her shoulder, his gaze landing on the urn. "He has to."

My hands balled as the rest of the congregation gathered. No one spoke. Dressed in black, some with a blue ribbon tied somewhere on their person in homage to my mother, they all waited for something.

Someone.

Me.

Swallowing my phobias of contact and caring, I strode from the treeline and into the sun.

A few gasps sounded.

Hope tried to come to me, but her father stopped her.

Aunt Cassie's and Grandpa John's eyes immediately welled with tears.

I kept my back straight and chin up, stoic and unbreakable as I held out my hands and waited until she placed my mother's ashes in them.

Aunt Cassie bit her lip, unable to stem more sadness as I nodded and carried the black vase to the same place where Mom and I had said goodbye to Dad.

People followed me, not giving me peace, expecting me to be the one to say the eulogy.

I had nothing to say.

Only that life was cruel.

And fighting for love wasn't worth it.

Dad had been forty-three when he passed.

Mom was the same age.

Ten years apart, but both gone so young.

A cruel twist of fate or just rotten bad luck?

I no longer cared about figuring out existence and the rhythm of the heart.

My family was gone.

And soon, I would be too.

Removing the lid, I stared at the grey dust inside, searching for words of wisdom and consolation. Mom had said the tribute at my father's funeral. She'd held the attention of townsfolk and doctors with her penned paragraphs destined for the book that would make their love story famous.

I had nothing like that.

I wasn't a writer.

Or special.

Or gifted.

I was just their son.

The orphan.

Turning around, I faced the crowd…and shrugged.

Tears erupted Aunt Cassie and Hope, and Nina turned into her father with sobs.

For the longest moment, I was wordless. But then the desire to get this over and done with shoved simple, almost heartless things from my mouth. "There's nothing to say apart from goodbye." I cursed the heavy hardness in my chest. The knives and swords that stabbed my every breath. "She wanted to be scattered here. So…I'll honour her wishes."

The breeze whipped harder as I tipped an urn for the second time in my life and let the mortal remains of my mother free. They fluttered and flew, cascading over earth and leaves, leaving the barest of silver traces behind.

Grandpa John sucked in a heavy sob before turning to the small gathering.

And he did what I could not.

His deep baritone blanketed the hillside with tales of my mother when she first found Cherry River, of her many years of friendship with Aunt Cassie, and of her star-crossed marriage to my father.

I didn't listen.

I couldn't stay.

Leaving the empty urn against a twisted tree root, I shoved my dirty hands into grubby pockets and strode away.

For a second, I was alone in my exit.

But then, tiny footfalls chased me, not stopping until the shadows of the forest kissed me, and I stopped to face the inevitable.

"Jacob." Hope dashed the final distance, her eyes red-rimmed and puffy. "I was so worried about you. Dad and I searched for two days looking for you."

I studied her, taking in the black dress and midnight boots. "I didn't want to be found."

"Well, you're here now. Please…stay." Her forehead scrunched as if she was fighting something before her eyes watered and she plastered a hand over her mouth. A loud cough escaped her, rattling and wet, thick and sick.

I backed up. My hand swooped up on its own accord to stop her as she moved toward me. "Stay away."

She wrung her fingers. "It's just the flu. That's why I kept my distance from you after our kiss…. The cough sounds worse than I am. Truly. I'm much better now."

My skin prickled with horror as she coughed again.

My ears rang with other coughing, other dying, other goodbyes.

And I'd officially reached my limit.

No more.

Just…no more.

"Leave, Hope. Leave and never come back."

She froze. "Wh-what did you say?"

"I said you're no longer welcome here."

"But…Jacob." She inched closer. "What about us? What about—"

"There is no us." I backed away again, stumbling in my haste.

"Not anymore. I can't."

"You can. It's just a stupid flu, Jake."

"Don't call me that."

"Well, don't say such idiotic things about asking me to leave."

"I'm not asking. I'm telling you."

Her eyes welled with liquid. "Don't do this, Jacob. Don't push me away."

"It's already done." My spine ached with pain.

I couldn't be near her.

I no longer had a heart.

I was empty.

Dead.

Gone.

If I'm dead, why does this hurt so goddamn much?

"There's nothing left for you here."

"There is." Her voice tangled with pleas. "There's you."

"No." Pointing toward the boundary of Cherry River, I commanded, "Go. I won't tell you again."

"But, Jacob—"

"Do as I say, Hope."

"You're upset. I want to be there for you—" Another cough interrupted her, splintering my tattered heart into fragmented pieces that would never fit together again. "I-I'm in love with you, Jacob. I *love* you. Don't you see? You can't ask me to turn my back on that. Della would want us—"

"Don't tell me what my mother would've wanted."

"It's true," she begged. "Please. Just come home."

"Leave, Hope."

"I can't. I belong here." She coughed again, worked up and breathless with panic. "I belong here…with you."

Graham appeared in the distance, watching me destroy his daughter. He'd hate me forever, but I welcomed that hate because it was the opposite of love.

Opposite of agony.

Hate was survivable.

Stalking toward Hope, I whispered under my breath, "Remember your promise?"

Her eyes searched mine, her hair loose around her shoulders. "What promise?"

"The one where you said you'd leave if I ever asked you to. You swore on your mother."

My voice deepened on that word. Neither of us had one of

those now. But at least, she still had a father. She had family.

I no longer wanted such a thing.

I wanted to be left the hell alone.

Whatever feelings I'd had for her were gone.

She was in love with a man incapable of loving her back.

I warned her.

I told her.

But she didn't listen.

"Jacob...please don't." Her tears tracked glitter paths down her cheeks. "Stop."

"I'm making you keep that promise, Hope. I'm telling you I can't do this."

"I don't want to go."

"I don't care."

"But I do. I care about *you*." She reached for me.

I grabbed her wrists and shoved her hands to her sides. "Don't touch me. Don't talk to me. Abide by your promise and leave."

"Don't you care that I'm in love with you?" She squirmed in my hold. "Don't you care you're breaking my heart?"

"I don't care about anything anymore."

I can't.

I just fucking can't.

"But what about you? You shouldn't be alone."

"I *want* to be alone."

She winced, tearing her wrists from my fingers and wrapping arms around her stomach. "I don't believe that. I want to help you. You need *someone* to help you. There's something between us, Jacob. There always has been. You have to feel it too."

"There's nothing," I hissed. "All I need is for you to keep your promise."

"But—"

"Are you not listening? I can't do this. Don't make me fucking do this." My temper clawed at my voice. I trembled with destruction. I was seconds away from breaking. Of falling to my knees and *begging* her to help me.

Of admitting that I *did* need someone.

Someone to take away my pain.

Someone to act like a drug, a blanket, a cure.

My heart didn't know how to live without such things.

But my mind didn't know how to survive with them.

I was stuck—locked between opposing, destroying forces—

and I would die if she kept pushing me.

Holding her gaze, I growled. "I'm done, do you hear me? Done. There is nothing left for you here."

More tears flowed down her cheeks, making her even more beautiful. Dark-haired and green-eyed—an empress of misery. "Jacob..."

"Fine. If you won't go willingly, I'll force you." Tearing my gaze from hers, I shouted at Graham lurking in the background. "Take your daughter, Mr. Murphy. *Leave.*"

Her body turned wild, reaching for me, scratching at my forearm, trying to keep me. "Don't do this. I'll go away. I'll leave for a few days. When I'm better and have stopped coughing, I'll come back. I'll give you some space. Then...we'll go back to being friends. Okay? Just friends. You need a friend, Jacob. Now more than ever. You *need* me."

"I don't need a friend. I've always hated that word."

"You didn't hate me."

"Are you so sure about that?" I narrowed my eyes, determined to crush her so she never came back.

She flinched. Goosebumps pebbled her arms. "Please, Jacob. I-I can't leave you." Tears rolled round and heavy down her cheeks. "*Please*, don't make me leave you."

Her vulnerability almost ruined me.

Her love so pure. Her care so bright.

It closed a coffin around my already dead soul and threw away the key.

I had no strength left.

I would run like the coward I was.

"Stay. I'll leave." Taking a few steps, I glowered at her not to follow.

She didn't obey. Eyes wide as emeralds, tears as bright as stars, she chased me.

So I did the only thing left.

The last option before she slaughtered me.

Looking past her, I locked gazes with her father. He wouldn't be on my side, but if he wanted to keep his daughter safe, he'd do this for me. "Graham, I'm seconds away from hurting your daughter. Get her away from me before I do something I'll regret."

He broke into a jog. "Don't you lay a finger on her."

"Get her off my property then. I want her gone from Cherry River."

Hope sobbed as her father wrapped his arms around her and tugged her away from me. He death-stared me with fury. "I appreciate you just lost your mother, Jacob, but if you *ever* speak to Hope or me like that again, I'll punch you in the goddamn jaw."

"Noted." I stayed emotionless. Calmer now that Hope was trapped.

I was safe.

Almost free. "Lucky for you, you won't have to see me again."

Hope struggled in her father's grip. "Jacob. This isn't you. I *know* this isn't you. You just need time to accept this."

Accept?

Accept?

Fuck that word.

That motherfucking god-awful word.

Black wrath consumed me as I stalked toward her.

Graham clutched her close as if he could protect her from the pain she'd caused me. The pain I wanted to share with her. "I will *never* accept this. Never. Do you understand? There is nothing to accept. Life is not a gift; it's a curse. Death is the gift because then the madness is over. You want me to accept that nothing is safe or sacred? That everything can be stolen at fate's whim? Well, fuck that."

"No," she cried, unable to untangle herself from Graham's arms. "I mean accept that they are gone. *Grieve*, Jacob. Remember, but don't fight the truth. Don't hurt yourself by refusing to accept that they're dead."

I spun around and walked away.

My tolerance was finished.

"Jacob!" Hope screamed after me. *"Jacob!"*

I didn't turn around.

My ears were immune to her cries, and I steeled myself against every inch of agony she'd caused.

"Let him go, Little Lace," Graham muttered. "Let him go."

Breaking into a run, I did my best to outrun tragedy and persecution.

Tried to outrun the awful things I'd said.

The terrible truth I'd uttered.

Her broken heart.

My broken soul.

I tried to run from life.

Chapter Forty-One

JACOB
***** *

ENTERING MY MOTHER'S house, I sucked in a breath at her lingering scent.

The smell of home and togetherness and family.

My eyes saw illusions and holograms—of her dancing with my dad in the living room, cooking us Christmas dinner, folding laundry in the sun.

Now, she was cinders and scattered in the wind.

Hope had finally left, dragged away by Graham.

My family had withdrawn into their grief.

I was alone.

Officially and totally.

Just like I always feared.

Just like I always wanted.

The past few days in the forest had solidified my resolution to leave. I was an oath keeper, and the time had come to honour my mother's dying wish.

I no longer had to abide by my father's.

I wasn't bound to stay.

I was destined to leave.

Tonight, I would vanish.

Nothing trapped me here anymore. I'd said goodbye at Mom's funeral. I'd left instructions with a local contractor to maintain the harvests, planting, and maintenance of my legacy and farm.

Cherry River would be cared for.

Forrest would be fed.

Grandpa John had Aunt Cassie and her family to care for him.

I was free to go.

Striding through the house, I ran my fingers over the couch and table, along the walls and pictures.

I touched it all, imprinted it all, because I doubted I'd ever see it again.

Entering my parents' bedroom, the quicksilver moon revealed the three blue packages that'd been discarded into the dirt when Mom died. Someone had collected them and brought them here, into a bedroom that would never be slept in again.

The shiny paper was smudged and soiled. Areas of sticky tape came undone, begging someone to open them.

That someone was no longer capable of such a thing, and I had no right to pry.

My hands shook as I gathered them off the bed and hugged them close.

Gifts destined for one deceased parent from the other.

They didn't belong in this world anymore, just like them.

Turning around, my eyes fell on the two books that were never far from Mom's bedside. A blue cover and a yellow cover.

Two paperbacks entombing their love story.

They didn't belong, just like the gifts didn't.

Grabbing the books, and nestling them with the parcels in my arms, I left the house I was raised in and jogged over the field and up the hill to my place.

There, I placed the blue packages and paperbacks on my table while I shrugged off my filthy clothing, had a quick shower, and packed a bag.

Inside the duffel, I tossed mere necessities. A passport that Mom insisted I kept valid, cash, and a few changes of clothes.

Nothing else.

Nothing else was important.

Hope was gone.

My life here was over.

With a last look around my home, I slung on my bag, scooped up the gifts and books, turned off the lights, and scaled the steps of my deck.

The night sky was grey like human ash as I strode into the forest and kept walking.

My feet knew the terrain. My body knew the location even blind.

My thoughts were calm and cold as I entered the clearing where my parents' dust had mixed and fell to my knees beneath the tree I'd carved our initials into.

There was no breeze tonight.

The sky hushed and hurting.

No owls, no mice, no life—as if it were all afraid of me.

With gritted teeth, I used my hands to dig a small hole.

A grave.

Once deep enough, I dropped the blue boxes into it.

One, two, three.

All unopened.

Curiosity gnawed at me to open just one.

But they weren't mine to open, so I shovelled dirt onto them instead.

Next to that grave, I dug another, this one to cradle the paperbacks until they rotted and became nothing but memories.

The two earthen coffins sat neatly side by side as I patted the last bit of earth, putting the past where it belonged, then climbed wearily to my feet.

I stood and stared at the small graveyard.

I tried to speak to my parents one last time.

But only ice slithered around my heart.

One promise broken.

One about to be honoured.

I collected my backpack, cut across Cherry River, and never looked back.

*****

Part Three

*****

Intermission

DELLA

✶ ✶ ✶ ✶ ✶ ✶

DEAR JACOB...

Oh, wait.

I have a question for you, dear reader, before I pen this letter to my son. How do you begin to write something for when you're dead? How do you compose something when you don't know when that will happen or how or why?

How did Ren do it?

How did he buy so many trinkets, pen simple notes, and wrap them tightly in pretty paper, all while knowing we wouldn't open them until he was gone?

That took courage.

That took undying affection.

And I find myself struggling in his position as I have no timeline on my death. I don't know if I'll be young or old. I don't even know if I'll outlive my son, in which case, this writing exercise is a waste of time.

All I want to do for Jacob is what Ren did for us.

Even gone, he reminds us we are not alone. He found ways to show his love, and even though it hurts—excruciatingly so—it's also the best thing in the world because even gone we feel cared for, watched over, and protected.

I'm wasting time.

I'm getting off topic.

If I die, I want Jacob to know I love him as much as his father does.

I want to remind him not to be afraid.

I want to force him to stay alive and somehow be happy.

I need your help, dear reader. I need your counsel on how to do such a thing because, in reality, I fear what will truly happen.

I'm afraid that if something happens to me too early, he'll turn his back on the living. He'll embrace the hopelessness. He'll accept the pain and sink into it forever.

So perhaps my letter shouldn't be about what he should do, or a lecture, or scolding, or guideline.

It should just be what he needs to hear.

I'll try again.

I'll keep it short.

I'll let my love speak instead of me.

Dear Jacob,

You are loved by the living and the dead.
You are watched by the caring and the callous.
You are real for now and for always.
Grief can't hurt you.
Regret can't define you.
Only you can do that.
So be who you want to be.
Love, hate, smile, or cry.
Be every emotion or none of them.
But don't be afraid to survive.
Fight.
Rejoice.
Grow old and happy.
Love.
Please, God, love. There is no other purpose for living.
And when you're through with this world...we'll meet again.
And when that day comes, I can tell you just how proud I am of you.
Of how wonderful you are.
Of how much I adore my son.
Until then, Wild One.
I love you.
Mom
xxx

Chapter Forty-Two

HOPE

* * * * * *

Twenty-One Years Old

I'D GROWN EXTREMELY intimate with the ceiling.

Lying in bed, night after night, struggling to sleep while Michael dreamed soundly beside me, I knew every shadow, imperfection, and discolouration.

It wasn't that I had a stressful job or crazy deadlines. It wasn't that Dad had met someone else and was hosting an engagement party in three months. It wasn't that I hadn't been on a horse in four very long years—although that probably had something to do with it—and it *definitely* wasn't thanks to unfinished business with a man who'd thrown me from his home and then vanished.

Not at all.

Then again…that was the *exact* reason.

But it shouldn't be.

Not after four years of *nothing*.

No letters, no phone calls, no visits.

For the first year, I'd stayed in touch with Cassie almost constantly. I'd ring and ask a thousand questions, all centring around if they'd seen Jacob or heard when he would return.

Each time, the answer was no.

And slowly, my questions dried up to just one.

'*Is he home yet?*'

After a while, I didn't even have to ask. The moment Cassie knew it was me ringing, she'd give me a sad *no*, then ask about my life as if to distract me from everything I was missing.

They'd hired contractors to run the farm in Jacob's absence. John Wilson hadn't bounced back since Della died, and his health was declining. Nina had opted to go to university away from Cherry River to get away from the perpetual grief. And Cassie and Chip were doing their best to stay strong.

It wasn't fair that sadness had swallowed up such a vibrant, wonderful place.

But that was life, wasn't it?

It came and went, far too fast and fleeting, leaving the ones not chosen to suffer.

Thanks to Della dying, I returned to my fascination with death.

I studied late into the night, reading research papers and theories that the brain stayed active even after death, which led to nightmares of still-alive cremations.

I trolled every internet site on afterlife, suicide, and soul-mates finding each other in the ether. I tried drinking special teas that forums said would give me dreams that would connect me to some spiritual awareness.

I Googled for any hint of where Jacob might've run to.

My internet provider probably had me flagged if Michael ever turned up dead.

And in the end, I had to let it go.

I couldn't let death drag me into some prison of my own making, and I couldn't let Jacob steal the future he didn't want with me.

When I'd returned to Scotland with Dad, I'd accepted the role in the crime drama he said I'd be perfect for and flew to England to begin shooting on location.

At least the cute countryside helped stitch together some of my missing pieces. The rolling paddocks and patchwork prettiness hinted at a different way of life if I'd only been brave enough to make Jacob accept me.

Every time he came into my mind, I resolutely shoved him back out again.

I'd shed enough tears over him.

I'd been broken on the plane ride home.

The way he'd looked at me, so cold and detached, ensured I'd cried myself to sleep for months. Between crying for Della and him, I'd drained myself to the point of having to move on or fade away into sorrow.

So I threw myself into acting and, although I did my best, I wasn't good enough. The script was awful and the directing subpar—a trifecta of disaster.

Reviews were scathing, and the show wasn't renewed, which meant after a year of being the actress I never wanted to be, I had a choice.

At eighteen, I was still so young, but I knew what I wanted to do, and thanks to Keeko's diligent teaching, I had eloquent writing skills and an imagination full of happy and sad things.

I couldn't be a farmer's girl.

But I would be the next best thing.

I bought myself a laptop with a long battery life and, for most of that year, I stayed in England, writing in open fields of farms I wasn't invited on. Watching men and women toil the land, rubbing my heart as it swelled with jealousy.

And slowly, that jealousy transmuted into a script.

Once it was finished, I asked Keeko to edit it for me, then grew enough balls to show it to a producer Dad put me in touch with.

The guy hated it.

Despised it.

And wasn't shy about telling me how atrocious it was.

I'd nodded and accepted yet another dream dashed but he'd patted my hand after tearing my work to shreds and said my story might be terrible, but my writing was not. He needed a co-writer on a TV show called *Rogue Rascal*—a simple plot of a morgue director who took it upon himself to hunt and kill those who murdered the clients he was hired to bury—and offered me a job.

It appealed to my morbid side, and the co-writer, Ashley Sleugh, was witty and smart, ensuring the script had punchy dialogue and imaginative ways of extermination.

I accepted.

And life crept forward.

Eighteen became nineteen.

Nineteen became twenty.

During the waking hours, I was totally fine. I'd schooled myself enough to forget about Jacob Wild. But during the witching hours? My heart was louder than my mind, and it opened dusty drawers where memories stayed hidden, tormenting me with everything I'd loved and lost.

I'd found who I wanted to be at Cherry River.

I'd found who I wanted to be *with*.

And both were ripped away the day Della died.

Despite my heartaches, *Rogue Rascal* was a hit and I stayed on for each new season. I spent more and more time on set doing last-minute line changes.

And that was how I met Michael.

Sweet, funny Michael who played a cadaver who'd been

murdered by a man-hating prostitute. He had no lines, and the make-up department made him look like a decomposing throttle victim who happened to love cream cheese bagels at lunchtime.

We'd bumped into each other in some cliché meet-cute that another scriptwriter would've rolled their eyes at penning. He reached for the same bagel I did. Our fingers touched. Something sparked.

He'd flirted.

I'd laughed.

He'd asked me out.

I couldn't find a reason to say no.

I'd be lying if I didn't say our first date had a third wheel in the shadows. My heart clung to Jacob, sending silent messages to wherever he was to come claim me before another did.

But he never came.

And Michael fell for me.

One date turned to two, then three, then four.

And on the sixth one, I had a choice to make.

A choice I'd hoped would always sort itself out.

My virginity.

For so long, I'd clutched to the stupid hope that Jacob would come back before it was too late. He'd grieve for his parents. He'd shut himself off for a while. And then he'd return, not as broken, and ready to embrace a new life...with me.

My virginity was *his*.

But in the end, Michael took it.

It'd been the perfect end to my desire for Jacob.

Michael hired a hotel room, took me dancing, and booked in a day spa where we were pampered and relaxed until we fell together sleepily, softly in an over-pillowed bed and made love for the first time.

Not rough. Not explosive. Not crazed.

Just sweet and beautiful...just like my dark-haired, blue-eyed boy who'd played a cadaver.

Scrunching the covers up to my chin, I sighed in the darkness, looking over to that sweet, beautiful blue-eyed boy. His face was soft and slumbering. His forehead smooth. At twenty-five, Michael was the same age Jacob would be, yet he seemed so much younger.

Even at seventeen, Jacob had seemed more man than a lot of kids that age. He had the weight of acreage and seasons pressing on him to be responsible and reliable.

Michael didn't have that type of pressure, which left him

unruffled around the edges. He stayed in work with small TV parts here and there, but he wasn't well off. But that didn't matter because he was good to me.

I genuinely liked him.

A lot.

Cared deeply enough that we'd been going strong for a year, and most nights I spent at his one-bedroom apartment above a fish and chip shop. The English accents of people placing orders and the fried aroma of their dinner drifted through his window; a quintessential part to the new life I now led.

Staying with him was convenient as I hadn't put down roots of my own. I missed Cherry River's depthless peace with every fibre of my body, which stopped me from finding my own home.

On the nights where I missed the farm that was never mine, tears leaked silently in the dark, and I'd have to remind myself all over again that I was with a wonderful guy. I had a great job. I was set for life.

I was *unbelievably* lucky.

Eventually, I would buy my own piece of paradise. I would live a new dream somewhere else. *With* someone else.

With Michael?

I didn't know and that was what made guilt a constant companion.

Snuggling deeper into my pillows, I closed my eyes and did my best to fall asleep.

Michael rolled over, pulling the covers from my legs.

Ugh, I give up.

Sitting up, I slid from the sheets and reached for my phone. Carrying it into the small lounge in my purple pyjamas, I sat on the couch, pulled a fluffy blanket over me, and tapped the screen.

The device instantly lit up as if it'd been waiting impatiently.

I turned my sound off at night so I wouldn't be disturbed.

I really shouldn't have.

Three missed calls.

All from Cassie.

"Oh, no." My hands shook as I punched in the number for Cherry River. I bit my lip as it connected, ringing on the other phone. There was something fundamentally wrong about calling someone at four a.m., but this was an emergency.

This was life or death.

"Hello?" Cassie mumbled.

"Are you okay? Is John okay?" I blurted. "Do you need

anything? What about Nina or Chip? I can fly over right away if you need—"

"Whoa, Hope. Slow down." Her voice lost its fuzziness. "I called you three hours ago. I figured you might still be up writing."

Ever since leaving Cherry River, my morning routines had become more like night owl habits and bedtime was late. Sometimes, I'd be going to bed at the same time Jacob would wake to go to work.

"Oh." I didn't know what to do with my excess adrenaline. "So, you're saying everything is fine?" My stupid heart wouldn't calm down, racing, racing, racing. "Everyone is okay."

Cassie took her time replying. "You could say that."

"You said that weird."

She laughed softly. "Can't get anything past you, huh?"

"What is it? Why did you call me three times?"

"I heard from Jacob."

I bolted upright on the couch. The blanket tumbled from my legs to the carpet. "You did?"

"He sent us a letter."

"Wh-where is he?" I couldn't swallow. My throat closed up. It wasn't the first letter he'd sent. He wasn't totally heartless to leave his family without a goodbye or a heads-up that he was still alive. There hadn't been many—four in total. But at least he still thought about his aunt, uncle, and grandfather, even if he didn't think of me.

"He's in Indonesia."

"Indonesia? What on earth is he doing there?"

Cassie sighed. "Wandering."

"Do you have an address?" I plucked the cotton of my pyjamas. The other letters didn't have return addresses. He'd been in Thailand for one of them and New Zealand for another, followed by Australia and Finland. He'd travelled the world all while I wondered if he was okay.

"The envelope is from some cheap hotel stationery with their address printed on. I don't know if he's staying there or just used it passing through. But...it's the first concrete location we've had." Her voice dropped, rustling sounded as if she was leaving the bedroom so as not to disturb Chip. "Look, I can't leave. My horse business can't be run by just anyone. I need to oversee the contractors, and the recent rescues we've taken in are a handful."

I flinched.

As much as I appreciated Cassie taking in more rescues, the

fear that she'd be killed like Della hissed in the back of my mind. "What are you saying?"

"I don't really know." She groaned. "I shouldn't be asking this of you. You don't have any obligation to my family and after all the time that's passed after…after Della dying and Jacob leaving…I don't feel right. But…" Tears caught in her throat. "My dad isn't doing well. He's frail, Hope. He's no longer the big bear we all know and love. I'm so afraid he's going to pass before Jacob gets home. Jacob needs to say goodbye to his grandfather. Otherwise, it will chew him alive. It might be the last straw he needs before going completely crazy."

Tears welled. "You want me to find him."

"Yes."

"But…he doesn't want to see me. Not after—"

"His mother had just died, and you had a cough. Two things he couldn't cope with. Lots of time has passed. If you find him, I have no doubt he'll be happy to see you."

"I'm not so sure."

"I am." She paused, before saying softly, "He needs you, Hope. He needed you right from the start."

My eyes trailed to the bedroom where Michael slept peacefully. He trusted I was his girl. That he had my heart just as I had his. What sort of person was I if I contemplated running around the world to find a boy who'd shattered me instead of staying with the one who cared?

"I can tell him about John for you, but…I've moved on. There isn't room for an us anymore. I'm with Michael. I can't hurt or betray him."

"I'm not asking you to."

I had no reply.

"I understand this isn't easy." Cassie sighed. "I know how much you cared for Jacob. And I understand he pushed you away too much to earn a second chance. Just…find him and tell him to come home. That's all."

That's all?

That wasn't all.

That was just the beginning.

Say no.

Don't do it.

But Della wasn't here to save her son.

And I was.

My heart pounded as I whispered, "Okay, Cassie. I'll try."

"Oh, *thank you*, Hope. Thank you from the bottom of my heart."

"Send me the address, and I'll fly there."

"You're an angel."

"I'm not an angel. Far from it."

"Well, you are to me. And to Della and Ren who will be watching their son ruin his life somewhere on a tropical island."

"What if he's found happiness? He might be with someone and living contentedly on a beach somewhere for all you know."

"He's not," Cassie muttered. "His letters are dripping in pain. It's what he doesn't write that tells the truth and…"

"And?"

"He's getting worse."

"How so?"

"He's…" She groaned softly. "He's fading. If that makes sense? I don't know how to explain it. But the time alone hasn't done him any favours. His letters sound empty."

I gulped. "I'll book the tickets tonight."

"Thank you." Cassie's voice dropped. "Come visit us soon, okay? We miss you."

I hung up, unable to accept such an excruciating invitation.

Cassie had thanked me from the bottom of her heart.

But what about *my* heart?

What about that?

What about the mess this would cause, and the inevitable hurt Jacob would give me?

Chapter Forty-Three

HOPE

✳ ✳ ✳ ✳ ✳ ✳

"YOU HAVE TO leave now? Like *right now*, right now?" Michael yawned as he sat at the kitchen table and smiled gratefully at the bacon and egg bagel I'd made him. He blew me a kiss before taking a sip of his coffee.

"I've already booked a flight and cleared a few days with work. It's a family emergency. I wouldn't go if it wasn't urgent."

"It's urgent because you need to tell this guy his grandfather is dying?"

My heart sank, miserable and moping. "Yes."

"But his own family can't pick up a phone and tell him?"

"He hasn't got a phone—not answering his old number anyway. He's not on social media. There's not even a guarantee he'll still be at this hotel by the time I get there. But I have to try." I washed my hands in the sink from my own breakfast and eyed my suitcase by the door.

It hurt to admit, but I'd packed every stitch of my belongings—not just the necessities I needed to travel. I'd spent long enough living unofficially with Michael to be blasé about leaving stuff. An odd bra, a pair of mismatched socks. A dress or two.

However, in the inky dawn with Cassie's voice still in my head, I'd searched the apartment for any trace of me.

I'd stuffed it all into the suitcase.

I didn't leave a trace.

What did that say about me?

What were my intentions?

Was I saying goodbye to Michael?

Was I playing with fire that wouldn't just burn me, but char me to dust?

Since talking with Cassie, I'd managed to book a flight to Bali leaving this afternoon, arranged a room at the same hotel where Jacob sent the letter from, and emailed work that I could still do script edits and amendments, but I'd be out of the country for a few days.

How easy it was to wrap up my life.

How simple and straightforward to just walk away without any reluctance or dismay—the exact opposite of what it felt like to leave Cherry River.

I hated that.

I *cursed* that because it showed me—no matter how often I told myself I was over Jacob—I wasn't. And it wasn't just him I wasn't over. I wasn't over his mother or family or home or lifestyle. I was envious. Immensely envious such a wonderful place existed without me. And I was furious because Jacob turned his back on all of it.

Turned his back on me.

"I'll miss you, Hope." Michael abandoned his breakfast, coming to cocoon me at the sink.

"I'll miss you, too." I spun in his arms, rising on tiptoes to kiss him. "I'll video call you when I'm there."

"And every day you spend away from me."

"Every day." I smiled, all while my heart worried what sort of chaos I was about to head into. Jacob was a battlefield, and who knew if I'd stay scar free this time?

Then again, I had a giant scar from him already, gorged deep into my stupid heart.

Kissing me again, Michael murmured, "I love you, Hope. Perhaps, when you get back, we can go away together. A romantic holiday with lots of sex and cocktails and midnight strolls on the beach."

"I'd like that." Squeezing him tight, I wriggled out of his embrace and strode toward my suitcase. "I'll be counting the days until I'm home."

"Me too."

We stared and smiled, and with a slightly shaky hand, I opened the door, walked through it, and closed it.

The click was as loud as cannon fire.

The symbolism of shutting myself off from Michael was all too real.

Because the thought of going on a romantic holiday with him was nice. He was nice. Our relationship was nice. Everything was *nice.*

But…I didn't want nice.

I wanted rough and painful and hard work and sweat and tears and everything that made life beautiful and ugly.

I wanted those scars, those battles, those moments of utter calamity.

I wanted to get dirty and messy and sunburned.

I wanted to fight because fighting for what you wanted made it all the more sweeter when you won.

I want to live as violently and as vividly as possible.

As I hopped into the cab and rode to the airport, all I could think about was a fourteen-year-old boy I'd met at a movie premiere.

A boy who feared hugs.

A boy who'd grown into a man.

A man I'd never stop loving.

* * * * *

For two days, I searched.

The hotel was basic but clean. My room small and Balinese in its decoration with a lovely balcony overlooking a sunset-perfect beach, manicured gardens with palm trees, and graceful turquoise pools.

It was heaven on earth, but Jacob wasn't here.

When I'd first arrived, I'd spent the evening patrolling the hotel grounds, ducking into restaurants, padding barefoot on warm sand as the moon highlighted boat sails and hotels along the coast, twinkling like diamonds.

The next day, I'd called Cassie and told her the hotel had no registration of a guest under the name Jacob Wild.

They'd never heard of him.

Our one clue had led to a dead end.

She'd apologised for sending me on a stupid chase, and told me to go back to Michael—to forget all about Jacob. But…as I stood on the balcony that second night and listened to the soft waves slap upon the sand, something inside me shook its head.

The same girl who'd befriended the stray dog that everyone else was afraid of poked up her head with curled fists and hot determination.

I hadn't let that dog chase me off.

I hadn't let Jacob chase me off until things happened that were too much to bear.

I'd flown halfway across the world to this tropical paradise, and Jacob was *here*.

I could feel it.

I would find him, even if it meant months of searching.

Months of nothing.

Months of turning my back on my carefully constructed life.

If I stayed here, I might lose everything. My job. My home. My boyfriend.

And the scary thing was…it was almost a relief more than a regret.

Calling Michael, while standing on that balcony, breathing in Bali air and my heart full of the past, I did my best to be present in our conversation. To laugh when he joked, to be sympathetic when he said he missed me, to be the girlfriend I'd been to him for the past year.

But I didn't know if it was the physical distance that shut off my heart or the fact I'd been thrust on a path that would hopefully lead me back to Jacob, but I no longer felt tethered to him.

I was adrift.

I was acting.

I hung up feeling like the biggest liar in history.

* * * * *

For a week, I searched.

I grew used to the local currency and way of life and travelled farther afield, leaving behind the hotel district and travelling to areas said to be hotspots for people who liked to get away from tourist mania. Beaches where only the locals hung out. Restaurants that didn't get flooded by guests at happy hour.

Each time I entered a new place, I scanned the crowds.

Luckily, by hunting in local areas, the tanned skin and black hair of the Balinese people were a perfect backdrop to highlight a blond-haired farmer who didn't belong.

Only, in each place, there was no such find.

At each bar and café, broad smiles and eager questions welcomed me. They happily answered mine, shaking their head without recognition at a photo Cassie sent of Jacob on my phone.

No one had seen him.

No one knew a man named Jacob Wild or even Ren Wild—in case he was using his father's name.

It was as if the letter was sent by a ghost.

By the end of the first week, I was disillusioned but not defeated. I gathered more maps from the hotel lobby and spent the evening circling off-the-grid beaches that didn't have road access.

The ones where only die-hard surfers made the pilgrimage, fighting jungle and rocky paths to surf waves only a select few had.

Instead of trying to catch a taxi to such places, I hired a driver for the day, giving him the list of locations I'd come up with.

To start with, the driver rolled his eyes and told me there was nothing of interest at the destinations I wanted. That the only people who went there were potheads or hippies. As I looked like neither in my calico dress with hair carefully brushed and a large floppy sunhat, he did his best to persuade me to see the silversmiths in Ubud or the turtles in Tanjung Benoa instead.

But then, he made a fateful error.

Pointing at one of the bays I'd circled, he tutted under his breath. "This one no good. This one where bad spirit hang out. Only one white man go there and he never come back."

Everything inside me stilled. "What do you mean bad spirit?"

"Temple there. Temple for the dead. If not given many sacrifices, it take your soul."

My heart soared. "I changed my mind. Take me there first."

"No. Cannot. Too dangerous."

"You said one white man went there. How long ago?"

"Long time."

I kept my patience even though anxiety rushed through my veins. "How long is long?"

"Ten months?" The driver shrugged. "He dead for sure."

"Do other people go there? Not just the white man?"

"Of course." He rolled his eyes. "Locals go. They say prayer. Small village there. Fishermen village."

A muggy breeze sprang around my legs, kissing my sandals and up the back of my thighs. Goosebumps darted over every inch of me.

I felt *touched* by something other than air.

Was it fate or some kind of psychic knowing?

Was it Della pushing me in the right direction to find her son?

Either way, I wouldn't accept a refusal. I was going to that village.

Even if I have to drive myself.

Patting my nervous driver on his arm, I climbed into his rusty, air-conditioned Toyota. "Let's go there right now. Don't worry about the other places. I only want to go to that one."

He raised his eyebrows, shaking his head. "You crazy, lady."

"I know."

Crazy to chase after a man who'd almost resorted to physical violence to get me away from him.

Crazy to drive across Bali to an area where bad spirits lived.

Crazy to risk everything for one boy.

The driver looked at the heavens, shook the map in my window, then stalked to the front of the car.

I didn't say a word as he plopped into the driver's seat, cranked the engine, and weaved through chaotic traffic. "You not blame me if you die, lady."

I rested my chin on my hand, staring at colourful shrines and pretty sarongs blurring into a rainbow as we drove. "I won't die. Don't worry."

"I worry," he muttered. "I worry long time. You should not travel alone."

With an aching heart, I murmured, "If I find what I think I'll find in that village…I won't be alone for much longer."

"What you say?" The driver looked at me in the rear-view mirror.

"Nothing."

For the rest of the trip, I watched the world pass me by and hoped.

* * * * *

I'd come to the wrong place.

Four hours ago, I'd argued with my driver to wait for me, hiked down an overgrown trail he'd pointed at, and ignored the painful blisters from my sandals as I'd arrived at the prettiest beach imaginable.

Dense jungle cocooned turquoise sea and golden sand in a horseshoe of protection while an island just off the coast held a temple glittering with sharp spires and intricate woodwork against the sky.

If evil spirits lived here, their home was pure heaven.

For the first hour, I'd followed the shoreline to an area of jungle that'd been cleared, leaving behind a small community of huts and frond-roofed homes scattered amongst the foliage.

A few women noticed me, all brown and slim and part goddess living in this utopia.

They'd taken me under their wing, spoke enough English to understand I was looking for a blond-haired man called Jacob Wild, and took me to the elderly woman in charge for answers.

Desperate hope kept me company as I passed her my phone with Jacob's photo on it. "Do you know him?" My voice trembled.

The woman with skin still perfect and hair slightly less black than her fellow villagers shook her head. "If man don't want to be found. He won't be found." She passed my phone back to me.

I paused, trying to work out her riddle. "Is that a yes or a no?"

She shrugged. "You seek but not find."

My temper escalated, but I daren't get argumentative with a village elder in the middle of nowhere. Instead, I nodded. "Okay, I appreciate your time."

"Bye, bye." She nodded and carried on with whatever duties she was in charge of.

I left the clearing where fish dried on strings and coconuts lay in big piles ready to be used. The girls who'd helped me before had vanished.

Somewhere in the dense jungle, there was a path waiting to take me back to my driver.

This was yet another dead end.

Another false lead.

The sun slipped down the sky, and thick clouds brewed a storm on the horizon. My time was swiftly running out.

But I couldn't leave without trying one more time.

Another couple of hours passed as I made my way into the jungle, following the crushed seashell paths around simple but elegant homes. There was something so fundamentally perfect and in keeping with the landscape that the houses morphed into the forest as a friend rather than an enemy.

Children played in small gardens, and a few elderly men sat on decks smoking pipes. Everyone was gracious and kind when I encroached on their property, asking if they knew anyone by the name of Jacob Wild.

No one recognised the man in my photo.

However, occasionally, I'd be stared at, thoughts racing in dark eyes, and secrets swallowed down tanned throats, and I'd get a wash of unease—the sense that they were keeping something from me.

Even though I believed they hid something, I didn't know how to change their minds to tell me, and when the first fat raindrop plopped on my head, I knew my time was up.

If I didn't hike back now, I'd end up sleeping on a windswept beach with lightning for a blanket.

With rain falling lazily, teasing me with the downpour about to arrive, I traversed the sand with hunched shoulders.

Out to sea, the temple no longer glittered with sunshine but cast an ominous shadow over the bay. The clouds above it were blacker than I'd ever seen.

Was that what the driver meant about the temple of the dead?

That it lured in unsuspecting visitors only to murder them with a change of weather?

Clutching my phone, I walked faster. Raindrops landed on my eyelashes, blurring a pack of children playing in the shallows. They weren't fussed about the tennis ball-sized droplets hitting them intermittently.

I stopped.

I should just keep walking.

But the wind kicked up, blowing my dress, whipping it in their direction.

Fine, Della, one last try.

Kicking off my sandals, I jogged through the icing sugar sand toward the children. They paused as I drew close, eyeing me warily.

Slightly puffed, I kept one eye on the storm and one on them, dropping to my haunches. "Hello. Do you speak English?"

One tiny girl nodded. "Little."

Bringing up the photo of Jacob on my phone, doing my best to shield it from the rain, I turned the screen to her. "Have you seen this man?"

Her cute face wrinkled. "No." Backing away, she tucked herself next to a skinny boy who looked like her brother.

Another girl came close, her hair hanging down to her hips. She touched my phone, tracing Jacob's shaggy blond mop and the surly position of his mouth. Behind Jacob was Forrest, the horse staring into the distance with sunshine picking up the strawberry roan of his coat.

"Pretty."

I smiled. "Yes, very pretty. Have you seen him here?"

"Horse?" She pointed at Forrest. "Village over hill has horse."

"And the man? Do they have him too?"

She bit her lip. "No."

"What happening?" An older boy, early teens but as scrawny as a wiry monkey interrupted us, black glossy hair flopped over one eye as he squished between the girl and me. "You annoying my sister?"

I shook my head. "No. She's helping me." Angling the phone

so he could see clearly, I asked for the millionth time, "Do you know this man? His name is Jacob Wild. He's my friend, and I'm looking for him."

The boy frowned. "That not his name."

Everything inside me froze. "You mean…you know him?"

He crossed his arms over a powerful but skinny chest. "Sunyi."

"Sunyi?"

He scowled. "Sunyi. Name is Sunyi."

The girl pushed him aside. "That Sunyi?" She peered closer at the photo. "Not Sunyi. Hair not right."

I looked from child to child as they launched into squabbling Balinese. Their voices pierced my eardrums, almost as loud as the thunder rumbling in the distance. Both made my heart pound as electricity and violence crackled in the air.

The boy tapped his finger on my screen, smearing water, arguing some more.

I couldn't follow their fight, but finally, the girl sniffed. "Hair dark in photo. But guess is Sunyi."

Her older brother smirked, his chin shot in the air with victory. Looking at me, he said, "Sunyi. White hair now."

My knees weakened. My body tingled. I didn't know if I wanted to cry or jump for joy. "So…you're saying the man in this picture is here?"

The boy shook his head, a big grin on his face. "No."

"No?" My eager nervousness bounced around in my blood with nowhere to go. I felt sick. I wanted to grab the boy and shake him. "What do you mean?"

"I mean, he not here."

"Where is he?"

"In water."

Was that code? A sentence that didn't do well with translation?

I cocked my head. "In the water?"

The boy rolled his eyes at my slowness. "Yes. Water."

"No." His sister grabbed his bicep, pointing at the horizon. "Here."

Spinning around, I stood too fast.

My head swam, my fingers dropped my phone, and the heavens opened their torrent.

A sheet of water fell from above, a heavy wet curtain doing its best to block the truth.

But it was too late.

I'd seen.

A fishing boat haphazardly made its way to shore. A basic craft with nets bunched at the end and a balancing pole keeping the long boat upright, slapping against the chop. The captain stood at the back with his hand on a long mechanism leading to an engine beneath the surface, while two men sat in the middle, dripping with rain, not caring they were as wet out of the water as they would've been in it.

Three men in total.

Two of them had black hair.

And one had a shock of sun-bleached white-blond hair.

A man I would've recognised anywhere.

After four long years, Jacob Wild, I've found you.

Chapter Forty-Four

JACOB

* * * * * *

GODDAMN THIS STORM.

I was exhausted. I needed to rest. But with this monsoon, my hut would leak, my roof would pound, and the much-needed sleep I dreamed of would be non-existent.

Not for the first time, I thought about leaving.

I should've left months ago when the wet season started and the temple in the bay cried with raindrops more often than gleamed with sunshine.

But I had nowhere else to go.

Nowhere else I could be left alone, anyway.

The men here had grown used to my presence as I'd camped on their beach. I'd hitchhiked through Bali, seeking the quietest spots, and found this place purely by luck.

The fact that it had a temple dedicated to the dead seemed too much of a coincidence to leave.

For a week, I'd watched the locals depart at dawn and return at dusk with stingrays and crab and fish.

They worked just as hard as I did. The only difference was they worked the sea while I worked the land.

I'd aimed to stay a couple of weeks, pay my respects, and carry on wandering, but they had other plans. I couldn't remember exactly how I'd begun working with them, only that I did. One afternoon, I'd ambled over to inspect their haul, and the leader shoved a basket of dead fish in my arms.

I hadn't shoved it back.

Instead, I'd followed the procession into their village and gave the basket to a teenage girl who proceeded to gut, scale, and dry them on a string.

That night, I'd been invited to dinner, tucking into banana leaf-wrapped rice with a chargrilled fish from their fire. Afterward, they'd shared their pipe with me, and the heaviness of silence that filled my bloodstream as the marijuana smoke filled my lungs gave me peace for the first time since my mother died.

I'd slept without nightmares that night, beneath the stars outside my tent.

The next day, a man nudged me awake with his foot, and I'd found myself on a boat, bobbing on the unforgiving sea, my skin burning from sunshine and my hair steadily turning white.

No one had mentioned I didn't belong.

No one asked me to leave.

And so, I stayed.

I stayed one month, then two, then three.

I was now as much a fisherman as I was a farmer, and I didn't struggle against the new career fate had given me. I embraced it because it gave me purpose again.

And each night, the pipe was passed around, and the smoke helped soothe my damaged soul.

The drug kept memories away and banished the girl who haunted me—quietening my guilt, my pain, and the knowledge I'd done something unforgivable.

When I'd written to Aunt Cassie last month, heading into town for supplies and having a drink at a local hotel, I'd almost included a letter to Hope.

But I had nothing to say.

No apology to utter or news to deliver.

Our friendship was over.

Four years was a long time, and I hoped it'd distanced her from my mother's death and the awful ending between us. For me, it felt as if it happened yesterday, but that was why I'd made my home on the beach belonging to the temple of the dead.

Every day, I served my penance beneath the hot sun.

Every night, I found short-lived salvation within a pipe.

And the work I toiled with hopefully appeased the two ghosts who lived in the breeze and sky, watching me live, hopefully happy that I'd found a place of sanctuary.

"Sunyi. Your turn."

Gede's voice interrupted my mindless musings, dragging me back to a soaking boat and thundering rainstorm. The wind howled, picking up ferocity as if determined to drown us before we pulled ashore.

Pushing the fishnets away from my feet in the bottom of the boat, I stood. Kadek passed me the rope to secure the craft, and I dived into the ocean.

An embrace of salt and sea welcomed me back to a world I'd grown familiar with in the ten months I'd lived here, and I stayed under for a second or two.

It was quiet beneath the surface.

Heavy.

Oppressive.

Safe.

Kicking, I breached the chop and sucked in a breath. The ocean was warmer than the air with the storm rapidly cooling the constant humidity.

"Sunyi, tie up. We get off this boat."

Sunyi…

Just as I didn't understand how I'd become employed as a Balinese fisherman, I didn't know how I'd earned that name.

I'd asked one of the village girls a few months ago what it meant and ended up smoking double the usual amount that night.

The Indonesian word meant desolate, dead, lonely.

I thought I'd hidden who I was at heart.

But these people recognised me instantly.

"Sunyi. Go." Gede pointed at the horizon where lightning forked, dousing the evening with white electricity.

Shit.

Pushing off in a powerful stroke, I swam to the plastic bottle bobbing a metre or so away. The mooring was tethered to the reef below, ready to hold the boat as the swell grew bigger. With storms like this, it was safer to keep the boats offshore rather than hauling them up the sand.

The second I'd secured the small vessel, Gede threw the net overboard with the small catch from today and jumped in after me. Kadek turned off the engine, glanced at his most prized possession, then dived in and struck off for the beach, leaving Gede and me to haul the net and its bounty through choppy current.

What I loved about working with these guys was their quietness. Conversation was not needed amongst the serenity of fishing. And I didn't speak their language, so when they did talk, I had no pressure to participate.

However, in the middle of an angry ocean, Gede cocked his chin, and grunted, "*Orang kulit putih.*"

My eyes shot to the shore.

I didn't know their language, but I knew a few words. Just enough to get by, including the name they'd given me and *orang kulit putih.*

White person.

I scanned the beach, the sand no longer pristine but dark with rain. Kids ran toward the community tucked within the jungle, leaving a single woman staring out to sea.

A woman with white skin.

Chocolate hair.

Bravery and pushiness and home.

I let go of the net.

She'd found me.

Chapter Forty-Five

HOPE

* * * * * *

I COULDN'T MOVE as Jacob stepped from the ocean, dragging a net with a Balinese man, rain mixing with the saltwater already on his skin.

His shirtless chest was leaner than at Cherry River, but the muscles and strength I was accustomed to rippled with every stride. The blue swimming shorts he wore had a tear on one thigh and a hole by his hipbone, revealing a story of someone who'd spent more time in the ocean than on it.

Our eyes locked. My heart galloped. Jacob didn't look away as he muttered something to the man and gave him the net.

Striding toward me, he raked both hands through drenched hair—white hair that set off his rich tan and highlighted dark eyes. With the lightning framing him from behind and the droplets splashing on his perfect skin, he looked as if he was the missing son of Poseidon.

My knees shook as bare feet brought him closer. Four years had been cruel and kind to him. Cruel because they'd stolen any remainders of childhood and kind because, in the wake of a boy, the man who stood before me was utterly breath-taking.

Wild as his surname baptised him.

Savage as the loneliness in his heart.

Every inch of me trembled to touch him. To lick at the rivulets of liquid as they waterfalled down his flat stomach. To kiss the tight lips as he studied me. To hug the hardness he'd wrapped himself in.

I'd come here to give him more news of death.

To tell him his grandfather was dying, and that he had such a small window to say goodbye.

Yet in that rainy, stormy moment, my mouth forgot words and my heart forgot Michael.

I was just Hope.

The embodiment of faith, belief, wishes, and daydreams.

I *hoped* with every fibre of my soul that Jacob would be kind, that he'd healed, that he'd let me love him.

Because I couldn't lie anymore.

I'd loved him when I was a child, and I loved him as a woman.

But I wasn't *free* to love him.

I was with another who was gentle and sweet and did not deserve a harlot who stood on a tropical beach, her white sundress plastered to a body begging another man to take it.

I hated myself as lightning forked, lashing like a whip, punishing me for my sinful thoughts. I cursed myself as thunder cracked right above our heads, making us flinch.

I'd never stood a chance against Jacob. Even when I was a silly ten-year-old, the power he had over me was absolute.

"Jacob." I stumbled forward, summoned to him and unable to fight it.

He didn't move, but his hand came up. A hand that used to drive a tractor and ride a horse and clutched my locket deep in a forest.

For the longest second, he didn't speak. His dark eyes gleamed, looking part storm, part mystery, endless in their torment. Then he sighed, and his heady voice barely carried over the slap and hiss of rain. "What are you doing here, Hope?"

No hello.

No embrace.

No hint of our past or friendship.

It was the reality check I needed.

My foot returned to its original position, removing me from his closeness, putting distance between us that reeked of strangers and strangeness.

How could I tell him that I'd come on Cassie's request? How could I tear out the heart he probably hadn't mended?

I gulped as the Balinese man dragged the fishing net along the beach, eyeing me up before glancing at Jacob.

Jacob didn't acknowledge him, his stare cold and full of warning, branding me with ice. His rejection made tears burn hotter than any lightning.

But then, I grew angry.

Angry with him and me and Cassie and John and even Della.

I'd been given a task. I'd walked away from my old life to find a man who didn't want to be found and tell him things he didn't want to hear.

The least he could do was say hello.

But then again, my feelings had nothing to do with this.

Jacob had been abundantly clear on where I stood with him.

I couldn't be angry that he hadn't changed those rules.

I could only be angry with myself.

I'd cheated on Michael just by getting on that plane.

I didn't deserve any other form of welcome because I *wasn't* welcome and that had never been more obvious. "Ca-can we go somewhere to talk?"

He squinted at the sky as another sheet of rain fell harder. "How did you get here?"

"Driver." I turned to point up the dense jungle-covered hill. "Up there."

"How long ago?"

"Four hours or so."

"Shit." He shook his head. "You stayed too long. He'll have left you. No one lingers here. Not with the superstition of this temple's bay."

I nodded. "I feared as much. I guess…I'll have to wait for the storm to pass and then call a taxi."

"Taxis don't come out this far, Hope." He sighed again, pinching the bridge of his nose before glaring at me. "Why did you come?"

My skin prickled. "Can we talk somewhere drier?"

"How did you find me?"

"A roof, Jacob. Give me a roof, and I'll answer any question you want."

"Any question?" His eyes narrowed.

I flinched. "What question do you have in mind?"

Another lightning bolt blinded us, followed by its friend the eardrum-smashing thunder. Rain turned into buckets, gods tossing litres of liquid from the clouds.

My dress hugged every curve, the lacy bra I wore underneath revealing pebbled nipples and quaking stomach. I was exposed and vulnerable yet Jacob didn't study my body.

His eyes stayed resolutely on mine, angry and black and unreadable. "I know all the answers I need."

I couldn't hold eye contact anymore. Instead, I looked at the sand and numerous tracks and river bends caused by the rain. I should just spit out about John. I should walk back to the hotel even if it would take all night.

I should never have come.

Familiar sadness and worry when it came to Jacob engulfed me. "I-I—"

What, Hope?

Say something!

Walk away.

Turn around.

Forget him.

My shoulders slouched, and the girl who'd befriended a rabid dog disappeared.

I'd made a mistake.

Twisting in the sand, I shrugged. "I'll go. I'll—"

"Aw, shit." In a burst of kindness, Jacob closed the distance between us and hesitantly placed a large, strong hand on my shoulder. "God, forgive me. I don't know why I'm such an asshole to you."

I blinked, trapped in his hold. "We haven't seen each other in a long time. It's understandable to be—"

"Don't do that."

"Do what?"

"Make up excuses for my shitty behaviour." He squeezed me gently before letting me go. "I'm sorry. Truly."

Rain blurred his handsomeness, hushing his apology so it didn't seem real.

Perhaps travelling had healed him? Maybe he wasn't the same farmer who'd broken my heart, after all.

"Look, it's not safe here. The storm is directly overhead. You'll, um, have to stay the night. I'll drive you back tomorrow."

"You'll…let me stay?"

His throat worked as he swallowed. The rage in his gaze faded into worried resignation. "We were friends once. What sort of friend would I be if I made you sleep in this?"

I bit back all the questions I wanted to ask.

Where would I stay?

Would he stay with me or expect me to hide away?

What would he do when he knew why I'd come?

I wanted to accept this truce, but my heart still carried too much pain. My chin rose. I willingly stepped into battle. "You made it pretty clear you didn't want my friendship the day you threw me out of Cherry River."

He froze.

Part of me wanted to scramble for cover, to take it back. But the other part wanted to hurt him as successfully as he hurt me.

He hurt me just by breathing.

That couldn't be normal.

It couldn't be healthy.

We weren't good for each other.

We never had been.

His voice was low and untamed as thunder. "You really want to go there? Right now? Standing in this downpour?"

Yes.

No.

I don't know.

I hugged my sodden dress. "Not one word, Jacob. You just kicked me from your life as if I meant nothing."

"You made a promise. You didn't keep it."

"I promised I'd leave if I didn't do the work you requested."

"No, you promised you'd leave if it became too much for me." He stalked toward me, his height pressing against me like another storm cloud. "It became too much. I asked you to go. You didn't. What else was I supposed to do?"

I hid my shiver; buried my shakes. "Oh, I don't know. How about let me be your friend? How about letting me love you at your mother's funeral?"

His entire body locked down. "Don't talk about that day."

"Why? Because it's too painful? Do you know what else is painful? Not knowing if you're alive. Not hearing from you in four long years."

"Whether I was alive or not was none of your concern."

I wanted to punch him. "Really? You really have the nerve to say that to me? Don't you remember what I said to you that day? I told you I was *in love* with you, and you broke my heart."

"What do you want? An apology? Is that why you came here?"

"I came here to tell you—" I slammed my lips together. No way would I blurt out John's ill health while we fought. I wouldn't do that to him.

God, why are we fighting?

This was my fault. I'd thought I could see him again and not bring up the past. It shouldn't matter that I had unresolved issues. He'd obviously moved on, and it was time to be professional.

I was a message bearer, that was all.

My bloodthirsty desire to hurt him as much as he hurt me vanished, and I looked at the sky, letting fat raindrops wash away my stupidity. "I-I didn't mean to say that. I…ugh—" I pressed fingers into my eyes, trying to be an adult and not some heartbroken fool. "I didn't come to discuss the past. I'm sorry."

He crossed his arms, our battle still tainting him.

I braced myself for another argument, but he slowly nodded. A sad smirk played on his lips. "Only a few minutes together and we're already back to fighting and apologising."

I laughed morosely. "Suppose that happens when you don't know how to act around the other person."

"You don't know how to act around me?"

My eyebrows shot up. "Seriously? I've never known. You terrify me."

He cocked his head, droplets kissing the cheeks I wanted to, rainwater licking the throat I never would. "That's a lie. You were never scared of me."

"You never truly saw me if you think that."

His forehead furrowed. His lips parted to say something, but he stopped and shook his head. "Come on." He broke into a walk, spine straight and face tilted against the storm. He didn't hunch away from it. Didn't flinch against the hailstones of moisture. "Let's continue this where it's safer."

Lightning flashed, casting us in dangerous voltage. Another boom of thunder hurt my ears as I fell into step with him. We didn't speak again as he led me over the beach toward the huts I'd visited earlier. Walking beneath palm trees and thick foliage, the storm was louder, the leaves percussion and the jungle an orchestra of violence.

Goosebumps leapt over my skin as lightning forked again, sending its crackling light through the trees to the seashell paths we followed.

Huts bunkered down against the rain, keeping their families dry and safe—or as safe as thatched roofs and bamboo walls could.

Jacob didn't stop until we reached the outskirts of the village. He turned toward a tiny shack that needed a lot of tender loving care. The three steps to the porch had holes to the dirt below, and the door hinges hung at an odd angle.

Using his shoulder to barge the door inward, he waited until I'd stepped inside before closing it and shutting out the elements. Unlike previous houses I'd been in, this one wasn't weatherproof, and the storm hammered louder, the crackle of lightning seeped through the walls, and the smash of droplets found roof weaknesses, plopping to the floor in triumph.

Leaving me by the door, Jacob strode through the one-bedroom place with a familiarity that came from living here a while. He switched on a solar-powered lantern hanging over a small table with two chairs, lit three candles by a queen-sized bed with just a white sheet to sleep on and black sheet to cover, before coming toward me and clicking a switch by the door.

A weak electrical bulb above us flickered on, intermittent with the raindrops above.

"Not sure how long we'll have power." Padding away, his sandy feet left a trail as he entered the small bathroom at the back of the room and returned with two towels. Threadbare and faded, he tossed one to me before using the other to attack his wet hair.

I tried to keep my eyes on the floor as I wiped rain off my arms and soaked up what I could from my dress, but Jacob was too much to ignore. His motions too swift and sharp not to command my full attention.

The way he scrubbed his hair until the salt-bleached strands tangled and tousled almost to his shoulders. The way he wiped his chest and arms with focused purpose but only made my heart race to touch.

"You done?" His voice made me jump.

"What?"

"With the towel." He pointed at it scrunched in my hands.

"Oh." I held it up. "Yes. Thank you."

"Welcome." With a stern look, he took it and deposited both in the bathroom. Heading toward a suitcase tucked in the corner with clothes folded neatly inside, he selected a white T-shirt and pulled it on.

My tummy clenched. I missed seeing his naked chest, but the white made his tan skin pop even more, and the fairness of his head became almost at odds with the depths of his eyes.

Dark eyes from his father.

Light hair from his mother.

Fight and fury from loneliness.

"Do you want some clothes?" Finally, his gaze drifted over my body. The translucent calico didn't hide a thing, and the urge to cup my breasts and wedge arms against my lower belly was out of propriety for Michael.

I'd already been a terrible person to him.

I wouldn't make my sins worse by showing off a body that by rights belonged to him—even though I burned for Jacob to stare.

But I didn't move because I didn't want to seem weak. "I'm not cold. This will dry quickly."

His jaw clenched as his eyes traced the shadow of my belly and down my legs to my feet. "Sure." Turning away, he wiped his jaw with a slightly shaky hand.

Another boom of thunder made me jump.

For so long, I'd wanted to be close to Jacob.

But now that I was, I didn't know how to relax.

All I could think about was how inappropriate this was. How being alone in a cabin in the middle of a storm with a boy I'd never forgotten was the exact opposite of being a good girlfriend.

And I couldn't leave.

Not yet.

I had an entire night in this tiny hut with him.

God, it was a fantasy turned nightmare.

My conscience condemned me, and I moved to the small table, fumbling with my bag that I hoped was waterproof enough to protect the one asset that connected me to the outside world.

I turned on my phone that I'd scooped from the sand. Granules and raindrops turned it into a mess.

But it still worked.

And my heart sank. Guilt filled up the space left behind, drowning me.

Three missed calls from Michael.

God.

"You okay?" Jacob asked, moving to sit on the bed. The sight of him on a mattress scrambled up my insides, adding more shame to my disgrace.

I can't do this.

Squinting at the top corner of my phone, I sighed in relief at the two bars of reception. I didn't know how the local infrastructure worked where electricity and phone reception existed on a remote beach, but I was incredibly grateful.

"I-I'm just going outside for a sec."

"What?" His tone wrenched my eyes up. "It's pissing down outside."

"I know, but there's something I need to do."

"Something more important than staying away from a potential lightning strike?"

I smiled sadly. "Yes."

If I didn't make this phone call, I deserved to be struck by lightning.

He shrugged, sitting on his bed with sprawled legs and a perfection I'd never get over. "Fine. Don't leave the deck. I have no intention of walking in the rain to find you if you get lost."

I nodded. "Noted." Clutching my phone, I looked at Jacob. Truly looked at him.

I drank in the barriers, the fears, the anger.

I knew him perhaps better than anyone alive today, yet we'd only ever kissed twice.

He'd successfully ruined me for anyone else just by being my friend.

And if I could be this in love with him, this *heartsick* over him, I wasn't being fair to such a nice guy like Michael.

I was being my mother.

Ungrateful for everything I had, only wanting what I couldn't, ruining lives with my greed.

I'd made an oath never to be like that…yet there I was, coveting something that wasn't mine.

This phone call wasn't about Jacob. Or me. Or even Michael.

It was about doing the right thing.

Because that was all that was left.

"I'll be back in a moment." Turning around, I struggled with the door and stepped into the raging rainfall.

Jacob didn't speak as I closed the door and prepared to break up with my boyfriend.

Chapter Forty-Six

JACOB

✳ ✳ ✳ ✳ ✳ ✳

THE MOMENT THE door closed behind her, I attacked my bedside cabinet.

Wrenching open the top drawer, I grabbed the local mixture of weed laced with some other ingredients and snatched the pipe I'd bought last time I was in town.

Doing what I'd been taught by Kadek, I opened the bag containing the drug, pinched some, and pushed it tight into the pipe.

Hope's voice threaded with thunder and raindrops as whatever call she'd made connected. If I wasn't so shaken by her visit—if I wasn't hanging on by a fucking thread with how gorgeous she was, how her wet dress showed me things I'd wanted forever, and revealed just how much I'd missed her—I'd stand by the door and eavesdrop.

But I couldn't.

I needed help.

And tonight, I didn't have a whiskey bottle.

Tonight, I had a pipe and a concoction guaranteed to take away my desire, calm my need, and remind me why I could never have Hope in all the ways I'd dreamed since sending her away.

Why did she have to tell me she was in love with me that day?

Why did it have to imprint in my infernal memory?

For four long years, my mind had obsessed over two things. One, the way my mother suffocated into death with a rib bone sticking through her lungs. And two, the way Hope cried as I ordered her from my life.

I'd done it out of self-preservation.

And I'd do it again.

Tomorrow, I'd drive her into town with Gede's car and tell her to get on a plane to return to wherever she came from.

I'd rip out a bleeding heart all because I wasn't strong enough to handle another person dying on me.

Hope's cough from four years ago echoed in my ears as I clutched my lighter and held it to the pipe. She'd been sick. She'd deliberately kept that from me knowing my phobia of losing those I loved.

Her lies were almost as bad as her flu.

Wrapping my lips around the intake, I inhaled deep and long.

Hot, heavy smoke filled my lungs, spreading its numbness in seconds.

Hope's voice broke through the pouring rain, raised and in pain.

My legs bunched to go out there. To fight whatever was hurting her and to kiss away her sorrows.

You can't.

Remember?

With trembling hands, I inhaled again, dragging the smoke as deep as I could into my lungs.

Normally, I'd take two or three hits and exist in a happy cloud of calmness for the rest of the evening.

Two or three wouldn't be enough tonight.

Hope was going to sleep here.

With me.

In my bed.

Holy fuck.

My lighter hissed as the weed blazed, delivering another shot of serenity.

How the hell did I stop her affecting me this way? I'd hoped distance would prove what I'd felt for her at Cherry River was just a stupid crush.

But time hadn't done what I wanted.

It'd thrown Hope in my face, again and again. Dreams of her sleeping beside me, nightmares of her dying, truth and lies of a relationship, a life, a marriage.

My mother had made me promise to wander.

I'd wandered.

I'd travelled through hot countries and cold, Asia and Europe, fascinating and bland. I'd stuck to myself, only spoken if it was unavoidable and been around people only if necessary.

A few girls had asked me out. One had even kissed me as I'd patrolled the streets, seeking peace, when she'd tumbled from a nightclub, tipsy and happy, and planted unwanted affection on my lips.

My body hadn't reacted. My lust a dead thing in my veins.

And I was grateful because I couldn't stomach the thought of sleeping with someone—even someone I'd never see again. Their death would not affect me. Their lives weren't my problem. But I still couldn't touch them.

So why did I continue to think about Hope?

And why was she goddamn here?

Another inhale, and the jittery panic in my blood slowly drained away. My eyes grew heavy, and I sighed in relief.

Thank God.

As long as the effects stayed in my system, I could handle having Hope in my room. I could be courteous and gentlemanly and treat her with the kindness she deserved, and then I would drive her into town tomorrow morning and never see her again.

No arguments.

No fights.

No kisses.

Nothing that would spike my heart rate, make me beg for a different life, or twist my thoughts into thinking I could love another.

One more hit for good measure.

Flicking my lighter on, I held it to the rapidly dwindling weed just as Hope fell into the room thanks to shoulder-ramming the wonky front door.

She tripped and almost tumbled, catching herself on the handle. Her phone skittered across the floor as her eyes soared to mine and her nose wrinkled at the smell.

For a second, she froze.

She took in the sight of me, pipe in hand, lighter burning, and for the quickest of heartbeats, she understood. But then, hell consumed her, and she bolted across the room, snatched my pipe and tossed it out the door.

She shook her hand where the hot metal had burned her, turning on me with undiluted rage. "What the fuck do you think you are doing!?"

I'd never heard Hope curse.

Not once.

I blinked, grateful of the haze, thankful that the energy she vibrated with didn't infect me to battle. "Geez, calm down."

"Calm down? *Calm down?*" Grabbing my cheeks, she dug fingernails into my flesh. "You're smoking. *Seriously?* You're putting carcinogens into your lungs! What the *hell* were you thinking, Jacob? Your *lungs* of all things!" Letting go, she paced in front of me, wild and wet from the rain. "You should protect your lungs at all costs. Your dad…" She choked. "Your dad died of lung issues. Didn't you think of that before sucking on smoke that can kill you?"

My temper steadily slithered through my buzz. Standing, I pointed a fairly steady finger in her face. "What I do with my lungs are none of your concern."

"Wrong. They *are* my concern. They've been my concern for eleven years!"

"I don't follow your logic." I scowled. "I'm not yours to worry about."

"You might not be, but it doesn't stop me from worrying!" She yanked hands through her drenched hair, sadness cloaking her. "What would your mother say? What about your aunt? Your grandfather? If they knew you were smoking after what you all went through with Ren….God, it would crush them."

That got my attention.

That got my fury boiling enough to shove away my self-induced fog. "My mother is dead, so she has no opinions."

"But the rest of your fam—"

"Shut up, Hope."

"I've shut up enough around you. I think I should speak. I think I should finally have the guts to say the truth."

"What truth?"

"The truth that you need to grow the hell up!"

"*Excuse me?*"

"You heard me. Stop being such a broken little boy."

Rage pumped my heart; furious blood filled my veins. "Don't go there, Hope. You won't like what'll happen if you do."

"Well, we have the whole night to entertain ourselves. What else is there to do, huh? Pussy-foot around each other?" She laughed coldly. "You just drugged yourself to avoid spending time with me. To avoid facing whatever it is you don't want to face." She came too close, bringing the scent of lemonade mixed with raindrops and the wildness of Cherry River.

Had she been home while I'd been gone?

Had she walked my paddocks and stroked my horses and infiltrated my family behind my back?

"Why are you even here? I didn't want you here. I didn't ask you to come."

"No, you'd never ask for something like that." Her eyes flashed. "You're Jacob Wild. The loner. The thief of hearts and destroyer of hope."

"You're saying I destroyed you?"

"I'm saying you don't deserve me."

I sneered, struggling to figure out what I could and couldn't say. "That's not news. I've known that all along."

"Wait...you have?"

"Why else do you think I stayed away?"

"Because you're afraid to love thanks to death."

"Yeah, but also because you scared me shitless."

She stopped pacing, her chest rose and fell. The see-through fabric of her dress drove me insane. Despite the weed in my system, my body hardened, reacted, wanted.

"I scared you?" Her head tilted like a bird; an innocent, sweet little bird which was a total lie because she was a master at manipulating me. Pushing me. Shoving me. *Breaking me.*

"You've known that from the beginning."

"No, I've known you barely tolerated me."

"Barely survived you, you mean." Shit, the drugs blurred my ability to keep secrets. What I shouldn't say blended with what I should. I couldn't distinguish the two.

Her temper simmered a little. "Why are you here, Jacob? Why did you run from your family when they needed you the most?"

My temper bubbled over. "I didn't run. I kept a promise to my mother. And they didn't need me. They have each other. They're not...blood."

"They're as much your family as I am."

"Yet you aren't my family so what a stupid point to prove."

"I'm your friend, even when you're being a jackass."

"I believe we agreed our friendship ended when I tossed you from Cherry River."

"You want to talk about that? Yes, let's talk about that." She inhaled deep. "Do you know how many nights I cried over you?" She resumed her pacing, our fight picking up heat. "How many times I wrote you letters I couldn't send? How many times I called numbers that didn't connect?" She tugged her silver locket as if she wanted to break the chain and throw it at me. "I took this off. I had no choice. For two years, it sulked in a box as I did my best to find where I belonged. But then I thought, *screw you*. I refused to give you the power to hurt me anymore, so I put it back on."

"What do you want me to say to that? That I should never

have bought it for you?"

"I'm saying you might hurt me over and over again, but I'm strong enough to keep coming back for more."

I eyed the storm whipping and howling through the front door. My pipe would've vanished into the mud by now. I'd have to survive the night with a screaming woman who made my body do things it shouldn't and a heart that begged for things it could never have.

I'd be better off sleeping on the beach and hoping a lightning strike put me out of my misery.

I stepped forward, intending to shut the door on the wild weather, but my toe nudged her phone. The phone discarded on the floor. And I remembered why she'd left in the first place. "Who did you call?"

Her entire demeanour changed from attack to defence. "No one."

I laughed. "Yeah, right. You want me to believe you stood on the deck in a monsoon to call no one?"

"No one you need to know about."

"Great. Not like you to be cryptic, Hope."

"It's none of your business." She crossed her arms, hugging herself as tears trickled down her face. "I hurt someone I cared about. That's all."

I frowned. "Hurt them how?"

She bit her lip, shaking her head. She couldn't reply as she fought another wash of sadness.

Her grief made my fury teeter. I wanted to push her for a change. To make her understand just how difficult it was to stay civil when someone backed you into a corner, but I also couldn't kick her when she was down.

I sighed. "Look, let's just get some sleep, okay? I've had a really long day and—"

"You think you can *sleep* this away?" Her melancholy switched again, catching fire with anger. "You can't just ignore this. Ignore me. Drugs and dreams won't protect you from the fact that I flew halfway across the world to find you."

"Yes, let's talk about that, shall we?" I stepped toward her, doing my best to hide the heaviness in my swimming shorts. I should've changed. I should've put something tighter on so the rapidly hardening disaster didn't do something irreversible.

"Okay, let's." She met me in the centre of the room, chest to chest, nose to nose. "Ask away then."

"Why are you here?"

"I came because Cassie is worried about you."

"I sent her a letter. She didn't need to be worried."

"And that letter had an address…ta-da."

"So *that's* how you found me." I nodded as it made perfect sense. Why hadn't I scribbled out the hotel stationery watermark?

"That's how I found you. And thank God I did if all you're doing is sitting in a boat getting sunburned and smoking pot. Are you trying to give yourself cancer? Because you're doing a damn good job."

"God, you're annoying."

"So you've told me."

"Like I said before, I can do whatever I want to my body."

"You're right. You do whatever you want apart from give it what it truly needs." Her eyes drifted to my hands clenched in front of my erection. A snide little sneer made me come so, *so* close to snapping. "Seems you like fighting with me, Jacob Wild. Not that you've ever given in."

"Given in? Fucked you, you mean?"

She gasped. "If you ever touched me in that way, it wouldn't be fucking. There is far too much between us to be so crude."

I bowed my head, moving much too close to her lips. "You need a good fucking. Perhaps it would teach you your place and that you can't boss me around."

"And you'd know because you've been with hundreds of women by now?" Her question dripped with acid, but her face blazed with vulnerability.

"Just like my body is none of your concern, what I do with it with other people isn't either."

"So you've figured out a way to be close to people and not get attached?"

"Attached?" I snickered with all the ice she injected me with. "Attached? You think I just get *attached?* That I sent you away because I was *attached?*"

"Yes." She nodded firmly. "That's exactly why. We only kissed twice, Jacob, but I fell madly in love with you. If a kiss has that much power, imagine what sex would do. I'd probably propose to you the minute you climbed on top of me."

A full body shudder epicentred in my heart and quaked through my limbs.

She stunned me silent.

Shocked me stupid.

I had no reply.

Her mouth opened and closed like a fish caught in my net, shock turning her eyes wide. "Um, forget I said that." Turning around, she buried her face into her hands. "God, what is it about you that makes me so *angry*?"

I still couldn't speak. The pot in my system highlighted the shivers she'd given me. Every inch of me felt foreign and alive and no longer in my control. My arms wanted to hug her. My legs wanted to go to her. My cock wanted to sink inside her and see if she truly would propose.

I should be fucking terrified.

I should bolt out the door and never come back.

But the damn weed mellowed my normal triggers. It muffled the coughing memories. It muted my phobia of affection.

And I moved toward her, hand outstretched to catch a few damp strands of her chocolate hair.

She tensed as I tugged the length. Even tangled from a raging monsoon, it was soft and silky, and the urge to press them to my nose and drink in her scent made me stumble.

"Wha-what are you doing?" She spun slowly, facing me, removing her hair from my grip.

"Nothing." I blinked, doing my best to eradicate the foggy lies that everything was okay. That there was nothing to fight or fear. I'd sought this kind of high. I'd begged for it to survive her company.

But now that I swam in serenity, it took away my power to run.

Why should I run?

What would I run from?

This was Hope. She knew me. She understood me.

She won't hurt me.

"I'm sorry." I stared into her beautiful green eyes. The colour reminded me of the ocean offshore where the depths flickered between turquoise and emerald.

She exhaled heavily. "No. I'm the one who should say sorry."

"There we go again." I chuckled. "Damn apologies."

"I wonder if we'll ever have a conversation where we don't use that word?"

"Doubt it." Her hair fascinated me again, dragging my attention to the slivers of fire dancing amongst copper and chocolate. The light bulb above crackled and flickered, shutting off as another boom of thunder punched the walls.

Darkness threatened to surround us, only held at bay thanks to the solar lantern and candles. The light turned buttery soft and sensual, adding another element to the drugs in my system. Layering heat to the overriding, overpowering need I had for this woman.

The nauseating need of wanting to kiss her so damn much.

My body swayed, my tongue licked my lips, my entire existence hinged on touching her.

But beneath the haze was horror. Recurring nightmares of corpses and funerals and caskets. Images of her dead and me alone, and the sick, sick sorrow it would leave me with.

Love had killed my parents.

Love was not kind.

To anyone.

Sighing heavily, I backed up and pinched the bridge of my nose. My erection throbbed, and the lust that had been absent in my travels compounded until my entire nervous system demanded I take her.

I hated the sensation of not being in control.

I hated Hope for the loss of it.

Turning away, I murmured, "Electricity is out. The storm will stick around for a few hours at least. I'm not suggesting we sleep to avoid talking; I'm suggesting we sleep because I'm tired and need to rest."

My back prickled as she came closer, stopping just behind me. "It's early. Don't you want to talk, just a little?" Her awkwardness pinched between my shoulder blades as she inhaled nervously. "I-I missed you, Jacob. Not a day went by that I didn't wonder if you were okay or where you were." Moving around me, she stood between me and the bed. "I want to know about your travels. Where did you go? What did you see?"

I didn't like her in the same vision as my mattress.

I didn't like the fantasies I suffered of tossing her down, kissing her deep, and peeling off that intoxicating white dress.

Shaking my head, I brushed past her, sitting heavily on the bed, hoping she'd take the hint and use the chair by the tiny table beneath the window.

Instead, she bit her lip, hesitated, then sat beside me.

The mattress creaked under our weight, and I remembered another bed a long time ago where she'd sat so close and berated me with questions about my concussion. She'd put up with my bullshit to drive me to the hospital. She'd cared so much even then.

Goddammit, why did she have to be so *real?*

Why did she have to affect me like a punch to the goddamn heart?

We sat stiffly side by side.

She gathered her hair over one shoulder, twisting the dampness into a rope. When I didn't speak, she whispered, "I haven't been on a horse since Cherry River." Her eyes caught mine. "You?"

Horses. The one subject I was happy to discuss.

"No." I shook my head. "I miss Forrest like hell."

"You could go visit him."

"No. He's not mine anymore."

"What do you mean?"

"I mean, Cherry River should be Aunt Cassie's. I don't deserve it."

Hope stiffened. "Of course you deserve it. You've worked that land since you were born."

I meant to stay silent, but my drugged consciousness decided to throw me under the bus. "I can't ever go back."

"What? Why?"

"Because death exists there."

She sucked in a breath. "There is also life. So, so much life. I know your parents dying left you with a—"

"New subject." I wedged my elbows on my knees, raking hands through my hair. "What have you done for the past four years?"

I expected her to be chatty and ease into stories that would lull me into exhaustion.

She didn't.

She sat silent and harsh, fingers plucking her dress. "Oh, you know. Not much."

Her resistance made me twist to face her. Our knees touched, and I shuddered at the contact, cursing the snarling desire for more. "Not much? What does that mean?"

"Just the usual. Working."

"Working on what?"

"I became a scriptwriter. On a small show in England."

"So no acting then?"

She chuckled. "I tried. Turns out, I'm not exactly talented like my father."

"I already knew that."

She glared. "Excuse me?"

"I knew you were terrible the moment you tried lying to my mother about my fall off Forrest." I smirked. "It was obvious."

Talking about my mother wasn't as hard as it should've been. Time had healed my wounds to scars, but I didn't deserve the pain to fade.

It felt wrong to move on.

But out here, living within the sacred grounds of a temple dedicated to the dead, my agony was easier to bear with her gone. And that made my guilt doubly cruel because I shouldn't feel any sort of relief. I shouldn't indulge in the fairy-tale she once had— that she was happy with my father in the afterlife.

The pressure was gone to be a good son.

And I was alone to fail, fall, and fake my way through life with people who didn't know me.

Hope's sudden smile made my heart beat hard, fast, and painful. "You put me in an uncomfortable position. I didn't want to lie to her."

"It wasn't lying. It was keeping my secret."

"Same thing."

"Not the same thing at all." I couldn't tear my eyes from her lips. Why couldn't I look away? Why did the air feel heavier and the light softer and the rain louder all at once?

Weed was supposed to dull the senses, not heighten them. "We all have secrets that need keeping, Hope."

She flinched, looking at the floor. "Do you have secrets?"

"Hundreds." My voice was as coarse as coral and just as poisonous. "All the time."

I want you.

I dream about you.

I'd give anything to be brave enough to claim you.

"Care to tell me any of them?" She blinked, her eyelashes painting spider webs on her cheeks. She'd never been so pretty, so innocent, so enticing.

She'd been seventeen the last time I'd seen her. She'd driven me insane back then. Now, she drove me out of my goddamn mind.

"Tell me one of yours." My voice was no longer coarse but gravel.

She blinked. "I don't have any."

"Sure you do. Everyone does."

"Nothing I want to share."

"And that's why they're called secrets." I sat taller, intrigued by her refusal. "You wanted to talk, Hope. So talk."

She looked away, staring at the door we still hadn't closed. Rain puddled on the floor, and I took the excuse to get away from her. Standing, I crossed the small space and wedged the exit shut.

Our eyes locked as I turned around.

Her cheeks pinked as she scanned my body. She jumped upright as if sitting on my bed had become quicksand into hell. "Um, you know what? I think...I think I'd like to sleep somewhere else."

My heart stopped beating. "Excuse me?"

"I don't think I can do this." Rubbing her face with her hands, she nodded to herself. "This was a mistake."

"What's a mistake?" I stepped toward her. "Flying across the world to find me? Why exactly did you, by the way? I don't believe Cassie was just worried about me. Or is the real reason a secret, too?"

She shrank into herself. "It's not a secret. It's just...hard to tell you."

"Hard?" Another step toward her. "Why?"

"Because you'll never speak to me again if I tell you and..." She shrugged. "I don't want you to cut me from your life again. But then again, I can barely be in the same room as you, so what's the difference?"

"Why can't you be in the same room as me?"

She rolled her eyes. "Oh, come on, Jacob. Don't be stupid."

"Stupid?" I poked a finger in my chest. "Did you just call me stupid?"

"Yep, just like I told you to grow up."

"Wow, the insults just keep coming."

She curled her hands into fists. "Not insults. Secrets. You wanted to know mine? Well, now you do."

I nodded condescendingly. "Ah, great. So all this time, while pretending to be my friend, you thought I should get my head out of my ass, grow up, and stop being stupid. That about right?"

"Don't forget about accepting death as a part of life."

"Ah, right. Can't forget about that one." My breathing was short and sharp. "I thought we agreed no more fighting. Why are you being like this?"

She winced. "I told you. I can't sleep in here with you. You want to go to bed. You want to rest. Well, I won't be able to do either, and it's too small for the both of us. I...I need some space."

"Space away from me?"

"Exactly."

"You just found me, and now you're running away?"

"Guess it's my turn to run this time, huh?"

"Wow, you really are on form tonight." I stalked toward her. "What the hell changed? We were having a normal conversation. We were getting along. Now you're jumping down my throat for things that aren't my fault."

She vibrated with temper. "That's the thing, Jacob. It *is* your fault. All of it is your fault. It's your fault I can't be around you when that's all I want to be. It's your fault I'm afraid of talking to you when I have so much to say. It's your fault I can't just be your friend when I tried so, so hard to be."

My feet locked to the floor. "What are you saying?"

"I'm saying I came here, all the while knowing this is how I'd react, and thought I'd be able to handle it. That I'd see you again and could ignore how I used to feel about you. Oh, who am I kidding? How I *used* to feel about you? It's more like how I *still* feel about you. It doesn't go away. As much as I wish it would, I'm still stupidly in love with you, and just being in this room is killing me because I know you'll never love me in return. It's torture living like this. I-I don't want to keep doing this to myself."

Everything inside me locked down. The weed no longer affected me. The gentle buzz evaporated thanks to rage and fear and temper. "What happened to your 'I'm strong enough to deal with being hurt' spiel?"

"I lied."

"You didn't lie. You're lying now." I studied her. "You're being weak by running. Which isn't happening by the way. I didn't ask you here, Hope. But I'm not letting you run around like a moron in an electrical storm. I'm sorry you can't stand the sight of me, but that's your issue, not mine. You're staying here until the weather clears and then I'll drive you back to—"

"No, I'll walk. I've walked home after a bad date before. I can do it again." Barging past me, her feet stomped the bare wood as she beelined for the door. Her hand wrapped around the handle, and something broke inside me.

Something splintered and shattered. The thought of her walking away crippled me. It crippled me worse than the thought of her staying.

Crossing the room in a few fast strides, I grabbed her

shoulders, spun her around, and pushed her against the door. "I'm not a bad date you get to abandon."

"You're right. You're not a date at all." She squirmed in my hold. "Now, let me go."

"No. You're not leaving."

"I am. Call your aunt. She has something important to tell you."

"I don't care what she has to say."

"You will. Believe me."

"Wrong." I brushed my nose against hers. "All I care about right now is keeping you safe from the rain."

"That's very chivalrous of you, Jacob, but faced with walking in the rain or sleeping here with you, I choose the rain." She tried to push me away. "Let go of me."

"Not until you stop fighting." I cupped her cheek. "You're staying."

"I'm not."

"For once in your life, you're going to do what I tell you."

She laughed coldly. "How about once in your life, you realise how much you're hurting me just by being you?"

My heart bled all over the floor. "*I* hurt *you*? What about the way *you* hurt *me*?"

Her cheeks pinked. "I don't hurt you. You're immune to me."

"You hurt me every fucking second. You hurt me just by existing."

"Why would you say something like that?"

"Because it's true." My thumb traced her bottom lip, disobeying my command to back away. "You call me stupid, Hope. But you're just as blind."

She shivered. "Let me go, Jacob."

"Can't." My feet inched closer, slipping my body against hers. She gasped as I wedged my weight on her, pressing her into the door. "Fuck, I can't."

I'd kissed this girl with a concussion, and when I was drunk. Both weren't of clear mind and rational thought.

What would kissing her be like after smoking a pipe?

"Don't do this, Jacob. Please, *please* don't do this."

I was intoxicated. My voice slurred with sex. "Do what?"

She whimpered as my mouth hovered over hers. "This."

"This?"

"Kiss me."

I knew she requested I stop, but in my current fog, all I heard was a command.

Kiss me.

God, yes, I'll kiss you.

I collapsed against her, slamming my lips to hers and erasing four long years apart.

She tasted just like she had that night in the stables. Sweet and heady and strong—so goddamn strong.

She wriggled in my embrace, her lips tight under mine, fighting me all while I begged her for welcome. "Stop." Her mumble against my mouth only spurred me on.

My hands fisted into her hair, holding her steady to kiss her deeper.

I groaned as I licked the seam of her lips, desperate for her to kiss me back.

Come on, Hope.

Give in.

Her legs shifted, angling her bottom half away.

Then, blinding white-hot agony.

I buckled over, letting her go and swimming in a roar of nausea. Cupping my balls, I fell to my knees, rocking in blistering pain. "You just kneed me!"

"You wouldn't let me go!" She stood over me, chest heaving.

I struggled to catch a breath, riding the shockwaves of injury. She ducked to her haunches, her face full of worry. "Oh, no, I didn't hurt you, did I? I barely put any pressure behind it. It was just a warning. That's all."

I laughed icily, cupping the boys and massaging the ache away. "That's *all*? Who the hell are you?"

She sighed. "I'm the girl who's very sorry. I shouldn't have done that."

"Damn right, you shouldn't." The pain faded, carried away by blood and heartbeats, leaving me angrier than I'd ever been. "I kiss you, and you try to kill me."

"I told you I didn't want to be kissed." She stood, towering over me on the floor. "I need to go. We're just...not right for each other, Jacob. We want different things. I...I truly am sorry for hurting you."

"I don't want your damn apology."

"It's all I have to give." She shrugged sadly. "Please...call Cassie. It's urgent. I promised her I'd give you the message, and I have. My task is complete. I need to leave."

My hand lashed out, fingers locking around her ankle.

"You're not leaving."

She narrowed her eyes. "I am. You've been smoking pot. You're not in your right mind."

"I didn't kiss you because of the weed, Hope." My thumb followed her ankle bone, loving the way she shuddered. "I kissed you because I couldn't *not* kiss you."

"And I didn't kiss you back because I *can't* kiss you."

"You've kissed me before."

"And both were mistakes."

"You're afraid you're going to propose to me if I fuck you in a rainstorm?"

A full body shudder took her hostage as my fingers crept up her calf. Her skin was like satin. Like sea glass and marble. I couldn't stop myself. I shifted higher on my knees, praying to her as I continued stroking the softest skin I'd ever touched. Around her kneecap, dipping to inner thigh and up, up, up. "Or are you afraid I'd say yes if you did?"

She wobbled.

Her hand landed on my head, fingers curling around my shaggy hair. "Don't...please don't."

Wrapping my free arm around her waist, I tugged her into me. Her stomach was firm and flat as I pressed a kiss right on her belly button. "Don't you want to know what it would be like?"

"Be like?" Her head fell back as my fingers continued climbing. Goosebumps pebbled her skin. She shivered as if she stood in a snowstorm and not in a humid hut in Bali.

"Between us."

"There's nothing between us."

I nipped at her lower belly. "There's *everything* between us."

My fingers grazed her underwear. She jolted as if lightning forked through the roof and hit her directly in the heart. "God, Jacob, please...you're not rational. It's the weed. This isn't you. God, it's not—"

I lashed my thumb over the most intimate part of her. The cotton between her legs was wet from rain and the sizzling heat between us. My throat became a wasteland of want. My body a nucleus of raging hot need. "It's not the pot." I nuzzled into her belly, pressing harder against her. A flood of warmth shocked me as her back bowed, opening her body to my control.

And that was it.

I broke.

Scrambling to my feet, I wrapped a fist in her hair and pulled.

With my other hand, I cupped her heat, rocking my palm against the part I'd read was the most sensitive.

She buckled in my hold. Her head fell back. Her lips parted. And I kissed her.

Goddammit, I kissed her.

Just as we fought with words, we fought in action too.

She kissed me back, violence for violence.

We tripped into the middle of the room, almost falling. But our lips never unlocked. Our bodies never unglued. Our hands roaming, claiming, possessing.

I did my best to fall toward the bed, guiding her as we spun and fought, kissing, always kissing.

Pushing her the final distance, she tumbled backward, bouncing on the bed where I'd been so goddamn lonely. Where she'd found me in my dreams and haunted my nightmares. Where I'd loved her, wanted her, watched her die, and realised I wanted this girl enough to face my awful fears, but I wasn't strong enough to fight for a forever.

She was the most dangerous thing to me.

She was the one person who could end my life all by loving me.

Hope scrambled up the bed, her dress bunching around her legs, her hair wild and tangled. Her eyes searched mine as I crawled toward her, hovering over her with shaking arms.

"You do this, and everything changes."

I ducked to kiss her, twisting her tongue with mine. "It's just sex."

"Sex you've avoided."

"Sex I want with you."

She pulled away, her palm cupping my cheek. "I need you to know how this will affect me. You already own my heart, Jacob Wild. If you take my body too, you can't have my friendship. It would be love. Unequivocally."

I kissed her again, wishing she'd shut up and let me focus on being with her here and not the terrifying future.

She kissed me back but pulled away with a moan. "Please, tell me you understand. I don't know what's going on with you. I don't know why you're doing this."

"Just understand I want you."

She sighed sadly. "But that's not enough for me." Pushing me, she groaned. "I don't just want one night with you."

My patience frayed; more blood swelled in my cock. "What *do* you want?"

Her eyes glittered with every emotion I was petrified of. "You really want an answer to that question?"

"I want the truth."

She looked away, breathing shallow. For a second, she shrank into herself, but then her shoulders braced and her green, powerful gaze froze me above her. "I want everything. All of it. You, Cherry River, *us*. I want more than you can ever give me." Tears rolled down her cheeks. "And that's why I can't do this."

I couldn't stop myself from kissing away her sadness, tasting salt and heartache. "I'm not trying to hurt you. I'm trying to give you want you want."

"No, you're trying to sleep with me." She huffed with false humour.

"That too." I nuzzled into her, kissing the side of her neck until her head flopped sideways. "Is it working?"

"You're not playing fair."

"You've never played fair with me."

"I've always respected your boundaries."

I laughed coldly, pulling away to kiss the tip of her nose. "I'm sorry but that's bullshit. You've pushed me to the point of breaking every damn day we've spent together."

She bit her lip, eyes searching mine. She must've seen the truth because regret coloured her. "You're right. I wasn't fair."

"You weren't." I bent to kiss her again, hovering over her mouth. "But I forgive you."

As my lips grazed hers, she murmured, "You're not being fair now. You're pushing me to do something I can't."

"And how does that feel? Does it tear you up inside? Does it hurt you to the point of excruciation? Does it make you want to run as far away as possible?"

She nodded as I kissed my way along her collarbone. "Um-hum." She shivered as I blew on the wetness left by my tongue. "I need to leave."

"You need to stay."

"If I stay I'll—"

"Sleep with me. Yes."

She moaned, long and needy, making me ten times harder. "I've wanted you for years, Jacob. You're making me run out of willpower to say no."

"Good. Give in." I didn't know where my aversions had gone. Our roles had reversed. I was the one asking for contact. I finally understood how it felt to want someone who didn't want you.

It sucked.

It hurt.

I wanted to stop.

But I was in too deep. Far, far too deep. My body controlled me now, not my mind, and my body begged, fucking *begged* to have her.

To have someone.

Just once.

To know what it felt like to be normal.

Hope groaned as I tangled fingers in her hair, holding her prisoner.

Her eyes blazed. "If we do this, it's on you. I refuse to feel guilty for pressuring you. I won't berate myself that I forced you to sleep with me. I'll—"

I kissed her, biting her lower lip. "Does it look like you're forcing me to do something I don't want to do?" I rocked my erection against her.

She gasped, her skin flushing with heat. "The pot has ruined you."

"Hope." I lowered myself on her, pinning her to the bed. "Shut up."

"But—"

"You're not forcing me to do anything."

"But you—"

"I want you. I want you so fucking much." I wedged my hips deeper between her legs, rocking until lightning sizzled up my spine. "See? Just be here with me. Let's see if all that fighting is for a reason."

"And after?"

"Who cares about after?"

"I care. I worry."

"There is no after. No past or future. Just this."

"I've tried living in the present, Jacob, and the past and future always have a way of intruding on it."

I sighed. She was right. I knew that far too well. But my heart no longer beat—it suffocated with need. My body made me reckless and hungry. I knew the suffering this would cause, but I'd pay it to enjoy one night with her. "It doesn't change that I need you so much I'm going out of my mind."

She looked away, her lips wet and pink. "I want you too…but

I need to know what you want from me...*after* you've had me. I need to know so I can prepare myself." She couldn't meet my eyes. "Do you understand? Do you see how hard this will be for me to have something I've always wanted, not knowing if it's mine forever or just for a little while?"

I flinched, looking at the flickering candles. What sort of answer could I give? I couldn't lie to her and say things would change. That I wanted her to marry me, move to Bali, and bear my children.

Those things would never happen.

I knew that in the depths of my soul.

My voice softened with sorrow. "There's no one else I'd rather love, Hope Jacinta Murphy, but out of anyone...you know me. You know I can't..."

She swallowed back tears. "Can't get close to me."

I nodded. My eyes burned. My heart drowned in an ocean of misery. "I'm sorry." I shifted to climb off her. My lust was a monstrous thing, but I'd deal with it on my own instead of forcing it on Hope. I'd hurt her enough. "Just...forget it."

I'd let myself give in for just a moment. I'd been brave enough just for a second.

And she didn't want me.

She wasn't prepared to share my pain.

It's for the best.

Her hands caught my shoulders, her stare far too intense. "Why do you want to do this?"

I struggled to find an answer that wouldn't promise things I couldn't promise and words that wouldn't hurt. Finally, I settled on the simplest. "'Cause when I'm with you, I forget about loneliness."

Her gaze danced over mine, swift and serious, reading whatever secrets I couldn't hide. "Do you accept that I love you? That this won't be fucking to me. This will be so much more."

I stiffened. The price was far too high. The offer far too tempting.

She loves me.

Yet...I can't love her.

What sort of bastard did that make me to steal her heart, all because I wanted her body?

I wedged my forehead on hers, searching for the strength to stop this. It wasn't right. It wasn't fair.

The weed in my system flickered and faltered, mixing my phobias with desires. "You're my only friend, Hope."

I winced.

I hadn't meant to say that but the aching defencelessness of my voice made her arms loop around my shoulders and pull me into her. "I said something similar to you, once upon a time."

"Friends can fight." I studied her mouth.

"Friends can also make up." She licked her lips.

"Friends can sometimes be more…for a night," I whispered, shivering as she opened her legs.

Time stood still for a moment.

The rain stopped falling for a second.

And slowly, Hope nodded.

She granted damnation and salvation.

She gave me something I should never have asked for, successfully ruining me forever.

Her hand cupped my cheek, her body welcomed mine, she brought my head down and kissed me. "Okay, Jacob. Okay…"

Chapter Forty-Seven

JACOB

* * * * * *

TWO THINGS I learned the moment I gave in to Hope and she gave in to me.

One, it hurt when I touched her. The pain reached into my gut, tore out my innards, and fractured my heart with how perfect she felt, how sweet, how soft, how sexy.

But it was nothing, *nothing* compared to the pain when *she* touched *me*. Her caresses were excruciating. Her kisses agony. Her hugs annihilating.

I wanted to sleep with her.

I'd wanted it for years.

I'd fought with her to agree, but now that she had...I didn't know if I had the strength to go through with it.

The pain.

Fuck, the *pain*.

The battle between keeping my heart out of the physical and the overwhelming desire to fall head over heels for her. To say *screw you* to a dismal future—the future where she'd grow old and die, or get sick and die, or one day just hate me and leave.

Those futures were unacceptable, and each kiss and stroke taunted me to tread that path. To believe it wouldn't happen. To blindly accept I'd somehow found an immortal goddess who would never perish.

That I would be the one who died first.

The one who left.

The one who hurt her just like my father had hurt my mother.

She loves me.

I was already killing her slowly. The only difference between us was she was strong enough to endure such a thing...and I was not.

I squeezed my eyes shut against the noise. I wanted another

hit on my pipe to focus on one thing and one thing only.

But Hope was my new drug, and her kisses were pure addiction.

She made me come alive.

She coaxed dormant parts of me to roar awake, all while encouraging timid things to claim. Dirty thoughts blended with scared thoughts, and I trembled as I collapsed on top of her, pressing my hips deeper into hers.

Her breath hitched as I kissed her hard—harder than I ever had before. Her damp hair curled over my pillow, and the bed creaked as she wriggled closer.

She was the only one to ever get this close to me. The only one I could stomach touching me, kissing me...

She would be my first.

But was I hers?

The acidic question laced our kiss. Had she found love with another? Had she been with many men? Why did that make fury unfurl and possession turn me sick with loathing?

Loathing for myself because I could've had her when she was seventeen while secreted away on my farm. She could've been mine from the very start.

Instead, I'd pushed her away.

She'd had a life without me.

She would continue to have a life without me after this.

My lips punished hers, bruising both of us as my disgusting thoughts pressured me to break—to either run or rush this. To find the climax I needed without the annihilation of being loved by her.

My right hand skated down her body, tugging on the wet fabric of her dress. "Off. I want this off."

Her eyes flared as I pulled away and gave her space. Hesitantly, her fingers hitched the hem, pausing around her hips. "Before I do, can I, um, ask one more question...and then I'm all yours."

My cock hardened to agony levels. "You're already mine." I dragged a fingertip along her collarbone. "You're in my bed, after all."

"You know what I mean." Her eyelids lowered, turning brilliant green into sultry emerald.

"How about we avoid another fight by *not* talking?" Ducking, I kissed the collarbone I'd just stroked. Her skin tasted of rain, coconut, and lemonade.

I groaned, nipping at her. "We seem to do better when conversation isn't our main pastime."

"One question, Jacob." Her back bowed as I wedged an arm around her, bending her backward until I earned a mouthful of delicious Hope. I wanted to trail my tongue down to the nipple showing beneath her clothes.

I groaned again, but this time in annoyance. "Fine, one question."

She blinked, hazed and hot as I unwound my arm and hovered over her.

"Ask quickly. Patience isn't exactly my strong suit."

"Okay." She licked her lips. "A-are you happy? I mean, right now? With me?"

I froze.

Happy?

Try terrified.

"I'm horny; does that count?"

Hurt glistened in her gaze. She took a moment to reply. "I guess...seeing as that is the main reason I'm pinned beneath you."

"You did argue that I'd never given in." I rocked my hardness against her. "Aren't *you* happy now that I have?"

Her hand raised to cup my cheek. Her touch sent fire bolts and poison right to my heart. Instinct howled for me to move away, but I shivered and ignored it, allowing the connection, enduring it.

"If I'm being honest, I don't know what I am." She sighed heavily. "I want you so much that if you didn't mean so much to me, I'd already be naked with you inside me. But..."

I liked the sound of that, and I was happy to oblige, but the faint thread of fear in her tone made me ask gently, "But?"

"But...why do I already feel like crying?"

"Do you often cry before having sex?" I meant it as a joke— an idiotic attempt to lighten the suddenly stifling tension. But my ribcage cracked one rib at a time as her eyes darted away, hiding a spark of truth.

Shit.

So this *wasn't* her first time.

That *killed* me. Here I was, the inexperienced, scared little virgin, and Hope had been touched before. *Adored* before. Cared for in ways I was too broken to achieve.

Great, now *I* felt like crying. Or tearing the goddamn walls apart. Or yelling at her for being my only friend, which meant she had all the power in the world to butcher me.

It wasn't fair.

I hated that she'd been intimate with others, all while I'd wrapped myself up in loneliness. It was my own stupid fault.

I *knew* that.

But it didn't mean I could live with it.

I wanted to hurt her. I wanted her to feel a tenth of the agony and longing I had for her.

At least then she'd have a justified reason to cry.

"What are you thinking about?" Her fingers trailed my spine. "You've gone rigid." Her other hand ran along my jawline. "If you don't stop clenching, you'll break your teeth."

A lance of pain struck from nowhere. My mother had said that exact thing on the red carpet for *The Boy & His Ribbon*. Hope had known my mother. She'd loved her. She'd met me when I was an idiotic fourteen-year-old mess.

Yet here she still was…tormenting me.

"Why are you here?" I narrowed my eyes.

She stiffened. "I told you…it's difficult to discuss. If you want to talk, we should stop…and talk." She moved beneath me, but I clamped hands on her shoulders, keeping her down.

"I don't mean why you're here, here. We'll deal with that later. I meant why are you still *here*? With me…after all this time? Why are you still…my friend?"

Her lips parted. The air crackled with electricity caused by lust and lightning. "What sort of question is that?"

"A good one, so answer it."

"Friends are there for the good and bad, Jacob. I'm loyal."

"Loyalty can be a curse."

"You're right." She nodded, her body heat scorching mine, sending more blood between my legs. "But it can also be rewarding…especially when the friend in question accepts there's something more between them."

"There's that word again."

"What, friend?"

I brushed my nose against hers. "No, *accept*."

She nuzzled me, kissing my cheek, working her way to my eyelashes and forehead. The sensation of being kissed so sweetly ripped up my stomach and set fire to the carnage left behind.

"Acceptance is the key to freedom." She kissed my cheekbone. "It's a cage of your own making." A kiss on my earlobe. "I only wish you could see that…if you could, your life wouldn't be so painful."

I reared back. "Would it take away the pain of knowing you've been with someone else?"

"Excuse me?" She sat bolt upright, shoving me away. "What the hell, Jacob?"

"This isn't your first time."

"How on earth do you know that?"

I snorted. "Oh, believe me. I know."

"It's none of your business." Her nose shot up with airs and graces. "None whatsoever."

"You sure about that? Don't *friends* have authority to approve or disapprove potential lovers?"

Rage dotted her cheeks. She laughed coldly. "Wait a minute, let me get this straight. After four years of nothing—no letter, email, phone call, *nothing*—you think you have the right to tell me who I can or cannot date?"

"Are you dating him now?" I sat on my knees, vibrating with anger. "Are you with someone else while you're here with me?"

"Wow, you have some nerve, Jacob Wild." She pushed storm-curled hair from her eyes. "Do you think that low of me? That I would sleep with you while with someone else? That I'd *cheat?*"

My heart slammed against a brick wall. "I don't know. You might've changed a lot in four years."

"Yet you haven't changed at all!"

Her yell pounded against the war drum of my heart. Regret squashed me, but I had to know—had to keep digging at my pain. I deliberately used my fears to push her away. To halt this raw and vulnerable connection between us.

I thought I was done pushing her away—at least for the night. I believed my lust was stronger than my terror.

Turned out, it was just waiting.

Waiting for the perfect moment to make me suffer and her despise me. I wished I could take it back. I wanted to touch her again. But the sickness inside lowered my head and grunted, "Just answer me, Hope."

"Answer what?"

"Are you or are you not with someone?"

"I can't believe this. No, I will not answer you!" Huffing with disbelief, she sprang off the bed. "Forget it. I'm leaving. I feared this was a mistake, and it is." Smoothing down her dress, she spun to face me. "Why couldn't you just let whatever was about to happen, happen, huh? Why couldn't you be brave enough to let love guide you for once, instead of fighting it all the time?" Tears spilled down her cheeks. "And why do I keep falling for it? Why do I think I can be strong enough for both of us? That one day, I'll be able to fix you?"

I tried to ignore the question. If I hadn't smoked weed and mellowed certain triggers, I wouldn't be able to reply.

But I *had* smoked. And I had to reply. Because I was in the wrong, just like always. "You keep trying because you know the truth."

"What truth?"

"The truth that if anyone can fix me...it's you."

"Ugh!" She hugged herself tight. "You can't say things like that. It sends mixed signals."

"I'm not sending anything. I'm trying to understand."

Trying to understand how to stop being like this.

"Understand what?"

"Why I feel this way about you when it fucking petrifies me. Why I'm furious that you've been with someone else when I know it's my fault. Why I can't seem to forget about you. Why I have dreams about you. Why, after all this time, I wish you *could* fix me so I didn't have to keep hurting you or myself."

She stood there, shaking, her dress dancing around her legs. We stared for a few quick breaths, trapped in honesty.

Finally, she stepped toward the bed. Her voice caught with a fresh spill of tears. "You want an answer? Fine. I *was* with someone. I was with him when I stepped on the plane to find you. I was with him when I saw you on the beach. I've been with him for over a year."

My entire body locked down. My hands curled into fists. "Were you with him when you kissed me?"

She shrugged dejectedly. "No."

I studied her, read her tears, heard her sorrow, and knew.

My shoulders slouched. "The phone call. That was who was more important than staying dry."

"Yes."

"You broke up with him?"

"Yes."

My voice thickened. "Why?"

Her gaze was too intense, too consuming. "You know why."

My entire body trembled as I climbed off the bed. The sandy floor stuck to my feet as I stepped toward her.

Her gaze dropped to my tented shorts, then glided over my chest to find my eyes.

She looked so sad it broke my heart.

I should stop this.

I shouldn't be so awfully selfish.

My voice was ash as I murmured, "You broke up with him...because of me."

She bit her lip as I moved closer.

"You broke another guy's heart all because I keep breaking yours."

She gasped as I threaded fingers in her hair, cupping the back of her neck.

"Stop putting me first, Hope. I don't deserve it." Pulling her into me, I kissed her deeply.

Her mouth opened. She let me control her, challenge her, then her tongue tentatively touched mine.

I licked her.

A tiny moan fell from her, tangled with frustration and anger.

And I was done.

Done with talking.

With hurting.

With denying.

Urgency ripped through my drug-haze, and I clutched her as if I'd fallen overboard into an endless sea of suffocation.

She clutched me back, pressing her body against mine until nothing was between us.

"Jake—"

"Quiet." I nipped her bottom lip. "No more talking. I'm done with talking." Walking backward, I dragged her with me until the back of my knees hit the bed.

"But—"

"Stop." I silenced her argument with a vicious kiss. I kissed her so damn hard our teeth clacked, our breaths knotted, and we clawed to get closer.

She cried out as I plunged my tongue deeper. My head swam as I dared cup her breast, squeezing her, loving the way my large hand enveloped her delicate flesh.

"Ah, God..." Her body went loose, giving up all control.

I took full advantage.

Ducking, I gathered the damp material of her dress, pulling it over her hips. "Take it off."

Her eyes flashed as she tried to pull away, but I didn't give her space. Pushing the fabric up, I gave her a single second to pull it over her head before my lips sought hers again.

The second the dress tumbled to the floor, my hand found her breast, grazing soft lace hiding softer flesh. "Now this."

Her lips twitched under mine. "You do it."

I kissed her, running my free hand to find the bra clasp, fumbling a little. I wasn't exactly savvy on getting women naked.

Fear returned, hissing with lack and limitation. I had no idea what I was doing. I didn't know how to satisfy her.

She had experience.

What if she laughed at my beginner attempts? What if she meant it when she said this was a terrible mistake?

Chasing such thoughts from my mind, I kissed her harder, making her squirm in my arms as I finally figured out the catch and the lace popped free. She wriggled, allowing the straps to cascade from her shoulders and the lingerie to fall to the floor.

I tore away, studying her pearly perfection for the first time. My breath came short and ragged as I imprinted the shadows and fullness that I'd dreamed of. The feminine muscles, the contour of her waist, the slenderness hiding such strength.

"Fuck, you're beautiful."

She blushed before tipping her chin. "Your turn." Her hands gathered my T-shirt, and with a quick glare and heavy shot of lust, I raised my arms obediently.

My T-shirt sailed down to land with her dress and bra.

"You're beautiful too." She traced my scars and imperfections, her breath turning just as papery as mine. "I've always thought so."

She leaned in and placed a kiss right over my heart. "The amount of times I watched you at Cherry River is embarrassing."

"Don't be embarrassed. I watched you too."

"Don't talk," she murmured, her hand dipping lower, travelling over muscles I'd honed with a life of labour. "Don't think about anything but this, just in case you run again." She teased me, stroking me when I wanted something harder.

Something *more*.

I reached out and captured her tight nipple. "I'm not running anywhere." The second my thumb circled her, she broke out in goosebumps. "You like that?"

She nodded with hooded eyes. "Um-hum."

I pinched her gently. "And that?"

Her eyelids fluttered lower. "Yes."

"And this?" I squeezed harder, bowing my head and taking her small nipple into my mouth.

Her back bowed as I caught her, pressing her breasts against my face. I didn't need an answer to know she liked this better.

I knew her.

I knew violence ran in Hope as it ran in me.

My teeth teased her skin, nipping my way to the other side. Finding her other nipple, I sucked it hard.

She jerked. "Jacob...." Her fingers turned to talons, dragging over my shoulders.

I loved seeing her come undone.

I loved the slices of sharpness as her desperation etched into my skin.

While my tongue stayed busy, my hands skated down her waist, fingers hooking into her underwear. "I want these off."

She teetered as I nipped at her nipple again, sucking deep. Rising up, I captured her mouth as I pushed the lacy material away from her hips.

She shook her head. "Wait...um, shouldn't we slow—"

"Can't." With a quick push, I said goodbye to the final piece of clothing hiding her from me. I couldn't breathe as she stepped from the puddle of lace, bare and beautiful.

My heart stopped beating. Literally stopped. My chest no longer held organs keeping me alive; it was filled with fiery lust and fantasy instead.

With a grunt, I fell to my knees, running my hands down the back of her ass and thighs as I went.

She flinched as my mouth lined up perfectly with her core. "Jacob...what are you—"

She never finished her question.

My tongue connected with her silky flesh, and she convulsed in my arms. Her hands landed on my head for balance as I hugged her upper thighs, pressing all of her into my mouth.

I didn't know if I did it right or if it felt good or if I'd royally screwed up.

But I let Hope guide me.

For every lick I gave, she quivered and quaked. For every bite and suck, she moaned and wobbled. I repeated what made her weak, and tweaked what made her stiffen.

The more I licked her, the hotter her skin became.

Her breath turned thin. Her fingers turned loose.

And her hips rocked toward me of their own accord.

I smiled against her, tasting her, drinking her, regretting so many things between us. Why was I so afraid of this? This wonderful, delicious girl who loved me?

I delved deeper, thrusting my tongue inside her, wanting to punish her for all my shortcomings.

"Holy—" A strangled cry fell from her mouth as wet warmth coated my tongue. She shivered harder, her knees buckling.

I didn't let her get away.

I dipped inside her again, biting her clit as my self-control threatened to snap.

I was so fucking hard, I couldn't see anymore.

I could only feel.

Heat and wet and want.

"Jacob...I'm—God, I'm..." Her head hung heavy as her entire body jolted.

I followed the satiny softness of her inner thigh and pressed a finger deep inside her.

She swayed, granting her entire body into my safekeeping as my one finger became two and my tongue fought to pleasure her.

I'd never felt something so good.

So silky and carnal.

My body strained with hunger, ready to grind, ready to thrust.

I was needy and angry and impatient.

And when Hope came all over my fingers, I couldn't hold myself back any more.

Her groan made my hair stand on end as her inner muscles squeezed around my invasion. Over and over, ripple after ripple, her wetness drugged me better than any pipe or alcohol.

Pulling her down, I yanked at my swimming shorts.

Her body folded like a fallen flower onto my lap. Her hazy eyes locked on my groin, watching as my erection popped from my shorts and the blue material trapped my thighs.

I pushed them as far as I could without moving.

Because I couldn't move.

I couldn't do a damn thing because I'd reached the end of my limit.

"Come here." I grabbed her around the back of the neck, smashing our lips together. Our kiss was sloppy and savage, teeth and tongue and temper.

Her thighs slipped over mine, sitting on me, caging me.

Her hands found my hair, tugging the length, fighting my need with her own. Her lips claimed mine, our tongues tangling with passion.

It reminded me of the other times we'd kissed. How a single kiss always turned into aggression. How aggression turned to war. How war escalated to the point of insanity.

I was insane. Pure and simple.

Inching forward on her knees, she angled herself over me.

Her eyes studied my nakedness, filling me with complex persecution.

I'd never been naked in front of a girl before. Never suffocated with hunger or trembled with self-consciousness. Having her see me made me powerful and vulnerable all at once.

The two emotions did not combine well with my fear and fury.

Clamping hands on her hips, I pushed her down.

She fought me for a second, her hand lashing around my hardness as if she wanted to repay what I'd done for her. "No." I pushed again, hissing as the heat of her met my tip. "I can't wait."

Her fingers unwrapped from around me, her cheeks pink and lips red. With a moan and a shiver, she nodded and sank.

Down and down, her wetness made me slip smoothly inside her, inch by inch.

I was wrong before when I thought my heart had stopped beating.

This was where I died.

This moment trapped in her body where I felt so many fucking things.

Good things.

Bad things.

Terrible and wonderful things.

"Goddammit, Hope." I buried a fist in her hair, yanking her closer. I thrust up, not gentle, not kind…just hungry.

So, so fucking hungry.

The same thunderstorm that echoed outside vibrated in my blood, demanding I claim more.

My bones bruised against the floor as I forced her all the way onto my lap, driving as deep as I could inside her.

She moaned as her forehead crashed against my shoulder and her arms wrapped tight around me.

Her hug hurt me. Fuck, it hurt.

But being inside her cancelled out that hurt, layering it with something else instead.

Something I wanted more than life itself.

I couldn't pretend I didn't crave her. I couldn't lie and say I could live without her anymore. I was done being alone when all I wanted was to have a family.

To love.

Even when people died.

To care.

Even when people left.

To be open to loss.

Even when love was so fucking cruel.

I thrust again and again, holding her prisoner as I made her mine.

I kissed her as I drove into her.

Deeper and deeper, over and over.

She cried out as I hit the top of her, my eyes snapping closed at the surreal sensation of being inside this girl.

She rocked against me for each thrust, fucking me as I fucked her, bruise for bruise.

There was nothing gentle or soft about us.

Both chasing a desire we'd danced around for years.

I took her.

Rough and ruthless.

She took me.

Determined and damned.

Everything inside me wanted to erupt. Her heat. Her kindness. Her blind belief that she could save me.

I slipped on the sandy floor as I thrust again. Sweat rivered down my back and Hope's skin turned just as slippery.

Her teeth sank into her bottom lip as her eyes met mine. Forehead to forehead, arms locked around each other, bodies riding the other.

And I fell into her.

I felt the tug to tumble.

I fought the call to commit.

I closed my eyes and forced my body to stay well away from my heart. All while knowing I was too late because as the first tingle and shiver of an orgasm brewed, I almost believed I could have this.

Have her.

For eternity.

As my hips rolled, I almost made the fatal error that all marriages were based on.

The belief that this would never end.

The faith that the preciousness of what we'd found would never die.

The trading of hearts in the face of death's rebellion. A declaration against life itself.

My face contorted as I let go, gave in, and allowed myself to taste such a gift for the shortest moment.

And the intensity, the relief, the all-consuming need I buckled with didn't kill me like I feared, it made wings sprout from my back and fortunes scatter at my feet. I believed I was invincible. I basked in the sacred glow of absolute untainted happiness.

And I wanted that.

With all my broken, stupid heart.

But then fear smoked inside me, whispering of sobbing goodbyes and tear-washed funerals, and my violence to avoid such pain became worse.

So, *so* much worse.

I bit her neck, cursing her even as I claimed her, thrusting again and again, arching my hips until every inch of me pounded into her. "I'll never forgive you for this."

She reared back, her breasts bouncing as I rode her. Her mouth opened to speak, but then her eyes burned with the same bloodthirsty fear, and in that second, she looked as if she hated me.

But then it was gone, replaced with the ever-suffering affection. "I know. But I won't forgive you either."

"Forgive me for what?"

"For stealing my heart forever."

I grimaced as a wave of dark desire clutched my lower belly. "I never asked for your heart."

She rocked against me, her fingers digging into my shoulders, pressing herself as deep as she could. "Yet you stole it anyway."

My eyes snapped closed as I struggled to fight the creeping cloud of an orgasm. A thunder strike clapped over ahead, making Hope flinch in my arms.

Rain hammered the roof as pain hammered my soul.

But I never stopped thrusting, hoping, living in that tiny piece of bliss with the girl I would give anything to keep.

I rode her until I couldn't fight my climax any longer.

She left me lost and alone, gasping for answers—throwing me to the mercy of two futures I didn't know how to survive.

One with her.

One without her.

And animalistic aggression soared over the weakness of my heart. It thought for me. It shut up awful worries and focused on the only thing it could survive.

Coming.

My orgasm brewed full of pain and goodbyes, pushing me over the edge.

I opened my mouth to howl, but Hope kissed me instead.

So I groaned into her.

I hugged her. I loved her. I came for her.

And I poured everything I was into her hands, knowing all along I'd lived a half-life, a broken life, and after this...I'd have no life at all.

Chapter Forty-Eight

JACOB

* * * * * *

EVEN EXHAUSTED—IN mind, body, and spirit—I couldn't sleep.

Lying on my back, staring at the ceiling, I re-lived being inside Hope until I grew hard all over again.

I was no longer a virgin.

After we finished, we'd shared the tiny cold-water shower, skirted around each other with timid smiles and worried words, then climbed into bed to rest.

I'd steeled myself against the torture of cuddling with her, knowing I wouldn't be able to ever let her go if she curled into me, trusted me enough to fall asleep in my arms, and dreamed beside me of a happier future.

But my fears were for nothing because she kissed me gently, then rolled onto her side, facing away as if this whole evening had been as overwhelming for her as it had been for me.

Space existed between us again, rapidly filling with cruel finality.

She knew me better than anyone. She loved me for, Christ's sake. All it would take was one word. A simple request.

Stay.

Stay here…with me.

But as the swell of soul-deep affection almost brought idiotic tears to my eyes, I knew I could never ask such a thing.

If I did, I would smother her in my need to keep her safe.

I would drive her mad, like I was mad, and together we'd spiral into lunacy.

Goddammit.

I rubbed at my broken heart, glowering in the darkness.

She was the reason I couldn't sleep. The reason I was a bastard.

Her silent, sleeping form made blood seep from my pores. Her sweet, strong personality made agony thrum down my spine. She wasn't pushing me or challenging me while she slumbered, and that made it worse. She was softer than she'd ever been, and it gave me far too much silence to be tormented by thoughts.

Around three a.m., the thunderstorm petered out, the rain stopped as if someone turned off a tap, and the jungle hissed and sighed as leaves dried and earth slurped up moisture.

The sudden quietness should've drifted me off to sleep.

It only made me more awake.

Anxiety quivered through me. Nerves and concern about how I'd go back to my regular life now that I'd tasted what one could be like with Hope. And terror because as much as I wanted her…I still wasn't capable of signing my heart over to the agony my parents had suffered.

Marrying into a future that was only happy as long as Hope was alive.

And life was such a fickle, fragile thing.

Keeping my distance from Hope was the only way I could avoid that lifetime of torture. But it also granted a different type of torture.

I didn't know how I'd survive without her either.

At four a.m., I climbed carefully out of bed, doing my best not to disturb Hope. I needed some fresh air.

I'd sit on the rotten deck and watch the sunrise; perhaps then I'd have a clear answer on what I would do about the mess my heart had become.

Striding away from a sleeping Hope, my foot nudged her phone, still abandoned and forgotten on the floor. I stooped to pick it up, but the screen blared bright with an incoming call, searching for the girl who'd stolen my world.

I scrambled to turn the volume down before the first ring could come through. I wasn't ready for her to wake up yet. She'd want answers. She'd push me for conversation. I wouldn't do well being pushed without contemplating my own questions first.

However, a name popped up on her screen.

A name I hadn't seen in a very long time.

And my thumb swiped to answer, holding the phone to my ear as I cut across the room and opened the wonky door as quietly as I could.

The second I was out of the hut and down the seashell path, I rubbed my face, gathered my courage, and prepared to apologise to someone I hadn't seen in four very long years.

"Hello, Aunt Cassie."

Chapter Forty-Nine

HOPE

✳ ✳ ✳ ✳ ✳ ✳

I KNEELED NEXT to Jacob's suitcase.

He'd left all his belongings…just like he'd left me.

I'd woken with a mixture of happiness and heartache, searched for him in stupidity, and headed to the beach to see if he'd been summoned to work.

Last night had been….

Insane.

Crazy.

Perfect.

I'd tried to say no.

I'd broken up with another boy with the fear of such a thing happening.

I'd given up protecting my heart and threw it into Jacob's hands the moment he called me his friend.

Couldn't he see we'd *always* been more than that?

Friends didn't desire as deeply as us. Friends didn't hurt as painfully as us. Friends didn't fit together as wonderfully as we did last night.

I had smudges of his fingerprints on my arms from his aggression. I had sore lips from his rough kisses and a heart winging with butterflies from his need.

I'd fallen for his imploring eyes and possessive touches. I'd felt so many, many things.

And just like Jacob had known I'd been with someone else, I'd known he hadn't been with anyone. Just the way he stared at my nakedness told me the truth. His blatant hunger and disbelief that he finally had the courage to be close to me made my belly clench and soul soar. He'd licked and kissed me and given me pleasure before taking his own.

He was the quintessential, well-mannered country boy with a

healthy dose of caveman.

The orgasm he'd given me was the best I'd ever had…not because I was his first or his fingers had never been in another woman or his tongue was virgin on my body, but because his tenderness, eagerness, and sheer-minded determination to make it good for me made me tumble even deeper into love.

Every part of my body felt like crying.

To cry for the incredible way he worshiped me, all while cursing me.

To get on my knees for more. For always. For eternity.

But it had all been a lie.

A horrible, *horrible* lie.

He's…gone.

How could he?

How did I not see it coming?

Why did I keep letting him kill me piece by stupid piece?

An hour ago, I'd been wary but hopefully. Content but grateful. Ready to face the man I loved and bargain with him for a life together.

The temple in the bay glittered with golden sunshine as I'd searched for him, looking like an alter for gods not ghosts. I could've floated across the turquoise water to give an offering— that was how tentatively happy I'd been.

I hadn't worried when I'd found an empty bed beside me.

I didn't grow concerned when I couldn't find him.

After all, Jacob was reliable. He had employment here, and he wouldn't let people down just because we'd lived an impossibility last night.

I didn't expect him to interrupt his life for me. He was a fisherman. He had responsibilities, and I loved that he upheld those responsibilities as diligently as he upheld them at Cherry River.

Last night, Jacob had given in to *us*. He'd accepted that I loved him. He'd willingly asked for contact and kisses and a connection as old as time.

That was the hardest part, wasn't it?

He'd crossed the biggest hurdle. We'd been *together*. His body in my body. His heart against my heart.

Surely, he would find it simple to accept the rest. To see that being alive meant celebrating togetherness, claiming your soul-mate, and loving your best-friend.

Those thoughts kept me trusting as I stood in the warm

shallows, daydreaming of a future with horses and husbands, smiling at the boats twinkling in the distance, imagining Jacob on one.

I'd wait all day if I had to. I'd be there when he sailed home, glittering in fish scales and dusted in sea salt, and I'd kiss him so, so deep. I'd prepare a meal for him, I'd bathe him, listen to him, laugh with him, then fall into his arms and his bed.

There was nowhere else I wanted to be.

The beach mirrored back the tentative newness inside me. The sand soft and white, the sky crisp and clear. The world had been washed clean, ready to inscribe anything we wanted.

And in a way, the storm washed away my own transgressions. I'd cried when I'd called Michael.

I'd felt so dirty breaking up with him on a crackly line with thunder booming overhead. My guilt hung heavy on my shoulders for hurting him.

I'd been a terrible person even as I broke up with him because he deserved someone better—someone who hadn't given their heart away when they were ten years old. I'd been a lousy girlfriend and deserved to repent.

I was willing to pay that price.

But I didn't think the cost would be higher than I could pay.

Standing on that beach with a fantastical future within my grasp, karma decided I wasn't worthy. That I deserved punishment…for everything.

The Balinese man Jacob had fished with yesterday tapped me on the shoulder, ripping apart my daydreams.

I'd spun around with a gentle smile, serene and calm…trusting.

Stupidly, stupidly trusting.

And that was when it happened.

When I died.

When I stopped hoping.

When I stopped *existing*.

My heart that had already been fractured far too many times thanks to Jacob, broke for good.

Snap.

Just like that.

All the little cracks here and little cracks there were too weak to weather another blow.

I'd given him my everything last night. I'd fought the inevitable for as long as I could. I'd asked him not to make me do it. I'd warned him what would happen if he took me.

But he hadn't listened.

He'd taken me, destroyed me…and now…he'd left me.

Left me to the rubble and ruin proving, once and for all, I was still a stupid little girl with stupid little hopes who would never earn a happily ever after with Jacob Ren Wild.

The local fisherman hunched his shoulders with reluctance, pitied me as my smile fell, and then swung a spiritual sledgehammer into my heart.

"Sunyi gone home. Isn't coming back. He tell me take you to hotel. We leave now."

I almost buckled to the sand.

I switched from whole to fragmented, tinkling with tiny broken pieces.

I had nothing left. I'd tried everything. I'd held him close and given him all I had to give. I'd hurt others. I'd left my job, my life, my world all to be worthy of him.

And it still wasn't enough.

Those pieces tumbled to my toes, utterly irreparable.

There would be no more sticky-tape. No glue strong enough in the world to fix what he'd done.

Jacob had gone.

Without a word.

Without a goodbye.

He'd hurt me for the last time.

I was no longer a friend turned lover. I was an unwanted woman in a village where I knew no one, abandoned by the boy she'd pinned all her hopes on.

Shock slowly morphed to rage.

Rage magnified to fury and I couldn't contain it anymore.

I couldn't pretend I wasn't affected as I nodded at the fisherman and somehow made my way back to Jacob's hut with tear-blind eyes and a dead heart.

Villagers smiled and waved but I just kept walking. Walking until I sank to my knees in front of Jacob's forgotten suitcase. His scent of grass and sea lingered as I slowly fell out of love into hate.

My hands shook as I reached forward and yanked clothes from the neatly packed case, one after another, throwing them against the wall with tears raining and agony spilling.

"How could you?!"

A pair of shorts floated to the floor as I tossed them.

"How could you run after last night?"

A pair of flip-flops bashed against the bathroom door.

"You son of a bitch!"

I threw a can of deodorant at the bed.

Needing to destroy something, to destroy him, I rummaged in the bottom of the case, looking for something heavy to throw.

I froze as my fingers latched around something metallic and round.

Pulling it free from boxer-briefs he didn't need and a sun-faded T-shirt he'd left behind, I gasped as the compass his dead father gave him sat accusing in my palm.

A compass to show direction.

A compass with an inscription to follow Jacob's true path.

Yet another casualty in Jacob's disappearance.

A treasured belonging—now a left-behind relic.

A strange, frosty silence filled me, replacing my fragmented heart, transforming my affection with icy annihilation.

This compass meant so much to Jacob. His father was the reason he wouldn't love me.

If he could leave this behind? I didn't stand a chance.

Nothing had been more final or so black and white.

A tear plopped off the tip of my nose as my fury receded into emptiness.

So be it.

No more.

I couldn't keep doing this.

I was done.

Officially. Totally.

Done.

My phone rang, shattering my oppressive ending.

I had no energy. I wanted to stay slumped like a marionette with a compass for her only friend.

But the shrill cell phone demanded I pick up, forcing me from my knees to my feet and dragging me in a stupor to the bedside table.

I didn't want to talk to anyone.

I wanted to throw the contraption out the window.

But as I glanced at the screen, obligation made me accept the call.

I owed this person an explanation.

I'd tried.

I'd done as she said.

I'd failed.

Holding it to my ear, I sighed and bit back my tears. "Cassie."

"Hope, thank goodness I got you. I've been trying for hours. It wouldn't connect."

I shrugged. Was that my fault too? Just as I hadn't told Jacob about his grandfather was my fault? Or the fact that I wasn't good enough for Jacob to give me his heart?

I wallowed in my soul-break. "I'm not in the mood to talk, Cassie. He's gone. He left before I could tell him."

"Oh, sweetie....what happened?"

Her concern made my back prickle with anger. "Nothing happened."

"Why do you sound so upset?"

"I don't want to talk about it."

"Did he hurt you?" Her voice lowered.

"When has he not hurt me?"

"Oh, God, I'm sorry." She paused before whispering, "Shit, this is all my fault."

I stood staring at the compass in my hand, clutching it with hatred. The temptation to chuck it through the open door sent fire down my arm. "What do you mean, your fault?"

A hitch in her voice echoed in my ear. "I...I spoke to him a few hours ago."

I froze. *"What?"*

"I was calling to talk to you, but he answered instead. I wasn't expecting it. And..."

"And what?"

"I told him. About his grandfather."

The strength in my knees gave out. I collapsed onto the bed. "He knows."

"He knows he has a limited amount of time to get here. Even if he could somehow get here today, I think he'll be too late."

"John's dying?"

Cassie cried quietly. "He's hours away from leaving us."

Cold tears trickled down my cheeks, and I knew exactly where Jacob had gone. Why he hadn't left a note. Why he chose not to wake me.

His fears had come true.

He'd indulged in love for one night, and his grandfather would die because of it.

Death had proven to be stronger than life.

"He's gone home...to John." I traced the compass with a shaking thumb. "He might make it."

Cassie's voice shuddered. "I hope he does…if he doesn't, I don't know what it will do to him."

I did.

Just like my heart had broken for the last time, Jacob's would too.

He would no longer be capable of caring.

He'd shut down, give up…die.

A corpse going through the motions of the living, inching closer to the grave he so craved.

Because death was so much simpler than fighting a war with no end.

The compass warmed in my hand. A breeze creaked through the hut, rustling in the thatched roof. Goosebumps ghosted down my arms as a presence touched me.

It felt like a hug from beyond of understanding and acceptance.

It brought freedom. It whispered of release. It felt like Della.

I'd tried to save him for her.

I'd tried to show him happiness for me.

But I'd done all I could, and there was no shame in admitting I wasn't strong enough.

I closed my eyes and nodded.

My sadness lifted a little, settling into bone-deep scaring. My pain manifested into resolution and sorrow—a recipe I would carry for the rest of my life.

And I knew what I had to do.

I would see Jacob one last time.

I would return to Cherry River.

I would give him his compass so he might find his way.

But then…I would put ghosts to rest, let my heart crumple to dust…

…and move on.

Chapter Fifty

JACOB

* * * * * *

I WAS TOO late.

Grandpa John died six hours before I arrived home at Cherry River.

I'd travelled as fast as I could. I'd caught the soonest plane, paid for the fastest service, and I still hadn't made it.

From the moment Aunt Cassie asked me to hurry, I'd lived in a tornado of fear and anxiety. The inability to hasten my journey, my incompetence at speaking to Grandpa John on the phone when she'd offered me to say goodbye, my rapidly swirling panic at losing another loved one.

I'd done this.

I'd been the cause of his passing.

I'd believed I could be happy.

Yet someone else had died instead.

It was the last straw.

The final stone on my sorry excuse of a soul.

No more.

Just…no more.

Stepping onto the property where I'd been born, I felt nothing. I'd burned through my panic, I'd used up my frenzied dread, I'd slipped straight past denial.

It was done.

Over.

All of it.

I'd left Cherry River on the wake of a funeral, and now, I returned to attend another.

My home was a cemetery all over again.

Walking over the paddocks I'd been raised on and into a farmhouse where I'd listened to the wisdom of an old man and grown up in the embrace of affection, all I felt was emptiness.

A vast void of hissing emptiness.

Even sadness couldn't creep into my chest. My heart had forgotten how to feel. And as Aunt Cassie threw herself into my arms and Uncle Chip patted me on the back and Cousin Nina cried quietly in the corner, I couldn't pretend anymore.

I couldn't act human when I no longer knew what that was.

I'd stopped being human the moment I stood over a sleeping Hope and left without a goodbye.

I'd left my heart with her.

I'd left my soul in her care.

And I was ready for a coffin as surely as my dead grandfather.

I should hold my family close and grieve with them. I should share antidotes about Grandpa John and shed tears for the dead. I should think about Hope and the callous way I'd run from her.

I should attempt to fix all the things I had broken.

Instead, I extracted myself from Aunt Cassie's embrace and went into the bedroom where Grandpa John had died. His body had been removed, but the medical equipment still hung in the corners like mercenaries of suffering.

He must've had an in-home carer as the end grew nearer, and the reek of disinfectant and drugs stung my nose.

I sat on the rocking chair where a plaid blanket draped with an embroidered donkey cushion, and I stared at the bed where a brilliant farmer had died.

I waited for some epiphany, some lesson, some way to say goodbye to someone who had already gone.

But that emptiness only grew worse, slithering cold and chilling, freezing me into nothing.

I tried to cry, to feel, to live.

But I had nothing.

No grief.

No regret.

No shame.

Just a severing, sombre silence, cutting me from the world of the living.

I screamed in my mind, searching for a way from the icy loneliness. I ran wild, looking for a way to be what others were.

To be brave.

To call Hope and beg for her forgiveness.

To hug my grandfather one last time.

I did none of those things.

I was a screwed-up, unforgivable bastard who finally got his wish.

I'd wanted to be heartless so I didn't feel pain.

Congratu-fucking-lations.

I stayed in his room for seven hours.

I studied his empty bed, imagined his body in a lonely morgue, pictured the wake and eulogy.

No one interrupted me.

They all stayed away—conditioned by my behaviour to avoid me.

And I didn't go to them.

I didn't seek solace or food; no drink or sleep.

I just stared.

And stared.

And stared.

And when I'd stared enough, I stood and walked out.

I headed to Forrest's paddock and waited for the rush of guilt for leaving the loyal roan, but as he came to nuzzle me, wuffling in my hair with contentment at having me home, I felt nothing.

No kick of affection. No crush of agony.

Nothing.

I sank to the ground and waited for horse hooves to trample me or lightning to strike me—anything to put me out of this strange, silent misery.

But Forrest merely stood guard, protecting me from things I no longer understood and watched as night fell, casting shadows until finally the darkness claimed me.

Darkness.

An old friend.

A new acquaintance.

The only family where I truly belonged.

Chapter Fifty-One

HOPE

✱ ✱ ✱ ✱ ✱ ✱

"JACOB."

His eyes shot to where I stood on the threshold of his home.

I didn't step into the living room. I didn't take all the years between us for granted that I would be welcome.

Not after the last time we'd seen each other.

Not after twenty-nine hours of travelling and stress and chasing after him like I'd chased him my entire life.

I'd caught three planes, hired a car, and flown and driven more miles than I could count.

But where Jacob Wild was concerned, those years and distance meant nothing.

Our past meant nothing.

We were nothing.

I understood that now.

Every time he mellowed and allowed me to be his friend, I'd believed progress had been made. But really, only a temporary truce had been formed. Once we returned to our separate worlds, we became strangers once again.

And as a stranger, I had no right to worry about him.

No obligation to hurt over his hurt or cry over his pain.

There was no smashing his walls and being accepted. There was only chip, chip, chipping away, knowing full well whatever progress I made would be undone the moment we said goodbye.

And this?

It was our final goodbye.

"What are you doing here?" He wiped his face with both hands, coming toward me and the open doors. He looked haggard and weathered as if he hadn't slept in weeks.

No sign of the boy I might have been able to save. Only a man I'd lost to his demons.

I hadn't been to see Cassie yet.

I hadn't told my father I'd flown halfway around the world.

I'd merely followed Jacob to the end.

"You left something behind. I wanted to return it to you."

I hated how, even with all my promises and declarations to move on, my fragmented heart still tried to piece itself back together. To be whole enough to cure him all while being too injured to be repaired.

I'd been with him a single night.

I'd had more than any other woman would be allowed.

And for that, I was grateful.

I wasn't grateful for the pain or the hole he'd left behind, but I *was* thankful he'd trusted me enough to be with me.

"I didn't leave you behind, Hope. I had no choice but to come." The monotone of his voice sent icicles through my blood. He sounded vacant and as empty as I felt.

"I didn't mean me." I flinched, enduring the pain.

The pain that Della had warned me about. The pain that was the price to share time and space with Jacob...but it was finally too hard to bear.

His forehead furrowed. He stepped from his home to face me on the deck. "What did I leave behind?"

Reaching into my bag, blinking with travel-gritty eyes and a brain fuzzy from lack of sleep, I pulled out his compass.

I expected him to stiffen. To wince. To show some emotion of leaving his precious belonging behind. He merely sighed as if I'd brought another death to his door and held out his hand. "Thanks."

Tears caught in my throat as I placed the cool metal into his grip. "Have you lost your way so much you're not even grateful to see your father's compass?"

He didn't make eye contact. Didn't reply.

Eleven years of knowing him.

Multiple moments of kinship.

A few indescribable days of friendship.

A single night of togetherness.

And the awful knowledge that Jacob Wild would never love me.

I already knew that.

I'd lived with that knowledge for over a decade.

But I still wanted to sob in that moment.

"I'm sorry about your grandfather."

He nodded, still staring at the ground. "Thanks."

"I should've been braver and told you the moment I saw you."

"Wouldn't have changed anything."

I bit back tears. "When...when is the funeral?"

He shrugged. "Not sure. Aunt Cassie is arranging it."

"You're not helping?"

He caught my eye. "I'm helping by staying away."

"She'll want you close, Jacob. Family should be close at times like this."

He didn't move. "She has Chip and Nina. And her brothers Liam and Adam."

I should go.

I should walk away with my heartbreak tucked in my handbag and my tears hidden from view, but this was the last time I would ever see him.

And I had to know.

"I've loved you since I was a little girl. I would've waited forever for you to love me back."

He placed his hands into his jeans pockets, the compass vanishing into the depths. "You were right."

"About what?"

"Being together was a mistake. I should've stopped."

I nodded on reflex, buffering against the hurt. "Did you feel anything for me that night? Anything at all?"

His face darkened. "I can't answer that, Hope. I can't give you what you want."

"How can you be so sure when you haven't even tried?"

For an eternal second, he just stared. Stared and stared and *stared* as if he could delete the truth before finding the courage to admit it. "I have. I *have* tried."

And that broke me even more.

Because that meant he'd tried to love me and failed.

He'd attempted to give me his heart and couldn't.

Gasoline added to my shattered pieces and caught fire, incinerating the final shards of hope.

I looked at the heavens, then looked down at hell and nodded. "Okay, Jacob."

He didn't even apologise. Didn't say a word.

But I had enough for both of us.

Curling my hands, I studied him, committing him to memory. "You won't see me again. All I ever wanted was to be there for you, but you were never there for me. I left my life, my work, my boyfriend the *moment* Cassie asked me to find you. I gave up everything for you, over and over again. I let you trample my heart. I allowed you excuse after excuse for your behaviour. I nursed my patience and schooled my annoyance and believed that one day, *one day,* I would be rewarded because you'd finally see that no one will love you the way I do. No one will understand you the way I do. But I have nothing left to give. You truly are alone now, aren't you? Just like you always wanted."

Brushing aside awful tears, I held my head higher. "I want you to know—it wasn't your moods or temper that pushed me away. It's this. Right now. Your indifference. Your cold-heartedness when I'm pouring out my soul to you."

Backing up, I shook my head. "I actually feel sorry for you. Sorry that you've already died before you've experienced life. You're happier to live a life of solitude than be brave enough to try. But that's on you now because I'm done."

I cried openly, unable to stop the thick wash of grief. "I'm leaving you, Jacob Ren Wild. And I'm never coming back. You've gotten your wish. I'm dead to you. Just another person you used to know. A memory that will slowly fade."

I trembled so badly my teeth chattered as I hugged myself before him.

I hugged myself because he would never hug me.

I comforted myself because he didn't know how.

And I waited for a single moment.

For *one* sign that he'd been affected by what I'd said. For one hint of redemption.

But he just stood there as if I'd shot him with bullets instead of goodbyes.

His stony eyes, tense body, and clenched jaw all screamed to be left alone.

So I did.

With one last look, I gave him the saddest smile and left Cherry River forever.

Chapter Fifty-Two

JACOB

* * * * * *

I SAT ON my deck, looking at my vegetable garden that had died and been invaded by weeds, watching the paddocks and meadows that needed better care than a casual contractor could do, and waited to succumb to the pain of losing everything.

I waited to break into a thousand brilliant pieces.

Hope had left me.

She'd cut me off, severed our connection, done what I'd pushed her to do.

Goodbye.

Forever.

I wanted to feel agony.

I *deserved* to feel it.

To cripple and crumple as my heart split down the middle, and all the light in my life drained free.

But the miserable silence clutched me deeper, protecting me from sorrow, muting death and breakups and the terrible knowledge that Hope was right.

I was alone.

I'd successfully shoved everyone who cared about me away.

I'd gotten my wish multiple times over.

And I felt nothing.

Fucking nothing.

I didn't know when Hope had left me.

Five minutes or five hours ago?

Time was just a sequence of numbers that no longer had any relevance.

What should I do? Where should I go? Return to Bali and continue to be Sunyi? Stay at Cherry River and tend the land I was born for? Or run into the forest like my father and forget about humanity for good?

To regress to baser instincts. To be the animal I'd embraced.

At least those questions kept me company; they hid the emptiness inside while pretending I had thoughts and feelings when both had been stripped from me.

But then my phone rang.

Snapping me back into the present, filling me with ice once again.

Graham Murphy.

Why would he call me? To commiserate on my grandfather's death? To discuss yet another family member who had passed?

My thumb hovered over the decline button. I was in no mood to talk—especially after his daughter had done her best to destroy me—but a breeze kicked through the meadow.

A harsh, cutting wind that hissed angry and judgmental.

I hadn't felt my father's presence while I wandered the globe, but in that moment he breathed down my neck, crushing me with his disappointment.

And even that didn't make me break.

But it did make me accept the call.

To speak to another human before I turned my back on them completely.

Pressing the screen, I held the phone to my ear. Slow and methodical. No rush or panic. Vacant of normal nervousness. "Hello, Graham."

"Jacob, fuck, thank God." Graham rushed. Graham panicked. His voice wobbled with tears and terror. "I can't get there in time. Shit, you need to go. Right now. I beg you. *Please*, go."

I sat taller, his emotions pouring down the line, doing their best to infect me. "Slow down. What's going on?"

His voice caught like any worried father. A father who'd felt death threaten his world. "It's Hope. She's been in a car accident."

I was running before the phone hit the ground.

Chapter Fifty-Three

JACOB

* * * * * *

"HOPE MURPHY, WHERE is she?" I yelled, barging into the hospital where Hope had defended my honour against town gossip, where Hope had cared enough to get me treatment, where Hope had driven me, sulking and arguing, when she barely knew me.

Fuck, Hope.

A nurse manning the reception desk for the emergency department jumped as I slammed my hands on the counter. "Where is she?"

My temper was real.

My fear was real.

Hot emotion thawed massive chasms in the ice around my heart.

"I'm sorry, who?" She blinked, shying away from me as I towered over her.

"Hope Jacinta Murphy. She was brought here."

I welcomed the panic.

I embraced the anxiety.

It meant I was still alive when all I'd wanted was to be dead. I couldn't die.

Not when she needed me.

"When?" She scooted forward on her chair, tapping the keyboard.

"I don't fucking know when. She was in a car accident."

"No need for profanity, sir. I'm only trying to help." Her fingers shook a little on the keys. "Um, there doesn't seem to be anyone by that name."

"What do you mean? There has to be. Her father told me you guys called him." My temper unfolded into fury, dragging me back into humanness. "Check again. *Now!*"

My voice had power. My hands had strength. My chest

crawled with concern and cowardice, dismay and dread.

Emotions. So, so many emotions.

All of them.

All at once.

Bombarded and alive.

"Oh…" She squinted at the screen. "Ah, okay, wait a minute, please." She scrolled with the mouse, stealing every shred of my patience.

"*Well?*"

She bit her lip, her eyes locking on medical text. "Ah, yes, here we go. Hope." She slouched. "Oh, dear. I'm so sorry." Her gaze met mine, no longer full of fear but sympathy.

Sympathy?

Why motherfucking *sympathy*?

"*What?* What is it?" I wanted to snatch the goddamn computer and look for myself. "Tell me!" My roar echoed around patients awaiting help, dragging their attention, pinning me in place.

My dread turned to depression. My cowardice to grief.

I'd been here before.

I'd stood at this counter and demanded they give my father back to me.

I'd been a kid then.

Now, I was a man, and the same childish terror that they'd keep Hope from me snaked around my heart.

"I'm so sorry to tell you this, s—"

"Tell me what? Spit it out. Goddammit, just take me to her."

"I'm sorry, that's not possible. She passed away."

"*What?*"

"She, um, she died due to surgery complications. I'm so very sor—"

The world vanished.

Light and sound and people and furniture all sucked up in a hurricane.

White noise muffled everything else.

Horror replaced heartbeats.

The ice that suffocated my chest exploded in a mushroom cloud of black, dripping disaster.

Dead?

Dead?

She's dead?

No…

That can't be.

My lungs constricted, and my heart decided it no longer wanted to pump blood but acid instead.

I clutched my chest, clawing at the suffocation, gasping at the horror.

She's...dead?

I killed her.

I let her leave Cherry River.

I should've stopped her.

I should've told her the goddamn truth.

I should've been *better.*

Kinder.

Softer.

I should've—

I couldn't breathe.

I can't breathe.

Dead.

All of them.

Dead.

I gasped for air even though I didn't want it. My body overrode my attempts to just die and be done with it. Instinct made me grunt and groan, tripping sideways as fog crept over my brain.

"Are you okay? Sir?"

I fell forward, clutching at the counter as my knees gave out.

Grandpa John died hours before.

Hope died only minutes ago.

And I'd been too late to save either of them.

The nurse leapt upright as I stumbled, my vision shooting grey, my ears ringing louder and louder and *louder.*

Death.

All I saw was death.

Coffins.

Cremations.

Ash and dust and *death.*

No.

I-I can't—

My strength vanished, slamming me to the floor. I grabbed something, anything to stay upright, but my hands didn't work anymore, my arms had no power, and I plummeted to the hospital linoleum with a rain of sign-in forms and pens scattering morbidly like mourners to Hope's funeral.

She's dead!

And I fucking killed her.

Then the trembling began.

The awful nausea and vertigo and stress and panic.

Panic.

Bone-deep, skeleton-crushing *panic*.

It gushed through me, suffocated me until I had a heart attack and begged for death to take me instead.

To no longer be the one left behind.

To be the one with the ticket for a change.

A ticket to a new destination where hopefully pain didn't exist.

Loud shouts sounded.

Hands grabbed me.

My panic turned to sheer rage, and I shoved them back.

"Don't touch me! For fuck's sake, don't touch me!"

My eyes flickered with grey and light—grey for the grave and light for life. Orderlies and doctors came running. Someone tried to speak to me, only to be sucker-punched in the jaw.

My throat closed up, squeezing and strangling.

My fingernails scratched for oxygen as I fell on all fours, becoming the beast I truly was.

Hands grabbed again.

Panic swirled faster.

Nightmares sucked me deep.

Hope was dead.

Dead.

How could life be so cruel? Why take her? Why take my father, my mother, my grandfather…now her?

Goddamn you!

Goddamn you all.

Fuck life and love and every-fucking-thing.

My chest grew hotter. My brain inched closer to stroking. My lungs turned to shreds.

Another minute and I wouldn't exist either.

I welcomed such a fate.

Hope was dead.

Her eyes were glass. Her body vacant. Her soul somewhere else.

I'll never see her again.

Tears were poison as they blinded me.

Air was toxic as I gulped for the end.

Hope was a corpse.

Naked and alone on some mortuary table.

Ah, fuck.

Something tight with spikes and knives twined around my stomach, making me retch. Panic befriended sickness, drowning me in both.

The one girl who I needed more than anything.

The one person who stood any chance at saving me, and what had I done?

I'd never shown her an ounce of gratefulness.

I'd pushed away again and again.

I'd pushed her into the ground.

God.

What…what have I done?

Her last words howled in my head.

"You've gotten your wish. I'm dead to you. Just another person you used to know. A memory that will slowly fade."

I'd done nothing to stop her.

Nothing to show her how much I needed her.

How much I loved her.

How much she meant to me from the very moment we met.

I did nothing to stop her from walking out of my life and into the arms of my enemy.

Darkness descended, fissuring through my veins and breaking apart arteries, feeding me destitution and despair.

I couldn't handle the pressure, the pain, the pounding realisation that she'd gone.

Gone.

Fuck, she's…gone.

No.

No

"Nooooo!"

A broken howl of something animalistic and pure monster ricocheted around the E.R. More hands clawed at me, and I fought them back. I roared, noticing the howls weren't from a monster but from me.

My panic spilled outward. I wanted to inflict violence on anyone who came too close.

I wanted to make them suffer.

These devils of death had taken everyone I had ever loved.

They deserved to die.

I'd kill them.

I'll—

A sharp prick pierced my arm.

And the blackness faded.

And the howling silenced.

And the loss of the girl I loved more than anything was no more.

* * * * *

"Mr. Wild?" A gentle pressure around my wrist dragged me back.

Sour thorns laced my throat as I swallowed and winced against a splitting headache.

"Don't rush it. Let yourself wake up naturally." The hand squeezed my wrist again. A feminine voice, sweet and concerned.

I didn't want sweet or concerned.

I didn't deserve it.

Wrenching my eyes open, I flinched against the brightness, grunting against a thick wash of sickness.

"That's it. You're okay. You'll feel a bit woozy because of the sedation. It will pass." She stopped touching my wrist, moving to the bedside table. Picking up a glass of water, she urged me to take it. "Here, drink this. You're dehydrated, which is making the effects worse."

I wanted to slap the glass from her grip, but I steeled myself against such tendencies and accepted it with a curt nod.

Throwing it back, I found it did ease the tightness around my temples and the thorns in my throat. Giving her the empty glass, I rasped, "Where am I?"

"You're in the hospital. Do you remember why you came?"

My thoughts skipped backward only to slam into a wall of horror.

She's gone.

The trembling returned, followed by the heart palpitations, and lack of air, and adrenaline, and *holy fuck, she's dead.*

They're all dead.

Everyone I've ever loved dies.

I fell deeper and deeper into the abyss.

"Hey, Mr. Wild." The doctor came closer, placing her hand on my shoulder. "It's okay. Breathe. You're okay. Just relax."

Relax?

How the hell could I relax?

Hope is dead!

The attack grew worse. I retched, but nothing came up. I

cried, but no tears came. I opened my lips to howl, but my throat was too raw to operate.

The doctor grabbed my cheeks, forcing me to look into her green eyes.

Green.

Like Hope's.

Eyes that had closed and would never reopen.

Eyes that were milky and—

"She's alive, Mr. Wild." She shook me. "Are you listening to me? Hope Jacinta Murphy is alive."

I froze, gasping for breath and heart pounding with arrhythmia. "Wh-what?"

"The nurse got it wrong. I'm so, so sorry. She's new and doesn't have a grasp on our filing system yet. That's not an excuse, of course. She's been heavily reprimanded and I assure you, it won't happen again."

I shook, trying to understand this upside-down reality. "So she's...she's not dead?"

"Not the Hope you enquired after. No." She sighed. "A Hope Mckinnock died this morning from complications in surgery. Your Hope is still very much alive. A huge oversight and I'm once again so sorry for the distress this has caused you."

The adrenaline in my system didn't fade. It only shook me harder.

How was this possible?

The same hospital that'd stolen my father, mother, and grandfather had somehow granted a miracle and given Hope back to me.

I didn't know if I should kill the doctor or faint in relief.

My head pounded, desperate to shed the fog and get away from these morbid riddles.

I rubbed my eyes. "Wh-where is she?"

"She's here. She's been patched up and settled in a room above this one. I can take you to her if you'd like."

For a second, I was weightless, grateful, comforted.

She was okay.

I wasn't alone.

But then, a wracking heave worked its way from the depth of my belly, wriggling through my ribcage, gathering pressure and power.

Black power. Ruthless pressure. Cremation coal and shadowy caskets, just waiting for me to step into the pyre and *burn*.

Flames engulfed me as the hellish force imploded in my chest.

An explosion of everything I'd been running from my entire life.

The terror of losing loved ones.

The pain of giving them my heart.

The aching, quaking knowledge that I would rather die than endure another funeral.

And the horror that I'd condemned myself to all of it because I loved Hope.

I *loved* her.

And I didn't know how to process that.

I didn't have the skills to put away my panic and *breathe*.

I'd lost enough.

I was done with the roulette of burying loved ones and being unable to move on.

And now, I faced a worse reality.

A thousand times worse because I'd willingly chosen to suffer by handing over my hole-patched, torn-stitched heart that still carried agony from decades ago.

A heart that never healed. A heart that would rather hide than be whole. A heart that now belonged to a girl who had all the power to kill me.

I love her.

It's not possible.

But...I love her.

Barbwire slithered around my chest, dragging me deeper into unmarked graves and weeping forests.

Hope was alive...but for how long?

I loved her.

I had no choice but to accept that tragedy.

All my fears had come true.

But how *long* would I love her?

When would she leave me?

Who would die first?

Me or her?

Who would be left behind—a shell, a figment...alone?

Oh, God.

My panic crept higher, overriding the sludge of whatever drug they'd given me, making me shaky and breathless and clutching starched sheets as if they could protect me from the impending attack.

Yet another attack.

Because I was weak and broken and so fucking scared of losing her.

I can't lose her.

My heave turned into a growl, which tangled with a sob, escaping my lips with the sound of something mortally wounded. Something that was only seconds away from ceasing to exist.

I crumpled over my knees.

My mind filled with pictures of my dead family.

My ears rang with coughs and laughs and 'I love yous.'

And I lost myself to the panic that was my oldest friend.

I wanted to be alone.

I needed space to shatter and pick up the pieces, but the doctor didn't give me space—she stole more of it.

The hospital bed shuddered as she pressed close. I flinched as her arm landed over my shoulders. Violence commanded I shove her back, but instead, I curled forward, bowing to touch, condemning myself to grief.

Grief over Grandpa John dying.

Grief over Hope dying.

Relief over Hope still alive.

Horror at knowing she'd die anyway.

I gasped for breath, hating myself for such weakness but unable to stop the panic, the memories, the fears.

"It's okay. Get it out." The doctor rubbed my arm like any kind mother.

Her sympathy made me shatter worse because I no longer had a mother.

I was a twenty-five-year-old man who'd avoided the steadily compounding issues of death since childhood. I'd bottled it up. I'd swallowed it down. I'd used distance as a shield and loneliness as invisibility against love.

Yet in that bed, as a stranger stroked me in comfort, I couldn't fight it anymore.

I wasn't strong enough.

I couldn't hide.

I couldn't run.

I broke.

My body sagged.

My panic stole me...and I sobbed.

I cried for my father, my mother, my grandfather, for Hope.

I cried for all the days I'd pushed them away and all the moments I hadn't appreciated. I cried for all the hugs I'd refused and the family kindness I'd pretended I didn't want.

And I cried for me.

For my phobias and panics.

For my tempers and torments.

I cried for all of it.

And the doctor's touch transformed from something I hated into something I needed. Touch was an affirmation of life, and life hadn't taken Hope from me.

She was still alive.

And...I love her.

Pain could find me anywhere—regardless of where I hid.

Therefore, I wasn't safe anywhere.

There was relief in that.

To know I would feel this agony if Hope was with me or away from me. I would feel it now and in the future. I would *feel* it. I would *permit* myself to feel it because pain was the price of love, and I finally saw that.

Finally *accepted* that it was the cost of being human.

My belief that I could endure a life without another wasn't healthy. Being alone was no way to live.

I was still the same ten-year-old mess my father had left behind.

In fact, I was worse.

But I'd had enough of being so afraid.

I...I need to get better.

The doctor spoke softly. "It's a panic attack. I'm sure you're aware as you've had them before, but if you calm down, you'll be okay."

I nodded, sitting tall and shaking her arm from my shoulders. "I'm all right." My voice crackled and cracked.

She shifted to standing, but her hand continued stroking up and down my arm. For a long time, she didn't speak, just let me re-centre, dry the wetness from my cheeks, and breathe a little easier.

When I no longer shook the bed with my sadness, she smiled gently. "I'm aware of your history, Jacob Wild. I read up on you while you were sleeping." Her hand carried on soothing me. "That's the second attack you've had in front of that ER counter. The first was when you rode your pony here against your mother's wishes when your father passed. Do you remember?"

I gritted my teeth.

I'd done my best to forget, but the memory was far too strong.

Nodding, I pulled away, thankful when she moved and stood with her hands looped in front of her white coat.

"I remember."

"Have you had many panic attacks?"

I looked away. "A few."

"What brings them on?"

I stiffened. "Does it matter?"

Her eyes burned into me. "It matters if you want to get better."

"Better how?"

I'd only just made that promise to myself. It was still sparkly and new. I needed time to live with the idea before leaping straight into treatment.

She smiled as if it was obvious. "To no longer be afraid."

I studied the sterile cleanliness of the room. I wanted to be free to love Hope the way she deserved, and I was prepared to do that. But I didn't want to be locked away in some asylum and treated as if my mind was deformed.

It wasn't my mind.

It was my heart.

And the only person who could fix that was Hope.

I shifted to climb off the bed. "I'll be fine."

"Stay there, just for another moment." She held up her hand. "Let your body recalibrate."

I huffed, dragging hands through my hair.

I was jittery and strung out but also strangely light. As if I'd purged myself from years' worth of denials and angers, hauntings and depressions.

She ducked her head, brown hair tied neatly at her nape. Her eyes were kind but professional. "I believe you suffer from untreated post-traumatic stress disorder."

My attention shot to her. "Excuse me?"

"It's nothing to be ashamed of."

I swung my legs to the floor, ready to leave. "I'm not ashamed because I don't have it. PTSD is for soldiers who come back from war. It's for men who have done things. Terrible things. Not a kid who lost his parents."

And more recently a grandfather...

She sighed. "You're wrong. PTSD is for anyone with unresolved trauma. You didn't just lose your dad; you watched him fade away during your entire childhood. I'm also aware you recently lost your mother, and your grandfather is currently in our morgue. Couple that with being told incorrect news of a young woman you obviously care about…and you're displaying all the signs of triggers you can't control."

"Triggers?" I hated that I knew that word well. That my mother had used it to help me cope—to show there was no shame in being affected by things other people weren't.

"It's treatable." She reached into her pocket for a pad and paper. "I don't know if it's fully curable, but you don't have to keep living this way, okay? If it's stealing your quality of life, it's worth asking for help."

"What sort of help?"

Images of being handcuffed and hauled into a psychiatric ward made me stand.

She stopped writing on her little pad, looking me dead in the eye. "Talking to a therapist to start. Perhaps drug therapy if needed."

"I don't want drugs."

"That's a discussion for another day. All I'm saying is…think about it." Tearing a page from her notepad, she passed it to me. "This is the name of a colleague who specialises in PTSD. Contact him. What have you got to lose?"

The paper shook in my hand as I took it. Part of me wanted to scrunch it up and throw it away, but the newer part—the hurt and healing part—folded it carefully and tucked it into my jeans pocket. "So I don't have to stay somewhere? Have…tests and things?"

"No. Just a simple office and someone to talk to."

That sounded doable.

But only once I'd seen Hope.

I had stuff to tell her.

Epiphanies to share.

My love to profess.

I swayed a little and swallowed back a final crest of nausea. "Where is she? I need to see her."

"I'll take you to her."

I stepped toward the door, then paused. "Um, just so I don't embarrass myself with yet another attack, is she…okay?"

The doctor, whose name I still didn't know but would always remember, smiled. "She's a little dinged up, but she's not dying anytime soon. She's a strong wee thing."

Strong.

That was Hope.

Stronger than me. Braver than me. The death of me.

"That's good." My heart stopped its irregular beating, gulping a huge sigh of relief. "Her father will be grateful to hear that."

She opened the door and guided me down the stark hospital corridor. "And you too, I suspect."

I gave her half a smile.

"Does she know?"

I stiffened. "Know what?"

"That you love her."

"Ah." I shrugged, wedging shaky hands into my pockets. "If she doesn't, she's about to."

An elevator pinged, swallowed us, and spat us out on the upper floor. She smiled as I waited for her to step onto the new level first. "I have a feeling she probably already knows."

"I'm not so sure." My boots thudded on the lino. "I did a pretty good job of proving I didn't." I winced, unable to stop the memory of her sleeping in my bed, my fingerprints on her skin, my release still inside her.

I'd wanted her so much that I hadn't used protection.

I'd taken everything from her...and then I'd left her.

To add contempt to my remorse, I'd just stood there at Cherry River when she'd flown halfway around the world to return my compass. She'd poured out her soul, then driven tear-blurred and exhausted straight into an accident that could have cost her, her life.

"I've been a bastard."

The doctor pointed at a door and squeezed my elbow. "It's in the past. I'm sure if you're honest with her, she'll understand."

God, I hope so.

I swallowed hard as she added, "She's in there. Good luck."

"Thanks."

She left, and I stood alone, inhaling deep, bracing myself for the hardest thing I would ever do. Hardest because I wasn't about to do what other men had done before me. I wasn't about to fulfil a timeless requirement and tell Hope I was in love with her.

I was about to admit I was wrong. About everything. That I wasn't happy. That I'd never be happy unless I had her.

And I honestly didn't know if she'd accept me.

I'd lived through her death.

I'd felt the loss of her before it had already happened.

And I'd learned I *was* strong enough.

Strong enough to love her.

For always.
If she'd forgive me.

Chapter Fifty-Four

HOPE

* * * * * *

I'D HAD DRIVING lessons after I'd taken Jacob to the hospital with his back injury.

Wow, how many years ago is that again?

It felt like an eternity.

I'd studied, taken my test, and had a licence tucked in my purse that said I was legal to be on the road.

But it hadn't stopped me from crashing.

Hadn't stopped my tears from blinding me or the shaky sadness from stealing my reactions.

It was my fault.

I hadn't seen the lady walking her dog across the street until it was too late. I'd slipped on the brake pedal and careened into the brick wall of Mr. Pickering's Personals—the only antique store in town.

The rental car exploded with airbags, the front crumpled, and whiplash smashed my head against the steering wheel.

And that was all I remembered.

Until I came to with the sounds of ambulance sirens and paramedics and the embarrassment of being hauled from my ruined rental and placed on a stretcher.

I'd argued.

I'd assured them I was fine and didn't need such fanfare.

But it turned out…I did.

"So as you know, we called your father. He's on his way."

I blinked, pressing a hand against my pounding temple. I'd been here for hours, and my head still hurt. Stupid painkillers were totally ineffective. "He's in Iceland, though, on a film set. He won't be here for days."

"Yeah, he did say he'd be late arriving." Dr Jorge smiled kindly. His bushy salt-and-pepper beard looked odd against his bald head. "He said he'd call someone close by to take you to their place. They'll care for you until he can get to you."

My heart stopped beating. "Who did he call?"

"He didn't say." His gaze flittered over the cast on my left leg, resuming his instructions. "Now, the cast has to stay on for six weeks, and you're to use the crutches assigned. Okay?"

I groaned. "Isn't there a quicker way to heal a broken bone?"

He chuckled. "Not one that has been invented yet. I recommend you don't fly for a few days or at all if you can help it. The cast will make long-haul a nightmare."

That left me one option.

I'd have to somehow drive one-legged across the country to get as far as I could from Jacob and Cherry River. I needed to leave immediately just in case Dad called Cassie to fetch me, and I was placed under house arrest in the very same place I was trying to escape.

I wouldn't be able to bear it.

Tears stung for the billionth time, but I refused to let them fall. My head ached harder.

I winced, rubbing my forehead.

Why did this have to happen?

I could've been on a plane back to England by now.

High above the earth where Jacob Wild walked, putting miles upon miles between us so I never had to see him and his indifferent face again.

I hated that I'd been so stupid not to use a condom with him. I was on the pill, but the knowledge that some part of him still existed inside me made me *furious*. I hated that we'd been that intimate. I hated that I'd given in. I hated that I'd given him back his compass.

I should've kept it—used it to navigate my own way through this giant catastrophe called life.

I hate him.

I will always, always hate him.

The doctor leaned closer, shining a torch in my eyes.

I cringed away like a vampire in noonday sun. "Hey, ouch."

He took the light away, inputting something on an e-tablet. "Light sensitivity should fade soon." He waggled a finger at me. "But just like you need to rest your leg, you need to avoid any exercises or strenuous activities for a week thanks to your minor concussion."

I laughed under my breath even though it made sickness wash over me. I had a concussion. How ironic.

Was it fate's cruel joke? I hurt Jacob, so it hurt me?

Don't think about him.

The space where my heart used to beat was an empty black-hole, sucking up my grief.

I'd done the right thing by cutting him from my life.

But it still hurt worse than anything I'd ever felt.

Including this accident.

"Anyway, you're all treated, and you have the script for your required pills. Just wait here until your lift arrives, and we'll see each other for a check-up soon. Okay?" He beamed. "Any questions?"

I shook my head, instantly regretting the painful sloshing. "No."

"Alrighty. Get better and no more reckless driving." He moved toward the door.

I smiled thinly. I wasn't reckless. I was barely going faster than a jog. But I guessed he was right because I shouldn't have been driving when I could barely see through my tears.

Would the police be after me? What about the rental car? What sort of mess would I face trying to claim insurance?

Think about that another day.

I closed my eyes as the doctor opened and closed the door, leaving me on my own to wallow in bad decisions, worse choices, and a body I'd stupidly broken.

The drugs better kill the pain in my heart as well as my head when they finally started working.

A soft click sounded as the door opened again.

I didn't bother opening my eyes, preferring to stay in the darkness. "I promised no flying or strenuous activity already. I'll obey, Dr Jorge."

"Hello, Hope."

My eyes soared open, smarting at the light and the fact that Jacob stood at the bottom of my bed.

His shaggy white Bali-blond hair. His hardened dark gaze. His air of perpetual loneliness. He looked the same but different: the boy I'd known since childhood with broad shoulders and brute power to work the land and sea, yet there was something new too.

His eyes were weary and beaten. His body battle-scared and suffering.

He looked as if he'd faced death and lost.

He wasn't someone I knew anymore.

Rage slithered through my bloodstream, making my leg ache

and cast tighten and concussion throb. "What the hell are you doing here?"

He flinched like a broken man. "Your father called."

"That's just great." I snorted. "Wonderful. Uh-huh, just what I need. You showing up when I never wanted to see you again. Just go away, okay? I don't need you. In fact, I want you gone."

What had my father been *thinking*?

He disliked Jacob as much as I hated him.

How dare he put me in this position!

Rage was a good antidote to my misery. The misery that cloaked and cradled, reaching out with wet fingers to touch the boy I didn't know.

Even in my hate, I wanted him.

Even in my rage, I needed him.

And that hurt me the most because my heart should be mine to command, not his to bury.

"Go away."

He merely shook his head and moved to the side of my bed, his hand landing on the white sheet so, so close to where my own fingers played with the blankets.

For the longest second, we stared.

Electricity surged and pulsed along my skin. My stomach quaked as Jacob killed me all over again.

I sucked in a ragged breath as his pinkie grazed mine.

We jolted; the electricity in the air completed its circuit, burning us, searing us together.

He licked his lips, and his barriers came down. Everything he ever was and pretended not to be blazed for me to see.

The truth.

The honesty.

The end.

He revealed a boy who'd lost more than he could cope with. A man who'd fought to be free of such pain.

And I didn't want to see anymore.

I pulled away, swallowing against a great ball of sadness. "Leave me alone, Jacob."

His breath caught, his voice hitched, and the tell-tale sign of grief roughened his tone. "If you still want me to go after I've said what I need, I'll go. No questions asked."

"Just go now," I whispered. "I don't want to hear what you have to say."

"Please, Hope." His pinkie kissed mine again.

I jerked my hand away.

He shook his head with a sad smirk, deeply desolate. "I just lied. I have no intention of going anywhere…even if you yell and scream at me, I'm not leaving."

My eyes narrowed. "You don't have a choice."

"I do. I do have a choice."

"You threw that choice away when you left me in Bali."

His head hung, contrition and regret painting every bone and muscle. "I know."

My lower lip wobbled as I fought back anger. "You got your wish. You're free of me."

His eyes snapped to mine. "I'll never be free of you. I don't *want* to be free of you."

Stop it!

"I don't care anymore. *I* want to be free of *you*. So just walk out that door and do what you're so good at doing." I leaned forward, bracing myself on the bed. "Run away, Jacob Wild. Run away."

I expected him to rise to my challenge. To fight my anger with his own. Instead, he stayed calm, his voice slipping into a soft murmur. "I deserved that. I deserve everything you have to say to me."

"Everything, huh? How about I'll never forgive you for leaving me? For sleeping with me when I begged you not to? For flying away without even saying goodbye?"

"I was wrong. I was an idiot."

"Idiot is too light a word for what you are."

He nodded. "True again. How about imbecile? That has a nice ring to it."

I crossed my arms. "What are you doing?"

"What do you mean?"

"Why are you agreeing with me?"

"Because you're right. And I'm wrong."

"Since when?"

"Since now."

I huffed. I hated that I was in bed, unable to run away from him. "I'm not playing this game with you. Just leave me alone."

"You want me to leave you alone after you've made me fall madly in love with you?" He pressed against the steel frame of my mattress. "I'm sorry, but that's not going to happen." He sat on the edge of the bed, scooting my cast over to make room for his size. "I'm not leaving you ever again, and you sure as hell aren't leaving me."

My body locked down.

Did he just say he's in love with me?

When I didn't speak, Jacob murmured, "Leaving you in Bali was the worst thing I've ever done. I regretted it instantly, but my heart...it stopped working the moment I heard about Grandpa John." He raked a hand through his hair. "I'm not telling you this to excuse my behaviour. I'm not seeking your forgiveness. I'm telling you this because you deserve to know. Deserve to know that I love you. I'm *in* love with you. I have been for years, but I've been too weak to admit it."

I couldn't breathe.

This was too much. This wasn't him. It wasn't real. My concussion played tricks on me. The drugs were hallucinogenic. "Wha-what did you just say?"

He stole my hand, holding it tight with dry, masculine strength. "You heard me."

"I—" I closed my eyes, ears ringing. "I don't understand."

"What's not to understand?" He squeezed my fingers as I tried to wriggle free. "I love y—"

"Stop saying that." I tore my hand free, wiping it on the sheets as if he'd contaminated me with whatever illness he suffered from. "I don't know what's going on, but this isn't real."

"It's real. *I'm* real. And I'm telling you I'm in—"

"Stop!" I pressed my temples. "I can't handle this. I need you to leave. Can you do that? If you truly love me, you'll leave me alone."

He smiled softly, kindly—with more emotion and love than I'd ever seen. It transformed him from temperamental loner to brave friend.

A friend who loves me.

"It's because I love you that I have no intention of walking out that door."

"Why?"

"Why won't I leave you?"

"No, why do you love me? Why now? Because you think that's what I want to hear? That I deliberately did this to myself to force such a declaration?" I glowered. "I had an accident. That's all. It's nothing to do with you."

"I love you, Hope Jacinta Murphy. I love you because I've run out of reasons why I shouldn't."

"That sounds as if you're angry about it."

"I am." He nodded. "I'm terrified. But it doesn't mean I can change it or that I *want* to. It's done." His eyes burned into mine. "So I hope you've enjoyed your little hospital stay because it's the last time you'll ever be away from me."

I looked at the closed door, contemplating if I should scream for my doctor. To demand he remove this crazy person from my bedside.

The tug to believe in this fantasy grew stronger.

The hope that this might be true crippled me to give in.

But I couldn't.

I'd given in far too many times.

I'd loved Jacob too painfully to do it again.

My shoulders slouched and tears prickled. "Please…just go away."

He reached forward, his thumb tracing my cheekbone, wiping away a single tear. "Never again. I promise this will be the last time I make you cry."

I ripped my face from his touch. "Why are you doing this?"

He dropped his hand to his lap. "I had some sense knocked into me."

My head throbbed harder. "What does that mean?"

"It means I was told you were dead."

I sucked in a breath. "Who would tell you such an awful thing?"

"If you stop asking questions, I'll tell you."

My teeth gritted.

His smile was totally at odds to this strange conversation, yet so perfect. The smile said he truly did love me. He was exasperated that I wouldn't accept it but patient enough to convince me.

I just didn't know if I wanted convincing when I didn't trust him to stay.

"I came here as a favour to your father," he said softly. "I believed, when you drove away from Cherry River, that I was doing the right thing by letting you go. That I couldn't survive giving you what you needed. But when he called, Hope? Fuck, it all came crashing down, and I finally understood. I didn't have a choice. I'd *never* had a choice because I'd already fallen for you. I'd already claimed you as mine."

"I'm not yours."

"But you are. You have been since that night we first met."

"No." I shook my head. "You could have had me, but you turned me down. Not once, not twice…I've forgotten how many times you pushed me away. But you don't have to push me away now because I'm done, do you hear me?"

"I'm not pushing you away, Hope. I'm asking you to give me another chance."

"No more chances." I blinked back tears. "I have no more to give."

"Yet you'll crash your car and let some nurse tell me you're dead?"

"Excuse me?" My mouth fell open. "Oh, I'm sorry. You're saying that's *my* fault?"

Whoa, the *audacity*.

My crutches were in reaching distance. He deserved a good swat on the head.

He didn't stiffen, challenge, or rebuff. He just nodded in that sage, wise way. A blanket of calm and acceptance over him. Nothing at all like the Jacob I used to know. "Hearing you'd died brought me to my knees, Hope." His voice was barely audible as he studied my cast. "I might have come on behalf of your father, but that's the biggest lie I could tell. I came here for me. I came for all the mistakes I've made and all the—"

"I didn't ask you to come."

He ignored me, carrying on as if I hadn't spoken. "I came because I knew I would rather have you for the shortest time than not at all. I finally understand why my parents accepted such pain. But by the time I arrived at the hospital, I was losing my mind. When the nurse couldn't find your record, I steadily suffocated with panic. And when she told me you were dead?" He shrugged with such dejection, my heart wept. "I broke."

The sentence hung monstrous and honest between us, sinking heavily to the floor while Jacob sucked in a breath and I stayed deathly silent.

He didn't meet my eyes as he confessed, "I lost everything when I lost you. Everything I've been running from, my fears, my triggers, my unresolved grief—it all found me. I-I'm not proud of what happened. I hate that people saw me that way, knowing the gossipers will spread my breakdown with glee. I wish I weren't so fucked up that it took two doctors and a syringe to put me out of my misery. But I—"

"Wait…" I jerked. "They…sedated you?"

He gave me a wry smile. "Something like that."

"Are you okay?"

He gave me the most adoring smile. "Even after everything

I've done to you, you still ask if I'm okay."

My body reacted to the echoes of shame and sorrow in his tone. My arms begged to hug him. My heart cried to love him. I still had the undying need to offer sanctuary and comfort.

But those were lies.

Jacob had suffered a panic attack.

That's all.

He was cracked open and vulnerable. His emotions frayed and existence tested. He might mean what he said. He might believe he would stand by his declarations.

But I knew how strong his safety mechanisms were. Once he'd patched up his hurt and hidden away his tears, he wouldn't be able to be so unguarded again.

He'd push me from his heart.

He'd gather himself in loneliness because that was all he'd ever known.

"I can't do this, Jacob," I whispered. "I can't put myself through this again."

He froze. "But—"

"Please...you have to let me go." I forced myself to meet his eyes, tears streaming down my cheeks. "I'm not strong enough."

"But I love you."

"It's not enough."

Familiar temper glittered in his onyx gemstone eyes. "What is enough? What do I have to do to prove to you that I'm serious?"

"I—"

The door swung open.

Dr Jorge bustled in with his e-tablet and large physique. "Ah, sorry. Thought you'd left and this room was free." He glanced between Jacob and me. Saw my tears. Read Jacob's anger.

He backed over the threshold. "Um, sorry to interrupt, but we have another patient that requires this room." He hugged his tablet to his chest like armour as he reached for the door handle. "Everything okay?"

I nodded curtly as Jacob shook his head.

We spoke at the same time.

"No."

"Yes."

The doctor frowned. "Well...anything I can do to help?" He looked at his watch. "I can delay the other patient, I suppose."

"No, it's fine." I swiped at my tears and swung my legs—cast and all—to the floor. I braced myself for the pain, realising too late I'd climbed off the wrong side. My crutches mocked me against the wall.

Damn.

Jacob noticed. Grabbing the two sticks, he brought them around the bed for me. "Here."

I didn't thank him.

Taking the crutches stiffly, I placed them under my arms. My first step forward was awkward, and Jacob hovered behind me, ready to catch me, willing to hurt me even more with his consideration.

My back prickled from his stare as I straightened my spine and hopped faster. I moved toward Dr Jorge. "Don't worry. We're leaving."

"Okay then. See you for a check-up soon." He stepped sideways so I could hop from the room and do my best to run from this hospital.

The hospital that had taken Jacob's family.

The hospital that kept me prisoner in Jacob's care.

By the time I made it outside, the sun hurt my concussed head, and I hissed between my teeth with discomfort. Jacob jogged ahead of me, vanishing amongst a row of parked cars.

A snarl of an ancient growly engine reached my ears just before Jacob swung in front of me in his truck. Climbing out, he opened the passenger door and gave me a stern smile. "Get in."

"No."

"We're not finished with this conversation."

"We are. I'm going to a hotel."

"Get in the car, or I'll throw you in myself."

My chin came up, my hands squeezing my padded crutches. "Call your aunt. I'll stay with her until my dad arrives."

His jaw clenched as his fist latched around the door. "Give me time to talk to you. Give me that, and if you still hate my guts, I'll drive you wherever you want to go. Even if it's across borders and continents."

I studied him.

I hated and loved him.

I lost to the soul-deep plea in his gaze.

"One hour. But once we've talked, it's over."

"Okay."

"Good." I sniffed.

And in that emptiness following a single word, Jacob stepped into me, his chest brushed my chest, his eyes found my lips, and his heart offered me to take it.

One simple word.

Four tiny letters.

An entire lifetime of love behind it.

His hand cupped my cheek, and his forehead kissed mine. "Fine."

Chapter Fifty-Five

HOPE

* * * * * *

FOR THE PAST two hours, Jacob had avoided the so-called conversation we were meant to have. He'd driven me back to his place, placed pillows on his couch, layered me with blankets, snacks, and the TV remote, then vanished in his dinged-up truck to who knew where.

So much for only being here an hour.

When he returned, he carted grocery bags to the kitchen he most likely hadn't cooked in since leaving Cherry River four years ago and proceeded to prepare something to eat.

I pretended to ignore him.

Whenever I felt his eyes on me, I studied whatever stupid show played on the TV. Whenever he cleared his throat as if looking for a right sentence to begin yet another fight, I turned up the volume and hunkered down in my blankets.

I wanted to be invisible.

But when my head hurt, he gave me painkillers.

When my broken leg ached, he gently positioned a cushion beneath it.

I merely had to wince, and he was there, doing his best to eradicate my pain.

I'd never been so fussed over, so watched or loved or wanted.

It made me cry deep inside because I'd wanted that sort of care all along.

I'd wanted the give and take of a true connection.

The domestication of lovers and friends with rolling meadows all around us, forests sheltering us, and the knowledge that we belonged to one another.

If one hurt, the other found a cure. If one was tired, the other let them rest.

A partnership until death did us part.

To see what such a life could be like with Jacob left my heart in a steady flux of throbbing agony. Whenever I looked at him in the kitchen or smelled the delicious scents of butter and pesto or caught him staring at me as if he wanted to kiss me stupid and then drag me back to his bedroom, it upset me in the most agonising way.

I thought he couldn't hurt me any more than what he'd done in Bali.

I'd been wrong.

This was where pain manifested.

This was where I fell apart piece by piece.

Right there on Jacob Wild's couch.

"Dinner's ready." He skipped his stare over me, cocking his head at the dining room table. Placing two plates on the wooden surface and returning to the kitchen for salt, pepper, and a carafe of water, he finally came to a stop before me. "Do you need help getting up?"

I flinched. I didn't want him touching me, but unfortunately, I needed his strength.

The bruises from the crash steadily became known as time passed. My hip hurt. My knee. My ankle.

Gritting my teeth, I held out a hand, wordlessly accepting his assistance.

He shot forward as if I'd finally given him permission to everything he wanted. Ignoring my outstretched hand, he wrapped his arms around me, plucking me effortlessly from the couch.

Standing in his embrace, our eyes knotted, and I sucked in a breath.

He was so warm and strong and reeked of protection and affection. If I were weaker, I'd lay my head on his shoulder and be done with it.

I'd accept whatever scraps he could give me.

I'd be the old Hope who happily took heartache for a snippet of his love.

But I was jaded these days.

I wasn't the idealistic girl who believed horses and farmers could fix everything.

I knew the truth, and the truth was Jacob would always be a loner.

Pushing him away, I reached for my crutches.

He let me go with a heavy sigh, moving to pull a chair from the table for me. I sat as nimbly as I could with my cast sticking out in front of me and hated the way he scooted me closer to the table like a child. Hated the way he bent down and placed a kiss on my hair, his nose nuzzling me far longer than permitted.

Goosebumps darted down my arms as he kissed me again, then headed to his own chair and the delicious looking avocado, pesto pasta he'd created.

Cracking some salt onto his plate, he looked up. "Want some?"

I shook my head, spearing a piece of penne and placing it on my tongue.

The awkwardness of everything unsaid between us squeezed viciously around my ribs. It made food taste like ash and time tick as slowly as centuries.

We ate in silence; the TV a quiet drone behind me.

Jacob had brought me here to talk. He effectively held me prisoner, and I didn't know how much longer I could take.

I'd never felt welcome in his home.

It was even worse now.

Halfway through my meal, I asked, "Are you going to say anything or just pretend you didn't kidnap me?"

He looked up with a soft smirk. "I didn't kidnap you."

"Does anyone else know I'm here?"

"Your father."

"Cassie?"

He shook his head.

"It's getting late, Jacob." I pushed aside my half-eaten dinner. "I want to rest."

"My bed is clean. Fresh sheets and blankets. I can help you shower if you want."

I laughed coldly. "You're not helping me shower, and I'm definitely not sleeping in your bed."

"I'd take the spare," he grumbled. "If you can't stand the thought of sharing with me."

"I can't stay in this house. Call Cassie and ask if I can stay with her. My father won't be much longer, I'm sure."

He shot to his feet, snatching my dinner plate and carrying both into the kitchen. They clattered as he tossed them into the sink. "I know I deserve your temper, Hope, but fuck it's hard to keep mine in check and not start a fight with you."

I swivelled around to face him.

He stood with both hands braced on either side of the sink. His shoulders bunched and lips thin, his muscles taut and ready to battle.

I did my best to stay calm. "I'm not trying to draw you into a fight."

"Then stop giving me the silent treatment."

"The indifferent treatment, don't you mean?" I pinned him with a deliberate stare. "Doesn't feel nice, does it? To have someone you care about just shut you out. No anger. No connection. Nothing but coldness. How are you supposed to fight with coldness? You can't."

"So you're giving me a dose of my own medicine, is that it?" He stalked toward me, fists by his sides.

I scrambled upright, grabbing my crutches and shuffling backward. "I'm not doing anything. I'm merely waiting until I can leave."

"We need to talk."

"We talked enough at the hospital."

"We didn't even begin." He came closer.

I moved toward the corridor and the bedrooms, hopping backward gingerly. My cast clunked on the hardwood floor as I navigated the space. "I don't want to do this again, Jacob."

"I told you I'm in love with you. I expected some resistance but not a flat-out refusal to accept."

"Then you have no idea how much you truly hurt me."

He sighed with torment etching him. "I'm beginning to see that now."

"Good."

His eyes narrowed on mine. "What can I do to make you believe I'm in love with you?"

Words sank into my stomach, leaving me mute—giving him the opportunity to sneak closer.

I scrambled backward, stupidly slamming against a wall.

He caged me in, hands landing by my ears with a thud. "I love you, Hope. I think I've loved you since the moment I met you. I was just too fucking afraid to admit it."

I couldn't breathe.

Why was he doing this? Why was he determined to be so awfully cruel?

Tears pricked my eyes as I tried to look away but couldn't.

"I'm sorry," he murmured. "Eternally sorry for all that I put you through."

Tinder sparked, setting fire to my blood. "Don't you *dare* apologise. I don't want your apology."

"But you need to hear it. You need to hear everything that

I'm saying. You need to believe me when I say I'm never leaving you again."

"That's because *I'm* the one who's walking away this time."

He chuckled, staring at my cast. "You won't be walking anywhere for a while."

"You know what I mean." I glowered.

"I know what you mean." He nodded. "But I hope you don't."

"Why? Why this sudden change of heart? You could've kept me forever. We could've started a life together the moment we slept together in Bali. But you didn't want me then, and you don't want me now. Do you feel guilty all of a sudden? Do you feel like you owe me?" I breathed hard. "I'm sorry about your grandfather, I truly am. I'm sorry I didn't tell you about him when I first found you. Perhaps if I had, you would've been home in time to say goodbye. I'm sorry for all of it, but I can't be what you want because you don't even know what that is."

"I do know what I want. It's you." His nose kissed mine. "I know I ruined what happened between us. I know I hurt you by leaving. But you have to know what that night meant to me. I'm sure you guessed I was a virgin. And I would've stayed one until my dying day if I didn't want you more than my own sanity."

"Is that supposed to be a compliment?"

"It's supposed to show you how much I love you. How much I need you." He leaned against me, wedging his hips into mine. The piece of him I'd only touched briefly steadily hardened the longer we stayed pressed together. "Can't you feel that, Hope? Can't you see how much I mean it when I say I love—"

"*Argh!*" I ducked under his arm, shoving him away from me. My crutches smashed to the ground, leaving me to scuttle along the wall for balance. "Enough. Okay? Enough."

"Why? Because I'm finally getting through to you? Finally making you believe?"

"You're driving me crazy."

"Good. You drive me crazy all the damn time."

"You're impossible."

"No, I'm in love. Big difference." He followed me, step for step. His bedroom offered salvation. If I could throw myself inside and lock the door, I could be free of this madness.

I could sit and weep and wait for my father to take me away like he did when I was younger. I could place my problems in some other person's control so I didn't have to suffer.

I wanted to believe Jacob so, so much.

I wanted to let down my walls and open my arms to him.

I wanted to smile and cry and tell him he'd won.

That I loved him too.

I always would.

But I couldn't because I knew what would happen.

He believed he'd changed.

I believed he couldn't.

The fear that he would forever be the boy who'd spent the past eleven years pushing me away was too painful to ignore.

I would end up being the Michael of the relationship—the victim instead of the villain. I'd made Michael believe we were equals. That his heart bought my heart and our togetherness was on mutual grounds.

He hadn't known my true thoughts. He never guessed my love for him wasn't like the love he had for me.

I'd been a terrible, terrible person. I deserved to love someone more than they loved me because that was the punishment required, but then again, I'd *already* lived that sentence. Most of my life, I'd lived it, and I didn't want to live it anymore.

My shoulders fell, and I stopped trying to inch away. "I know you think you love me, Jacob, but you don't. Not really."

"Don't tell me what I do or don't feel, Hope."

"Well, don't ask me to believe in fantasises."

"You're really starting to get on my nerves." His eyes tightened. "I lived through your death. I know what it feels like to lose you. Truly, *truly* lose you. And if you think you're going to take away my right to love you—after I've been through that agony—then you don't know me very well."

"I know you plenty. I know you *too* well. That's why I'm saying—"

"You're not saying anything—unless it's that you love me back."

"Threats won't make me love you, you know."

He grumbled under his breath. "You won't win this argument. You loved me when we spent the night together. You *still* love me even though you hate me right now. I can wait. I can grovel. I can show you that things have changed between us because I know what it feels like to lose you and—"

"Stop repeating that. You're saying my 'death' didn't hurt you as much as you feared? Therefore, you can love me because…what? My dying won't break you apart like your parents' death did?" My voice hitched as a tear escaped my control.

His temper gathered power. He stomped toward me, slamming his hands against the wall, trapping me once again. "You're not listening. That's not what I'm saying at all." His voice was more of a growl, twisting my stomach with hunger and hesitation.

"It's not important." Another tear rolled from my lashes. "I just need to leave."

"You're not leaving. I told you that. You're stuck with me for life."

Exhaustion fell over me. "I'm tired, Jacob. Just please...leave me alone." I was tired from the accident and tired from dealing with him for eleven eternally long years. When I'd wanted him to fight for me, he never did. Now, when I wanted him to let me go, he refused.

He tangled me up and made me spin.

And I was *tired* of this. So, so tired.

"Thinking you were dead was the worst thing I've ever felt, Hope. I wanted to die too. My system overloaded. I...anyway, it doesn't matter. What *does* matter is I realised, despite my issues, I *am* strong enough to love you. *I love you.* I love you so fucking much, and I need you way more than you need me." His head bowed, his lips seeking mine. "All I'm asking is for you to believe me."

I turned my mouth away at the last second, wincing as he kissed my cheek. "Believe you?"

He licked my skin as another droplet of sadness trickled free.

He nodded, pressing his body along mine. "Please."

I shuddered. "What's to stop you from changing your mind tomorrow? What if you decide it's not worth the grief, after all?"

"I won't. It's not possible." He tried to kiss me again.

I avoided it, earning half a kiss and a lusty growl. "I know what will happen, Jacob. I'll fall for you until I can't live without you. I'll accept all your moods and messes. I'll agree to be with you forever. But then, when it gets hard or we fight or something sets off your triggers, you'll shove me from your life all over again."

He pulled back a little, his dark eyes gleaming with ferocity. "You're right about my triggers."

I wanted to cry harder. "Exactly."

"But I won't let them rule my life anymore."

For the first time, a spark of hope appeared. "And how exactly are you going to do that?"

He reached into his pocket and pulled out a piece of paper with a name on it. "This is a therapist. I'm...I'm going to make an appointment to see him."

Softness did its best to replace my hardness. "I'm happy for you. I'm glad you're ready to accept help. I truly hope it makes your life more bearable. But...it's too late for us. I...I can't trust you. You've broken it too many times."

He rubbed his heart as if I'd stabbed him through the chest. "I can see why you wouldn't trust me."

"Zero trust." I held up a circle with my fingers. "None."

"I hurt you badly when I sent you away at my mother's funeral."

"*Hurt* me? You ripped out my heart and buried it with her."

His gaze fell to my cast. "I have so much to make up to you."

"Stop doing that."

His head tipped up, his sorrowful gaze swirling with honesty. "Stop what?"

"Agreeing with me like you did at the hospital. It's making it hard to have a proper fight with you."

"But you're right. You deserved better."

"I don't care. It's making me uncomfortable."

"Well, accept it because I don't want to fight with you. Not anymore."

"And I don't want to fight with you either." I sighed. "So please...just let me go."

His voice dropped to barely audible. "Please, Hope. I'm begging you...give me another chance."

The tiny pieces of my heart lurched to give him whatever he wanted. But I gritted my teeth and shook my head instead. "I still love you, Jacob, but I don't *want* to love you anymore. If you love me like you say you do, you'll let me go."

His eyes flared. "You can't mean that."

"I do."

He stood, towering over me. His hands curled into fists, falling by his sides. "You're asking me to rip out my heart the very moment I finally have one strong enough to give to you."

Tears rained faster. "I'm sorry."

"Don't do this, Hope."

"I have no choice."

He chewed his lip, looking wildly around the corridor as if something could make me change my mind. His chest rose and fell, quicker and quicker until his entire body trembled. Clenching his jaw, he closed his eyes and inhaled hard through his nose, getting his system under control, refusing to give in to the panic attack.

The fact I had power over him to cause such strife almost made me throw myself into his arms. To apologise. To tell him *of course* I wanted him. *Of course* I loved him. How stupid of me to convince him I wanted to live an empty life without him.

But he opened his eyes and a glint of something I'd never seen before rendered him unreachable. His hands came up, he imprisoned my cheeks, and his mouth smashed on mine with a violence he'd always kept leashed.

I stumbled as he hoisted me into his arms, dragging me into his bedroom with my cast bumping against his legs and his tongue hunting mine with heat.

A gush of anger and relief, rage and lust hijacked my control as I threw my arms around his neck, wordlessly agreeing to this attack. Giving in one last time.

I would stay firm to my word.

After.

I would walk away.

After.

But…I wanted him.

I wanted a true and final goodbye.

"Hope," he grunted as he tumbled onto his bed, cradling me protectively. The moment we were horizontal, he spun me around and wedged me on my back.

My cast couldn't stop the pain in my leg or the throbbing in my head, and I flinched as he kissed me harder.

His hand skated down my body, squeezing my breast and pinching my nipple. There was nothing seductive or sensual.

Our fight had spilled into sex, and it echoed with arguments and frustrations.

In a knot of body parts and fury, we permitted ourselves to drop our barriers and tangle with tempers. To be furious with one another. To be brutal and unkind and *honest.*

Honest about all the hurt we caused.

And the knowledge that we'd only cause more because we weren't meant to be.

I struggled to accept such heartbreak as his teeth caught my lower lip, sharp and punishing. I bit him back, nipping him all while nervous need fluttered in my stomach. I'd always feared Jacob would overwhelm me if we collided this way.

And I was right.

Before, I would've embraced his torment. I would've dropped my guard and been as wild as he—I would've entered the war he wanted to lavish.

Now, I just wanted to be selfish and take what he had to give me, all while begging my heart not to get involved.

This was purely an ending to a decade-long dance.

I gasped as Jacob cupped my head with both hands, his fingers slipping through my hair. His eyes caught mine, desperate and dark, daring me to deny him.

I wouldn't deny him because I was sick enough to crave him even when I hated him.

"This is where you belong, Hope. Right here. In my bed."

I didn't reply.

Our eyes battled before he finally sank over me, his mouth seeking mine in a vicious, brutal kiss.

One hand stayed locked in my hair, keeping me trapped for his plundering mouth while the other skated down my body. My clothes were wrinkly and travel-worn. Smudged with dirt from my accident and reeking of hospital, but none of that mattered as Jacob grabbed the hem of my grey skirt and hoisted it up to my hips.

He breathed hard as he looped his fingers in my underwear, his nails grazing the delicate skin on my hipbone. "Every night for the rest of our lives, I'm going to make love to you. I'm going to take my time to show you how much you are loved and remind you as the sun goes down that I will never hurt you again." His lips sought mine, feeding the words deep into my heart while I squirmed in his hold.

"But tonight, I can't wait. Tonight isn't about showing you I love you. Tonight is about showing you I literally can't breathe unless you are mine."

With a yank, he pulled my underwear down, growling under his breath when they caught on my cast. "Goddammit."

Wriggling, I helped him unhook the material, moaning as he got them off and pressed me into the mattress with his bulk between my thighs.

"I love you, Hope." His hand dived between my legs, finding me hot and wet.

It took everything I had not to repeat the vow to him.

He attacked my mouth with a feral kiss as he stroked me, pinched me, then slowly inserted a finger inside me.

My back bowed. My nails latched onto his lower back. I didn't want to show him the power he had over me, but my willpower rapidly unravelled.

His kiss scrambled my mind as he rocked his touch inside me. I couldn't stop the rush of urgency as I fumbled with his belt buckle, undoing the well-worn leather and unzipping his jeans.

He groaned as I pushed the denim down his butt along with his boxer-briefs. The moment his hot, naked flesh stuck to mine, I grabbed his hard length.

His entire body shot rigid. His face nuzzled into my hair as his hips rocked, seeking more of my touch.

I squeezed him hard, wanting to hurt him while also showing him we were equally matched in bed. He could make me come undone, but I could make him do the same.

"That feels so good," he breathed into my ear as I stroked him up and down, my skin sizzling with how hot he was.

"I want you," he grunted. "Only you. *Always* you."

I squeezed my eyes from more tears. The timbre and truth of his voice almost made me believe it.

Unfortunately, where I had limited jurisdiction over my heart, I had no control over my body. Not a scrap of authority as I turned shuddery and shivery and opened my legs wider in invitation.

This is just physical.

It means nothing.

Liar.

His grip on my hair tightened, tugging my head back so he could attack and kiss his way down my throat.

My cream T-shirt didn't protect me from the hot dampness of his mouth as he sucked my nipple through the material.

A flood of wetness crested through me.

He groaned as he inserted a second finger inside me, and I pumped him faster.

The longer he physically loved me, the harder I found it to keep emotional distance.

I wanted to burst into tears because this, *this* was what I'd begged for. The domestication and the dominance. The sweet and the surly. He'd finally given me everything, but I was too afraid to take it. Too confused and timid to trust.

His tongue circled my nipple over my T-shirt as he nipped and suckled his way back to my mouth, consuming me with his heady taste.

My breaths turned choppy and short as primal command made my skin spark with need.

With sudden fierceness, I pumped him once more, tugged on his wrist to remove his fingers from inside me, then lined up his tip to my entrance.

He reared over me, lips wet, eyes black, a wildness inside him that made me tumble into agony. "Wait, I want—"

"Fuck me, Jacob." I arched my spine, grazing my wetness on his erection.

He locked in place, a hiss trickling from his mouth. "But—"

"Finish this." I gritted my teeth.

I wanted him desperately to end this.

I wanted it over.

"No matter what you think, this isn't the end, Hope." He kissed me softly. "It's just the beginning." He planted hands into the mattress and pressed an inch inside me. "Tell me you understand that."

I pursed my lips and said nothing.

My eyes shot a challenge. My body screamed a goodbye.

And Jacob accepted my denial with a swift, deep thrust.

Taking me. Impaling me. Filling me with every part of him.

I cried out, raking my nails down his back, willing my body to accept him even though I'd banished my heart from such a thing.

His head tipped forward as he quaked with desire. His length inside me hardened, stretching me until I utterly belonged to him.

And then he moved.

A rock of his hips. A pound of his body.

He didn't make love or fuck me.

He claimed me, invaded me, surrounded me with every sense until I was molten despair in his arms.

"This is us, Hope. You and me. Forever." He thrust into me, his breath catching as a wash of pure pleasure engulfed us.

"Don't talk." I moaned, grabbing his hips and commanding him to take me faster.

He obeyed, driving me into the bed with the delicious speed of a frenzied beast and adoring lover. His mess of long blond hair tickled my cheeks as he kissed me. His few-day old beard rasped my lips and skin. He was as Wild as I'd ever seen and I shivered in his power.

I was merely his conquest, there to accept his temper all while he vowed to love me.

His tongue hunted mine again. His groan dark and heady,

twisting my belly with a tingling orgasm.

Somehow, he knew.

He felt how close I was.

He sank deeper, driving into me, consuming me until we were savage with lust.

He fought to climb into me, and I clawed to get closer to him.

Our bodies slowly slicked with sweat; our nerve endings quickly sought a mind-shattering release.

His hand shot between us, his rough farmer's thumb finding my clit.

His rhythm picked up speed, hammering into me as his touch gave me nowhere to hide. "I want to feel you come when I'm inside you." His breath caught, and his tone rasped with greed.

I savoured the sensation of him controlling every part of me.

I gave up rocking against him. I stopped screaming at my heart not to fall. I gave in because it was the only thing I could do with the man I wanted more than anything on top of me.

His free hand trailed to my neck. I dug my head into the pillow, giving him the column of my throat. But he didn't cup or stroke me.

He merely tangled his fingers in the chain of my locket and tugged—pulling me up to kiss him with the silver jewellery. "I bought this because I missed you."

A thrill shot down my spine as he thrust faster.

"I told myself it meant nothing. I believed it meant nothing. I lied."

A sick excitement sizzled deep, deep in my core, soaring me higher and higher, twining me tighter and tighter.

He didn't stop claiming me. His body pumping into mine. His touch all around me. His eyes entrapped mine with their gemstone glittering depths.

"I bought you a necklace when I was a teenager. Perhaps I should buy you a ring now that I'm a man. Then again, wasn't it you who was supposed to propose if I slept with you?" He cupped the locket, his jaw clenching and body driving deeper. "I'm inside you, Hope. Don't you owe me a question?"

I glowered at him, loose and drunk on the pleasure he gave. "I owe you nothing."

"You're right." His hand spread over my throat, squeezing gently as he increased his pressure, taking every last piece of me. "But I owe you my heart. And you have it. Forever."

His thumb pressed into my clit as he kissed me, attacking me from all angles.

And I lost it.

My desire supernovaed. A firework of heat and hope and heartache.

My broken leg didn't stop my orgasm. My concussion didn't prevent stars from exploding behind my eyes. And my bruises did nothing to prevent the way I came apart in his embrace.

As I rippled around him, he reared onto his fists and fucked me hard and deep, increasing the length of my orgasm, wringing me out until I was floppy and dazed—his captive to take whatever he wanted.

Then he joined me in bliss.

His climax raced down his spine, and he groaned the most guttural groan.

A groan that smashed down my final, flimsy walls and made tears leak from my eyes.

His essence spilled into me, and I had nowhere to hide.

I loved Jacob Wild with every molecule.

I wanted to believe him, trust him, forgive him.

But as my body lay sated and tingling, our limbs entwined and heartbeats pounding, my soul scrambled from the togetherness.

This had been yet another mistake.

It was a fantasy I couldn't have.

It was an ending that needed to happen.

I closed my eyes against the inevitable goodbye.

Chapter Fifty-Six

JACOB

✳ ✳ ✳ ✳ ✳ ✳

I WOKE GROGGY and slow as if I'd drunk heavily the night before and suffered a hangover from hell.

I hadn't drunk. But I had indulged in substances bad for my health.

I lay on my stomach, inching my arm across the bed to Hope.

Dawn only just lightened the sky. My body still sang with our ruthless connection, but I needed to touch her again. I needed to be inside her. To assure myself she'd finally accepted that I loved her and she wasn't going anywhere.

My heart went from sluggish to crazed as my hand met cool, empty sheets.

Bolting upright, I scanned the dawn-doused bedroom.

No Hope.

Leaping out of bed, I hopped into a pair of boxer-briefs and rushed to find her.

I dashed into my bathroom, expecting, *hoping* to see her in the shower.

She wasn't.

Where the hell is she?

The sweet, delicious tone of her voice came from the kitchen and energy bolted through my legs. I ran down the corridor, skidding into the living room.

She stood with her hand in her hair, crutches leaning against the dining table and her phone to her ear. "I'm not at Cassie's, Dad."

Graham was loud enough through the phone that his timbre sailed across the space to me. "Where the hell have you been staying then? I assumed Jacob would take you to his aunt's."

She winced, her back to me, either ignoring me or unaware of my presence. "He didn't. I'm at his place."

"You spent the night?"

"Yes. He was a...gracious host."

I wanted to snicker at her comment. To love the inside joke and relish in our secret. But her tone wasn't that of a girl in love. It was resigned and unhappy...resolute. "I'm ready to go, though, so feel free to come get me."

"Okay. I'll be right up."

"I'll be outside."

What?

Hope severed the call, then turned around with a heavy sigh. She froze as she saw me standing there, half-naked, chest heaving, my heart in pieces by my feet. "Last night meant nothing to you?" I padded toward her, arms spread in surrender. "You're leaving?"

Her lips pressed together as she fought another onslaught of tears. She pocketed her phone in clothes she'd changed into from her suitcase and grabbed the crutches. "I told you I can't do this again, Jacob."

"But we slept together."

"We did."

"And now you're leaving."

"Like you did." Her chin sliced the sky as she held her head high.

"So you're punishing me?" I closed the distance between us.

She backed up, her crutches squeaking in her haste. "No, I'm merely protecting myself from a future I can't survive."

"That's bullshit."

"It's the truth."

"But I'm in love with you. How many fucking times do I need to tell you?"

The crunch of tyres on gravel outside made my heart race with sickness. Her dad must've been parked at Aunt Cassie's house to get here so fast.

I'd run out of time.

I'd run out of hope.

My spine rolled even as I fought the urge to grab her. To kiss her again. To drag her back to my bed.

Graham knocked on my door, wrenching Hope's gaze to it.

I stepped in front of her. "Don't go. Let me prove to you. Let me show you that I'll never hurt you again." Grabbing her shoulders, I longed to wipe away the tear rolling down her cheek. "I promised I'd never make you cry again. These tears are your doing."

She shifted in my hold, trying to hide from my touch, but I

didn't let her. I merely moved with her, digging my fingertips into her delicate body, cupping a hand around the nape of the woman I loved with all my heart. "Hope, please—"

My front door opened. Graham stepped uninvited into my home.

Goddammit, I should really lock my door.

He froze, taking in the scene before him. His daughter with crutches, cast, and bruises, and a boy who'd broken her heart so many times half-naked before her.

"Hope?" He crept forward, his eyes narrowing on mine. "What's going on?"

Hope shook her head, doing her best to back away. "Nothing. I was just saying goodbye."

I let her go, turning to face Graham.

My skin prickled at being mostly naked. I felt vulnerable and bare and not at all worthy, but this was my one chance. My last shot at keeping the girl I needed. "I don't want her to go."

Graham cocked his head. "I don't think you have a choice in the matter."

"But…I love her. With all my sorry excuse of a heart."

Hope sucked in a breath as I moved away from her. I went to her father. I did the honourable thing and told the guardian of the girl I wanted more than anything the truth. Perhaps *he* would believe me. "I've hurt your daughter, sir. I know that. I know I have a lot to make amends on. I've been mean and idiotic and downright awful, but…I love her." I spread my hands. "I can't let her walk out that door because I know I'll never see her again and that just can't happen."

Graham crossed his arms. "If Hope wants to leave, then you won't stop her."

"And if she wants to stay. Will you let her?"

He looked past me to his daughter. "Hope is an adult. She can make her own decisions."

I studied him. I looked past my childish grudge about him playing my father. I put aside my grievances of his intrusion on our world, and I accepted him as a man. Just a man…like me. One who'd sinned and made mistakes and I knew what I had to do.

"You're a good man, Mr. Murphy. I'm sorry I didn't see that till now."

He froze.

"I hope to be as good a father as you are someday." My voice rasped with sincerity. "That's the honest to God truth."

Hope whimpered behind me, sending shivers down my back. I smiled softly as I turned to face her again.

I blocked out her father. I went to the most important person in my world, and with my heart aching and stomach in knots, I sank to my knee before her.

The air in the room vanished.

Graham cleared his throat. Hope moaned under her breath, and I bowed at the feet of someone who I would love until my dying day. Breath was hard to come by as my heart galloped in terror and acceptance.

"Hope Jacinta Murphy."

She shook her head, biting her lip. "Jake...what are you doing?"

"Hush." I captured her hand, bringing her knuckles to my lips. "Let me do this before I have another panic attack."

She wobbled in place.

I sucked in a gulp, looking into her gorgeous green eyes. "If you won't take me as your friend and you refuse to take me as your lover, I have only one option available."

Goosebumps exploded over my skin as she moaned again. "Jacob...stop."

I clutched her fingers tighter. "I love you, Hope. I don't care how many times I have to say it to make you believe me. I'll say it every hour of every day for the rest of our lives if I have to. In fact, I'll do that anyway. Just because you deserve to be told you are loved. You are loved so fucking much with all my heart. And I will continue to love you forever. I will never stop. You have my utmost vow. I will love you until you are old and grey. I will love you when we bicker and argue, and I will love you even past death. I know I've hurt you. I've broken your trust and been a jackass for years. I've been the worst kind of friend to you while you've been the best kind to me. But...you died yesterday. And I wanted to die, too. The thought of you gone didn't just butcher me; it stole the very essence of who I am. If you *had* died, I know I wouldn't be the same man. I would be changed. Irrevocably. Just like you would be changed if I died. We're already bound in every way that matters."

She stumbled. One of her crutches tumbled to the floor, and I grabbed her other hand, giving her something to cling to. "I thought I could avoid love so I wouldn't feel the pain my parents did. But the thing is...I've been feeling it every day of my life because I've been fighting the one thing that could make me whole."

I smiled as she cried openly.

"I was so afraid of losing you that I didn't realise I'd *already* lost you, and I would rather the pain of burying you than the numbness of not having you. So push me away, refuse to see me, find someone else who is worthy of you. But you have to know that I will always be there waiting. I will always love you because it's an impossibility *not* to love you. Love is worth any price—I see that now. No matter how long we'll have together, I'm strong enough to love you. I'm brave enough to accept."

My voice thickened as I murmured, "I accept this, Hope. *Us.* I accept that eventually one of us will die before the other. I accept one of us will be broken and the other will live a half-life until we're reunited. I even accept that love has the power to lead us back to each other past the grave. I *accept*, Hope. I finally fucking accept."

She cried harder, tears glittering like crystals on her white cheeks.

I turned her hands upside down and pressed two kisses to her palms. "Marry me. Accept me just like you taught me to accept you." I nuzzled into her sweet-smelling skin. "Please, Hope. Marry me."

Her father grunted, Hope crumpled, and I stayed on my knee with more fear than I'd ever felt.

My last chance.

My final attempt at deserving her.

A breeze blustered through the open door, whistling around my home, cool and warm, quick and calm. Two elements. Two sides.

My hair raised on the back of my neck as familiar whispers filled my ears. A familiar connection to ghosts I held so dear.

My parents.

United in the wind and there for my proposal.

I didn't care if it was pure imagination. It helped to know they saw me. That they celebrated my change of heart as much as I did and approved of my choice.

Mom had loved Hope already.

Dad would've loved her undoubtedly.

She was as much a Wild as I was and had been since she was ten years old.

The breeze died down, and Hope didn't give me an answer.

I waited for another heart-destroying second before slowly

climbing to my feet. Nudging her chin with my fingers, I asked softly, "Well...do you have an answer for me?"

Her gaze locked on mine. She didn't look past me to her father. She didn't seek approval or answers. She merely stared into me. Stared and stared and cupped my cheek with a shaking hand.

The moment lasted forever as she read my heart, inscribed my vow on hers, and finally, finally nodded. "I believe you."

The strength in my legs vanished. I stumbled. "Oh, thank God."

She gave me a tentative smile. "Want to borrow my crutches?"

I laughed. "Don't need them. I have you to hold onto." I dragged her to me, kissing her hard.

With her lips on mine and her acceptance softening my anxiety, my heart knitted itself together in ways it never could before, stitch by stitch, string by string until it was a new heart, an eager heart, a battered, bruised, and wizened heart.

A heart brave enough to accept a marriage, a family...a home.

I groaned into the kiss, not caring that her father was right there. Or that he was about to become my father-in-law. I only focused on Hope—like I would for the rest of my life.

She kissed me back, her tongue tangling with mine, making parts of me clench and swell.

I wanted to kiss her forever, but I also needed to hear her promise. To know she'd heard what I said and understood how deadly serious I was. Kissing her one last time, I pulled away and murmured, "So? You will marry me, right?"

She shivered in my arms, her mouth pink and eyes wide. "Is this real? Are you *really* proposing? This isn't just a—"

"It's real, Hope. I know what I'm asking. I know it includes a wedding and vows and everything else a marriage comes with."

She studied me. "But do you understand it's forever? You're signing on to arguments and make-ups and driving each other crazy."

"I said I did, didn't I?"

"Saying it and believing it are two different things." Her voice might be stern, but her eyes twinkled. "You can't get out of this. Divorce isn't something I'll give you. You'll be stuck with me."

"And you'll be stuck with me. With my overbearing, over-protectiveness. I'll drive you nuts." I pressed my lips together. Not sure why I was arguing against her agreeing to marry me when it was the only thing I needed. "Forget I said that."

She laughed under her breath. "Will you let me drive the tractor?"

I grinned. "No chance."

"In that case, my answer is n—"

"Fine! You can drive the tractor. I'll buy you your own tractor."

She snickered. "So you're saying you'll share Cherry River with me? You won't get grumpy if I want to work with you?"

I cupped her cheek, loving the way she pressed her palm into my touch. "I want you there every dawn. Working with you is one of the best things to ever happen to me."

"What are the other things?"

"Falling in love with you, of course." I kissed her again. "Definitely the best thing that's ever happened to me."

"A few days ago, you would've said that was the worst thing to happen to you."

"A few days ago, I was an idiot."

She laughed as I ran my thumb along her bottom lip. "Stop stalling. Yes or no, Hope."

Once again, she studied me. She didn't hold back, assessing and debating, not taking my proposal lightly.

And I was glad.

It meant her reply would be heartfelt and binding. We'd both enter into this arrangement with commitment and steadfast promises.

To his credit, Graham didn't make a sound, and Hope didn't look at him over my shoulder. We could've been alone with the intensity in which we watched each other. Loved each other.

Finally, she nodded. "Yes. I'll marry you."

Dragging her into me, I kissed her hard, heaving a sigh as darkness erased from my bleak, empty world.

She was mine.

She'd agreed to be mine for eternity.

Hope threw her arms around my shoulders, deepening our connection.

Our kiss swiftly changed from romantic to sinful.

Graham cleared his throat, dragging me back to reality and the fact that I couldn't maul his daughter with him watching.

Pulling away from Hope, I unashamedly positioned her in front of me, hugging her from behind, hiding the reaction she'd caused in my tight boxer-briefs.

Graham never looked away from me as he spoke to his

daughter. "Are you sure about this, Little Lace?"

She nodded, patting my hand splayed on her stomach. "I believe him...finally. So yes, I'm sure."

"But he hurt you."

"He did. But I hurt him."

"Perhaps sleep on it. There's no rush."

Hope stood taller in my embrace. "I would've agreed with you last night. I honestly thought I had the strength to walk away from him, and that it was for the best. But I was lying to myself, and I won't lie to you. I've always loved Jacob, Dad. I will always love him—whether I'm his or someone else's. *That* was what hurt me. That was what made dealing with Jacob so hard. But...I believe him." She twisted to look up at me. "I don't have to fight what I feel anymore because he feels the same. And...I trust him not to take that away from me."

I nuzzled her nose with mine. "Never. I'm all yours."

She smiled gently. "I know. That's what makes this so easy. I don't know how to explain it, but I see the truth in your eyes."

"And you'll see it every day for the rest of your life."

Graham came toward us, his gaze narrowing. "I can see you love my daughter, Jacob. I'm not denying that. I even saw it when you were young. But affection isn't enough if you intend to hurt her like you have in the past. Love can sometimes be the worst weapon."

I stiffened but didn't get angry. He deserved to judge me. He'd seen me strike out in fear. He'd lived his own tragedy with a woman who'd hurt him.

But thanks to Hope, I no longer had to be afraid. And thanks to my parents, I knew what a happy marriage entailed. It was about being there for each other through thick and thin—crying together and laughing together. Being best-friends.

Hope was already my best-friend. The rest would work out as it was supposed to. "I'll prove to you that I'm worthy. You have my word I won't intentionally hurt her ever again."

I hugged Hope closer.

We were a couple.

Husband and wife already in the eyes of gods and ghosts.

Hope twined her arm around mine, nestling into me like she'd always belonged. And that was the thing...she had. I was just too stupid to see it.

"He won't hurt me, Dad."

Graham came closer, eyeing my undressed state and the way I

glowed with relief and adoration. Slowly, he raised his hand in agreement.

I unwrapped an arm from Hope and clasped his grip.

We shook.

"I expect a wedding sooner rather than later," Graham muttered. "Make an honest woman of her."

I chuckled as we let go. "Is tomorrow too soon?"

Hope's laughter made me shudder with joy.

And I had no choice but to kiss her again.

"Excuse me a second." I nodded at Graham, spun Hope in my arms, and captured her lips with mine.

A kiss to seal our pact.

A kiss to bind ourselves for eternity.

A kiss to accept the inevitable.

Accept.

It was amazing what such a simple word could do.

The power it yielded. The fears it deleted. The serenity it granted.

Accept.

Our tongues touched.

A gentle breeze wrapped around us.

I belonged to her, and she belonged to me.

I was home.

HOPE

✳ ✳ ✳ ✳ ✳ ✳

"I DON'T THINK he's going to like this, Cassie."

Cassie glanced my way, her fingers wrapped tight around the steering wheel as she drove us through town with two new pony rescues on the back.

I'd been living at Cherry River for three months.

Jacob and I were getting married tomorrow.

My leg had healed, my concussion all gone, and we'd officially had two fights. Fights I'd caused by wanting to take on Della's old role and help Cassie save abused and kill-pen horses.

Jacob didn't want me anywhere near the freaked-out, unstable beasts. And I understood—of course, I did, but I also wasn't some city girl who didn't have equine experience.

I promised him I wouldn't get close unless I could read the situation correctly. I wouldn't take my eyes off them for a moment. I wouldn't go behind them or stand directly in front of them.

I agreed to all those terms, only drawing a line when he asked me to wear a helmet and body armour at all times.

"I did warn you." Cassie smirked. "You're the one getting the full blame."

"I know." I pouted. "But he was…. I mean, how could I leave him there?" A shiver worked up my spine as a horse kicked inside the trailer. "I hate people who don't treat animals with kindness."

Cassie sighed, her red-brown hair glinting in the sunshine. "I know. I'm surprised I haven't gone to jail yet for blowing up some of these so-called farmers for what they've done."

"We've done the right thing, though, by taking him."

"Yeah. Hopefully, Jacob sees it that way."

I rubbed my face with my hands. "Ugh, he's really going to kill me, isn't he?"

"Yup." She chuckled. "Maybe instead of a wedding tomorrow we'll have another funeral."

The fact she could laugh about so much tragedy showed how accepting of life she was.

Jacob had finally learned how to do the same—in smaller increments.

He'd accepted us.

There'd been no question that I would live with Jacob. I'd quit my job in England and returned to being a farmer's girl.

Cherry River was mine as surely as its owner. Dad had flown back to his film location the next afternoon, and Jacob never let me out of his sights.

For the first few days, his openness to love was absolute. We spent most of our time in bed followed by late evenings hanging in the fields with the horses, seeing as I couldn't ride with my cast.

For a few weeks, it was pure paradise.

But then his fears slowly tried to claim him again. He flinched when my cast was removed. He started second-guessing my mortality.

I didn't let it worry me. He'd made me a promise, and in return, I promised I'd help him work through those dismal days.

Highs and lows.

Learning and growth.

Family.

When his mind started teasing him with dark and morbid things, I hugged him close and reminded him we were alive. We had hearts that beat and blood that flowed, and that was all he needed to focus on.

Slowly, he managed to ignore his nightmares and accept that life had shades of all colours—happy and sad, hard and easy.

A week after his grandfather had passed away from lymphoma, Jacob, his remaining family, and I gathered at the local church where his grandmother Patricia had been laid to rest.

The church spilled with well-wishers there to say goodbye to such a wonderful, wise man.

Jacob didn't manage a eulogy, but he did take my hand once the service finished, and together, we sat by the freshly carved gravestone in the sun. We stayed for an hour in silence, saying our goodbyes in different ways.

I knew Jacob suffered from guilt for not being home in time. And I suffered from guilt for not telling him sooner. But touching that sun-warmed headstone filled me with a sense of peace that I hoped Jacob felt too.

That afternoon, we headed to the garden store and bought trays of vegetable seedlings and stayed up well past midnight planting fresh herbs and produce.

We bickered about what to cultivate.

We argued about which paddocks to turn into orchards.

It turned a stressful day into a restful night after yet another funeral.

And once we'd carefully tucked plants into dirt, Jacob had taken me to bed where we clung to the living, accepting touch and togetherness, saying no to death because we had so much to be grateful for.

The next week, I spent the afternoon feeding horses and cleaning out water troughs, while Jacob went to his first therapy session.

I didn't have to cajole him into going.

He booked and attended all on his own.

And he came back different. A new level of wisdom in his gaze. A strange kind of consent to life and all its lessons.

He also came back with a gift wrapped in a small black box from Mr. Pickering's Personals. The antique store I'd crashed into and the place where Jacob had bought my locket all those years ago.

As I cracked the lid, he'd lowered to one knee and proposed all over again, slipping a square solitaire with lacy gold filigree onto my wedding finger.

He said the lace was for the locket-wearing, lace-named girl who would always own his heart.

"Ah well, at least I don't have a thousand bridesmaids who will miss me if I don't walk down the aisle." I forced a laugh.

"You're walking down that aisle. I planned a wedding for you guys. Least you can do is go through with it." Cassie grinned. "I'll tell my nephew not to murder you. How about that?"

"Gee, you're so sweet."

She laughed.

Cassie had planned tomorrow and kept it simple at our request. She'd shown me photos of the wedding she'd put together for Ren and Della. A simple altar in the meadow, a marquee for after, and a guest list of mostly family.

That was what I wanted.

I'd ordered a dress online with a sleeveless lace top and full cream skirt, and Jacob sourced new jeans, boots, and a shirt.

Nice and easy.

Magazines called for rights to photograph the ceremony, but I told them I was no longer part of their world. I had never belonged, and they'd most likely never see me on the red carpet or on the big screen again.

I was soon to be a farmer's wife, and that role fit me better than any other.

As we pulled up to Cherry River, a horse kicked the trailer again.

"I'll have Chip help me with the ponies. You better go find Jacob before he sees the surprise on his own and has a heart attack."

I flinched. "I don't know if I'm ready."

"Too late." Cassie laughed. "God, I'm so glad I'm not you right now."

"Stop it. It won't be so bad. He'll be okay with it."

"Yeah, suuuuure he will." Parking outside the barn, she slapped the steering wheel, blew me a kiss, and leapt out. "Come find me if you need somewhere to sleep tonight!"

I slouched in my seat. "This is going to be bad." Twisting to look in the back, I steeled myself against my mistake. But two gorgeous eyes met mine. A nose sniffed in curiosity. And I melted all over again.

It's not a mistake.

I'd done my best to stop pushing Jacob—after all, he'd done so well dealing with his past and accepting that he couldn't control every little thing.

But this new addition? He might see it as a push.

He might resent me for doing something he wasn't ready for.

But...I couldn't leave him there.

The little dog was scruffy, flea-bitten, and skinny, but his eyes...they were pools of trust even after the scars left by cattle irons that'd been pressed into his puppy skin.

He wasn't pretty with grey and black fur, a muzzle of white and half an ear. But he belonged here. With us.

"He'll love you just like I love you," I murmured.

The dog wagged its tail once, timid and scared. His black, soulful gaze tracked me as I climbed from the truck and went to open the back door.

Only, Jacob was there.

Talking to his aunt.

His smile broad and cowboy hat tilted low against the sun's

glare. His Wranglers and plaid shirt were multi-colour with grass stains and mud, and his boots held a day's worth of grime.

He worked so hard.

He was so capable.

My heart melted for my husband-to-be just like it'd melted for the dog.

The dog who'd been hiding in a pile of horse manure to avoid the farmer's wife and her beatings.

After I'd helped Cassie round up the two rescue horses—seized by the SPCA and given to us for fostering—I'd seen a little shadow watching us before zipping away to hide in such filth.

As Cassie signed the paperwork, I'd snuck away, squatting down by the manure pile, whispering calm things.

It'd taken ten minutes for the dog to creep forward. Another twenty for him to come close enough to smell me.

Cassie wanted to leave.

But I couldn't leave without him.

I'd let one stray dog down by letting others give him away to an uncertain future. I wouldn't do it again.

With a quick plea not to bite me, I'd scooped him up, tossed him in the backseat and stole him.

Now, I was about to face the consequences.

Cassie laughed at something Jacob said, then turned to face me, pointing.

Tattle tale.

Jacob followed her finger, his grin growing wider when he saw me. His white-blond hair from Bali had grown with darker regrowth, framing his perfect face with the shaggy length tied in a knot at his nape.

He was rugged and rough and utterly sublime.

And he's probably going to kill me.

Striding away from his aunt, he pushed his cowboy hat farther up his head, then ducked and kissed me, sweaty and salty and so deliciously him.

I let him dictate the kiss, partly because he short-circuited my brain every time his mouth claimed mine, and partly because I didn't know if I should reveal the mutt or squirrel him away until I'd trained and earned his trust.

But Jacob pulled away, his eyes warm as molasses. "Aunt Cassie said you had something to show me?"

"Oh, she did, did she?" I glowered over his shoulder at her.

She threw her head back and laughed.

"What's going on?" Jacob's smile faltered a little. "Everything okay?"

"Um." I bit my lip. "I did something."

"What did you do?" His gaze dropped over me, scanning me from head to toe. "Are you okay? You're not hurt, are you?" Panic I hadn't seen in a while filled his eyes. "Goddammit, Hope. I told you I didn't want you around those rescues. Not after what happened with Mom—" He went to grab me, but I spun out of his reach and yanked open the back door.

"I'm not hurt, but this little guy is. I know you find it hard, and I know I'm asking so much of you, but...please?" I held out my hand, inviting the little dog to creep forward. "Give him a chance?"

Jacob froze, his attention locked on the scruffy mutt. "Where the hell did he come from?"

"The farm where the horses were abused."

"Why did you bring him here?"

"To save him." I shrugged. "But only if you can handle it. If not, I'll fatten him up, show him what love feels like, then find him a forever home." I didn't want to give him up, but I also didn't want to hurt Jacob.

"Goddammit, Hope." He rubbed his face with a shaking hand. "What are you trying to do? Kill me?"

I abandoned the pup and went to my best-friend and lover. "Not kill...set free." I nuzzled into him, hugging him tight. "You love Forrest. You have a bond with him. That doesn't hurt...does it?"

He hugged me back, wedging his chin on my head. "It hurts, just like loving you hurts."

I kissed the dirty shirt over his heart. "But worth it."

He nodded with a heavy sigh. "Yeah, worth it."

I held him until his shakes subsided.

A thud sounded behind us, followed by a little squeak.

I spun in Jacob's arms. "Oh, no. He fell out of the truck." I moved to leave Jacob's embrace—to check on the dog now splayed in the dirt, but Jacob held me back.

His fingers feathered and tightened, then let me go reluctantly.

With a smile, I moved away and ducked by the little dog.

The canine trembled, his tiny muzzle pulling back to reveal pointy teeth in warning.

I cringed.

Jacob wouldn't tolerate a dog that might bite me—begging or no begging.

I stiffened as Jacob crept forward, expecting him to pull me away and order the dog off his property. Instead, he dropped to his haunches, murmuring soft things, his voice calm and soothing.

And the dog listened.

His teeth no longer bared, and his tail wagged. Slowly, he inched with his belly gliding the ground toward Jacob's boots.

Jacob didn't touch him. Just let him sniff.

The dog took the invitation and circled him, sniffing his jeans, his wrists, his knees, everything he could reach.

After he'd sniffed his fill, he stared Jacob dead in the eye, then flopped onto his back, revealing his gaunt belly.

I burst out laughing as Jacob groaned under his breath.

His eyes met mine, rueful and exasperated. "Just like you, huh? Bit of fight to start with, then full-on warfare to make me fall in love with you instantly."

I giggled. "I did nothing of the sort."

He scratched the dog's belly, shaking his head. "You know exactly what you did. I didn't stand a chance against you."

"And he doesn't stand a chance against you. You're the favourite." Even though I'd rescued him, he'd chosen his pack, and the leader was Jacob. "He's madly in love with you already, just so you know."

Jacob caught my eyes, his tan face and handsome smile stealing my breath. "And you're madly in love with me too, right?"

"Every day of my life." I smiled.

"For the rest of forever?"

"For the rest of forever." I leaned forward and kissed him, still shocked even now at the privilege of being able to touch this man. Kiss him. Make love to him. Sleep beside him when he was at his most vulnerable.

Jacob grabbed me, squishing me close until we tumbled into the dirt together. But he didn't stop kissing me. He didn't stop when dust covered us or the dog jumped on us or when Cassie got out the hose and sprayed us with a laugh.

We rolled and hugged and kissed and played, and I'd never been so stupidly happy.

"He can stay, Hope Jacinta Murphy." Climbing to his feet, he held out a hand to help me up. When I stood, he brushed the worst of the mess off me before yanking me close and whispering into my ear. "That's the last time I call you Murphy, by the way.

After tomorrow, you're a Wild. Hope Jacinta Wild. For always."

* * * * *

As I stood at the top of the aisle with our family surrounding us, my dad doing his best not to cry after giving me away, and staring into the eyes of my soul-mate, my heart threatened to burst from my ribcage and frolic in the meadows beyond.

I wasn't just marrying the boy I'd be born for.

I was inheriting a farm that I'd always belonged to.

I was completing the life I was destined for.

The celebrant gave us lines to bind and promise us, and Jacob and I repeated them.

The little dog we'd called Arlo ran around our legs as we turned to face our family with hands joined and hearts united and souls stitched together for eternity.

The sun hung low and golden in the sky, and Cassie took photo after photo as Jacob and I signed the wedding certificate, then drifted toward the forest where Ren and Della were scattered.

I missed Della so much. I hoped Jacob was right that the dead had a choice to linger or leave, and Della had lingered to see this moment.

I wanted her to know I would forever look after her son. I would care for him, protect him, and be the best wife he could ever ask for.

A gentle breeze swirled in my wedding dress as Jacob gave me a smile blended of joy and sadness, then used his father's Swiss Army knife to carve another set of initials into a tree that already carried his parents'.

J.W 4 H.W with a rudimentary heart sketched around the two.

Our names beneath Della and Ren's.

Our love story mingled with theirs.

A true family.

Jacob put his knife away as the breeze kicked harder, tugging at my veil and ruffling Jacob's hair. He pulled me into him, and we hugged beneath the tree that carried such memories and troths.

"I love you, Hope. For richer and for poorer."

I clutched him closer. "And I love you, Jacob. In sickness and in health."

He nudged my chin up, pressing his lips to mine in an endless kiss, and the breeze died down with the softest sigh.

He murmured into my mouth. "I'll love you during life and well past death."

"Forever."

The world stood still.

We were at the epicentre of our happiness.

And as he pulled away, we linked hands, smiled, and walked side by side into our new beginning.

Extended Epilogue

JACOB

✶ ✶ ✶ ✶ ✶ ✶

TWO YEARS LATER

CROSSING THE MEADOW that I'd crossed so many times before, I steeled myself for the task ahead.

I hadn't entered my parents' house since my mother died and I left Cherry River. I hadn't visited when I returned. I hadn't cleaned or sorted out their belongings in the two years that I'd been married to Hope.

But today, I had no choice.

Today, I crossed the meadow to do something that should've been done a long time ago: release ghosts from the rooms and air out the lonely house for new occupants.

Hope and I had been happy in my small cabin.

We'd worked hard, turned Cherry River into a fledgling orchard, and cultivated the ground to grant even bigger grass yields.

Hope continued to help Aunt Cassie with the horse rescues, and I'd learned to hide my fear. I had to trust if Hope got hurt...that was okay. I wouldn't stop her from doing what she loved just because my mother had died dealing with such creatures.

I'd gotten better at accepting.

Arlo, the little dog that was my personal shadow, had helped with that.

He was just so happy, so utterly alive in each moment. No worry about what he would do that night or the next day. No stress over things he couldn't change.

He was as good on my mental health as my therapist Dr Mont.

Pulling the key from my pocket, I sucked in a deep breath as I opened the door and stepped over the threshold.

Instantly, the familiar smell dragged me back through time to when I was a child and both my parents loved and laughed in this place.

I let memories surround me, I let highlight reels overwhelm me, and then I moved forward with my shoulders squared and heart sad but not bleeding.

Hope didn't know my plan. I didn't know if she'd like it or disagree.

But we'd been to the doctors this morning.

Our third check-up on our baby.

I flushed.

Our baby.

I would be a father soon.

And thanks to today, we knew what we were having.

A daughter.

A little girl who would ruin me for the rest of my days just as surely as her mother did.

Striding through the house, I bypassed my parents' bedroom and entered my old one where Hope had stayed. Her scent blended with mine, and I smiled.

Perhaps this should be the nursery.

Move out the furniture, paint, renovate, and give the old house a new family to shelter.

Plans unravelled in my head, ideas of changing a few walls, and amending the property so it became ours instead of just my parents.

Needing a paper and pen to sketch my ideas, I followed the corridor to the room my father had built for my mother. A writing room. A small square looking over the willow grotto where her desk could store her manuscripts while her gaze followed her husband on his tractor.

The feel of this room was soft and welcoming, and I sighed as I opened one of her desk drawers, searching for a pen.

I froze.

My hands shook as I pulled out two green boxes that'd once had the power to cut me apart.

The gifts from my father.

Mom had kept them, waiting for a time when she could give the last two presents. A time that never came, just like the boxes she hadn't opened. The ones I'd buried by her ashes.

My mind shot back to the greenhouse the day before she died

when she'd given me the ribbon lace for the girl I'd fallen in love with. I'd shoved that gift into a cupboard, fighting my own lies that Hope meant nothing.

I should've given it to her. After all, the gift was to her from my father.

Who were these gifts to? Hope or me?

Two remaining boxes.

One for when I got married.

One for when I had a child.

Our wedding had already happened.

The birth of our child was a few months away.

A gust of air blew through the room. I didn't know where it originated from as the windows were closed. It wasn't chilly like the autumn breeze outside but warm and imploring.

I didn't want to.

I didn't know if I could handle such things, but I owed the two people who had died to open them.

Ripping into the paper, I cracked open the first box.

Inside rested a small photo frame. Silver and simple, empty and needing one of the many photos Cassie took of Hope and me at our wedding.

A piece of paper fluttered to the floor.

Gritting my teeth, I picked it up and read.

Dear Wild One,

Congratulations on getting hitched.

If you're anything like me, it would've been the best day of your life. Not because family and friends watched you pledge yourself to your chosen one, but because you've laughed death in the face. You've made a solemn vow that you will never be alone. Ever. You will always find each other now you are wed.

I'm so happy for you to find your other half to share your life with.

I love both of you,
Dad

Clearing my throat from a wash of emotion, I rushed to open the last box before I broke and had to go back to Hope. Before I had to see my wife, hug her close, and remind myself that all this pain was worth it.

To look at her rounding belly and know she created a miracle. To accept that sometimes miracles came to pass and sometimes tragedy came in its place. But through it all, we survived.

The paper ripped loudly on the final box, the lid tight over its contents.

Pulling it open, I tipped a silver bangle into my palm.

A bracelet for a baby.

Inside an inscription glinted: *Live Wild. Love Freely. Be Blessed.*

I clutched the precious metal in my fist as I read the last message I would ever have from my father.

But it wasn't addressed to me.

It was addressed to my daughter.

The little person Hope and I were yet to meet.

Dear Baby Wild.

You are so loved.
You were born to parents who will lay down their lives for you.
You were created by love that no amount of pain can shatter.
You have the world at your feet, and I wish you every blessing and happiness.

Love,
Your grandfather.

The strength in my legs buckled.

I'd pushed myself too far, and I tumbled into my mother's writing chair. Wedging my elbows on the desk, I breathed deep, using tricks the therapist had given me to stay in the present and not focus on all the things I could lose. All the scenarios that could go wrong. All the worries that drove me mad.

Slowly, my heart stopped racing, and I looked up again.

In the distance, amongst wildflowers slowly fading with autumn and trees turning orange, stood Hope. She had one hand on Forrest's whither while she scratched the nose of a white mare called Snowy. A rescue horse turned heart horse that I trusted to protect my wife impeccably.

I stood to go to her.

To celebrate the news of our daughter and brainstorm names well into the night, only my boots nudged something beneath the desk, dragging my eyes to the darkness.

A box.

Another goddamn box.

This one bigger and heavier than all the rest as I bent to claim it from the floor.

Placing the silver bangle to the side, I hoisted the bulk onto the desk. My hands shook as I smoothed the lid.

Was it my place to open? Was it an invasion of my mother's privacy?

I waited for a while. Paused for a breeze or a sign that I was permitted to see such things, but the air stayed still, watchful.

This house held so many secrets, but if it were to shelter a new family, prior history would have to be dealt with. Precious belongings would have to be stored in safekeeping, ready to make room for more secrets.

I told myself my curiosity was purely from a renovation point of view even though I knew whatever was in the box would butcher me.

Gritting my teeth, I opened the lid and raked a hand through my hair as I found hundreds upon hundreds of letters, all addressed to my father.

A few held just one lines, others multiple paragraphs, and some with sheets and sheets of news.

My mother had always been a writer. Her journaling was mostly why their love story was fashioned into a book, and instead of stopping a lifelong calling, Mom had turned to writing to Dad when he died.

The paper felt otherworldly as I claimed a small note and held it in the light.

My Dearest Ren,

It's hot today.
Hot enough for a swim in a stream in some empty forest, just the two of us. I had a dream last night of our many camping trips—of you when you were just a boy looking after an annoying little girl. Remember those days? God, I do.
I wonder if we'll have that again…when I find you.

I stopped reading, placing the letter face down on the desk.

It felt like an intrusion. It filled me with grief.

Scooping the massive pile of paper from the box, I placed the tower before me. So many notes. So many little snippets of her life she'd wanted to share with the ghost that watched over her. I wanted to hide them somewhere safe, but I reached for another, adding salt to my wounds.

My Ren,

Today is a hard day.
I miss you more than I can bear.

My heart lurched, tasting my mother's sorrow.

Dear Beloved Ren,

Jacob adopted a new horse today.
They're both as broken as the other, so one of two things will happen:
they'll end up killing each other or will heal together, but for now, they have a
friendship no one else truly understands.
Jacob has called him Forrest.
There's so much of you in him, Ren.
It's unbearable sometimes.
Then again, there's me in there too. His temper and stubbornness, for
one.
Anyway, I have to go cook dinner.
I'll see you in my dreams.

Another page fell from the stack as I pushed the letters neatly
to the side. My eyes skimmed it before I could stop myself.

Ren,

Hope is slowly winning, you'll be glad to know. She's not afraid of
Jacob's temper. You'd be so proud of the way she pushes him to be happier. I
know she loves our son. And I love her. She truly is a Wild, Ren.
She belongs here, and I hope, one day, she officially becomes family.

Turned out, I'd kept her wish and fate's design.

Hope was family. A true Wild.

With my wedding ring glinting on my finger, I ran my touch
along the stack of letters.

Declarations of love and loss—a life my mother had to live
without her husband by her side.

I had no idea what to do with them. They couldn't be given
away, and they definitely couldn't be destroyed.

They would have to be protected and guarded—a talisman
for our own love story; a reminder to adore each and every day,
even if it killed us.

Bracing myself for yet more tragic notes to ghosts, I looked inside the box again.

Tucked at the very bottom was a piece of soft leather tied with tan string.

I pulled it free and undid the fasten, flopping open the leather to reveal yet another piece of paper.

This was different, though. This one wasn't a love note but a short manuscript. Written in secret, stored in dust, and dedicated to the family she'd left behind.

I looked out the window again, searching for Hope and the horses. She'd guided the creatures to the stable where she'd begun tacking up Snowy for our evening ride.

The world of the living summoned me to join it, but the whispers of ghosts made my eyes fall back to the pages.

Should I read it?

Was it private?

I didn't have a choice as my attention fell on my wife's name in the dedication.

To Ren, my husband who lives in my heart.
To Jacob, my son who keeps me whole.
To Cassie, my sister who keeps me brave.
To John, my father who keeps me smiling.
To Hope, my daughter who I hope becomes family.

My hands trembled as I turned over the page, committing myself to this tale. I couldn't trap away my mother's words again without honouring them.

The description page was neatly typed.

'Come Find Me'
A Short Story
by
Della Wild

I swallowed hard as I turned the page and began.

A SHORT STORY might be a single paragraph, a simple page, or a complex novella.
It should have a beginning, middle, and an end.
It can be fact, fiction, or fantasy.

This is none of those things.

It doesn't have a beginning. There is no middle. There is only an end.

An end I have dreamed about, fantasied about, researched about.

I'm still alive, and I'm grateful. I don't want to rush time or seek death. But I do live in two worlds. A world where I stay with the living. The world we all know to be true. It's governed by gravity and seasons and rules imposed by reality. But the other world? The one after this is a mystery. Is it all light and angels like some texts? Is it all red and flames like some warnings? Or is it just another place?

A place with its own rules and parameters…as real as the one we are born to. A place where we visit when we dream, a place we feel on lonely nights and touch in shadowy corners?

A place where our loved ones wait to find us.

In my world, that place is real.

So real, I dream about it.

I visit there so often, it's as much home as the one I breathe and exist in.

The only thing is…there is no breath required in this other world. There are no limitations on bodies or fragility caused by sickness or strife. There is no sorrow or struggle.

Just a place of utmost satisfaction.

And that is where my story begins…or ends, as the case may be.

This is my prediction, my hope, my prayer for when my final day on earth occurs.

I will die, and I am not afraid.

I will pass over, and I am ready.

I will close my eyes on the family I love, but open them again to a husband I've missed for eternity.

I will never publish this tale as it's purely for me. An exercise in creation. A tool to help me cope.

And when my dying day comes, I am no longer human but a ghost.

A phantom.

No longer belonging to bone and body but to wind and wishes.

I belong to magic.

I belong to love.

And I feel it…tugging me.

The world is still around me, but it's different.

I recognise trees and flowers and sunshine, yet they feel so much more. More alive. More colourful. More knowing.

My feet are bare, yet I don't feel the green, green grass between my toes.

My white dress is fabric, yet I am naked and free.

I feel alive even though I am dead.

I no longer have pain from long-ago injuries. I no longer feel the twist of ligaments or strength of sinew. I walk, but really, I skim the ground below me.

I am weightless with freedom and marvel at the exquisite wash of nothingness. The complete lack of sensation from taste or sound or touch. My mortal senses are no longer master here, and slowly, step by step, wing by wing, I embrace a new way of existing.

A way of all-knowing, all-feeling, all-encompassing.

I am no longer a woman.

I am a spirit tapped into the wonders of creation itself.

The shimmer and shine of this new existence fades somewhat as my feet descend to sink into spongy, dew-wet grass.

And this time, I feel it.

I feel breath in my lungs and blood in my heart.

Yet I know I am no longer human.

This is just the form I am most comfortable in...for now. The form this new world has given me until I'm ready to take on a new one. To fashion a different existence, to live in the elements and explore the galaxies.

But for now, I am limited by my imagination and tolerance.

And besides, I'm searching.

Searching for something I lost so long ago. Something I know is still waiting for me.

I keep walking, dazzled by trees rustling and sun shining and the sky glittering like every sapphire and turquoise gem has been used to create the heavens.

There's no dirt or sullied imperfection. No rushing or stressing or worry.

Just me in an endless summer meadow, floating, walking, manifesting my way to what I'd lost.

I still remember my previous life. I remember the son I created and the family who adopted me. I remember more in this form than I ever could in my human shell. My thoughts are free. My mind is a universe of teachings and past lives, and I've been given the key to all of them.

Some ended young. Some ended badly. But almost all of them had a partner.

A boy.

A man.

Different faces, different hearts, but one soul.

The soul intrinsically entwined with mine.

It's as if I summoned him.

A silver shadow appears on the horizon. A silhouette blinded by sterling light.

And I am home.

It takes a single thought to cross the distance. To sail from meadow to horizon and stop before him.

In this world, he could take any shape, be any power, exist in anything. Yet I recognise him.

The sable bronze hair, the soft brown eyes, the jawline I've kissed and the body I've hugged.

His hand reaches for mine.

I place it into his touch.

Our connection lashes our fingers together with bolts of gilded gold. The sensation is tenfold. His skin is satin. His heat so comforting. His strength god-like as he pulls me into his embrace.

And there, we stand.

We stand in each other for heartbeats, but in the other world, it is years.

Time has no jurisdiction here, and as the seasons roll and people grow older in the place called earth, we just stand in serenity. Peace. Togetherness.

Saying hello.

Our heartbeats sync into one. Our fingers mesh and glide through each other's. We are air and water and love and lust all at once.

The magic of touch slowly wraps us in skin once again, allowing voices to work and eyes to blink, granting the power of speech and conversation.

Soon, we will no longer need these forms. We will choose another to start a different life or we will stay here together. It's up to us. All options are available. Reincarnate or remain. Watch or go.

No pressure to choose any.

Right now, I'm in heaven with the husband I lost so young.

His face transforms into a smile, and I fall for him all over again. But this time, my heart has no limits. It can tumble far, far deeper than before. It can splash into my soul because that is what keeps us tethered. Bound as one no matter where we go.

His hand cups my cheek, and he kisses my forehead. "You found me, Della Ribbon."

His voice is the same but not. The rough timbre plaits with golden grace.

I rise on my tiptoes and kiss him.

This man who is more than just my husband but my soul-mate. The missing piece of my being. "I always do, don't I?"

And I do.

In multiple lifetimes, we are drawn and delivered. No age, race, or circumstance can keep us apart. It's impossible because when we came into being, we were one. We were whole, then split down the middle to become two. Our one task is to find each other in every lifetime to complete the circle and be happy.

"Tell me...what did I miss?" His lips meet mine, and we kiss for a month on earth. A month where the moon crests and wanes and waxes.

When we pull away, I smile. "You saw it all. I felt you watching me."

"I did. I watched it all."

"I'm glad."

Locking me against him, he walks through the softest flowers with me by his side. "I saw our son fall in love and get married."

"Yes, he chose well."

"I saw John pass and find Patricia."

"As it should be."

Ren spins me in his arms, brushing aside my hair before kissing me again. "And I saw our grandchild. A girl."

"She's the perfect embodiment of hope and stubbornness."

"She is." He smiles, white and blinding. "Her name suits her perfectly, don't you think?"

I nod. "Perfectly."

His body shimmers, teasing with solid and figment. "Our son has made me proud, Della Ribbon. I'm so glad he's no longer alone."

"He's found his Hope and his heart. But he still misses you. Deeply."

"I know."

Together, we turn and look through the veil of this world and the other. A rainbow shimmer, a curtain of protection where souls can guard over the living.

And there we watch Jacob and Hope riding over fields with their daughter trotting behind. A daughter who is the perfect blend of all of us.

A daughter named after a grandfather she wouldn't meet in her lifetime but perhaps in another…someday.

"She's a pretty thing," Ren murmurs into my hair.

"Pretty and stubborn and bold."

"A perfect child for a perfect name then."

We kiss again, letting our son and his wife canter off with their daughter.

A daughter who will grow to experience her own trials and tribulations—to find her own soul-mate.

A daughter named Wren.

In a daze, I wrapped the manuscript inside its leather cover, placed it into the box, and closed the lid. When had Mom written such a thing?

It felt so *real*. As if she'd already visited such a place and returned to pen it for others.

How did she know we would have a daughter? How did she know I'd marry Hope and find a way to be happy?

What other stories and love notes would I find if I pressed forward with the renovation? Had she written any to me? To Hope? Had she done what Dad had and pre-empted her death with gifts of remembrance?

Goosebumps never faded as I turned my back on the writing room and strode warily through the house. I'd entered this place with new beginnings on my mind, yet the past had found me instead. A manuscript that Mom had written in privacy yet predicted a future that had come to pass.

Wren.

She called my daughter Wren.

After my father.

After love.

I needed to see Hope. I needed to feel the sunshine on my skin and her arms around my waist—to remind myself I was alive and not in the astral plane that my mother's words had painted so well.

Striding out of the house, I braced my shoulders and strode across the meadow where Hope waited for me. She sat on the fence line with a bottle of water in her hand and a cowboy hat on her head.

She grinned, jumping from the railing and jogging to launch herself into my arms. "I missed you. I thought you said you'd only be a few minutes."

"Yeah, sorry." I hugged her hard before placing her on her feet. Her belly nudged me, pregnant and protecting our daughter.

Wren.

Her hand touched my cheek, dragging my attention from my mother's manuscript. "What's wrong?"

I forced myself to focus on her and not on the sudden, overwhelming need to tell Hope our unborn daughter already had a name, selected by ghosts and predicted by a storyteller.

"Nothing." I kissed her gently. "Ready for a ride?"

"Yep." She rubbed her belly. "I want to get in as many as I can before I can't."

"If I didn't like that mare of yours so much, I wouldn't let you ride in your current condition."

She winked, moving toward Snowy and stroking the pretty mare's mane. "We have a connection, me and her. She won't hurt me."

I went to my own horse, and my heart softened with affection as Forrest nudged my hand for a scratch. "I know the feeling."

Hope still rode in a saddle and bridle, but she'd made me promise to teach her how I did it tackless after she'd given birth. She hoisted herself up with the aid of her stirrups while I backed up and ran at Forrest, vaulting up and into position.

"Show-off," she muttered.

I laughed, but my eyes kept trailing to my parents' house. The presence of both of them pressed on me. I swear I caught glimpses of them on the meadow and heard the echo of their voices in the air.

Hope guided Snowy forward, and Forrest followed. She twisted in her saddle to look at me. "Spit it out, Jacob Wild. What happened in there?"

I shook my head. "To be honest, I don't really know."

"What do you mean?"

"I mean…I went inside with ideas to do a renovation. To ask if you would be okay moving into a bigger place now…now we have a little one on the way."

Her smile split her beautiful face. "That sounds amazing."

"Okay, great." I grinned, doing my best not to mention anything else but knowing Hope would get it out of me anyway.

"And the rest…" She cocked her head. "The bit you're trying to hide?"

"Can't I have any secrets, woman?"

"Nope." She laughed gently. "Spill."

I sighed heavily. "Turns out my mother had been writing letters to my dad. I found them."

Hope halted Snowy. I caught up with her. "Wow. That would've been hard to read."

"Yeah." I raked a hand through my hair. "Not as hard as reading a manuscript that she never intended to publish and is just gathering dust in a box."

"Oh?"

I kicked Forrest ahead, needing some space. Should I tell her what it was about? Should I reveal the name? The most perfect name? The only name I could imagine calling our daughter now that I'd seen it?

Hope trotted Snowy to appear beside me. Her hand reached for mine, and her touch gave me courage. Bringing her hand to my lips, I kissed her knuckles. "I'll show you the manuscript. You should read it."

"What's it about?"

"Death." I smiled. "Death and reuniting and love."

"Okay…" She licked her lips. "I'd be honoured to read it."

I sucked in a breath, forcing myself to be brave. "There's something else."

"I thought there might be." She sat serious and patient in her saddle. "Do you need time or—"

"Mom predicted we'd get married."

"Wow, really?"

"She also wrote we'd have a daughter."

"Whoa, that's rather—"

"And we'd call her Wren."

Hope fell silent.

The same goosebumps that infected me washed up her bare arms. She opened and closed her mouth, her eyes skating to the horizon. The horizon where ghosts apparently knew our tale before it even came to pass.

Our horses ambled forward, swaying us with their steps, taking us closer to the treeline.

For the longest minutes, we said nothing as we let the word settle between us, sink into us, become a part of us.

"Wren," Hope breathed.

I stiffened. "We don't have to—"

She stopped Snowy and turned to me. Tears glittered in her gaze, shock whitened her cheeks, and love glowed on her skin. "Wren Della Wild."

A name in honour of my father and mother. For love, impossibilities, and miracles.

The force of such a name fractured my heart, and I slipped off Forrest. Going to my wife, I tugged her from the saddle and into my arms. "Are you sure?"

She kissed me, deep and true and long.

And I kissed her back.

I thanked the universe for making me worthy of loving her.

My heart belonged to her as surely as it belonged to the little girl we had yet to meet.

The little girl who already had a name.

A perfect name for a perfect life ahead of her.

The breeze that existed between this world and the next wrapped around us like a ribbon. A ribbon of air, dancing in our hair, kissing our cheeks, then soaring to rustle in the treetops.

And it was done.

Kissing my wife one last time, I pulled away and rested my forehead on hers.

Hope just smiled and whispered, "Our daughter is called Wren."

I nodded. "Just as it should be."

The End

If you haven't read the epic love story of Ren and Della before Jacob existed, both books are out now!

Start with The Boy & His Ribbon **and complete their journey in** The Girl & Her Ren.

Reviews on The Ribbon Duet (Ren & Della's tale)

5 Stars

Pepper Winters has penned the novel of the century with this masterpiece! I'd even go so far as to say it's her best work ever! There is no real way of describing this book! Other than it's breathtaking, gut-wrenchingly beautiful, superbly poetic, and brutally raw! —Heather Pollock

5 Stars

This book has all the feels. Sadness, anger, gut wrenching heart ache, relief, hope and happiness, I felt it all. This book will forever be one of my all time favourite books, definitely one I'll never forget and it's left me desperate for more from Ren and Della. —Vickie Leaf

5 Stars

Pepper Winters I am sitting here with tears in my eyes and my heart utterly, irrevocably destroyed by your beautiful words and vision. You have written a masterpiece of unrequited love, a soul destroyer like no other. I don't want to say too much, but this tale is not like anything I've read before. It will be one of my favourite stories for years to come.— Effie

UPCOMING BOOKS 2019

The Body Painter
Other titles to be announced on website.

**For more up to date announcements and releases please
visit:**

www.pepperwinters.com

Playlist

Too Good at Goodbyes by Sam Smith
Thanks for Nothing by Poison
Broken by Lovelytheband
Hurt Somebody by Noah Kahan
Misery by Maroon Five
Nothing Breaks like a Heart by Miley Cyrus
Bad Liar by Imagine Dragons
Wild Things by Alessia Cara

Acknowledgements

Thank you so much for your patience while I wrote The Son & His Hope.

This story was a labour of love and took the longest I've ever taken to write a book.

The Boy & His Ribbon was the easiest story I've ever had to write.

The Girl & Her Ren the hardest.

And now, The Son & His Hope is the longest.

Only fair I suppose as they were the most emotional books I've penned so should hold titles to their name. 2018 really took a toll on me emotionally with my beloved horses and rabbit suffering injuries and illnesses and my own wellbeing tested too. So I truly do thank you for your patience and understanding.

Thank you to all my beta readers who helped polish their tale: Heather, Melissa, Melissa, Tamicka, Yaya, Julia, Heather, Nicole, Vickie, Selena.

Thank you to my editors and team around me.

Thank you to my audio narrators on this book Will and Hayden.

And thank you to you, the reader, for spending time in Hope and Jacob's world.

I have a lot planned for 2019 so keep your eye on my newsletter and instagram for news!

Thanks again.

Pepper xx

Made in the USA
Middletown, DE
07 May 2023

30169838R00312